Josie's Way

Other books by Winifred Wolfe

Ask Any Girl
If a Man Answers
Never Step on a Rainbow
Yesterday's Child

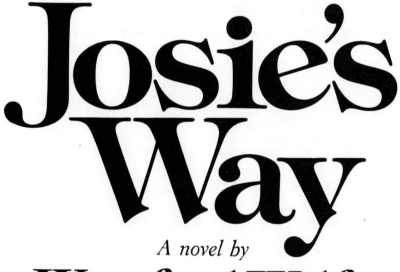

Josie's Way

A *novel by*

Winifred Wolfe

ARBOR HOUSE
New York

To the memory of Malvina Hoffman
    Whose artistry I admired
    And who asked me to write this book.
And to Jack,
    Who introduced us.

Chapter One

He came into her life uninvited and through the back door. He brought mud on his boots from the rain that struck the road outside with a savage violence, making it bounce back up again in silver-tipped checks. A quiet violence fell about the man, as he waited inside a stranger's kitchen for the storm to exhaust itself.

Josephine missed him by minutes. She had gone into another room to end an argument. A clash between a thirteen-year-old boy and an eleven-year-old girl shut in after school was inevitable. In addition, there was the trauma of simply being alone together for more than ten minutes.

She found Peter stretched on the rug in front of the cold fireplace, and tried to remember when he had sprung so tall. One day while she had been busy doing ordinary things, he had extraordinarily grown. The sense of relief at having brought him safely this far mingled with a sharp pang for the little boy greedily swallowed whole in the bigger body.

"He started it," Elsie said.

"Screw you," the tall boy answered, and the little boy within him disappeared like dried tears. "All gone," Josephine used to say to the baby, "all gone."

"Don't use that language to your sister," she said.

1

IN THE kitchen, the man lit a cigarette. His stubbly bristled cheeks hollowed as he inhaled. Since he couldn't find an ashtray, he tucked the burned-out match into the top of his boot and listened to the voices. If their owners stayed where they were a few minutes longer, there was a chance the rain would let up and he could be gone with no one the wiser. But if they returned too soon and found him, it would be their fault.

"LET'S GO into the kitchen," Josephine suggested, "and see my anniversary cake."

"You mean it's finished?" The thick coating of resentment on Elsie's tongue let her mother know she didn't particularly care. Not anymore. Small feelings, Josephine thought, upset, bruised so much more easily than small knees and elbows. . . .

SHE HAD been at the table when from a distance someone had said, "Mother, you're not listening to me." Then she had realized it wasn't really from a distance at all. Elsie was in the kitchen with her.

"What did you say, dear? I'm sorry."

Bending so closely over the elaborate garden that topped the freshly baked cake, she had been oddly drawn into the heart of it for an instant. Or was it a few minutes? Longer than that? She had fashioned a frosting cone of wax paper and moved about planting, rather than picking, tiny blooms that burst into life under her fingers. She hadn't known anyone had come into the room.

Suddenly she was impatient, not with Elsie, but with herself—for all the times in her life she had been caught not listening. When she was eleven, the apology had been to *her* mother. For the circle to complete itself, shouldn't her own daughter give back the words now: "What did you say? I'm sorry." Only it was still Josephine, at thirty-six, who didn't always listen and didn't always hear.

"I said it was raining."

"Why, it's a downpour," surprised. "When did it start?"

"You mean you didn't even know?"

"I was busy doing this." Heavy sheets of rain slashed across the road.

"I can't go out," Elsie complained, "and there's absolutely nothing to do in this house."

Josephine looked at her and wondered why she had always found

2

something to do at that age even if it was only holding her hand up to an electric light bulb to see the red around the dark shadows. And after that she was always conscious of the fact that everywhere she went, she carried her own skeleton around with her. Sometimes she couldn't sleep nights thinking about it. She was glad Elsie had less imagination; Elsie would sleep better nights.

"What are you putting on the cake?" Elsie wanted to know.

"A garden—like the one we had this summer."

"Okay, I'll help by making one of the roses."

"No, don't! I don't want you to!" A sharpness in her voice startled them both. She tried to explain. "It's almost done. If you had come before—"

"You're afraid I'll spoil it, aren't you?"

"No," too quickly.

"Never mind. I'll go bother Peter instead."

Her mother stretched out an over-solicitous arm to pull her back. The girl was gone. I should have let her see the cake if she really wanted to, Josephine thought. Why did it seem so important for it to be finished first? And why didn't I let her make a rose? Would anyone else have noticed that one flower spoiled it? . . .

Now, IN the living room, she told herself again that she would never deliberately hurt her own child. "Did you ever see such rain? It reminds me of wet pine needles."

"The biggest raindrop," Peter informed them, "is hardly ever more than one-tenth of an inch wide. The smallest is usually about one-fiftieth of an inch wide."

"You think you're so brilliant," his sister said.

"Personally, I'm impressed," his mother said.

He took the gibe and the compliment in his usual stride. "If Fran's caught in this, she'll drown."

"How many times have I told you not to call your grandmother Fran?"

"You and dad do."

"Because she's his mother."

"Okay, I'll call you Josie."

"I wouldn't advise it." She pushed back the drapery. The sky was hung with great curtains of water. "I shouldn't have let her go to the square.

3

The cake could have done without candles."

"Why couldn't she have waited until I got home? I'd have been glad to go."

Unexpectedly, Elsie said, "Is it really finished?"

"There wasn't much left to do. Next time work with me from the beginning. I'll teach you how."

"Who says I want to learn?" The coating of resentment was still on her tongue.

"Let's talk about it another time. Come tell me if you like this one."

THE MAN was in the kitchen when they got there. He wasn't waiting for them; he was just there. He seemed to have brought the outside in with him—in his corduroy coat that hung heavy with dampness, pulling it unevenly at the hem; in his misshapen hat, whose brim tipped water when he nodded at them. He looked at them as if they were the intruders and they stared back at him, like one terrified great eye.

Instinctively, the way she always did behind the wheel of a car, Josephine shot out a protective arm to keep the children from falling forward into danger.

Peter added to her confusion by wrenching free. At that moment, even in the presence of the unknown, the greater threat to her immediate future was realizing that her firstborn no longer wanted her protection.

She watched Peter clench his fists and assume an air of almost comic masculine authority. "What do you want?"

"If this keeps up," the stranger said, "God may command one of us to build an ark. If you're the Chosen, how good are you with your hands, boy?" His indifference was a tolerant pat on the head. It turned the man into a boy again.

Josephine had her child back, but could have cried for him. "He asked you what you want."

In reply she received a shadowed appraisal, from under the shrunken hat brim, that dismissed her with equal tolerance. Without stopping to think, she heard herself trying to prove this was still her house. "Take off your hat."

The stranger obliged with a broad solemnity, crushing it in his hand and stuffing it into his coat pocket.

She felt like a fool. Did it matter if he took off that sad, misshapen

4

hat? What mattered was that he was there.

"I knocked first," he said. "You didn't hear me."

"So you just walked in." She decided it was best not to let him know she was afraid.

As if he often let them speak for him, he spread his hands in a vague gesture of apology. Big as he was, they seemed oversized. Short bristly hairs curled over the broad backs. The fingers were long and square-tipped. Between two of them he waved the stub of a cigarette. "How do I get rid of this?"

When no one answered, he tossed it into the sink. "There's a sign at the crossroad: 'Welcome to Ditchling—a Friendly Town.' I was sure such a friendly town wouldn't want me to stay out in that deluge."

"Evidently you believe in signs."

"Only when they don't try to sell me something."

The first shock of discovery was over, and somehow Josephine knew he wasn't there to harm them. His hair was long enough to be caught and held by an elastic band. He needed a shave, and his teeth, when he showed them, were yellowed with nicotine. Once he was gone, she was the one who would have to clean the sink of his drowned-out cigarette and mop up the marks of muddy boots. She was annoyed because he was there, but knew he hadn't come to harm them.

Outside, a blade of lightning split a cloud, followed seconds later by a dry crackle of thunder. It sounded farther off. The storm would be moving away fast now.

"As long as you're here," she offered in a constrained voice, "why don't you stay until this lets up?"

"How very nice of you." The sarcasm was thinly veiled.

It was nice of me, she thought resentfully, wondering how she could have asked him to leave. His leaving couldn't have been less gracious than his staying.

He moved closer to the table and looked down at her cake.

Because of what had happened between them before, Josephine was warmed to hear Elsie boast, "She did that. My mother."

"Isn't it too bad you can't see the garden for the flowers?"

"It's decoration," Josephine told him stiffly.

"I'm sorry. I shouldn't have said that."

She was sorry, too. A few minutes ago she had wanted her children to look at what she had done. *They* wouldn't have criticized. *They* wouldn't have spoiled it for her.

5

Determined to change the subject, she asked, "Are you just passing through town? You're not from this one."

"Do you really know everyone in this town?" His question was polite, but his smile made it a carefully chosen insult.

"Well—almost everyone. I was born here."

He raised uneven reddish brows, as if he were just a little sorry for her. Then he said, "I was headed for the River Road when the sky opened."

"To get to the River Road," Peter told him, "you should have walked the other way."

"I know. This looked like a nicer road."

"That's so stupid," Elsie said. "If you go in the opposite direction, how do you ever expect to get where you started out for?"

Out of habit, Josephine was on the verge of reprimanding her for being rude when the man said, "You must have a name. What is it?"

"Elsie."

"The truth is, Elsie, people who only get where they start out for sometimes haven't any other place to go. Why don't I introduce myself, so you'll have a name to give what the rain blew into your kitchen? Ben Goudy."

"Goudy?" Josephine said.

"You knew my uncle?"

"Everyone in town knew Jess. We didn't know he had any relatives, though."

"Most of us have. Somewhere. We never met."

Elsie felt cheated. This person with the interesting rasp in his voice might at least have turned out to be an escaped convict. Instead he was only the relative of a stupid old man who used to tease her about the color of her hair.

Once too often he had said, "Some day, I'll toss a bucket of cold water over your head and see if the blaze goes out." And every time he said it, he thought it was twice as funny as the last time. But the very last time she ran home and upstairs to the bathroom and, with a big pair of scissors, cut off most of the magnificent mass. It had been awful to see that electric hair that used to bounce on her shoulders lying dead in the colorless basin.

She had started to cry and couldn't stop and wished Jess Goudy dead, too. A week later he was.

"He died," she informed his nephew with a childish lack of sweetness.

6

"It happens," he answered with equal lack of sweetness, and swiveled the cake plate around. "He left me his house. There was no one else, I guess, and I don't want it."

Josephine wished he would stay away from her garden, since he didn't like it, and heard herself running words together to distract him. "Jess was a sweet old man. At Christmas he used to fill bags of candy and give them to all the children. My Elsie was especially fond of him. I remember how upset she was when he died. They had their little secrets. Didn't you, Elsie? They were very good friends, your uncle and my—"

"That house is a big white elephant. I hope I can unload it."

Personally, Elsie was grateful for the interruption because she hadn't known how to manage one herself and stop her mother's tongue. Her own little secret was that she murdered the old man by wishing him dead that day over the bathroom sink. Didn't it *have* to be her fault if she had wished it so hard? . . .

"Mr. Goudy," Josephine said, "don't you want to hear about your uncle?"

"Frankly? Not particularly. The world's full of old men who give candy to kids and die when they have nothing else to do. Sometimes it's the only way they have left of getting anyone to pay attention to them. Do I have to be interested in someone I didn't know? There's damn little chance of ever getting to know him now."

She checked a fresh spasm of annoyance. "You've come to sell his house?"

"If I can. In the meantime I've been living there. Not in the house. In the barn."

"Whoever heard of anyone living in a barn?" Elsie asked.

"Someone was even born in a stable once." He walked to the window. The rain had stopped and sun was trying to break through. He flung open the kitchen door and started out to welcome it. As an afterthought, he turned to Josephine. "Sorry I messed up your clean floor." For a moment, he smiled at her, showing those strong, even, if slightly yellowed, teeth. Then, seeming to fold the dampness around him like a cape, he was gone.

Josephine folded her own arms about her because she felt a chill in the warm kitchen. It was over quickly and then the room seemed almost suffocatingly empty.

"Why do you suppose he wants to live in a barn if he has a whole house?" Elsie asked.

"I couldn't care less," Josephine snapped, "why he wants to do anything."

The children drew back in surprise.

"Don't you have homework? You probably have homework. Both of you. Go do it."

They left, not understanding any more than she did why she was so suddenly angry and so badly out of temper.

Without stopping to think, she picked up the thin knife and lifted off a ribbon of icing that bordered the cake. Following that, she removed a cluster of roses and a clump of leaves. For several minutes she worked feverishly without stopping. When she was done, she was sickened. An invisible hand seemed to have guided her own unwilling one in silent struggle and won. She wanted to cry. It had been better her way. She was sure it had been better her way. Frantically, she felt the wax cones. There was still icing left. Maybe even enough.

As carefully as she had just removed it, she laid down a fresh candied ribbon. Then she restored the leaves, refashioned the flowers, adding more for good measure. She had barely finished when the door, still unlocked, opened again.

"Hi," Frieda said cheerfully. "You look funny."

"Do I?"

"Sort of red in the face."

"I've been working." How could she explain that in a kind of delirium she had deliberately destroyed her work because a stranger hadn't liked it—only to change her mind moments later and build it over again?

"Who did that to your floor?"

"It's easy enough to clean." Grateful for something to hold onto, she took a mop from the broom closet.

"Honest to God, Josie, that can wait."

Reluctantly, the mop was put aside.

"What a marvelous-looking cake! Cover it up, so I won't be able to see it. I'll gain weight looking."

"That's ridiculous." Now she seemed to be scolding Frieda. Poor blameless Frieda.

"What's the matter?"

"Peter and Elsie—they're always at each other. I was an only child. I would have loved having an older brother. We would have been good friends."

"So, when he's thirty-five and she's thirty-three," her neighbor pre-

8

dicted helpfully, "they'll be good friends. My kids are impossible today, too. Maybe it's the weather. I can't stand them. It's one of the reasons I ran over. Here's the other." From behind her broad back, she produced a gift-wrapped package. "Happy anniversary. Don't say 'You shouldn't have' until you open it. Then return it."

"Thank you, and of course I won't return it."

"Oh, I don't mind. I have a thick skin." A grin bulged her wide cheeks. "You've probably noticed. I also have lousy taste. You've probably noticed that, too."

"Frieda, why are you always running yourself down?"

"I'm good in bed," she conceded. "I've got to be good at something, don't I? Anyway, Tony's not complaining. Josie, I've got something to ask you, but I don't know how sympathetic you're going to be."

"Try me." She was already resigned.

"Could we have our luncheon here instead of at my house?"

"But that's two months away!"

"It's keeping me awake nights now. It'll be a total disaster—worse than last time." She widened her big eyes pitifully. They were, she knew, her most persuasive weapon. "You toss off things like that with absolutely no effort."

"All right."

"You'll do it?"

"You knew I would."

"You're an angel. I'll owe you one. Say, I think I do have a good proposal for the meeting, though. Since we're supposed to be the Cultural Society, isn't it time we did something cultural?" She was standing next to a cupboard. A door close to her was slightly ajar. She swung it open accusingly. All the glasses were arranged according to size. "Look at those goddamn things."

"What's wrong with them?"

"Big, little, littler. Sometimes I wonder if you're for real. Never mind. What would you think of an art exhibition and auction? We could get the fine arts students from the college to submit their work—proceeds to go to a scholarship fund."

Josephine nodded quick approval. "Ted would give us a lot of publicity in the *Digest.*"

"Terrific. Tell you how I happened to think of it. Ben Goudy moved to Ditchling. We'll make him head of the judge's committee."

9

"Ben Goudy?" She repeated his name only because it came as an unpleasant shock to hear it again.

"You'd never know what was going on in this town if you didn't read your husband's paper or if I didn't tell you first. And I usually scoop the *Digest.* Admit it. He's old Jess's nephew and a famous painter or something—one of those real arty characters from the look of him."

"You've seen him?" For some reason she was deliberately putting off telling her that she had seen him in her own kitchen minutes before.

"I got a quick look at him the other day in the square. Picture this, Josie, a screaming plaid shirt, a huge silver belt buckle—even high boots and a wide hammered bracelet on his arm. And would you believe a pony tail? As if we didn't have enough trouble with the way some of the kids are freaking themselves up."

"It sounds as if you got more than just a quick look at him."

"Only in passing," Frieda insisted with dignity.

"I met him," Josephine said quietly, and hoped Frieda hadn't heard. It would save her the bother of discussing the man.

"Why didn't you tell me?"

"Because you didn't give me a chance." Then she described how the three of them had discovered Ben Goudy. She described his lack of manners, his complete lack of interest in the dead uncle who had willed him a house, even told her about the barn, where he was going to live temporarily, but she didn't mention his unflattering opinion of her cake or how she had come close to destroying it afterward because of it.

Unexpectedly Frieda said, "You know, I wanted to slap his face. Men who look like that bother me. Too much man, I guess. Now that I've heard what he's like, I wish you had done it for me."

In fairness, Josephine felt compelled to say, "You only have my fast impression of him. He wasn't here that long."

"Just the same, that makes you the logical choice."

"For what?"

"To ask him to judge the contest if we decide to hold it. You're the only one who knows him."

"I don't know him. Not really."

"You took him in out of the rain."

"No. He did that himself. I didn't invite him."

"Okay, so don't ask him, if you'd rather not."

"I'd rather not."

"Forget it, then." Frieda started to test the cake frosting with the tip of her finger but controlled the impulse. "We'll get one of the others."

"It won't matter who asks him. He'll refuse."

"What makes you so sure?"

"Because I know him." It was such a complete contradiction of what she had just said; she was glad the wall phone rang and saved her from trying to explain. It would be difficult, since she didn't understand herself.

"That was Fran," she said after she hung up. "She's driving home with Ted."

"Fran was out in that rain?"

"She left before it started. She went to the square to buy candles for the cake. I was worried about her. Pete said she'd probably drown."

"Isn't it like you to have a mother-in-law like Fran?"

"What's wrong with her?"

"Not a thing. She's perfect. She wouldn't dare to be otherwise. Not in *your* house."

Confused, Josephine thought, I know she meant that as a compliment. What's the matter with me today?

It was the rain that was just over. It colored the most innocent remarks gray. The rain had put her out of temper, first with her children and now with her best friend. The weather bureau promised clearing for tomorrow. Tomorrow everything would be back to normal.

"What's a disgusting thing like that doing in your sink?" Frieda demanded.

Josephine looked and saw the stub of a cigarette. It clung as if it had grown like a wet and shriveled brown scar on the clean white porcelain. . . .

When Frieda left, Josephine threw away the offensive cigarette stub, picking it up gingerly between her thumb and forefinger and tossing it with revulsion into the sanitary liner of the garbage can. She scrubbed the white vinyl floor with a wet and soapy mop until every suspicion of a boot smudge was removed. Cooly, methodically, with an economy of motion, she purified her kitchen again.

But when it was all over, she was dismayed to find his portfolio tucked into the space between the sink and the stove—a flat black leather carrying case spotted gray from dried rain. Part of him was still there.

Since nothing about the man was of any real interest to her, only curiosity could have prompted her to undo the string ties. The portfolio fell open to a carefully drawn study of a hand—broad-backed with fingers long and squared off at the tips. No one had to tell her it was his hand seen through his eyes.

Terrified beyond reason, she slapped the case together and retied the strings. She had worked so hard to wipe out all traces of him. Now he was forcing his way back in again behind a shrunken and disembodied hand.

Chapter Two

LATER, HER husband saw it for what it really was—the forgotten property of an unpleasant stranger who had happened by a few hours earlier. She couldn't imagine why it had unnerved her the way it did. With Ted next to her on the edge of the bed, she could examine, with detached interest, the other sketches. She could look calmly at precise studies of an arm, dissected and carefully drawn, sectioned off to show the relationship between bone and muscle; a piece of skull; the elevator of the upper lip; the wing of the nose.

On other pages were floating fingers bent at the joints, details of toes and ankle bones.

"He's got talent," Ted said.

"There should be something nice to say about everyone."

"How long was he here?"

"Only a few minutes until the storm blew over. By this time he's probably forgotten he was here at all. Making no impression is worse than making a bad one."

"Do you care whether or not you made an impression on him, Josie?"

"No."

"Then forget about him. There's been enough talk on our anniversary about another man."

"I don't think of him that way," she protested, self-consciously

13

remembering suddenly how Frieda said she wanted to slap Ben Goudy's face because he was too much man.

"He seemed masculine enough to me."

"You met him?"

"He came into the *Digest* around three to place an ad."

"Then he must have been coming from the square when he got caught in the rain. What kind of an ad? Oh, the house."

"He was right; it is a white elephant. I don't know who'll be interested. I suggested that instead of an ad he'd do better letting the real estate people handle it."

"His ad wouldn't have made us rich," tightly. "And we're still talking about him. Talk about something pleasant. The weather we've been having, for instance."

"That's pleasant?"

"By comparison."

"Come on, Josie. Don't be too hard on that either. Read the next issue of the *Digest.* I spring gallantly to its defense."

"You think it deserves defense?"

He was, he told her, giving people a chance to count their blessings by recalling that in 1911, in Chicago, the temperature dropped sixty-one degrees overnight. "One day, two people fainted from the heat. The next day, a man froze to death."

"Your son told me that the biggest raindrop is hardly ever more than one-tenth of an inch wide, and that the smallest is usually about one-fiftieth of an inch wide. Both of you," she said with fond exasperation, "love to collect useless trivia."

"Facts, madam, are not to be considered trivia." But he looked pleased. "If Pete keeps it up, there's a chance he'll turn into a good newspaperman. He can take over the *Digest,* if it's still around."

"If?"

"Well," lightly, "that's a long way off, isn't it?"

She couldn't argue that. It was a long way off, but the next morning was only twelve hours away. "Ted? Do me a favor? On your way to the paper tomorrow morning, drop that portfolio at the Goudy barn. If you don't, he's sure to remember where he left it."

"Not tomorrow. I won't have time."

"Ted, I really don't want him in this house again."

"Then leave it on the back porch."

"And let him think I'm afraid to see him?"

14

"If you're not," he suggested, "return it yourself."

He was concentrating too intently on adjusting his tie. Seen in the mirror, he was a double image of a man clearly parading the authority of a husband who preferred keeping unpleasant things to himself.

"What's wrong?" she asked.

"Nothing, only tomorrow's the day I go to Middleburg to set up the *Digest.* You know that."

"Since when do you have to be there so early that you don't have time for a small detour?"

"Okay, Josie, if it'll be that unpleasant for you, I'll leave earlier. But don't you think you're making too much of this?"

"All right. I'll do it." She forgot all about Ben Goudy. "Come here. Let me fix your tie."

He came obediently, the way Peter used to come to her, without resistance. A grown man and a small boy, she thought, are never too proud nor too unsure of themselves to accept help from the women who love them. In the difficult years between, like the ones Peter just stepped into, they foolishly deny themselves.

"Now tell me what's wrong."

He yanked the knot of his tie into place. "What did I say to give you that idea?"

"Oh, a lot of little things."

"I've been invited to breakfast."

"By—?"

"Harris Bartlett. Friendly?"

"Suspicious. He never invites you to breakfast on makeup day."

"Don't worry. I won't tell him what I think of his lousy rag."

Ted had only contempt for the Middleburg *Banner,* a weekly pasted together from syndicated mat services.

"Our contract is coming up for renewal soon," Josephine remembered anxiously.

"Not for months."

"If he doesn't renew it and we can't use his presses, how do we get our paper printed?"

"I've been invited to breakfast," Ted repeated, and he was still smiling.

"You're sure it doesn't mean anything?"

"It means he has the good taste to enjoy my company. Darling, the *Digest* isn't the only weekly in this part of the state using Bartlett's plant.

And no one else has been invited."

"There'd be no reason for him to single us out, would there?"

"No," patiently, "and after you return the portfolio, be a good girl and return Frieda's gift." He picked up a cheese board, half-hidden in the tissue paper of the gift box, then dropped it back again. In the center, on a mottled tile, strutted a small black skunk.

"It's meant for strong-smelling cheeses."

"Tell her we already have a cheese board."

Josephine shook her head stubbornly. "And insult her? Learn to live with it."

Without warning he pulled her to him. "Think you can live with me another fifteen years?"

If she didn't answer, it was only because she was amazed he could think there was a choice. "We should go down now," she said. "Everybody's waiting for us."

"We're the guests of honor. Let 'em wait. Does it seem fifteen years, Josie?"

"Yes. When I look at the children."

"A decade and a half! How did you let it happen? You're such a good manager. How could you let it happen to us?"

Straight-faced, she answered, "Careless."

"I wish we could do it again."

"What would you do differently?"

"Nothing," without hesitation, "not a thing. That's just it. It's going too fast. Before you know it, we'll be married two decades."

"And you'll be asking me how I let it happen." She had changed into a yellow silk shirt and a long dark green wool skirt.

"You wanted to match my flowers," he realized suddenly. The yellow shirt was almost the exact shade of the roses he had brought home, and the skirt was the color of the dark leaves. "Who else but Josie would have thought of that? You're terrific. Look at you. Two children and fifteen years and your waist is exactly the same."

"Maybe not exactly."

His hand slid down around it. "I can tell." He was wearing the freshly pressed jacket he had found waiting on the bed and the tie, carefully selected, that had been placed beside it. He had put both on without argument.

"You didn't mind changing too much, did you?"

"For such a special occasion?"

16

"It is, for me."

"As a woman, my mother will probably welcome the excuse to dress up. What about the kids?"

"I asked them—as a favor."

"I got yellow roses to go with your hair," he said.

"The best thing to call my hair," matter-of-factly, "is ash. I've always been a 'somewhat' blonde."

"Not the color—the glow. My father noticed that about you the first time he met you. I had told him there was a girl at the university I wanted them both to meet."

Josephine remembered . . . and hoped her mother-in-law wouldn't. Not tonight. Not again. For Fran, occasions for the living, like birthdays or anniversaries, invariably occasioned talk about the dead.

PETER WAS slumped in his father's chair reading *The Fellowship of the Ring.* He had washed his hands and face and put on a clean sport shirt. His mother was grateful and didn't ask for more.

Elsie, in jeans, looked no different than she had earlier.

"I wanted to see you in a dress," Josephine reminded her.

"I couldn't find one."

"I'll help you look."

"This is so dumb."

"We're having a party," her grandmother said. "Don't be stubborn, honey."

"Come on, Cinderella," Josephine said briskly, pushing her ahead to the stairs. "Let's find some tattered old rags for you."

During the exchange, Peter didn't once glance up from his book. It was as if there was no one else in the room. "Turn on the lamp next to you," Fran said. "You need more light if you're going to read."

Without taking his eyes from the page, he reached up and fumbled until he found the switch.

"That's better." Her skirt wasn't floor-length, but she was wearing her best black, and she had taken out her good pearls. Her short dark hair, severely brushed off her forehead, was relieved by a smoke-colored streak artfully applied at the temple.

"Josie used my best cut-glass vase for your roses," Fran said, pleased. "Didn't she arrange them beautifully, Teddy?"

Ted nodded. Alone with his mother, he dropped the forced cheerfulness he had feigned upstairs, and his shoulders drooped.

"Come on in and watch me put the candles on the cake," she suggested, throwing a warning look at the silent boy. "It's the least you can do after I almost caught pneumonia getting them for you. I'm still not so sure I haven't."

"Think you're coming down with something?" he asked, concerned.

"Oh, I'll be just fine." He followed her into the kitchen. Fifteen candles had been removed from the small box. Fran picked up one of them, waved it with uncertainty over the cake, then dropped it with frustration. "No, I didn't," Ted said abruptly, answering her unspoken question.

"You're absolutely sure you didn't tell Josie why you think Mr. Bartlett wants to have breakfast with you?"

"Yes," he said dryly, "but I'm not absolutely sure she didn't come close to guessing."

"Don't upset her, Teddy. Not tonight."

"Well, if I'm right, she's going to be very upset tomorrow."

"You're still not sure he wants to buy you out."

"What I am sure of is that he can if he wants to. All he has to do is shut down his presses and squeeze us out."

"Please don't discuss it tonight. Not on your anniversary. Does it seem like fifteen years ago? Your father was still with us then. If I could really believe he's gone, maybe I could cry for him."

"Fix the candles for Josie." There was a soft urgency in his voice. "Go on."

Fran looked down at the cake. "Isn't this a work of art? I just hate to spoil it."

Quickly, he picked up a candle. "I'll show you how it's done." He jabbed one into the center of the frosted garden and she let out a little cry: "Not there! Maybe around the border."

"Stick them anywhere," Ted said carelessly. "You really think Josie will mind? She tosses this stuff off practically with her eyes closed."

But later, when it was time to cut the cake, Josephine was the one most anxious to remove those candles that stood afterward like smoking branchless trees. She wanted to root them out quickly because they had destroyed her garden even before she put a blade to it.

But the cake was forgotten when Ted gave her a gold circle set with fifteen diamonds. Since Elsie had changed reluctantly from jeans to a dress, her mother pinned it on her.

18

"Give it to me for good when I'm married?"

"Let your own husband buy one for you," Ted said. "My girl keeps this one."

"Girl!" Peter snorted. "Hey, you've got to be kidding. She's a lady."

"And don't either of you ever forget it," Ted warned.

After the children went upstairs to bed, Josephine and Ted sat with Fran around the fire, sipped brandy and listened to her talk of the wedding fifteen years before and of people who had been there then and couldn't be now.

"Your blessed mother, Josie, and Ted's father, rest-in-peace. . . . Sometimes," she sighed, "I think I know more people in the cemetery than out of it."

"Get back to the wedding," Ted suggested gently.

"I've never been to a nicer one," his mother said.

Josephine smiled and reached for her husband's hand. "I enjoyed every minute myself."

"Because you were different from most brides, Josie."

"That's not true." She didn't want to have been different.

"Well, I've certainly never seen a calmer one."

"Serene's a better word," Ted said.

"A perfect word," Fran agreed. "Serene and lovely. Oh, you should have seen me at mine." Unexpectedly, her voice became high-pitched and she speeded up the monologue. "I was at sixes and sevens. It was a very long time ago. I hardly remember any of it."

What she did remember, in a voluptuous flow, were some of the things that happened afterward—the early years, the struggles and successes, the lovely daughter killed in an automobile accident, who would never grow old, the loving husband who did. . . .

" 'I'm going to take a nap, Fran.' You remember how I told you he said that. 'Don't let me sleep too long,' he said. But I couldn't wake him up again. I tried, but I couldn't wake him." Every remembrance was like telling the beads in a rosary.

In the middle of one of his mother's reminiscences, Ted glanced at his watch. He'd be less cruel, Josephine thought, if he were more subtle.

"Two o'clock!" Fran said, with genuine surprise. "I don't believe it. Go on, children. Go upstairs. I'm going to stay down here for a while."

So they went upstairs and made love. On the aniversary of the day they married, Josephine gave her husband the gift of dishonesty—of feigned passion and simulated desire. Ted never suspected. He proved it by falling asleep satisfied almost immediately, leaving her with a blessed sense of privacy.

Relieved of his weight, her entire body ached. There wasn't one muscle or nerve in it that had reacted spontaneously. The breathing next to her was even and relaxed, but she felt worn and lonely.

She hadn't wanted to lie to him on their anniversary and decided it was probably because she was so tired by the time they got into bed.

Or perhaps it had been because she wasn't able to forget the woman still sitting alone in the living room, sitting in the dark, not abandoned, but all alone.

Chapter Three

JOSEPHINE SLEPT restlessly. The purest, the most comfortable sleep didn't come until just after dawn.

When she came out of it, the loneliness was gone with the morning star. So was her husband. Josephine smiled up at a ceiling she could see clearly now. Ted had left early, she was sure, to allow himself extra time, to save her the unpleasantness of having to meet Ben Goudy again. She smiled, pleased to have helped give him that good night's sleep.

But the first thing she saw when she got out of bed was the rain-spotted black portfolio. It was still leaning against the wall. More puzzled than disappointed, Josephine stared at it. She had been so sure Ted had taken it with him. She was still sure he meant to. Something more important must have been on his mind. Whatever it was, he had brought it home with him the night before. Although she had sensed it, she hadn't really tried very hard to find out what it was. A stranger had somehow cluttered her mind. She didn't deserve to have Ted make it easier for her. She would drive to the River Road and the Goudy barn herself. She was a big girl. "A lady," he said the night before, "and don't you forget it."

In another way, she was glad he hadn't done her job for her. If she wasn't careful, there was a danger of leaning too heavily—of one day becoming like Fran.

Josephine opened the bedroom door and listened for familiar sounds from the end of the upstairs hall—a faucet running, doors banging. Peter and Elsie were up and would be down in time for breakfast.

She went into her own bathroom, showered and dressed quickly. She looked in the mirror only long enough to run a fast comb through her hair. And all the time she kept thinking of Fran who had leaned too heavily on a husband.

This morning, Josephine thought, I am entering the sixteenth year of the safety of a small harbor my own husband has built for me.

It was comfortable in the harbor, and never a need to leave it. But if, selfishly, she managed to outlive Ted, there would be the same need there had been for her mother-in-law and she wondered if she would find being set adrift any easier.

Death had only taken from Fran; it had left nothing. Even the memories she held out with both hands before the fire last night were a source of never-ending heartache. Because she couldn't warm them back to life, they counted for nothing.

The branch of the tree beyond the window cast only a very thin shadow. It was wrong to reflect on future sadness. It was much too nice a morning.

"DOWNSTAIRS ISN'T being used for anything except junk," Peter said. The sun, playing on his hair and the chrome of the flatware, apologized for yesterday's weather.

Scraping scrambled eggs from pan to plate, his mother answered, "That junk is important—back issues of the *Digest.*" The toaster gave up two golden brown slices. Josephine dropped them still hot onto a plate and pushed them toward her son. "Marmalade, Pete?"

"I can reach it."

"More milk, Elsie?"

"Okay."

There was always pleasure in watching them eat. They took the food she gave them and when they swallowed it, it seemed to give her strength.

"Isn't there plenty of room in the basement of the *Digest?*" Peter asked. "I'll even help dad clean it up and make more room."

"You won't make him do it himself? Well, that should deserve something."

"Are you saying if I do, I can have this basement? Fix it any way I want?" In his enthusiasm, his voice cracked. Fortunately, his sister didn't notice. His mother pretended she hadn't.

But, oh, she thought with curious wonder, that voice is so right for that body—an undeveloped voice sliding and stumbling for a comfortable new level. And those undisciplined arms and legs, not quite used to their new length. A perfect design, only she hadn't made it. This boy had come through her, not from her. It was a silent confession of envy for the Master Craftsman who had really created her son and who was still stretching and rounding, changing and perfecting.

"Ask your father later. If he says okay, I'll even help you fix it. If you want my help."

"Sure. Why not? Dad's late this morning." The tone of voice left unsaid, *And wouldn't you know it? Just this particular morning when it's so important to me.*

"Your father was up and out long before you were. By now he's halfway to Middleburg." She tried to calm a flutter in her stomach and wondered again what it was Ted had been thinking about when he walked unseeing past Ben Goudy's portfolio. "Ask him about the store-room tonight. It won't go away."

"That's what I mean. If it just sits there, it's a waste of good space. I've got some fantastic ideas for it. You wouldn't believe them."

Unexpectedly, Elsie said, "I would."

Her brother shot her a sharp suspicious look, but she had said the words so simply that there was no doubt she meant them. "Could I help, too?"

He shrugged with pretended indifference. "If you do as you're told."

She promised.

"Okay, then."

"Thanks." In her excitement, even her hair seemed to catch fire.

Looking at them, their mother pleaded silently, Please go on being happy. Do it for me. I'm responsible for your being here.

She wanted to say, Your father loves you, too, but I was the one who wanted you more. He wanted you, only later, he said. I didn't want to wait. That's why I feel responsible when you're unhappy.

Only she didn't say any of it.

Listen, she wanted to tell them, this day will never be as young as it is this moment. And neither will you, so make the most of it.

She didn't tell them that either. All she did say was: "Elsie? Run upstairs before you leave and ask your grandmother if she'd like a cup of tea."

"Fran's still asleep."

"Gran," she corrected automatically. "How do you know?"

"She was snoring when I walked by her room."

"Your grandmother doesn't snore."

Elsie drained her glass and with a quick flick of her tongue blotted the white droplets at the corners of her mouth like a cat. "I ought to know. She snored most of the time when I slept with her. Except most of the time I couldn't sleep."

"When was that?"

"When you and daddy were in Europe."

"You were such a little girl," surprised. "Do you really remember?"

"Only some. Like that part. She said I missed you, and that I wouldn't feel so lonely if she let me sleep with her."

"That was thoughtful."

Elsie's eyes narrowed slightly. With unchildlike perceptiveness she said, "I think she was the one who didn't feel so lonely—with me in her bed."

Peter announced suddenly. "We're going to be late."

Every morning Josephine did more than feed them. She sympathized with their small problems and minimized their bigger ones. She settled an argument, sewed a button, spread a Band-aid. For as long as they were there, the house was full of them. They sat at the kitchen table and reached into every corner of every room.

Then they were gone, and the house screamed it. Josephine turned the faucet on full to drown the noise their silence made.

Upstairs the black portfolio waited, but more important things came first. She wouldn't do a thorough cleaning, but no dishes would be left in the sink. If a fire happened while she was gone, no strangers would look upon the intimate untidiness of unmade beds. And bathrooms belonged to members of the family. Personal idiosyncracies would be recapped and rehung, kept private from alien eyes. It was left to her to guard even their unimportant secrets.

She went to look in on her mother-in-law first. Elsie had been wrong. Fran wasn't really snoring. It was more a rumbling protest, dredged from the bottom of an uneasy dream. Whatever the dream was, it was making the soft pillow hard. She went into the other rooms—Elsie's first, then

Peter's. In many ways, his room had been left less chaotic than his sister's.

That girl is so untidy, Josephine thought, exasperated. She sees how I keep our room—her father's and mine. . . .

In the light of day, the double bed in the master bedroom was only an impersonal piece of furniture, but it had a vaguely offended look. With a wide sweeping gesture, she flung the quilted spread over it to hide the deceit she had put there in darkness. She lavished extra care into the arranging of the small decorator pillows. The bed still looked reproachful, so she deliberately turned her back on it and came face to face, as if it were alive, with the black portfolio.

How much longer could she put off getting it out of her house? How far to the barn on the River Road? Twelve minutes by car? Back again in twelve? A twenty-four minute slice out of a twenty-four hour day, that's all. All right, add two minutes more—possibly less.

"Mr. Goudy? You left this in my kitchen yesterday. Yes, I was sure you remembered. I wanted to save you the trouble of coming back for it. As it happened, I had an errand to do." The lie would come effortlessly. "It took me directly past this house. No, no trouble at all. Please don't bother to thank me. Good-by, Mr. Goudy." Oh, it would take less than two minutes.

She grasped the handles of the case and half-ran down the stairs.

Minutes later she was headed for the River Road, driving along other roads already bordered with dead leaves. She had never liked the late autumn, "Nature's bloodless triumph." She didn't like the maples screaming scarlet while they still lived, or the yellow before dying that was all around her.

Neither of her children seemed to feel the same ache she felt when she walked on fallen leaves. They ran through them joyously while she turned her head away and couldn't look. And the smell of burning leaves Ted loved always made her a little sick.

The thought of Ted brought one hand off the steering wheel to touch the spot where he had fastened the diamond pin the night before. He had no right to have spent so much money on a gift, but fifteen years, she supposed, was a milestone and her husband enjoyed erecting milestones. It was incredible to her that an intelligent man like Ted didn't recognize them for what they really were—headstones to the years.

She had driven almost all the way up to the old house before she remembered that Ben Goudy was using the barn, not the house.

The big barn door was slightly ajar, leaving just enough room for her to slide in without disturbing it further. She moved inside and left the dying summer outside.

She intended to leave the portfolio and go away again. Even the words were well rehearsed: Mr. Goudy? You left this in my kitchen yesterday. Yes, I was sure you remembered. I wanted to save you the trouble of—"

But no words came. For the first time in her life, she was in one place and not even a small part of her wanted to be anywhere else in the world.

Josephine stood hardly breathing, and listened to a strange new sound. It was the sound frozen movement makes, and it was everywhere. She could hear it in the wire sculpture of an elongated horse that whinnied close by. She could hear it in the naked marble of a young girl who covered her face with her hands and wept silently. She could hear it in the thud that the powerful stone man had just made as he bent his enormous knees in supplication.

These sounds were as real to her as the one she could actually hear —the tap-tapping of a mallet against a chisel.

Without warning, Josephine felt she was on the verge of the greatest happiness—the most intense joy of her life. The feeling passed as quickly as it had overcome her, and she wondered what had caused it. Perhaps there was something about the barn, bathed in mysterious color. After a moment she realized it was the sun vibrating through a north-light exposure that seemed to form an enchanted dome. It produced a curious effect on her. She could control it now.

Ben Goudy sensed rather than saw her there. "Who is it?" without looking away from his work. "Is someone there?"

She wondered why she felt the way she did when she was in a church. "You left this in my house yesterday."

He stopped tapping and looked around. "Oh, it's you."

"I came to return this." There was an echo quality about her voice, as if she were listening to herself talk in her sleep. He didn't seem to notice. The truth was he didn't seem to notice anything about her. He was simply patiently aware of her presence. The muscles under his jaw were working. It was as if he were feeding on her confusion.

"Put it down anywhere and go away."

Josephine felt herself color and grow hot. She put the portfolio on a worn bench. The door was still open. The station wagon was waiting outside. There were so many things left undone at home. Afterward she never could say how it happened that she found herself standing behind him. Under the marble he was flaking off, a form was coming to life.

"That's very good."

He spun around violently and she started back as if he had struck her. "Careful!"

She had backed into a skeleton on the wall, jolting the bones to rattling. Her throat contracted in terror.

For the first time Ben Goudy looked amused. "Did the machine frighten you?"

"Machine?"

"The most perfect ever devised."

She looked at the skeleton with new respect.

"I don't expect you to agree with me."

"You've done all . . . this? Everything here?"

Suddenly he threw his mallet violently to the planked floor. The sight of his hands paralyzed her. If she had never seen the man again she would have forgotten his face, but his hands had reached out and taken a fist-hold on her memory.

"I'm extremely grateful to you," he was saying, "for taking me out of the rain yesterday. I'm grateful to you for returning my sketches today. I'll be even more grateful if you'll get the hell out and let me alone."

"This makes a wonderful studio. So much light." She began to pull nervously at her fingers.

"What do you want?"

"I don't know."

"What's the matter with you?"

"Matter?"

"Look at your hands. They're trembling."

She hid them behind her and, without intending to ask it, blurted out, "What didn't you like about my cake?" She didn't blame him for letting out a spurt of laughter, but she said, "Don't laugh at me."

The expression on her face, more than her words, stopped him. "You're serious."

"I know it was only made of sugar, and it wasn't important, but when I did it, it was very important to me. Tell me what was wrong with it."

"What was it supposed to be?"

"A garden. Like one I had last summer. That was beautiful."

"How did it grow—choked like that?"

"Well," she admitted, "it wasn't exactly like that. I added to it. Did I add too much?"

27

"What makes you think you can improve on nature? Try to capture its spirit. Don't try to improve on it."

"Don't add green to summer? Is that what you're saying?"

"It can't be done."

"I see. I really am sorry to have bothered you," she apologized. Once more she tried to leave. This time she stopped by the statue of the sobbing girl. If she touched it, she was sure she would find the body warm. "When I was very young," she told him, "I had a little talent for drawing and then one day my mother bought me some clay. I cried because I didn't know what to do with it."

"What did you do with it?"

"Let her take it away from me. She didn't like to see me cry. Good-by, Mr. Goudy."

"Wait a minute." Something in his voice gave her the courage to face him. "There's some clay," he told her, nodding toward the wooden table.

She let the cardigan sweater she had carefully taken from her neat well-ordered bureau drawer slip carelessly from her shoulders.

"There's something hidden in there. Look for it."

The clay was soft and hungry. When her fingers dug into it, it devoured them.

ONCE, WHEN her little boy was six, she wanted to chase him from underfoot.

"Petey, dear," she suggested, "wouldn't you like to go out and play?"

"There's nobody to play with," he told her. "I have only one friend and he's my enemy."

She wanted to pull her rejected child to her, but knew he'd fight her, twisting his hard little body from the hollow of her arms as if it were caught in the hollow of a wave. And she didn't tell him, because he wouldn't understand, that she had an enemy, too. Hers sat on the face of the electric clock in the kitchen. It had two hands—one long, one short—and they never stopped moving. Pulling the plug wouldn't make any difference. It was only one member of a vast army of timepieces everywhere. She was simply more conscious of this particular one because they were together in the same room so often. And the vast army served one invisible master. Everyone called it Time, and it crunched hours while they were still warm. In the beginning it was Monday and the beginning of the week. And she was very young. Then it was Friday

28

and sunset and another weekend. There was the budding and the flowering and the fruiting and the falling leaves, and no stopping any of it, and then she was married and twenty-one and waiting for her first baby.

"Nine months," Fran had said. "The first eight aren't hard to take. It's those endless last four weeks."

Only for Josephine, the last flew by as the others, and Peter wasn't an infant totally dependent on her nearly long enough. Two years later Elsie came. She had Elsie, too, only a little while, and both children were growing so quickly. They had no intention of stopping, either. Then, instead of being twenty-two or twenty-nine or thirty—never mind, never mind, she had told herself on that particular birthday, how old is spring? . . . but am I really thirty-six? Impossible. And the creature kept devouring hours while messengers continued to sit on the faces of clocks to remind her. She had to accept the fact that she could never destroy it. She could only try to outrun it, knowing that in the end she'd lose the race.

Then came the morning in Ben Goudy's studio barn, the day after fifteen years of marriage when she stopped running, and she and time collided head on.

The impact caused no more noise than all those other sounds that frozen movement made: the whinnying of the wire horse, the sobbing of the marble girl, the thud of the stone man kneeling.

It had never happened to her before. What time took from her, she took back with both hands and used completely. Even as she submitted to it, she knew she was exhausting it. When it was all over, they were both satisfied. She had wrung out every second and for once they had been as equals. . . .

SHE HEARD a voice. It belonged to Ben Goudy. "Don't you think you ought to take a break?"

There was the smell of fresh coffee.

Josephine glanced at her watch. "I've been here three hours? I don't believe it."

"Let me see what you did."

"I had no idea what I was going to do," standing aside for him. "I just felt with my fingers until I found her inside the clay. Is she any good at all?"

"You tell me."

"Something wrong," slowly. "She hasn't started to breathe."

"Who told you clay should breathe?"

"I just know it should." She looked around for her sweater. It had been tossed over a crate. "Sometimes my children come home for lunch."

"Then by all means go and feed them."

"Is it all right if I come back tomorrow?"

"You haven't finished, have you?"

"No."

His shrug said, "Then you'll have to come back." She knew what he meant and smiled in relief.

"By the way, what's your name?"

"Trask. My husband publishes the *Digest*. He said you met him yesterday. You wanted to place an ad."

"Your first name."

"Oh—Josephine."

"Do you know that the woman you found in that lump of clay looks something like you?"

She looked at it again, but uncomfortably this time. "Perhaps, it's because I made it like that, just a face looking up; but all of a sudden it reminds me a little of a death mask."

"Have some coffee with me," he suggested, going to the burner. "I make terrible coffee, by the way."

She looked at her watch again. "Well, I have a few minutes."

"Is that the way you live, Mrs. Trask? Only minutes to spend on yourself?"

It was a conclusion more than a question. He took two cups from the low shelf next to the burner, poured coffee into both and offered her the one without the crack. "I'm sorry I don't have any milk. There's sugar somewhere."

"It's fine this way."

"Try it before you say that."

She sat next to him on the bench and sipped. After a moment she admitted, "It is terrible."

"I warned you."

"I make good coffee. At least my husband thinks so."

"If there's a trick to it, I've never learned it."

"You might," she said, smiling suspiciously at the stained percolator, "start with a clean pot." She wondered why she had ever been afraid of him. And she must have been, or she wouldn't have tried so hard to persuade Ted to return the portfolio. "I'll make coffee whenever I come—if you like."

"You're really coming back?"

"If you'll really let me."

Unexpectedly, he raised his head and demanded sharply, "What time is it?"

"What?"

"Come on, you're the one with the watch."

"Almost a quarter of," she said, confused. "Sixteen of—exactly."

"You know it exactly."

"I have to. I lead a very busy life, Mr. Goudy."

"What makes you think your life will suddenly become less busy, Mrs. Trask? Where will you find the time to come? Do you plan to give it from fourteen of until sixteen past?"

She forced herself to look directly at him. "I want to come very much."

"There are three primaries required to do sculpture," he told her. "You've just named the first: inclination. You want me to believe you have that?"

She replied at once and without blinking, "Yes."

"The other two primaries are time and material. I'll see that you have the material to work with." Still holding his cup he stood up and looked down at her. "But I can't find the time for you. You'll have to do that yourself."

"I will," she promised. "But starting tomorrow." She had risen to her feet again, and standing, finished the last of the bitter liquid in the cup. "Good-by, Mr. Goudy."

"Good-by."

"Thank you."

He didn't answer.

Josephine left the barn the way she had entered it. The burst of color was an ache behind her eyes—old gold and claret and russet. Inhaling the clear air, she looked up at the ripe sun and wondered why she had always called summer "dying" and never "harvest." Overhead, a flock of birds flew away from summer without a backward look.

Because they know they'll be back, she thought, climbing into the station wagon her husband had bought her. And so will I. Tomorrow, I'll be back.

Chapter Four

With her mother-in-law to take her place in case the children did show up for lunch, Josephine could have stayed at Ben Goudy's studio longer. Instead, she forced herself to leave. It was a teasing perverseness to hold back what had amounted to an almost purely physical pleasure until the next day. She couldn't keep herself from smiling and actually heard herself laughing softly at something she, herself, didn't completely understand. All she knew, as she backed into the driveway, was that she was happy. The flowers in her garden were dead. The leaves were dying, and pretty soon winter hail would pit the frozen gravel. But she was happy.

Sometimes Ted came home for lunch, too. Today his car wasn't in the driveway. She was relieved not to see it because that meant there were no problems at the paper. She remembered—it seemed such a long time ago—how upset she had been because Ted forgot to take the portfolio with him when he left that morning. She had read dire reasons into a trifling oversight.

Perhaps, she rationalized, if I have a new interest, I won't have to invent things to be upset about.

Later she would tell Ted what happened at the barn. He'll say it's good for me to have a hobby, she decided confidently. Of course, he'll say I have enough to do now, but I'll tell him I'll give it an hour, two at the most. I won't give it any more time. Ben Goudy doesn't understand that I simply don't have it to give. Still, I can easily manage a couple of hours.

Having resolved it to her own satisfaction, she ran up the back steps to the kitchen. At the open door, she stopped and looked at the children with an uneasy sense of guilt. She found herself staring at them with a detached curiosity, wondering how they got to be hers in the first place. There was even something disturbingly unfamiliar about them.

"Careful," her son said with a faintly superior smile. "That's programmed to self-destruct in five minutes." And there was something reassuringly familiar about them again.

The lid of the grill was open. A runny yellowish mixture dribbled over the sides of the stove and Elsie, armed with a spatula, was waving it helplessly over the fast-spreading, bubbling cartwheel.

"Would you mind telling me what you're doing?"

"Making pancakes."

Peter had pushed two kitchen chairs together and was sprawled across them eating a sandwich. "I said thanks, but no thanks. I'm too young to die."

"Maybe I used too much milk," Elsie admitted. "Is it too late to shake some more flour into it?"

"Yes," shortly. Some of the liquid had trickled down onto the scrubbed floor. The clean sink was cluttered with an unwashed collection of assorted utensils. A wooden spoon and an eggbeater coated with what had started to be pancake batter stuck out of a large red mixing bowl. Peter had added his own contribution to the bowl: a knife generously dipped in peanut butter and a jellied spoon. Nothing was the way she had left it. In rearranging the chairs, Peter had even managed to shove the table closer to the window.

"Where's your grandmother?"

"Still in bed," Elsie answered. "Is it okay if I spread this on an English muffin? It doesn't look so good, but it'll probably taste okay."

"Just turn off the grill. When you go back to school, I'll scrape off that mess and throw it away. What do you mean she's still in bed?"

"She's sick." Obviously offended by the assault on her culinary effort, Elsie added spitefully, "Maybe she's dying."

"Oh, shut up," her brother said. "She's just got a cold."

"I'm going up to see her," Josephine said anxiously. At that moment, the barn, the River Road, the statue of the powerful kneeling man and the upturned face of the woman who didn't look like her, but had

33

something of her in it, were so far away that if someone told her they had disappeared altogether she would have accepted it without question. She wouldn't even have taken the time to feel sorry. She simply didn't have the time to take.

"I don't want you to be late getting back to school. I'll open a can of soup and make you a fast sandwich to go with it."

"I don't want soup and I can make my own sandwich," Elsie told her.

"Well, all right. There's chicken salad in the refrigerator, or cheese and tomato if you don't want peanut butter. Maybe," she added, "it'll be safer if I make it for you."

Her daughter refused with a quick shake of her head. The face under the mop of red hair was flushed from more than standing over a hot grill. Her expression was a curious mixture of tragedy and belligerence.

"Never mind about the pancakes," Josephine said, attempting an understanding smile. But really, it was so simple to follow printed directions on a box. She herself had done it when she was much younger than Elsie. "Saturday I'll show you how to make them. Then next time they'll come out perfect."

Unexpectedly, Elsie said, "I hate pancakes."

"You mean you don't want to learn?"

"If I hate them, why should I learn?"

Mothers, Josephine thought bewildered, are supposed to understand daughters better than sons. Elsie and I are so unlike. I've got to try to understand her better. "All right," she said gently, "fix something yourself. I'm going upstairs."

IT TOOK a moment to adjust to the lack of light.

"Fran?"

Outside was such a pure and lovely day. On the way back from the barn, she had to squint into the bright sun. She switched on the floor lamp. The silk shade with the old-fashioned fringe gave off only a pale light, but it was easier to see now.

"Fran?" She spoke the name a little louder this time.

The older woman was lying without moving, eyes closed. One hand hung limply on the blanket. Beneath the stretched skin, bluish veins rose to the surface, trying to escape the prison of flesh, aging and often in pain, that still held them in. Lately, Fran complained a lot about arthritis.

"Sometimes," she had said wistfully, "my hands don't seem to belong to me anymore. They won't do anything I want them to do."

Remembering, Josephine clenched her own still strong ones. What would I do, she wondered with sudden panic, if mine stopped doing what I wanted them to do?

The hand on the blanket was almost gray, but the face on the pillow showed too much color. Fran's head turned slowly toward her. When her eyes opened, they overflowed with gratitude and apology.

She shouldn't apologize every time she isn't well, Josephine thought. It makes me uncomfortable. It's never her fault. And this time it's mine.

"I'm so sorry," Fran said.

"I had no right letting you go after candles yesterday. The forecast was for rain."

"I'm going to be a terrible bother to you." She managed to lift a drooping hand to her mouth. It stiffened when she coughed convulsively behind it.

"I'm calling Dr. Cullen."

"Oh, now, honey. All I've got is a touch of . . . something. He'll charge for a house call and prescribe exactly what I would—bed rest, juices and aspirins—if I've got a fever. Josie? What are you doing?"

"Finding out how much of a fever you have."

Fran tried to wave her away. "I'm running way under a hundred. I can tell."

A minute later Josephine held the thermometer under the light and announced, "One hundred and three."

"Really?" amazed.

"I'm calling him now. Have you eaten anything?"

"I hadn't the strength to get out of bed. I was sure part of it was being tired because we sat up so late last night. Wasn't it a nice anniversary party, though?"

"Yes," absentmindedly. "After I call the doctor and get Pete and Elsie off to school, I'll bring you some juice. Or do you want something to drink right away? Your lips look parched." Without waiting for an answer, she went into the adjoining bathroom and returned with a glass of water.

Fran took it, protesting, "You shouldn't have bothered. I don't want to be a bother. I'm sorry about the children. I told them to get lunch themselves. Did they manage all right?"

"Smooth as silk," Josephine lied, at the same time wincing inwardly at a vision of pancake batter hardening on the griddle. Every nerve end in her fingers itched to clean up her kitchen.

"You didn't say anything last night about going anywhere this morning."

"I know."

"Why didn't you tell me?"

For the first time since her mother-in-law came to live with them, Josephine found herself gripped by an unfamiliar resentment. She almost answered, "because I shouldn't have to account for all of my time. Maybe *fourteen of* until *sixteen past* should belong just to me."

Instead she said, "I'll tell you later," and added, "It's not important anyway." Because she wasn't sure exactly how important it really had been, she knew she wouldn't tell her.

"Josie? Before I forget, Frieda was here. She stood at the foot of the stairs and called, 'Anybody home?' "

Few people ever locked back doors in Ditchling. Yesterday, a stranger had walked in uninvited. He brought mud on his boots and his clothes dripped with the rain. What else had he brought?

"She woke me out of a sound sleep. I was too groggy to answer."

"Never mind. I'll call her. I'll do everything I have to do. Let me go now."

From that moment, she moved with her own special kind of efficiency —telephoned John Cullen who promised to come by as soon as possible, saw her children off\to afternoon classes, then carried up a tray with freshly squeezed orange juice to her mother-in-law along with lightly buttered toast and a pot of weak tea. She sat with her, then left behind a pitcher of fresh water and carried the tray downstairs again. After that there was time to clean the kitchen. The grill had to be scraped with a knife. There were even a few minutes left over to telephone Frieda.

"You didn't say anything about going anywhere this morning," Frieda said.

"There was some . . . business I had to attend to, something Ted wasn't able to do himself." Half a lie was also half a truth.

"Did Fran go with you? She wasn't home either. I yelled loud enough for her to know I was there."

Josephine explained about Fran.

"Oh, that's too bad," sympathetically. "You weren't wrong yesterday, worrying about her being out in the rain."

"She'll be fine. Dr. Cullen's on his way. With the antibiotics they have today—"

"It'll take a week to get over whatever it is she has," Frieda finished for her, "or seven days, if she just stays in bed and rests it out."

Josephine laughed. "You're probably right."

"It'll mess up your personal plans though, won't it? I know how much you were looking forward to going."

"Going where?"

"The outdoor auction, of course."

"I forgot. The outdoor auction."

"Josie, how could you? There are only two left. One this coming Saturday—and the week after that. Then it's over for the season."

"I better not count on this Saturday."

"Sure. With Fran laid up, you'll have your hands full."

"Yes," Josephine said, "my hands . . ."

Ben Goudy had said, "Look at your hands. They're trembling."

And she hid them behind her quickly and without intending to ask it, blurted out, "What didn't you like about my cake yesterday?"

Now the cake was eaten, and the clay he had given her used up.
. . .

A car stopped at the curb. Josephine abruptly ended the conversation. "John's here."

"I'll call you later."

Josephine knew with a certainty that she could count on the call, and for the second time in less than half a day she experienced an untamed and unfamiliar emotion. The first one had been resentment of Fran's questions about where she had been. What could she call this reaction to Frieda's genuine interest and constancy? Being crowded . . . This time she didn't even bother to reproach herself. If it was true, why deny it? She *did* feel crowded. Two new sensations in half a day. No, three. That other strange one in the studio. No name for that one yet, but she knew it was the opposite of being crowded. It was what a single tree might feel, alone in the forest, having the moonlight all to itself.

37

Chapter Five

DR. JOHN Cullen had an amiable, uncomplicated face that could look concerned and reassuring at the same time. It had worn the same expression through Pete's and Elsie's mumps, chicken pox and German measles, through Ted's bursitis and Fran's arthritis. The expression had been the same when on two occasions he informed Josephine that she was pregnant.

"But you know already, don't you?" he had said.

"I thought you might like to know, too."

"Very considerate." He thanked her soberly. "Boy or girl?"

"Boy. I've already painted a scene from 'Jack and the Beanstalk' on the nursery wall. Oh, it'll be a boy this time. Then a girl. Two years apart."

"To any other woman I'd suggest never to be too sure of a baby's sex or a baby's timing. There's too great a risk of disappointment."

"I've always believed in the right thing at the right time. I haven't been disappointed up to now. I won't this time."

"Somehow I don't think you will be."

"Long ago," she told him, "I decided exactly the direction my life was going to take."

"And in all things—order?"

She nodded. "I function best that way. Not everyone does."

"There's order, Josie, and there's the consummation of order."

She smiled. "You always were smarter than I am, John."

"The ultimate, the perfect objective . . ."

"Why is it wrong to plan for perfection?"

"Because life," he said, "is much too full of unknown factors for anyone to plan on the ultimate. The only true order is intangible space. Human beings aren't tossed like stars and satellites into orbit. No one down on this earth moves with invisible ties, in such mathematical precision."

"You don't understand. All my ties are invisible." Her voice was as strong as it was steady. "But I know they're there. Whenever crisis threatens the security around me, all I have to do is keep order in my own physical universe. The rest is simple."

"I think," he said, "I should be a little afraid of you, Josie. Instead, I'm a little afraid *for* you."

"Don't be. Order for me is as vital to my . . . fulfillment as breath is to the fulfillment of a newborn. My first," she told him confidently, "will be a boy. He'll be named Peter, after Ted's father."

The only jarring note was struck in his office on the last checkup before delivery. "Do you feel as well as you look?" He appeared to be taking stock of her from head to foot without taking his eyes from her face.

"I look ready to give birth," she said.

"What day?" There was teasing behind the smile.

"You know my date," impatiently.

"It could be the day after or the day before."

"It won't." Clumsily, she shifted her unaccustomed weight.

"What's bothering you?"

"It's been such an easy pregnancy."

"Is that a complaint?"

"Pregnancy is nothing at all."

"You are complaining."

"About the do-nothingness of it for me. My husband doesn't let me do a thing. And his mother's around to fill in for him when he isn't there. Last week I wanted to paint the nursery. She stopped me, so he did it. Now the color's all wrong. Ted wouldn't even let me mix it. He thought the fumes would make me nauseated. When Peter comes, I'll move him out for a few days and do it over again."

"What else won't they let you do?"

"Rearrange the furniture in the living room. I started pushing the couch to the window wall."

"That wasn't very bright," he suggested, "pushing furniture."

"It was wrong the way it was. All of a sudden I looked at it and knew it was in the wrong place. I had to make it right—but by myself. Don't you understand? For months now, I've been so totally uncreative."

"Josie," he reminded her, "you're creating life."

She shook her head stubbornly and stared at the marked protrusion of her stomach. "I'm not doing a thing. I'm practically a bystander. Everything's happening *to* me, not from me. And when nature completes its part, you'll take over and do what's left to be done."

He laughed. "Tell me, would you feel more creative if I left town when you go into labor and let you go off into the fields like a peasant and deliver the child alone?"

"Ted would just find another doctor." She wondered, knowing she'd never have the chance to prove it, if actually bringing forth life would make her own accomplishment seem any greater. "No," she said honestly, "I'd only be taking credit for God's work. I wouldn't deserve any more credit than you will."

He stopped laughing. "Josie? Are you jealous of Him?"

"Would it be a kind of blasphemy if I were?"

"I don't know," he admitted. "I really don't."

Dr. Cullen didn't leave town, and with his help Peter arrived exactly on the due date.

"Such fast easy labor, Josie," Fran said. "It was so difficult for me. Fifteen hours in labor. Did I ever tell you?"

"Being a grandmother," she promised, "will be much easier and a lot more fun."

"ALL RIGHT," Dr. Cullen was saying now, almost fourteen years later. "What's wrong with grandma?"

"She insists you'll examine her, tell her it's a touch of *something*, then charge her for a house call."

"She's right, and my price has gone up."

They smiled at each other and he reached out and squeezed her hand with affection.

"You okay?"

"I'm never sick. You know that."

"You look—" he hesitated.

"What?"

"I'm not sure. Not quite yourself."

She almost blurted out: For a while this morning, for the first time in my life, I forgot where I was—and who I was. I just know I wasn't myself at all. Have you anything in that bag that will tell me who I became for a while? Instead she said, "I've been rushing all morning. I'm fine." She ran up the stairs ahead of him.

Fran greeted him coolly. "It wasn't necessary for you to come, doctor."

"Don't begrudge me a fee, Mrs. Trask."

Josephine looked amused.

"Don't be sarcastic," Fran said flatly. "Josie shouldn't have bothered you to drive all the way here to prescribe aspirins."

A few minutes later, he wrote out a prescription.

"What's that?" Fran demanded suspiciously.

"An antibiotic. Take as directed, starting tomorrow morning."

"Ah!" triumphantly, "then I'll live through the day."

"Absolutely," he agreed, removing a small opaque bottle from the bag, "because there are enough pills here to last until then. One every three hours. These are my own samples, so I won't charge you for them. That should make you feel better about the bill I'll send." He turned to Josephine. "Give her one now. It'll probably make her groggy." He snapped shut his bag. "Before I leave, I'll suggest a diet for the next few days and maybe stop in again tomorrow."

For the first time, Fran appeared concerned. "What've I got?"

He winked at Josephine, then asked gravely, "Sure you can take it, Mrs. Trask?"

She bit her lip anxiously.

He took a deep breath. "I'd call it," he said, "a touch of . . . *something.*"

Fran glared furiously at him, as Josephine laughed and poured a glass of water from the pitcher.

"Capsules are better than pills," her mother-in-law said petulantly. "Pills melt on the way down."

"Don't be ungrateful," Dr. Cullen said good-naturedly. "Remember that's a sample."

Fran popped the yellow tablet into her mouth and gulped water. "It didn't melt," she announced, pleased with herself. "I'm a terrible patient. Poor Josie!"

"Never mind about me."

"With everything you have to do. This girl," she addressed the doctor, "is remarkable. Nobody else gets half as much done in one day."

"If I do," Josephine answered without thinking, "it's only because I don't waste any of my day on regrets." Puzzled, she wondered why she said what she did and exactly what she meant by it.

Downstairs, before he left, the doctor wrote out a diet. "With proper care, she'll be up and about in about a week."

"She'll get proper care."

"I don't doubt it." Unexpectedly he added, "What regrets would you have if you wasted some of your day having them, Josie?"

"I don't know why I said that. Maybe because I'm one of the lucky ones. I don't have any."

"You are lucky." As she closed the door behind him, she had the uncomfortable feeling that he hadn't been completely convinced.

She returned to the patient upstairs.

"Was I rude to the doctor?" Fran asked.

"I'm sure he didn't think so," flipping the pillow to the cooler side.

"Don't be insulted if I fall asleep on you. I feel floaty." She sounded intoxicated.

"It's a reaction to the pill. John said to expect it."

"Nice of him to leave his own samples." Fran stifled a yawn.

"He's a nice man." Josephine said it as if she were talking to her younger child and waited for invisible weights to close the eyelids.

Instead, a sudden thought gave them the energy to open wider than before. "Are you surprised he didn't remarry after his wife died?"

What surprised Josie was the abruptness of the question.

"Well, why don't you think he did?" Fran asked again.

"I never thought about it."

Her mother-in-law gave a swaggering little laugh. "Well, it's not because there wasn't anyone else. There was someone John Cullen would have married in a minute, only she wasn't available."

"Since when do you listen to gossip?"

"I never gossip. Of course, I love it when other people do it for me." Her shoulders sank even deeper into the pillow. "Aren't you interested in knowing who?"

"If it's true, it's his business."

"Not yours?"

"Any reason it should be?"

"There could be." Without warning she followed the suggestion with the statement. "You're the one he's in love with, Josie." This time, when her lids closed, they appeared sealed tightly. Josephine had the distinct impression that, behind them, eyes were alert, begging to be called back.

She obliged them. "What did you just say?"

Fran's eyes flew open again, brimming with innocence. Then she saw the anger in her daughter-in-law's face and a belated sense of discretion hastened to let her know, "Oh, I'm not the one who said it." It also made her very sorry to have been the one who repeated the story. She had thought—she realized now it had been a stupid blundering thought— that a touch of flattery might compensate for some of the extra work this "touch of *something*" was going to cause—the running up and down of stairs, the shakings of the thermometer, the turnings of the pillow—all her fault. The truth was she had expected a better reception for her well-intended compliment.

"I'm asking you who did say it?"

"Please, Josie, I really am light-headed. It's not important."

"Important enough for someone to tell it to you," stubbornly.

"Making so much of nothing. It's not like you."

"I hate gossip. It's so—" she searched for the right word to damn it and came up with "untidy." Then, after a moment, "Who said it, Fran?"

Fran threw out the words "Frieda Haines" like a sacrifice, as if hoping the offering would end the discussion.

"Frieda?" stunned.

"It came up just once—in idle conversation. And it was her own personal opinion. So you see, honey," soothingly, "it isn't actually gossip. Gossip is when something is spread. This was . . . just between us."

After a moment, Josephine half-whispered, "How dare she? Was that something for my best friend to talk over with my husband's mother?"

"As if I'd ever believe you'd encourage anything like that."

"You might have."

Fran raised offended eyes to her. "Your husband's mother! Aren't I any more to you than that, Josie?"

"Of course you are," unmoved, "but that's what you are to Frieda."

"You promised to forget I ever mentioned it," Fran said quickly, in the hope that Josie would be confused into believing she had actually made the promise.

If Josephine didn't answer immediately, it was because she was wondering how uncomfortable she was going to be next time she saw John Cullen, or if she would ever feel quite as comfortable with him again.

He had been more than a doctor to care for her physical needs. In the walled intimacy of his office, she had told him things she never told her husband in the walled intimacy of their bedroom. She couldn't have confessed to Ted, for instance, how uncreative she felt during pregnancy. Ted wouldn't have understood. It didn't matter if John did or not. He was only her doctor; he was impersonal and had other patients. A statement like that would have bothered her husband, but nothing she could say could ever disturb the rest of John Cullen's day or any part of John Cullen's life because she had no part in the rest of it.

Now there was Frieda saying that she had.

Suddenly she felt as if she was the one who had swallowed something that made her groggy. It had been a long day, longer than usual somehow, and still only half over. Already she was having difficulty remembering back to early morning when she had discovered the black portfolio still in the room.

"Never mind. I'll forget you mentioned it."

Maybe, she thought, I'm coming down with a touch of something myself. I resented it when Fran wondered why I wasn't here for lunch when I should have been. It's where I belong. And when Frieda asked me, I felt . . . crowded. To be upset with her for having a loose tongue is one thing, but to be angry with her for asking a simple question isn't fair. Where was I part of this morning? It doesn't matter. Only losing control matters. Fran's right. It's not like me. What's wrong with me today?

"You're sure you won't say anything to Frieda?"

"I told you I'd forget it." If it wasn't worth hearing, it wasn't worth remembering.

"Thank you, honey." The smile pulling at her cheeks showed her age. "Do something else for me? Go down to the square and get the prescription filled."

"I'll wait until the children are home from school. That way they'll be in the house if you need anything."

"The druggist is across the street from the *Digest.*"

She frowned. "I know that."

"While you're waiting for the prescription, stop in and see Ted."

Josephine placed both hands on her stomach to quiet it. "Any special reason?"

"I wouldn't let him say anything last night. It would have spoiled our party."

"Then I wasn't imagining it," softly.

"He was afraid you came close to guessing the truth."

What was the truth? But mixed with her natural alarm was a kind of relief. From the moment she returned from the River Road, she felt like a stranger in her own home. There had never before been a time when she was unsatisfied to be in it, never a time before when she felt there was somewhere more important, secret, dark and waiting, where she should be instead.

I felt I should be with my husband, of course, she tried to convince herself. My life is so bound up with his that when he's in trouble, I can sense it.

And that, very simply, was all that had been wrong with her. Even John said she looked different. At the time she thought it had to do with a few hours spent in Ben Goudy's barn. It had nothing to do with that at all.

"It's the paper," Fran was saying. "Something about—"

"Harris Bartlett?"

"And the plant. What do I know about these things? Let Teddy explain. Didn't they meet for breakfast?"

"Yes."

"Then he's been back a long time. He may need you."

"But I can't leave you."

"I'm so tired," Fran murmured. Her eyes closed and she was breathing heavily. Josephine had no way of knowing if sleep was a pretense. For the second time that day, she draped the cardigan around her shoulders and ran from the house.

Chapter Six

.

TED WASN'T in his office, but Millie was at her desk in the cubicle outside it. "He's at the Chamber of Commerce, Mrs. T."

The newspaper was the center of Millie's world. She spent the hours from nine to five at the *Digest,* sending out for lunch, moving within the small radius of telephone to typewriter, desk to files, and it was only here that she knew any personal freedom.

She was typing legals when Josephine arrived and she looked up from under uneven eyebrows she plucked herself. No professional could have done the job so inexpertly, and no hairdresser would have been guilty of half-hiding that shortened forehead with such a tangled fringe of graying hair.

Millie's features were useful: by the kindest stretch of the imagination, not one could be considered ornamental. Josephine often wondered if it bothered Millie that she had grown into her forties unloved by any man. If there had been one, someone in Ditchling would have known.

She wondered if Millie silently rebelled at the monotony of years spent caring for an ailing mother and a demanding, senile father who wouldn't eat dinner unless she made and served it and who refused to go to sleep unless she was in the house.

She never seemed to resent the fact that other people had been granted more from life. She lived hers with a simplicity almost childlike in its trust that the next day would be as uneventful and no worse than the one just ended. That was the only luxury she asked. Because it was so little, it was all she got.

"He'll be back any minute," she was saying. "Why don't you wait?"

"Sure."

They smiled at each other, Millie with lips that always appeared slightly swollen.

But for the first time, Josephine found herself thinking with surprise: she's not really ugly. God doesn't create anything that isn't beautiful, if only we have eyes to see it. She found herself wondering what Ben Goudy could make of a face like that. I could do something exciting, she thought, if I had his talent and his time. Unfortunately, I don't have either.

She had to remind herself that she wasn't there to think of anything except the paper. Millie might know something.

"He was at Middleburg this morning, wasn't he?" Josephine said, closely watching the face she had just decided was not ugly.

"This is his usual day for that," noncommittally.

"Did he say anything about his breakfast?"

Millie looked confused. "Didn't he have it before he left home this morning? He's feeling okay, isn't he?"

She knows even less than I do, Josephine decided. "Mr. Bartlett invited him to have breakfast with him in Middleburg."

"That must have been a fat thrill." She returned to typing legals.

Millie had strong feelings about Harris Bartlett. Josephine neither liked nor disliked him. It was difficult to feel anything toward someone who never let you know what he was thinking.

If Ted had been uneasy about the breakfast meeting, it was because he knew that, with a smile as neatly arranged on his face as the tie on his white shirt, Harris Bartlett was capable of offering a moist limp handshake while he announced with equal emphasis that it was nice seeing him again . . . or that he was going to stop letting them use his plant.

"And that," Ted told her when he came in a few minutes later, "is exactly what he's threatening to do."

"I suspected it last night," Josephine said, deliberately keeping her voice low. They had closed the door to his office to keep Millie from overhearing them. "Didn't I say so?"

"There was no reason to upset you until I was absolutely sure."

47

"Why should he do this to you?"

"Oh, it's nothing personal. You remember Ed Brucker? Oakdale *Press?*"

"What's he got to do with this?"

"Everything. Ed had enough of our New England winters and decided to sell. Bartlett offered him a better price than anyone else. Once he took over, he filled the *Press* with boilerplate, canned news, canned cartoons—"

"Like the Middleburg *Banner.*"

"It costs practically nothing to set up and he keeps all the profit. From Bartlett's point of view," banging the clutter on his desk in several places, "it's just good business."

"What are you looking for?"

"A pack of cigarettes buried somewhere under this mess."

"You gave up smoking," she reminded him, "a year ago."

"I started again on the way back to Middleburg." He spotted the edge of the pack of cigarettes, grabbed it and, shaking one out, quickly lit it. "Don't get on my back about it now, Josie."

She let him inhale deeply, then asked, "Did he make us an offer, too?"

"A pretty good one."

"Well, we're not selling."

"He offered me the job as editor."

"A lazy editor? Pasting a paper together from syndicated mat services? That's not what you had in mind when you started the *Digest.*"

"That's not what any of the others had in mind when they started, either."

"Others?"

"Bartlett's been moving in, buying up as many weeklies in the state as he can get his claws into. In most cases he's made the former owner the managing editor."

"How much editing do they do?"

"They make good enough caretakers."

She wiped her fingers across her forehead. It felt as dry as her throat. "So suddenly—with no warning."

"I've been afraid of this for a long time. I wanted to make it easier for you by not saying anything. Throwing it at you like this . . . is probably rougher. I'm sorry."

She reached over, gently took the cigarette from his mouth and firmly snuffed it out. He let her do so without protest. It would have been better if he fought her. It would have proved he had spirit left in him.

"There's isn't any use," he said. "In the end, he'll get what he wants."

"You'll figure out something." Lightly, she hoisted herself up on the desk beside him. "Listen," she began, then stopped and laughed.

"If you can see something funny in all this," he said, "tell me."

"Us. Look at us! This could be fifteen years ago, sitting side by side on the same desk. We had no choice then. We had no chairs."

"So we're back where we started."

"Oh, no. We've come a long way since. The children—"

"You know I didn't mean that."

She put an arm around his shoulder. It was rigid and unyielding. "If you really want a cigarette, I'll light another for you."

He shook his head.

"You really don't need it," she approved. "Listen, I'm not much good at business . . ."

"I wouldn't bet on that. You've got a mind like a computer." He patted her knee. "In this team, Josie, I'm the one with the imagination. I suppose it's because I'm more creative. It's you—and your fantastic sense of order—who could be the real business head in this family."

Josephine stiffened and turned her head. For a moment she wasn't with him at all. Inside the barn a north light formed an invisible dome, and she was telling Ben Goudy how her mother once gave her some clay, how she cried because she didn't know what to do with it. So he gave her other clay, and in it she found something. . . .

"It's true," Ted said. "Don't be modest, Josie. You are the clearer-thinking half of this team. Sometimes I let my enthusiasm run away with me, I admit it. It's never true with you."

"All right," she said almost politely, "suppose I throw some questions. You throw back the answers. Maybe you'll find the one you need."

From outside the office, Millie, holding two containers of coffee, knocked on the door with her elbow. "Anyone in there want coffee?"

"Love it," Ted called back.

"Then get it before it spills. Cardboard containers are hot."

A few minutes later she left them alone again.

"Cardboard containers," Ted said, "also make coffee taste like cardboard."

Josephine started to tell him how much better it was than the coffee Ben Goudy gave her earlier. "It's hot," she said instead, "and tastes fine. Ready?"

"Ready."

"You're president of the newspaper association in this area. How many others have been approached by Bartlett?"

"I don't know."

"How long do you have to make up your mind?"

"Until thirty days before the contract is up. Sometime in March."

"And if we don't sell?"

"It wouldn't take much for him to launch a rival paper in this town."

"But the *Digest* has a big following. Haven't we built a healthy circulation?"

"It takes more than circulation to keep a newspaper running. It takes ads."

"Why should our advertisers suddenly go over to him?"

"Because he could offer them lower rates and wider coverage, operating a system of block advertising."

"What's block advertising?"

"If he manages to get control over a lot of papers, the ones he has now plus those he hopes to gobble up, advertisers would get a lower rate for every additional paper."

"I understand," she said.

"Our circulation covers only Ditchling. How could I hope to match that?"

"Is looking for another plant the answer?"

"I've been to three within a seventy-mile radius."

"And never said a word to me?"

"The soonest any of them could take us on," he said, as if he hadn't heard her, "is eight months from now. That means we'd be out of business for three months while Bartlett begins to build here. So what would we be coming back to? Even if we had circulation left, there's that business of the ads again—or the lack of them."

He finished the last of his coffee and made an inept toss at the wastebasket. "Any more questions?" pleasantly. "I'm ready with a few more depressing answers."

"How many other locals are in our association?"

"Ten, including us."

"What if *all* of you hold out? What if he can't get any of you to sell?"

For the first time Ted grinned. "You know, I'd like to hit him over the head with *that,* just to see his face crack. We were together for over an hour this morning. In all that time his expression didn't change. Not once. It was . . . like sitting across the table from someone wearing a—"

"Death mask," she said, as she had earlier about another face.

Do you know that the woman you found in that lump of clay looks something like you? Ben Goudy had asked. . . .

That was then. This was now. Anyone so clear-thinking as Ted believed she was should be able to keep a simple conversation on track. There was no room for detours—not in their discussion, not in her life.

"Maybe this is a stupid question, but if he can form an advertising block, why can't you?"

"Oh, come on, Josie! With what?"

"Other locals who won't buckle under to him."

Ted looked uncertain, but his shoulders relaxed slightly. "For all I know, they already have."

"Ask them. If they haven't—"

"Maybe," he finished slowly, "we could form our own independent cooperative."

She was on the verge of asking exactly what that was, but thought— never mind, he's thinking out loud.

"A combine for advertising rates. We might even be able to give Bartlett a run for his money." He was on his feet now. "If we pooled our resources, maybe we could even start a plant of our own, start a corporation . . . sell stock. . . ."

"Would that be possible?"

"I'm beginning to think," he said, "anything's possible in this best or worst of all possible worlds—as long as you're in it with me. Didn't I just say you were clear-thinking?"

"Only not very creative." He was all wound up and didn't hear her murmur the words.

"A combine of our own, Josie, with our own papers for cooperative advertising! You're wonderful!"

She held up her hand. "Don't give me credit for any of it. I'm not even sure what it means."

"You started me thinking. Of course," he added soberly, "none of it'll come to anything if the others have already decided to go over to Bartlett."

"Then get them together and find out."

He flung wide the office door and shouted, "Millie!"

"I can hear you," she said. "Honest."

51

"Where's the list of names—office and home phone numbers of the members of the County Association of Publishers?"

"Filed under *A*," she said, "for Association. Or *P* for Publishers, or *C* for County, or *H*."

"*H* for what?"

"How Soon Do You Need It?"

"Actually," he told her, "I needed it this morning, before I kept a very unpleasant appointment." He let the door slam shut again and turned back to Josephine. "Was yours very unpleasant, too? Sorry, I forgot to ask."

"I don't know what you mean."

"That damn portfolio. I walked right by it. It wasn't deliberate, Josie."

"I was sure it wasn't."

"Halfway to Middleburg I remembered."

"It didn't matter."

"I know you didn't want to take it back yourself."

All she said was, "I shouldn't have bothered you about it."

"You did return it?"

"Yes."

"And?"

"He thanked me." Then she told him about his mother.

"You're sure John said it isn't serious?"

"She'll be fine, but I want to get back to her. I'm going to pick up the prescription now."

"Was he at least polite?"

"Ben Goudy?" as if she didn't understand. "I guess he was polite enough." What she really didn't understand was why she hadn't said anything more about what happened at the studio. She had planned to tell her husband that she could easily spare a few hours out of her busy schedule. She had even rehearsed: "Of course it won't be too much for me. I can manage. Actually, a hobby will be good to have. A nice healthy hobby is good for anybody to have."

Only he might laugh at her. After all, he was the creative member of their team.

"See you later," she said, and kissed him good-by.

He pulled her to him and in a low voice said, "I'm glad I didn't spoil last night by telling you then about the paper. It was a nice anniversary party, wasn't it?"

She shivered slightly when he laughed softly into her ear. "Did you notice the way Pete ate the cake? Saving the frosting for last?"

"I didn't notice."

"Like father, like son. I saved my frosting, too. The last part of the party was the best, wasn't it, Josie?"

She closed her eyes and clung to him. It was easier than looking at him.

"I love you, too," he whispered.

Chapter Seven

SHE DIDN'T go back to the barn the next day. There was a sick woman to be cared for in the room upstairs. As he promised, the doctor paid a second visit. There was, he told Josephine, an epidemic of flu going around. He stayed only a few minutes.

It wasn't until after he drove off that Josephine remembered she had forgotten to be ill at ease with him after what Fran had told her. Everything was the way it had always been between them. And she had dreaded seeing him again, just as she had dreaded seeing Ben Goudy again. That meant she could put the nonsense Frieda suggested out of her mind. It would be simple because it had been senseless. In retrospect, the meeting with Ben Goudy didn't make much more sense.

"Rice soup again," she announced, carrying in a tray. "Make a face if you want to."

"I hate to be such a bother," Fran said. "It looks delicious."

During the days that followed, her mother-in-law grew increasingly better, and the kitchen, since Josephine was in it more than usual, was increasingly filled with tantalizing baking smells. It wasn't too early to begin thinking of the holidays. Christmas cookies, fresh from the oven, were well sealed and stored in the freezer.

One day, when she had nothing else to do, she even baked bread.

"Nobody bakes bread anymore," Peter said.

"I do."

"What's dad decided about me fixing up the basement room?"

"He said okay."

"Hey, great."

"There's a condition."

"Isn't there always?"

"I'm to help you."

"But I want to fix it up myself. That was the whole idea."

"He meant help you clean it out first."

He favored her with a broad generous smile. "Be my guest."

"There has to be a system, Pete. There's so much that has to be looked through carefully and packed properly."

"Can we start today?"

"Sure. After you do your homework."

To PETER, all it meant was emptying the basement room. For his mother, it meant filling her arms and memory with the years that had happened. But at least she could hold in her arms for a little while the tangible proof that they had been.

Peter looked at her and laughed.

"What's so funny?"

"The way you're carrying that bundle of papers. Like a baby."

He wasn't so wrong. The *Digest* had been their firstborn. We can't let it die, she determined fiercely.

She had suggested to Ted that it might be best if she invited the publishers to a meeting at their house—a meeting that could decide a common fate.

"It's a good idea," he said, "if the calls aren't made from the office. Millie might overhear and I don't want her to suspect the paper could go. It means too much to her."

Now, packing back issues into crates, she remembered how she had answered, "It means too much to all of us."

"Dad's really counting on me taking over the paper one day, isn't he?" Peter was saying.

If there is still a paper, she thought. But all she said was, "I'm sure he'd like that very much."

"What if I don't want to?"

55

Perhaps it was because he was asking the question now, when they were trying desperately to save the paper, that the question came as a slap. She put her hand to her cheek. "You've always talked about being a newspaperman, too, Pete, ever since you were old enough to talk."

"But the Ditchling *Digest* isn't exactly the *New York Times.*"

"No, it isn't."

"Maybe I want something better than a little local. Maybe I don't want to settle for second best."

The young are so arrogant, Josephine thought. He's calling what we have "settling," what we are "second best." Maybe deep down, we know second best is all we were born to be. But right now, if we lose that, we have even less. Peter doesn't know how cruel he's being.

"I'm not knocking the *Digest.* It's great. For what it is."

She was sitting on the floor beside a packing case. "I hope," she said, "that when the time comes, your byline in the *New York Times* is the one people will look for first—if that's what you want. But how much do you really know about a weekly press?"

"I could probably run the *Digest.* It's not very big."

"I don't mean our own. I mean grassroots papers all over the country." She could see him wince at "grassroots."

"It sounds so folksy."

"A weekly press is very folksy. It's also been the breeding place for writers, editors and publishers all through our history. Ask your father. He'll tell you."

Suddenly, he was on the floor beside her. "I hurt your feelings."

She caressed the side of the box that held all of the issues that had been published during the first months of the *Digest*'s existence. "I don't want anything to happen to our paper."

"What's going to?" But the question was asked without any real concern. Why should she expect him to be either possessive or protective of anything he had never had to fight for?

She gave him a reassuring slap on the knee. "Nothing," briskly. "But we're going to catch pneumonia if we keep sitting on this cold basement floor. Fran will take the blame. She'll say we caught it from her."

"And apologize."

"Don't be fresh." But they exchanged a smile of secret understanding.

ANOTHER SATURDAY came.

For the first time in more than a week, Fran dressed and came downstairs. "There must be something I can do for tonight."

"Everything's done."

"Teddy nervous?"

"More excited, I think. Your son should have been a trial lawyer. He loves pleading—" she hesitated, then said, "worthy causes," catching herself in time from calling it a lost cause. It bothered her that the phrase even crossed her mind.

"Do the other publishers know what the meeting's all about?"

"Some of them may have been in touch with each other. It doesn't matter. What matters is getting together tonight and promising to stay together. Are you sure you won't need me if I go out for a while this afternoon?"

Fran gave her a pained look. "After I've kept you tied up over a week waiting on me?"

"I didn't feel tied down, and it gave me an excuse to get my Christmas baking done early."

"There was nothing you canceled on my account?"

"Just the auction," she lied, "last Saturday. It doesn't matter. I'm going today."

"Have a nice time. Come back with a treasure."

FRIEDA WAS at the front window, waiting. They drove to the auction in the station wagon.

"We couldn't have a better day for it," Frieda said once they arrived. They were wandering around the big yard examining items that would be going up on the block. "How do you feel—after your internment?"

Josephine picked up a brass inkstand. "You make it sound so grim."

"Well, wasn't it?"

"Since I saw you last, I got a lot of things done that needed doing. And Fran was no trouble."

"She was a perfect patient, I'll bet."

"As a matter of fact, she was."

"Naturally. What are you going to do with that inkstand?"

"Leave it where it is."

"Oh," disappointed. "I love to come to these auctions with you. You usually come up with so many fascinating ideas, like how to turn old spittoons into birdbaths."

Josephine had to admit it was good being out of the house, especially on such a ripe autumn day. She laughed into it. "I never turned a spittoon into a bird bath. You said once before that Fran was perfect, that in my house she wouldn't dare to be otherwise."

"Imagine you brooding over that."

"I wasn't brooding. It was just a statement."

"I also said you ran the perfect house."

"I remember that, too." She also remembered the day—rainwashed, not sunwashed like this one.

Frieda jerked her hands smartly upright in mock surrender. "Are you planning to shoot me for saying you run the perfect house? I meant it as a compliment. I'm jealous because I'm such a slob."

They continued to wander idly about the yard. There was nothing that particularly attracted her in the marble-topped nightstands or the empty bird cages. She kept looking. Fran had told her to come back with a treasure.

She saw her own face reflected in the convex surface of an old pitcher. Distorted in the gleaming curve, it looked more like her than the face she had found in the clay. It, at least, breathed in the silver. The face she had found in the clay hadn't breathed at all. *Who told you clay should breathe?* he had asked. And she had answered, *I just know it.*

Until today, she thought, I had an excuse: Fran was sick. Today, I had no excuse. Why didn't I go back? I could be at the barn, instead of here.

She felt Frieda tug at her sleeve. "They're starting. Anything here you're going to bid on?"

"I'm not sure . . ." Josephine began, and stopped. Moving toward the auction block, like scattered autumn leaves being swept together, was the crowd, regulars from Ditchling and familiar faces from nearby Middleburg and Mitford and Kingston. Mixed in with these were the unmistakable dealers from the city, hoping to snatch up a thumbprinted Waterford glass bowl from the wooden block and set it against a background of velvet in a Madison Avenue shop window, or a slipper chair that had been gathering dust in an attic, or an antique clock someone had been glad to get rid of because it hadn't run for years.

And leaning against a roll-away bed, watching with the semidetached interest of a puppet master, was Ben Goudy.

She guessed he was there before she saw him. She must have guessed it or she would have been more surprised to see him. After almost ten days of internment—Frieda was right, that's what it had been—she felt suddenly alive again. There was just the right amount of bite in the air.

"There's your friend," Frieda whispered.

Josephine pretended not to understand. "Who?"

"Ben Goudy. Over there. See? What do you think of that outfit?"

Secretly, Josephine thought he looked rather wonderful, with the wide hammered silver buckle of his belt flat against the buckskin shirt. He had pulled heavy lumberman's boots over black corduroy trousers. The oversized rings on his fingers had probably been made from twisted wire scraps. Because she had known the elongated wire horse, she felt she knew the rings.

"A real eccentric." Frieda dug her nails into Josephine's arm. "I think he's coming over here."

A moment later he was. "What do you think of all this junk, Mrs. Trask?"

"Well, you've heard the expression: one man's junk is another man's antique."

He nodded. "The only thing that interests me is that roll-away bed. You're probably an old hand at this. How much do you figure it'll go for?"

"If nobody else has a need for a roll-away bed, you can practically take it away for the asking."

"I dragged a mattress in from the house and put it on the floor. With the cold weather coming on, sleeping on it might not be such a good idea."

"Weren't there any beds in the house, Mr. Goudy?"

He shrugged. "Big four-poster affairs. What would I want with those? Four-posters were designed for women of another generation who had their babies at home and needed something to hold onto while they were whelping. I just need something to sleep on."

Josephine didn't know how to answer that and Frieda saved her from trying by deliberately brushing up against her.

"My friend, Mrs. Haines," Josephine said, suddenly remembering her friend was there.

"How do you do?" Frieda said in her best P.T.A. voice. "How do you like Ditchling, Mr. Goudy?"

"How do *you* like it?"

"Very much," she said, flustered.

59

"Good." He turned and walked away.

Josephine sensed Frieda's embarrassment. I should be embarrassed as much for him, she thought—for his indifference to what other people think about him. Or maybe it isn't indifference. It's possible he's deliberately rude. There are certain people he takes malicious pleasure in offending. Anyone outside his world and his interests is superfluous. It's presumptuous and affected and vain, but in his own way he's being honest. In his own way he was being honest that first time we met. I was tolerated only because my kitchen was dry, and he let me know it.

Frieda whirled on her. "Who the hell does he think he is?" Her ample figure swelled with rage. "I'd still like to slap his face."

"For the same reason you gave once before? Because he's too much man?"

"Probably a cover-up," Frieda snapped. "I'll bet he's homosexual."

"I don't think so," looking after him.

"The kind who hates women. Some gays like women, you know."

"I know very little about the subject," testily. "You're the one who seems to be the authority."

"I don't know why you're so mad at *me* all of a sudden."

"It's in poor taste to jump to conclusions about somebody you hardly know—somebody you met for a few minutes."

"That's how I get my mental exercise," Frieda quipped, "jumping to conclusions. What makes you so sure he's straight? How well do you know him? You just met him once yourself."

"Twice," without thinking.

Frieda frowned. "The first time was when he walked into your house without being asked, wasn't it?"

"And the second time," Josephine improvised quickly, "was a few minutes ago. Look, there's something I want coming up."

Frieda turned her attention to the auctioneer. "You don't always tell me the truth, do you?"

"Don't I?"

"You said you never turn old spittoons into birdbaths. Now you're going to bid on one."

"Not for a birdbath. I have something else in mind."

"Something marvelous and original?"

Josephine smiled suggestively, then answered, "I'm going to use it as a spittoon."

"You've got to be kidding."

Frieda looked as startled as Ben Goudy when Josephine bid a dollar
... *going* ... and a half ... *going* ... and two dollars. "Gone!" declared
the auctioneer and the gaudy spittoon was hers.

"You weren't kidding," Frieda gasped.

"Pete is fixing up the basement. I'm going to suggest doing it as an
old-fashioned Western saloon. If I can't, I've lost two dollars." And had
the fun, she thought, of seeing your face when I started bidding for it,
and Ben Goudy's jaw drop when I actually bought it. For a few moments, confusion had caused him to lose some of his superiority.

She had been right about the roll-away bed. Nobody else wanted it,
so he got it for three dollars.

"I hope it's lumpy," Frieda said spitefully.

"There's nothing else I want here. You?"

Frieda shook her head.

"I've got to get home then. There's a press association meeting at our
house tonight."

Just before they left, Josephine looked around. He was already gone.
As she slid behind the wheel, she admitted to herself that she had been
afraid all during the brief meeting that he would ask her why she hadn't
returned to finish what she had started. Now she was disappointed
because he hadn't.

Chapter Eight

EIGHT OF the publisher-editors who formed the County Association of Publishers arrived almost at the same time. Only Stan Ryder of the *Leader* came late, winking broadly at Josephine as he walked in. "I had to wait for kitten here. She was in the bathroom fussing with her hair."

"Oh, daddy," the girl in tight slacks said, "did you have to tell her that?"

"It's all right that I brought her, isn't it, Josie?"

"Of course."

"Mabel's at the country club. She's got herself all involved with the dance we're having. Hope you and Ted will make that."

"We'll try," she said, without meaning it, at the same time taking their coats and passing them on to Elsie who hung them in the guest closet.

"I didn't want to leave her home alone. You know the sort of thing that can happen if a young pretty girl's left alone in a house these days."

"Elsie," Josephine suggested, "take Judy downstairs. Maybe she'll be interested in what Pete's doing."

"He's putting down a new floor," Elsie said, studying the older girl with undisguised hostility, "only I'm helping."

"I'm not much good at things like that, but I'll watch, if he won't mind."

"I'm sure he won't." Josephine wondered if Judy's turtleneck sweater had shrunk in the wash, been outgrown or deliberately been bought a size too small.

"A knockout, isn't she?" Stan Ryder bragged. "She's got boyfriends like fish, a regular school of them."

"Oh, daddy!" Judy tossed long straight hair from one side to the other. As it flew by, she caught some of it between even rows of white teeth and began sucking on one end.

"Tell Pete I'll carry down a tray for the three of you a little later," Josephine said. "Go on."

"That's right," Stan said. "Go with Elsie, kitten." He shook his head after them. "Your girl's eleven, isn't she, Josie?"

"Yes."

"Isn't it something, the difference a couple of years makes?"

He put a comforting arm around her and they started toward the living room where the others were waiting. "Don't worry; one of these days your Elsie will change from a caterpillar into a regular butterfly. Just like my Judy."

"WELL," TED said getting up, "it's Stan. We're all here. Now we can start."

She seemed to spend part of the hour that followed underwater. Words swirled around her head, wrapped in little bubbles. Every once in a while, one of the bubbles burst and she was able to put a few together and make sentences—half sentences with no real meaning.

I'm not concentrating, she decided, because no matter what Ted believes, I don't really understand business. I'm not clever in business and I'm not really creative. I'm good only at arranging my cupboard so that the glasses are in steps. It drives Frieda insane. And I can make and decorate cakes.

The one she had decorated for that night had a frosted masthead of the *Digest.*

"Very effective, Josie," Stan Ryder told her. "Only an effigy of Harris Bartlett would have been better."

She had set a table with sandwiches and cold beer, and there was coffee in her big electric percolator. That table was her biggest contribution to the evening, except for lending Ted a certain comfort simply by being there, hands folded in her lap, only half-hearing under a depth of imaginary water.

Her thoughts had gone to other things, foolish things, like the spittoon. She wondered if Peter would like the idea of a Western saloon. It had been fun seeing the expression on Ben Goudy's face. But he hadn't asked her why she hadn't come back, and she hadn't asked him what he had done with the head she started. Squashed it back into a lump probably. It wasn't any good anyway.

"Let's take a break and have something to eat," she heard Ted say.

Since everything was set buffet-style, there was nothing to do for the men, so she kept her promise and carried a tray downstairs. "Why, Pete," she said pleased, "how much you've done!"

"I did some," Elsie informed her, at the same time giving a swift, unfriendly glance at Judy Ryder, who was perched, legs crossed, on a large crate, still sucking on a lock of her hair. She parted her lips and the strand dropped moist and pointed onto the sweater that rose in two hard-tipped points.

Josephine saw Peter swallow hard, then turn back to put down another tile.

"You know how she got up there?" Elsie whispered. "He lifted her."

"There's a lemon-lime for you, Judy. Your father said you liked it."

"I don't really," was the ungracious reply.

Peter shrugged. "Have my ginger ale then."

"You're awfully nice."

"Is there more cake," Elsie asked, "if I want more?"

"Have mine," Judy said. "I'm on a diet."

"I don't see why you have to be," Peter said; then, "Hey!" to his sister, "you're supposed to set those tiles in easy, not slap them down."

Upstairs, in Fran's room, Josephine set down a second tray. "I'm not sure if Elsie's jealous because Peter's paying so much attention to a girl, or if she's upset because the girl is Judy Ryder."

"What's she like?"

Josephine hesitated before admitting Judy was pretty. "But I don't like her and I'm glad she doesn't live in Ditchling."

"Mitford isn't that far away, honey."

"Far enough for a boy who isn't really interested in girls. Not yet anyway."

"How's the meeting going?"

"They're doing a lot of talking."

"How much of this came as a surprise to the others?"

"Bartlett had already approached every one of them. Unless somebody's not telling the truth, no one's agreed to sell out yet."

"Then this meeting of yours was a good idea."

"Ted would have thought of it if I hadn't." Before she left, she said, "If Elsie's going to turn into something like that, I hope she stays a caterpillar for a long time."

Fran stopped delicately blowing into her tea. "What caterpillar?"

"I'll tell you some other time. I've got to get back."

Downstairs, she slipped quietly into her chair. The meeting was about over. Ted was trying to give them something to think about on the drive home.

He reminded them that in the United States there were about ten thousand weeklies like theirs, that if they sold out, the others wouldn't miss them. But their towns would. "Because in these weeklies," he said, "the people see themselves. The kind of canned newspapers Bartlett would put out won't wake personal opinion because there won't be anything personal in them. If all the grass-roots papers were to die out, it would be as big a blow to the free press of this country as having a central government print the only news we're allowed to read."

When he finished, Stan Ryder leaped up, pumped his hand and said, "What I'd like you to do is type up copies of what you just said, so we can read it over and remember, if the going gets rough."

After they left, Ted said dryly, "And if they do start to sell, Stan Ryder will be the first to go."

"He inherited the *Leader,* didn't he?"

"It came with Mabel. Her father was twice the man at seventy when he died that his son-in-law is now. I could have counted on him, but Stan . . ."

"Go to bed," she suggested. "I'll finish down here."

"I want to be with you."

She smiled. How young he sounded, she thought. They were alone in the kitchen. Josephine dried the dishes and Ted, with his longer reach, put them up on the top shelf.

"Then the *Leader*'s only a hobby for Stan?"

"He makes a lot more from real estate. You know why he keeps the paper?"

"The title?"

"Publisher and editor. It's a joke. A couple of young guys do all his work for him on little better than cub reporter salaries. It's an open secret."

"What did you think of his Judy?"

He looked surprised. "I didn't really notice her."

"Your son did!"

"Oh?"

"Elsie heard him tell her he's going on fifteen."

"I guess that added year makes a big difference."

"Obviously, he hoped it would to Judy Ryder."

"So our Pete's got himself a girl."

That upset her so much she almost dropped the last plate.

"You're getting tired. Give me that."

"Judy doesn't live in Ditchling," Josephine said.

"But Mitford," he reminded her as his mother had, "isn't that far away."

Silently, she planned to encourage Pete to work on his new room. It shouldn't be too hard. He had thrown himself into it with such enthusiasm and it had been his idea in the first place. If he worked hard, and with her help, the room could be finished in time for him to have his birthday party there. His fourteenth, not his fifteenth.

"I bought a spittoon."

"A what?"

"Spittoon." She laughed. "It's funny what an effect that poor, inoffensive thing has on people. It's for Pete. We may be running a Western saloon in the basement."

"Great! If the paper goes under, I can help him run it."

"Don't even joke like that." She switched off the kitchen lights. Together they went upstairs.

"Stan Ryder did have one good idea," she said. "Wanting you to make copies of what you said tonight. I was proud."

He was still smiling at that as he undressed. "Where did you get a spittoon?" he asked suddenly.

"The auction." She pulled back the quilted bedspread. "Ben Goudy was there."

"Did you bother to say hello?"

"I even introduced him to Frieda. I think he frightened her."

"Then he doesn't frighten you anymore?"

"He never did."

"Then why did you try so hard to get me to return his portfolio?"

66

"I was busy that day," promptly. "It was the day Fran took sick."

"Oh, that's right."

Only it wasn't right. Fran did come down with the flu that day, but Josephine had been at the barn and didn't know about it until she finally came home.

Ted had more important things on his mind and accepted the half-truth. It was harder for her. If there was a difference between a half-truth and a half-lie, she didn't know what it was. One just sounded nicer. Either one was being secretive and evasive and slightly deceptive. She felt a sharp stab over her right eye. Ted heard her open the medicine cabinet over the bathroom sink. Then he heard the water.

"You okay, Josie?"

"I'm taking a couple of aspirins."

"I know what's bothering you."

She came to the door and stood leaning against it in her nightgown. "Do you?"

"The paper. Don't worry about it. We'll work it out."

Suddenly she wanted to shout, "Don't say *we!*" She wanted to tell him not to count on her to help him this time. For the first time in their married life she felt she had tried to do too much, give too much—to Ted, to the paper, to the house, to the children, to her mother-in-law. She was tired, and besides she had a damn headache.

"Come back to bed, darling."

Under the covers, she clenched her teeth and promised, "We will work it out, Ted. Somehow, we will."

THAT NIGHT she had a dream. The electric kitchen clock was striking. She started to count the hours, but lost interest almost immediately because time didn't matter. Knowing it didn't matter gave her a giddy sense of freedom. The familiar things were behind her—the stove, the sink, the refrigerator. She didn't bother to look at them because she knew they would all be hidden behind a black shroud. That didn't seem any more peculiar than an electric clock striking. And she simply accepted the fact that she couldn't feel the antiseptically scrubbed vinyl floor under her feet.

She was a figure floating in the air over it to get to her worktable. She had to finish decorating the cake. It lay face up in a pool of bluish light. The electric clock continued to strike and Ben Goudy began to laugh.

67

"Don't laugh at me!" In her dream she thought, I mustn't lose control. I'll disturb the whole house. The most important thing in my life is not to disturb my house, but to him she said, "It was the most important thing in my life when I did it. Tell me what's wrong?"

"It's a death mask. Don't you know that the woman you found in that lump of clay looks like you, Josephine Trask?"

"Go away. The clock isn't striking anymore. That means the rain's stopped."

"What time is it? Come on," he ordered roughly. "You're the one with the clock."

She began to whimper apologetically. "I have a lot of things to do, Mr. Goudy. I lead a very busy life."

"Then you won't need this," he said. She knew what he was planning to do, so she caught his wrist in a desperate grasp; but with broad open fingers, his hand smashed onto the clay and destroyed it. What had been the nose was disfigured by a broad thumbprint. The eyes were pushed in. They could never see now.

He was an evil man. A destructive man.

"It wasn't nice of you to say it looked like a death mask," Josephine said sadly.

"But I didn't say it. You did."

And in her dream she thought about it. "That's true," she admitted. "I'm sorry."

Then she realized with horror that she was still holding onto his wrist. Somehow it had separated from the rest of him. In her own two hands, she was holding one of his, shrunken and disembodied. She screamed, knocked against the worktable and the cake fell to the floor. The plate smashed to pieces.

THE NOISE woke her and she sat up in bed trembling and perspiring.

Ted stirred and sat up in the dark. "Josie?"

"I'm perspiring." She was so relieved to find she could talk she almost cried with gratitude. "Feel. Under my hair."

What she really wanted was the reassurance of his hand, his strong full-sized hand.

"It's those aspirins you took before you went to bed. How's your nightgown?"

"I'll have to peel it off."

68

The weight of the mattress redistributed itself and she knew he had got out of bed. "I'll get you a fresh one."

Huddled under the blanket, she started to remove the damp gown.

"Here," her husband said. "What else can I get you? Tea? Warm milk?"

"I'm fine now. Thanks."

"You don't think you caught what Fran had, do you?"

"No," she assured him, then added ridiculously, "Don't you know I can't be sick? I simply don't have the time."

A few minutes later, she was asleep again.

Chapter Nine

AWAKE, SHE moved in everybody else's world. Asleep, she always returned to her own.

It wasn't necessary for her to remember exactly what she had dreamed the night before. In the light of a new morning, she knew that unless she went back to the studio, she was risking other nightmares. That compulsion to finish what she had started there was more than a need. It was a nagging force that wouldn't let her rest—especially when she slept.

"You look better this morning," Ted said.

"I was overtired, that's all." She wasn't tired now, just determined.

"You try to do too much."

The school bus had come and gone. "Maybe I need a hobby," she said, pouring his coffee.

"Poor Josie"—he teased—"doesn't have enough to do."

"Pete finished laying the floor in the basement," she said. "Look at it before you go."

"Fixing up that room will be enough of a hobby if you really want one."

"No. That's his special project. He wants to do it himself."

"Has he seen the spittoon?"

"Not yet. I told you Ben Goudy was at the auction when I bought it, didn't I?"

"Yes. You said he frightened Frieda."

"She's easily frightened." She poured honey into the little pot. "Did I tell you what happened the day I returned his portfolio?" Ted looked up at her from his coffee. "He gave me some clay, and I . . . played around with it. He thought I might have some talent."

"Did he really tell you that?"

"He must have thought so because he asked me to come back. He even said he'd help me."

"But you didn't go."

"Wouldn't I have told you if I had? Anyway, I couldn't if I wanted to—not with your mother being sick and all this business with the paper. . . ."

"Today," he told her, "I'm going to start looking for other printing plants. But it can't be for the *Digest* alone. It has to be the whole combine or we won't be able to compete with Bartlett for cooperative advertising."

"Where are you going to start?"

"That," he told her, "is *my* special project. You're not to worry about it."

"Just how do you expect me not to worry?"

And he obliged her by suggesting, "Take Goudy up on his offer . . . if you really think he meant it."

For some reason she had wanted it to come from him. "He meant it."

"It might be fun for you, playing around with clay."

Be fair, she told herself sternly; you were the one to use the expression first. "If I do decide, I won't let it cut into anything else I have to do."

"Of course you won't," confidently. "I know you, darling."

Once he was gone, she took the tray upstairs. Fran had been talked into staying in bed a little later for a few more days. Josephine told her she might be a little late for lunch. This time she even told her where she was going.

"If you do it as well as everything else," her mother-in-law said, "you'll be better than Mr. Goudy in no time. I know you, honey."

When Josephine drove away from the house there was a brown paper bag on the seat beside her.

71

HE WAS sitting exactly the way she had left him on that other morning —holding a cracked cup and drinking from it. The barn was full of the smells of coffee and clay, flaked marble and dust and stale cigarette smoke. She knew he hadn't sat there all that time waiting for her. Hadn't she seen him since at the outdoor auction? Still, he seemed to have been waiting and finally she had come.

He raised the cup to her as if greeting an old accomplice. His mouth was an unsmiling triumph. For a moment, Josephine thought of leaving again. There was fresh clay on the table. He put it there for me, she thought, and had to clasp her hands behind her to prevent them from seizing it. Somehow that action forced her eyes to open wider. She felt them burning in her head. There were rings of fatigue around them. She had noticed them in the mirror that morning. Ben Goudy's own eyes narrowed and she knew he had noticed them, too.

"Have you been sick?"

She gave him a sad little smile. "I keep telling people I don't have the time for such waste." Then, by way of explanation, she added, "My husband's mother has been, though. That was one of the reasons I didn't come back."

"Tell me the real reason."

"I wasn't sure I had enough time."

"Are you sure now?"

"I have to be," she told him. "Something happened last night that didn't give me any choice."

"What happened?"

Her nightmare was none of his business, even though he had been in it. "Never mind," she said. "It's enough I'm here."

"How do you know I'll let you stay?" He put down the cracked cup and stood up. She took a deep breath and waited for him to come toward her.

"I don't," she admitted so softly she wondered if he even heard her.

"The coffee's probably no better than it was the last time, but it's hot and you're welcome to it." He nodded in the direction of a shelf that held an assortment of dishes, none of them matching, many of them cracked. The shelf itself, unpainted and obviously handmade, was nevertheless carefully put together with respect for whatever tree had died to give him the wood.

Josephine slipped out of her coat, went over and poured coffee from

72

the pot that was sitting on the stove. Ben Goudy had given her something to do with her hands and she was grateful.

"It's a little better this time," she said.

"I took your advice—cleaned the pot."

"I really do make very good coffee."

"I know. Your husband thinks so. You told me."

And it was my husband, she thought, who suggested I come here today. He thinks a hobby would be good for me. She didn't dare use the word to Ben Goudy.

"Tell me," he asked suddenly, "when did your life become less busy, Mrs. Trask?"

He was laughing at her without laughing. Josephine forced herself to return his accusing stare without flinching. "I want to come very much. This time it'll be different."

"Put that coffee down," he said, "and come here."

She went to him obediently.

"Let me see your hands."

She opened them and stood silently while he felt each of her fingers. "They'll do," he said. "They're not a woman's hands."

She had never been so pleased at such a dubious compliment.

He smiled back at her for the first time since she had returned. It warmed her more than the steaming liquid.

"Most people," he said, "know very little about their own hands. Their muscles are flabby, their fingers are weak. You can learn to make yours respond, to do anything you wish them to do—but only if you work at it. The tools I give you can become extensions of your fingers."

"Will you really show me?"

"Time," he said roughly, "is as important to me as it is to you. If I'm willing to give you any of mine, it'll be because I think you could be worth it."

"I brought a smock," she said.

He nodded approvingly.

While she was buttoning it, she moved about his studio. It was neater than she remembered. Everything seemed to be in its place and there was a place for everything. There was a lot here she didn't understand, a lot she had to learn, but this order was something she could understand and appreciate. The familiar hand-stitched blessing on her kitchen wall began, "The beauty of the house is order."

"I use a lot of tools," he said, as if he knew what she was thinking.

73

"They're always in use. I keep them neat and put them away clean."

"You've cut another window since I was last here," she observed.

"I needed that high sidelight as well as the overhead skylight. You'll understand why."

"No wonder you didn't want the house," she said. "You don't need anymore than you have here. This is ideal, isn't it?"

He laughed at her again. This time she could hear the laughter, and there was nothing unkind in it.

"Ideal? The floor's uneven and creaks. All kinds of peculiar fungi sprout out of cracks in the walls. The place is full of leaks, and it's damp most of the time."

"The stove," she said, "is friendly, and it glows."

"Don't let it fool you. It won't keep you warm."

"I won't mind."

"I'd better warn you about something else, too. Perhaps, because it is so primitive—anything can happen." He added disarmingly. "There's a kind of magic here, Mrs. Trask."

Her children had taken all the magic she had offered and thrown it back because they had outgrown it—Santa Claus and the tooth fairy, whispering sea shells and paper monsters that could be tamed, hand puppets that recited the alphabet. "I've always been fond of magic," Josephine said, smiling back at him. "Where is that head I started, please?"

"Where you left it."

She glanced at the worktable. Next to the fresh clay was something covered with a cloth.

The coffee was better than it had been. Maybe she would think the work she had done was better as well.

"I want to ask you something first," he said.

"What is it?"

"What the hell are you planning to do with a goddamn spittoon?"

"I'm going to use it," she said, delighted it had really bothered him.

"Bake a cake in it or plant petunias?"

"I'm going to use it as a spittoon," she insisted, and deliberately changed the subject by going to the table and lifting the cloth. It was damp.

"I've kept it that way to prevent the clay from drying up."

"You went to all that trouble?"

"I knew you'd be back to look at it again."

74

"You were so sure?"

"Very sure."

She removed the cloth, impatient to see once more what had been accomplished during those three hours. She remembered how she hadn't realized it had been three hours, and how she hadn't felt the least tired afterward, only wonderfully exhilarated.

Now she wasn't exhilarated and she was much more than tired. She was exhausted to the point of crying and wondered what kept her from it. In all her life, Josephine had never experienced such deep and terrible disappointment.

"What's the matter?" she heard him say.

"When I asked you the last time if I could come back, you said"—something was caught in her throat, like a lump of cold clay—"you said I hadn't finished. And I honestly thought you meant that anything that was started should be finished. But, looking at this . . ."

"All right," he dared, "what's wrong with it?"

"Everything." Tears were stinging behind her eyes. This is stupid—stupid, she kept repeating to herself. I really am going to cry. And over what? "Everything!" she began again. "I think it's because it was started wrong and developed wrong. If it had been right from the beginning, it would finish itself—"

"Good," he said, pleased. "And that's your first lesson."

"It is?"

"I could show you," he said, "how to stretch a polished crust over what you've done, but it wouldn't be right, would it?"

"No."

"There was no idea behind what you did. Sculpture without idea is without heart. Without a heart it can't breathe. You yourself said this looked like a death mask."

"It does."

"We'll start again, only this time you'll share the atmosphere with your work."

"I'm not sure I understand." Sculptors often fashioned busts of themselves. Did they ever—could they ever do a self-portrait of the entire body in stone? She found herself wondering, embarrassed, if he had been his own model for the gigantic nude stone man.

"Your work," he was saying, "will have the same space and air that you have all around you. The next head you do won't be flat."

"Round, of course."

He shook his head. "You'll start with the symbol of life, the oval, the shape the unborn baby takes, the shape we curl up into when we die. The basic shape of the world isn't round. Didn't you know that? It's oval."

He gave her some plasteline. "Cut this up," he ordered. "Knead it into large sausage shapes, the size of bananas. Then wash your hands and we'll start again . . ."

JOSEPHINE NEVER knew at what point she began to think of it as their studio, not just his. She was never sure just what day she began to hum or sing softly to herself when she worked. It simply happened.

Chapter Ten

No ONE in town happened to be looking when the last leaf blew away. Ben brought in another secondhand potbellied stove and Josephine insisted it had to be the same one she and Ted used when the *Digest* started.

"What other could possibly give off as little heat and as much coal dust? Did I ever tell you how we started? No ledger, no rate cards. Only an empty mat book. Did I ever tell you I wrote 'Ditchling Doings' for three years?"

He didn't answer, so she continued, "That paper means everything to us. Now someone's trying to take it away. The man whose presses we use . . ."

"I'm bored with this conversation," he said. "Let's get back to work."

"You sound angry," surprised. "Are you?"

"I don't like to waste time talking about things that don't matter."

"They matter very much to me, Ben."

"Then go home," he said, "and worry about them."

He was making it clear that the subject of the *Digest* held no interest for him. . . .

This world into which she came—at first twice a week, then little by little, with growing help from Fran, sometimes until night began to edge the high windows—that very special world of his was something apart from any other beyond. Entering it was always a slight shock to her nervous system. She even had trouble breathing for a few minutes. It was a very special world that existed on an entirely different plane.

"You go there a lot," Peter said one day.

"You and I are both busier than usual," she said. "How's your downstairs room coming along?"

"You'll see it when it's ready."

"Do you like my idea of a Western saloon?"

He grinned. "Want to tell me what you're making?"

All she did was smile back. "And you'll see *that* when it's ready," she told him.

What she didn't tell him was how slyly she was tricking him—letting him think she was writing a laundry or a grocery list while all the time she sketched him on the backs of envelopes or paper napkins, dozens of small sketches to be stacked next to the dozens of small scale models in the barn.

For weeks she filled his plate and studied the group of muscles that sprang from the shoulders to support the head, watched him eat and analyzed the muscles he used to chew. She listened to him complain about his sister's disregard for his personal property and, at the same time she commiserated with him, watched how his nostrils fluttered and which muscles caused the frown.

And he never guessed. It was all part of the wonderful surprise she would give him on his fourteenth birthday. She would surprise Ted, too. "Why, Josie," she could hear him say, "you did this?" And she would say, "Does it look anything like our Pete? Be honest."

That would come later if the work was good enough. Telling Ted now would be more than premature. It was trivial compared to the larger problem he had on his mind: keeping his newspaper from dying. . . .

"Jo," Ben said one afternoon. "Why can't you work without making noises?"

"What did you just call me?"

"Jo."

"Nobody else calls me that."

"That's all right. I don't mind."

"It's Josie usually. Sometimes Josephine. Somehow, nobody ever—"

"What were you humming?"

She thought about it a moment, and about her new name, and wondered why no one had ever called her that before. *Jo.* She liked the sound. *Jo.*

"I don't know what song it was," she answered. "Sometimes, lately, I feel like singing every song I ever knew—and all at the same time."

He looked at her curiously, then put his tools beside a stylized figure made up of masses of curves and angles. Josephine wasn't sure what other people would see in it. For herself, she could see clearly a woman agonizing to get out of the stone that held her prisoner.

Ben told her it was the best thing he had ever done. She didn't tell him the tortured figure made her feel uncomfortable. Until the woman was completely free, Josephine didn't really want to look at it.

"Take a break," he suggested. "Let's have a cigarette."

"Coat your own lungs black if you want to."

"Wouldn't it be simpler to say you don't smoke?"

"I don't smoke."

"Then drink your lousy coffee. You made it. And watch me coat my lungs." He sounded sullen, but she had stopped being afraid of him. And she knew he knew it.

Things were different between them now. Lately there was a telepathic hum between them. She could almost hear it, indiscernible to any other human ear—except perhaps his—but clear as the full-throated note of a bell. So many times she knew what he was going to say before he said it. So many times, he snatched a thought from her own mind as it was just beginning to take shape. It was probably because of the honest glow of companionship in the work they shared. Or the closeness of the place they worked. Or the place itself. He had warned her there was magic there.

One day she arrived breathless. "I couldn't get here any earlier."

"Why did you bother to come at all?"

If she let him, he would provoke her into an argument and minutes were precious. "You said you'd help me build an armature today. If you'd rather not now—"

"Shut up," he said, and almost immediately continued, "Every sculptor works in his own way to build an armature for modeling a head. Let me show you the way I do it."

It was as much of an apology as she needed.

By the time she was ready to leave, she had constructed, with the help of his strong, practiced hands, a framework on which clay could easily be manipulated and firmly pressed.

"Tomorrow," he said.

"Early," she began, then remembered. Tomorrow was the day she had promised to give Frieda, the day of the club luncheon. "I could," she offered, "come for a few hours." The tips of her fingers were pulsating in anticipation. "Everything," she said, "is so easy to prepare." She said it confidently because she knew it would be. Even the cookies, which would be served afterward with the coffee, had been baked and stored in the freezer weeks ago, when her mother-in-law was down with the flu.

Ben muttered an obscenity she pretended not to hear.

"Would you rather I didn't come tomorrow?" Josephine asked.

"You want to start working on that head, don't you?"

"I'll see you in the morning then," she said happily, and looking back at what they had done together added, "thank you."

She couldn't tell her son and didn't want to tell her husband, but the next morning she did confide in her mother-in-law and had to keep from laughing at the startled reaction.

"You mean you haven't done anything up to now? Nothing? In two months?"

"You're wrong. I've done a lot."

"Making sketches of his work? That's what you just said."

"I said drawings. Careful drawings. Sometimes Ben gave me plaster figures. I cut off the arms and legs." She laughed at the undisguised distaste. "The more I study his work," patiently, "the closer I come to developing a technique of my own."

Fran still looked unhappy. "And here I've been expecting you to come home with something—nice—that we could put on a coffee table. I hoped perhaps a cat. Remember my Tommy? The way he used to jump into the kitchen sink in our apartment in New York, and catch the drips from the faucet? He was so smart, that cat."

Josephine smiled. "He was a she."

"Oh, well, by the time Teddy's father and I discovered that, we were so used to calling her—*him.*"

"And busy finding homes for the litter *he* had dropped."

"Such a long time ago," Fran sighed. "Another life. Is that really all you've done, just drawings of ears? And some little practice models of Pete?"

"Are you beginning to wonder if I've taken advantage of your good nature," anxiously, "leaving part of the running of my house to you while I wasted my time?"

Only she knew none of it had been wasted.

"Anything I do here," Fran said, "I do because I live here, too."

"Of course you do," Josephine said. "We're a family."

"Only it's your husband, your children, your home. You have so much, Josie. Give me this little." Fran's low voice was a plea. "Let me do some of the unimportant things in 'our' house. They're important to me because they make me feel needed." Once she started to cry, she couldn't stop.

Josephine put her arms around her. "It'll be all right, it'll be all right."

Only both knew it was a lie. Nothing would ever be the way it once was when there was a cat that used to jump lightly into the kitchen sink and catch the drippings from the faucet. The cat was gone, and the husband and the home, and there were no children to depend on her anymore.

"Only those who are very young, like Pete and Elsie," Fran said, pulling a tissue from her sleeve, "look forward to growing old. What do they know?"

It was the first time since she had come to live with them six years ago that Josephine had ever seen her cry.

"On your anniversary," Fran recalled, blowing her nose in the tissue, "I told Teddy that if I could just cry for his father, maybe I could finally accept the fact that he's gone." She gave a sad forced laugh. "I think I just have."

"And I don't think I should leave you now."

"You're going somewhere?" startled.

"I told you. To the studio. This is the morning I'm starting that head of Peter. I want it to be finished in time for his birthday."

"But Frieda's luncheon . . ."

Josephine interrupted her with a laugh. "It's really funny the way you both call it Frieda's luncheon."

"But you did promise—"

"And I promise you I won't break it. I'll only be gone a short while."

BEN DIDN'T say hello when she arrived and didn't look at her for the few hours she was there, but somehow he sensed the moment she looked at her watch, because he stiffened.

At the door he called her back. "What's so easy to prepare?"

"Are you really interested?"

"Curious."

"Shrimp Newburg," she told him and amended, "quick shrimp."

"What the hell makes it quick?"

"Cans of frozen shrimp bisque and packages of frozen shrimp." She didn't bother to tell him she would serve it on rice from a silver chafing dish that had been a wedding present. "Well, never mind. I'll see you tomorrow. I'll have a whole day then."

"Put some of that goddamn shrimp in a jar. We'll heat it up."

THE LUNCHEON went smoothly with Frieda accepting the compliments graciously and straight-faced.

"As if you had anything to do with it," Alice Daly said crustily.

"Didn't I let Josie take over when she offered?" Frieda popped another mint cookie into her mouth and hoped Josephine was looking in another direction.

"I suppose I shouldn't say this," Frieda said, when the meeting was over and everyone else had gone, "but isn't Alice Daly a mess?"

Without warning, as if she had snapped a photographic portrait study and was looking at a negative, Josephine saw lids drooping over small eyes in a square face, and painted lips curled downward. There were no visible scars, but with terrifying clarity she knew that the makeup camouflaged silent suffering.

"No wonder her husband gets the hots for other women," Frieda was saying.

"Don't," Josephine reprimanded sharply, because she had recognized an unmistakable stamp of sickness on that face. It was possible Alice herself didn't know it yet. Josephine did, and the cold certainty made it impossible to sit still. She got up and began to clear the dishes.

"Josie's mad at me," Frieda said. "She doesn't approve of that kind of talk."

Fran continued to crochet the afghan she was planning to give her son and daughter-in-law for Christmas. "I didn't even hear you," she lied pleasantly, cross-stitching on the long panel.

"Are you mad, Josie?" Frieda asked plaintively.

"I like her." Josephine wondered just how sick Alice was. She couldn't ask John Cullen. It was possible the doctor didn't know yet either.

"Alice despises me," Frieda said matter-of-factly. "Who cares? It's mutual. The meeting went well, though, didn't it?"

"Very nice," Fran said, changing threads from green to brown.

"The girls liked my idea for the art contest. Don't forget you promised to ask Ben Goudy to be the judge."

"I didn't say he'd accept."

"The exhibition is a wonderful idea," Fran said. "The art student from the college who gets the scholarship will have you to thank."

Frieda looked pleased. "That's true. Only now I've got to be the chairman or chairperson or whatever we call it these days. Josie, I can't thank you enough for today."

"Forget it."

"I would have been up all night getting everything ready. How long did it take you?"

Fran answered for her with unmistakable pride. "She didn't get back until a little while before the meeting."

"You're kidding."

"I went to the studio for a few hours. I didn't want to kill the whole day."

"Kill?" There was a hollow sound when she repeated it.

"Josie didn't mean that the way it sounded," Fran said.

"Of course I didn't," quickly.

"You're at the barn an awful lot lately. You really enjoy those lessons?"

"Very much."

"I hardly get to see you anymore." She appealed to Fran. "Get her to stop going so much."

"Josephine is so artistic. It's a wonderful outlet for her. I've encouraged her."

"She's giving it too much of her time."

"I won't stop now," Josephine said simply. "I couldn't if I wanted to."

"That's ridiculous."

"No, it isn't. I may really accomplish something worthwhile there . . ." She let the words run on. "Sometimes I wonder what I did with myself before. Didn't I realize how bored I was?"

After a moment, Frieda said quietly, "In that case, I'm glad you've developed a hobby."

Chapter Eleven

THE NEXT day belonged only to her—and to Peter, the Peter she was creating with her hands. Her fingers glided over the clay head that was beginning to look like him—only a little, but it would happen if she kept working. Concentrate on the subject. Think of her son, the way he looked last night when he suddenly put strong young hands on her waist and lifted her off the floor.

"Don't," anxiously, "you'll strain yourself."

I'll never be able to carry him again, she had thought suddenly, which was stupid, because it was years since she had been able to lift him the way he was effortlessly lifting her, years since she lay against the pillows in the bed, her knees raised and the infant perched on them. "Down the magic mountain," she used to singsong, holding the baby hands and letting him slide down over her thighs to safety.

"Let's take a break," Ben Goudy said, but she kept on working and didn't bother to answer.

Afterward she could coax him back to good humor by showing him what she had accomplished and admiring what he had. Soon. Not just yet. Her fingers would leave off by themselves when they had done enough. Her hands would stop working as if they had a will and a mind of their own and knew better than she did when they said everything that needed to be said for the moment.

Think of Pete, she ordered herself, passing one of her hands over the clay head that was beginning to take form. Did she imagine electricity rising from the hair? Probably. But it was happening quickly, even better and faster than she dared hope. . . .

"I killed a lion with my club," Pete said. "Ha ha. There are ten thousand members in my club."

"That's an old one," Josephine had said, "and put me down."

"Did *your* club ladies leave us anything to eat? Bet Mrs. Haines had four helpings of everything."

She remembered how she had reprimanded him. But now she was also remembering how Frieda sounded as if she had been crying when she said, "I'm glad you've developed a hobby." . . .

"I'd like to take a break now," Josephine told Ben.

The remembering drained energy from her fingers; they stopped moving. If she was seeing Frieda and not her son in the clay face now, it wouldn't be any good. Hadn't she practically told her friend that all those afternoons they once spent together added up to a dull waste of time?

Yet—wasn't it part of what used to keep her so busy? She was always so busy, she never realized she had nothing to do.

She wiped her hands on her smock.

"You look tired," Ben said.

"I am." It had nothing to do with the work. It had to do with Frieda and that look of loyal and exclusive love. Frieda had no right to demand that kind of love in return from her. No one did.

"Shoulders hurt?"

"A little," she admitted.

He came behind her and massaged the tightness out of the muscles, starting at the nape of her neck and spreading his broad-tipped thumbs outward.

"Were you back in time yesterday?"

"Yes." Under his firm grip, the tightness was leaving her shoulders and she relaxed to the gentle rhythmical motion of his hands.

"While you were working, I heated up the stuff you brought this morning. It smells good."

"It is."

"Probably too good for your hens. What do you call yourselves?"

"The Ditchling Cultural Society."

"Jesus," he moaned.

85

"Nobody knows who branded us with the name."

"Probably someone's final revenge before getting out of town."

"I promised I'd ask if you'd judge our spring art exhibition."

"How do I know where I'll be in the spring?"

"I knew you'd say that." She took a deep breath and continued, her eyes still shut, "Something sad happened yesterday. I discovered that one of my friends is very sick." She explained how she knew. "But it isn't possible, is it?" And she waited for him to ridicule her and say that of course it wasn't.

"The more you analyze faces," he told her solemnly, "the more you'll discover there are not three dimensions, but four. The fourth is the revelation behind the mask people wear. Study the face, Jo, and you'll find it. I'm sorry about your friend, but if you saw death there, you were probably right."

Josephine hadn't been able to bring herself to use the word *death*, but she knew it described exactly what she had seen in Alice Daly—in that fourth and final dimension.

Her knees felt so weak she was surprised her legs could carry her as far as the coffee pot on the burner.

"Shoulders better?" Ben asked, concerned.

"Much. Thank you."

"You couldn't help what you saw."

"I could have been wrong," she said faintly.

"I hope so. . . . Pour some coffee for me, too."

When she gave it to him, they sat side by side on the bench.

"You've been happy these past two months, haven't you, Jo? You even look different than you did that day you took me in out of the rain."

She glanced at the modeling stand with its revolving top and at the work that was waiting for her—and she could forget about Alice for the moment and even be happy again. "You took yourself out of the rain."

"You didn't answer me. Have you been happy?"

She pushed her hair back from her forehead. "From the first time I came here," she remembered, "I felt I was in one place, and that not even a small part of me wanted to be anywhere else in the world."

"Do you realize what you've just said?"

"What?"

"That you've never been completely satisfied."

The charge was too fantastic to deserve a sensible reply, but she felt obliged to answer something. "I couldn't have said that because it just

86

isn't true. I have my home, my family—"

"And I've had myself. I don't need anyone else."

"Hasn't there ever been anyone you cared about?" She was glad to be able to turn the conversation to him. "Haven't you ever been in love?"

"A great many times."

"How fortunate for a great many women."

"I'd rather talk about you."

"Of course you would," she smiled. "It's safer."

"Lately," he said, annoyed, "I have the feeling you're laughing at me."

"Probably because I am. You say things just to be contrary. Then you sulk, like my Pete used to when he was little."

"I was never like your little Pete."

This time she couldn't control her amusement and broke into a laugh. "You were never a small boy?"

"I never enjoyed being one, so in a way I suppose I never really was one."

"I'm sorry," she said quietly.

"Be honest, Jo, would you want to suffer the agony of being that young again?"

"My children don't suffer."

"Either you don't really know them, or they're not very bright." He went to the potbellied stove and kicked it. "This goddamn thing. It's no better than that other. How did we get onto me? I said I'd rather talk about you. Remember the first day you came here?"

"I remember."

"And that head of a woman you started?"

"I never finished her because I knew I wouldn't be able to make her start to breathe. There was a wrong start there."

"Very wrong," he agreed, but said it more to himself than to her.

"But this head of my son—" She went back to her turntable. "He's actually coming to life under my fingers. It's the most glorious feeling."

"If you made love like that to conceive him, I envy your husband."

"When I finish this," she said, pretending she hadn't heard the remark, "I want to do a figure of my Elsie. Then I'll always have them just the way they are now."

"That's the only way you'll always have them."

"I don't believe you."

"Then you're a fool." He stood beside her and looked down at her work. "When we're through with that, we'll send it out and have a cast made."

"And the clay?"

"The clay will be destroyed."

She let out a little cry.

"It will come back to you in bronze," he promised. "When it does, it will be permanent. Clay is just mud."

"But this mud belongs to me. It has part of me in it now." She had a fleeting vision of Frieda's startled face—if she could hear her talking like this. Ben didn't act as if what she said was in the least peculiar . . . "What if somebody makes a mistake when they cast it?" she asked anxiously.

"You'll always worry about that, but it will come out right."

"Someday," Josephine vowed, "I'm going to learn how to cast it myself. I'm going to do it all, every step from the first to the last."

"You have a lot to learn then."

"I have time."

"Sure," Ben said. "But the question is, are you willing to give it?"

She looked at her watch, the gold one Ted gave her last Christmas. Almost another Christmas. With things so uncertain with the *Digest* this year, they would have to tighten their belts, be less extravagant with gifts, but do it in such a way that the children wouldn't notice. Nothing should spoil the holidays for the children. "I've got to leave," she said.

"There's enough light to work at least another half-hour."

She began to unbutton her smock. "I know, but I haven't time." She stopped.

Ben was triumphant. "I told you you weren't willing."

He went back to his own work and began to chip at stone again. It was a comforting sound. Every stroke brought the woman inside it closer to her release. Josephine glanced at him to make sure he wasn't watching and gently placed a kiss on the forehead of the small clay face that was Pete's. Then she covered it with a wet cloth. "Good night, darling," she whispered. It seemed to her she had whispered it very softly and was taken aback when from across the room she heard Ben's voice: "What did you say?"

"I was talking," she nodded at her work, "to him."

"Oh," he said.

Her coat was on a hook next to where she hung her smock. She sat on an orange crate to pull on her boots, and tied a kerchief under her chin. When she was ready to leave, she went over to him. "Good night. See you tomorrow."

"If you have time." It was a dismissal.

"You try so hard to make me dislike you," she said smiling. "I'm sorry. I do like you."

He put down his tools and faced her. "Why?"

"Because you're really a very nice person. You're warm and full of gentleness you think it's a weakness to admit."

"Go home. It'll be a pleasure to work without your humming."

When she reached the barn door, he called after her. "I didn't hear your car when you came."

"I didn't take it. I love to walk. Especially in new snow."

"Wait for me. I'll walk with you."

"You don't have to."

"If I had to, I wouldn't do it."

She laughed at him. "There you go again, sounding like my children —contrary."

"I would appreciate it," he snapped, "if you'd stop comparing me to your children."

"You force the comparison."

"Then keep it to yourself. I don't enjoy having you play little mother to me." He had wrapped a long wool scarf around his neck and, hatless, grabbed Josephine by the arm. "Let's go."

"You're not wearing a hat! And you haven't got any gloves."

"My, what big eyes you have, grandma."

"All right, catch pneumonia. I won't even come to bring you hot soup."

"Can I count on that?" Still holding onto her with one hand, he lifted the iron latch with the other and steered her out into the winter beyond the door.

The coldness stuck to her eyelids and she had to keep blinking them to keep her eyes from gluing shut. It burned her cheeks red and made everything she said come out wrapped in little puffs. Except for the infrequent coffee breaks they shared, they seldom talked during the session. Today had been the longest exchange between them yet. Now that they had the chance to talk without the pull of wanting to return to work, they said very little. There was something in the purity of the snow all around them that seemed to demand the purity of silence.

Finally, when they turned off River Road, he said, "I have an idea for some fighting cocks. Perhaps it'll interest you to see how I make them by bending strips of metal, using strips of wire for tail feathers."

"But you can't leave what you're doing, can you?" she said, upset, thinking of the woman in the stone who would have that much longer to wait.

"That one's finished."

"I thought you liked it."

"I do."

"You said it's the best piece you've done."

"I still think so."

"Then finish it."

"I told you. It is. Once I told you something else: every piece of sculpture, to be any good at all, must have an idea behind it."

"I remember."

"I've said everything that needed to be said, as far as it's gone. If I complete it, it would say nothing."

"What does it say now?" she asked angrily, wondering how he was capable of being so cruel.

"It says that the woman I found in the block isn't strong enough to free herself."

Josephine didn't answer.

"What's the matter?"

"I'm disappointed. I thought you were working on something beautiful. Now it seems . . . ugly."

"Whether you think it's ugly or not isn't important."

"Shouldn't a piece of sculpture be lovely to live with?—not just beautifully made?"

"It depends on how you respond to the miracle of life. You're not denying that you see life there, are you?"

"Looking at that," she said deliberately hoping to offend him, "makes me feel unhappy to be alive."

"Good! Then I was right to stop when I did. Sometimes it takes two people to paint a picture or carve a piece of sculpture—one to work, and the other to pull him off before he does too much. I hope you like the next thing I do better." They had reached sight of the brown and pink house. Ben stopped short, as if an invisible fence had been thrown up to bar his way.

"When you have a family," Josephine told him graciously, forgetting

90

that a moment before they had been arguing, "there's always room for one more. Have dinner with us."

"I want to get back to the studio."

"I'd like you to meet my family."

"I've already met them."

"Only the children. I'd like you to meet Ted, and my mother-in-law."

"I met your husband," he reminded her. "I wanted to put an ad in his paper and unload the property. He sent me to a real estate agent."

"I forgot."

Ted's car, she noticed, was parked at a careless angle in the drive. Evidently he hadn't bothered to take time to put it into the garage. If he had been in such a hurry to get to her, something must have happened.

"Maybe you'll come some other time," she said, glancing at the lighted windows over her shoulder. Even to her own ears, the words were surface-polite and she sounded eager to leave and go indoors.

"Some other time."

Already the barn and the person she had been there were fast fading into the afternoon just over. The light was gone, and the trees were a blue shadow, darker than the sky around them. It occurred to Josephine that the woman who worked in the studio by day with Ben Goudy and the woman who came home to Ted at night were two different people. They probably wouldn't even like each other and she made up her mind not to introduce them. She laughed.

"What's so funny?"

"I just had a ridiculous thought. Too foolish to repeat. Thanks for walking me home." She held out her hand. He touched it briefly and then, as if it had burned him, quickly dropped it and buried both his own deep in his pockets.

"What's the matter?"

"You were right," he said. "I should have worn gloves."

"You see?" she said. "Next time you'll take my motherly advice."

"Jo," he said, "do you really like me?"

"Yes."

"Don't."

"Why not?" she asked.

"Because I've made you dissatisfied with everything you have and everything you are; but you haven't found it out yet. I feel guilty enough without your liking me."

"You mean dissatisfied with the work I'm able to do? Because I recognize that you're so much better than I? Well, of course I don't expect to be as good. I haven't had your training or—"

"Never mind." A single winter star appeared without warning. They both looked up and saw it at the same time. "Man," Ben Goudy said, "couldn't possibly have started as a speck and become a seer. I refuse to accept that."

"I used to," she said. "I don't anymore. Now I'm sure that life had to begin through the love of creation."

"Good night, Jo," Ben said. He turned and walked away.

She watched him until he became as dark a shadow as the trees, but one that moved and grew smaller. Then she went into the house where it was warm.

TED WAS straddling a kitchen chair and watching his mother snap green beans. Even with the collander hugged between her knees, there was an aristocratic air about Fran. A face like hers should have a marble portrait carved, Josephine thought, but not by me—by someone who has the time to learn to do it well. Ben was right. *I'm not willing,* and these two are part of the reason.

She had a sickening sensation of having pushed away a vague, reprehensible thought. She wasn't sure what it was.

"Well," Ted greeted her dully, "it's happened."

Hadn't she known from the moment she saw the car abandoned in the drive?

"You two go into the living room and talk," Fran said understandingly. "I'll finish this and cut up the potatoes." She smiled up at her son. "Josie trusts me a lot more lately."

"It was never that I didn't trust you. You were a good cook long before I was."

"But every woman has her own way of doing things. I know that. I'm trying the best I can to do it your way. . . . Oh, Frieda wanted you to call her."

"Later. Where are the children?"

"Elsie's up in her room with her friend, Laurie. Laurie says it's all right with her mother if she stays for dinner."

"That's one way to get an invitation. And Pete?"

The crisp sound of a bean snapping answered before she did. "He came home from school, left his books and went out again. I didn't ask where."

Josephine began wondering where Peter was and ended by trying to recall exactly how his ears were set on his head. Now that she thought of it, were they as close as she had made them? Or did they stick out just a little? She'd have to remember to look at them later.

"Wherever he is," Ted said lightly, "he'll come home for dinner."

Fran smiled. "If there's food on the table, our boy will be here. I'm sorry, honey, I just couldn't ask him to account to me. He's not four years old, as he keeps reminding all of us. He'll be fourteen next month."

He told Judy Ryder he's going on fifteen, Josephine remembered uneasily. But he hadn't seen the girl since that night. He was like his father, never secretive. If he had made the trip to Mitford he would have told her. Of course she hadn't been home as much lately for him to have told her if he had wanted to.

"Frieda said she wanted to ask you something important."

Josephine glanced at Ted. "Later," she said again.

"It's okay," Ted told her.

"Isn't what we have to talk about more important?"

"It can wait."

"I won't let her keep me long," she promised, and went to the wall phone to dial.

Frieda answered on the first ring. "I'll tell you what I wanted," brightly. "I made reservations at the Towne House. Lunch tomorrow, you and me."

"Frieda—," Josephine began.

"After all, it's the least I can do to thank you for yesterday. I pushed that club buffet on you and you were a good enough sport not to object too much."

"I didn't object at all. It was nothing."

Words seemed to be chasing each other. "I want to take you to lunch as a token of appreciation."

Josephine looked impatiently at the door leading out. "I can't tomorrow. I have other plans."

"In the barn?"

"I'm working on something. I've only just started and—"

"If you only just started, pushing it off a day wouldn't be such a big deal, would it? I mean, the world wouldn't come to an end."

"If it means that much to you . . ." reluctantly.

Frieda said quickly, "Skip it. We can make it another time."

"Next week," Josephine offered. "One day next week."

"Oh, come on, I've been busy myself lately. Don't feel bad about turning me down. I'll cancel the reservations. I know," she said before she hung up, "you'd make it if you could."

I could have, if I had really wanted to, Josephine thought, amazed at her own selfishness. She considered calling Frieda back, but it was too late. To accept now would add insult.

In the living room, she curled up on the big couch and prepared to salve her conscience by giving all her attention to Ted's problem. With a start, she realized she had thought of it as Ted's problem, not theirs.

"Bartlett dropped in this afternoon and made me a flat offer for the *Digest.* As soon as he left, I came home to tell you."

"And I wasn't here! Oh, darling," she apologized, "I'm so sorry."

"I had to talk to someone. I was ready to explode. Thank God Fran was here."

"I should have been," she said, wondering at the same time what exactly Ben had meant, saying he had made her dissatisfied with everything she had, everything she was, but that she hadn't found it out yet. . . .

"How are they coming?"

"What?"

"The lessons."

She shrugged. "Slowly. I don't think I'm very good."

"Does he? Jess's nephew."

"I never think of him as Jess's nephew anymore. And you were right when you said he couldn't be that bad. He isn't, really. Anyway, let's not talk about him anymore."

"He's probably a lot more interesting than I am to be with lately," Ted said. "All I can talk about, because it's all I can *think* about, is my lousy paper."

"It's not lousy," she protested, "and it isn't yours alone. It never was. And I want to hear about it. Tell me."

So he told her about the visit from Harris Bartlett. After a few minutes, she realized uncomfortably that she was anticipating everything he said. But hadn't they both expected it to happen this way months ago? As Ted went on, telling her in detail about the offer, his refusal and Bartlett's lightly veiled threat not to renegotiate the contract when it came up for renewal in March, Josephine found she was forcing herself to concentrate on him by concentrating on his face as he talked.

What an interesting face! Mentally she drew a line where the brows would be placed. The tightly curled hair that made him seem even more boyish could be done simply in a solid mass. Surface detail could be eliminated if it interfered with the simplicity, the flow of the whole unit of shape. She studied him until she was startled to hear him say, "Isn't that what I expected of that guy?"

"Bartlett? Yes, of course. We both knew he'd—"

"I was talking about Stan Ryder. Didn't I predict he'd be the first to sell out? I feel a lot better," he said, coming to sit next to her once more. "Talking to you always makes me feel better. You don't have to say anything. Just being here and listening is enough."

She was too ashamed to tell him she hadn't been listening. The mantel clock told her she hadn't been listening for more than twenty minutes.

Chapter Twelve

"ALICE DALY's in the hospital," Frieda announced. She stood in the frame of the kitchen door and swayed forward as if she were being pushed.

"Are you all right?" Fran asked. Her concern for the moment was all for their neighbor.

"Never better." Frieda's round behind was encased in slacks that were too tight for her. She moved unsteadily to the table and grasped the chair for support before spreading herself over it. "Don't I look all right? What's the matter?"

"I don't know," Fran admitted.

"I'm on a diet. Again! I'm feeling a little woozy. This much"—she studied the air between her thumb and forefinger, then narrowed the space and amended—"hardly noticeable. I'm surprised you did."

"Have you had breakfast?"

"Tomato juice. That'll last me until lunch." She began to laugh. "I forgot which of my adorable twins told me this joke about tomato juice. Would you believe sometimes even I can't tell them apart? So I yell, 'Hey, you,' and one of them usually says, 'Who, me?' and I say, 'You're the one.'" She shook her head and pouted, "What were you asking me?"

"You were telling me a joke," Fran reminded her patiently. As if to give her hands something to do, she folded the letter she had been reading and carefully replaced it in its flowered envelope.

"Oh, that's right." Her large almost childlike eyes were bright again. "Well, this little girl says to her mother, 'Mommy, what's a vampire?' And the mother says, 'You're too young to know about such things, darling; drink your tomato juice before it clots.' Isn't that sick? Remembering it was probably the reason I choked swallowing the stuff. I had to put something in it to make it go down easier."

"I think you put in a little too much . . . something."

"For God's sake, a shot of vodka in my juice to pull me through the morning doesn't make me a lush."

"What's this about Alice Daly?" Fran asked, but she was thinking: I wonder if Josie knows about this drinking. Josie's her best friend. Josie could do something about it. "You were telling me about Alice," she prompted again.

"I just told you. She had a miscarriage."

"You didn't tell me that."

"You weren't listening." She began again, carefully picking her words. "Alice is on the sixth at Memorial. Don't ask me how I know it's the sixth. I have sources. I used to tell—" she hesitated and then said pointedly, "—your daughter-in-law that I usually scoop the *Digest* and she used to say it was true. That was when she used to see more of me." She raised her hand, poised it in midair, then let it fall heavily against her thick thigh. "Seeing much more of me would be asking too much, wouldn't it? Maybe that was part of it. Josie is so neat—a place for everything and everything in its place. Maybe I took up too much room in her life. That's it. She couldn't stand me anymore because I'm so fat."

"Ten pounds," soothingly, "maybe fifteen at the most."

"She isn't in now, is she?" But before Fran could answer Frieda went on, "Never mind. I know she's at the barn, pulling cow's tits." She laughed. "I know she isn't doing that, but it came to me all of a sudden. Sorry. You're a lady like my friend Josephine, proper and correct. She doesn't like it when I talk like that either. How the hell did we get on milking cows? I guess that's because that's what you usually do in a barn. Unless there's a hayloft. And my friend Josie isn't the type to go in for a little roll in the hay."

"I'm going to get you some coffee," Fran said. Without waiting for an answer, she filled a cup and set it down in front of Frieda. "I'm sorry about Alice if it's true."

"It's true all right. The sixth is the . . . gynecological —" She had difficulty with the word and smiled when she finally got it out. "—floor," she finished victoriously. "I ought to know because I had a D & C there a couple of years ago. Did you ever have a D & C? It's an extremely undignified procedure. There you are flat on your back, legs raised and spread, but when you come right down to it, sex isn't all that dignified either . . . but there is a difference if you care to analyze it. Would you care to?"

"Drink the coffee."

"I'd rather have a glass of water." She opened the cupboard, looked surprised and then ran the faucet full force, raising her voice over it. "Now, you can't convince me Sam Daly was carried away by a sudden passion. My God, you've seen Alice. I mean I'm fat, but when I get all dressed up I don't make a bad appearance. And Tony says there's just more of me to love. He said it last night. How do you like that? After all these years? But Sam would have had to be roaring drunk—I don't mean a little . . . happy, like I am now, because of a couple of shots of vodka. It had to have been deliberate and, my God, she's old enough at forty-three to know how to keep from getting knocked up. And why anyone with an eighteen-year-old old daughter—Jennie is eighteen you know, and Andy is going on sixteen . . ." She took a deep breath, paused and then said wistfully, "I could never give a buffet luncheon like the one Josie did."

"You should have more confidence in yourself," Fran said.

"I don't do anything well, Mrs. Trask." She changed her mind about the coffee and drained the cup in one gulp. "That wasn't always true. Before I was married, I was a production assistant at this TV agency where Tony and I met. I weighed one hundred and ten pounds. Would you believe it? Anyway, they hated to lose me. Believe it or not, I was very efficient . . . very capable."

"What happened to change all that?"

"I don't know. I really don't. I changed. Maybe it's living out here. Basically, I'm a city girl."

"So was I," Fran said, "before the children invited me to live here for a while. Why don't you call me Fran, instead of Mrs. Trask? If they do . . ."

"It's a throwback to my fast fading youth," Frieda said. "A well brought-up girl always called her friends' mothers Mrs. or aunt. If I called my mother by her first name . . ."

Fran smiled. "I don't honestly remember how old Teddy was when he started. He was probably seeing how much he could get away with. His father—his name was Ted, too, did you know that? Anyway, he didn't like it, but I didn't really care."

"My mother would have said that in life we have only one person we can call mother." The strong black coffee was beginning to have its effect. "Oh, boy, can I just hear her saying that? My mother was very big on the subject. Very sentimental. Forget Mother's Day and she'd break your arm."

"When Teddy and Josie call me Fran, it's like being thought of as a friend. That's rather nice, too."

"You said something just now about living here only for a while. You're not planning to leave Ditchling?"

"Oh, no." To herself she added, because I'm needed here now. I wasn't before, but I am now. Maybe one day she would even stop calling her room upstairs "the guest room." She took the letter she had been reading out of the envelope again and smoothed it. "This is from my friend, Anne Harris. She used to be my next-door neighbor in the building on Central Park West. For years we were as close as you and Josie—" A faint cloud passed over Frieda's face and Fran realized she had said the wrong thing.

"Used to be," Frieda corrected softly.

"We still correspond, Anne and I," Fran said, as if she hadn't heard. "Sometimes we talk on the phone. She's a widow, too." She waved the letter. "I give Anne credit, living alone in a city like New York. But she goes to lectures and theater matinees, even, yoga classes. She loves to travel. She's going on another cruise. To the Caribbean this time. That's what she wrote in this. She begged me to go with her."

"I wish someone would beg *me*. Why don't you go?"

"I just told you. I'm needed here. Ask Josie."

"Who sees her anymore?" Frieda asked tightly and looked stunned when Josephine came down the stairs and into the kitchen. "Good morning," she said warmly. "I didn't know you were here."

Frieda's head snapped sharply in Fran's direction. "Why didn't you tell me *she* was?"

"I started to," Fran said, looking away quickly because she couldn't bear the accusing weight of the stare. "You didn't give me a chance."

Frieda turned to Josie instead, "What are you doing here?"

"I live here," she answered pleasantly, pouring herself half a cup of coffee. She was anxious to leave for the River Road, but rushing off would probably hurt Frieda's feelings. Hadn't she hurt them enough only a few days ago? Or was it last week? She couldn't remember.

"You usually leave here earlier. I watch you from the window." It was a biting voice, full of lightly veiled resentment.

"I was stripping the beds and filling the laundry basket." The mental picture of Frieda at the window clocking her made her uncomfortable. "I've already remade them, and I'll put everything into the machine when I get back."

"I can do it," Fran offered obligingly.

"No, please don't. You do enough around here. When Pete comes home after school, ask him to carry the basket down. I'll take care of the rest later." To Frieda she said, "You're really sticking to your diet this time, aren't you? You're thinner."

"You're a liar, but thanks."

"I mean it," she insisted, in an effort to please and encourage her. There was no real harm in a lie wrapped in such good intentions. "You look definitely thinner since the meeting last week."

"Two weeks ago," Fran corrected. There was a sweetness in her voice that sounded almost solicitous.

"It couldn't have . . ." she began, then broke off self-consciously because she realized it had been.

Frieda bit her lip, then blurted out, "What's happened to your glasses?"

Josephine looked puzzled.

"In your cupboard. They're not in steps anymore. I got one down before and noticed. Everything's just . . . put away."

"All of a sudden one day it seemed unnecessary to keep it all like that. I didn't need to anymore."

"Did you need to before?"

"I thought I did." She wondered why she ever had.

She finished her coffee. Fran took that cup and the one Frieda had used to the sink. It was a conscious gesture to leave the two younger women to themselves. She hoped Josie would notice that Frieda had been drinking, but the coffee seemed to have worked wonders.

What had actually sobered Frieda was Josephine's unexpected appearance.

"You're not planning to go to the barn as much now, are you, with Christmas coming up and everything?" For the first time she smiled at her. It was a gentle, pleading smile.

"Probably not," Josephine said.

"I've decided to give a little supper sometime during the holidays. I'm not going to ask you to help. Not even a little."

"You know I'd be glad to."

"No," stubbornly. "All I ask from you is a small vote of confidence."

"You've got it."

"What about New Year's Day? You'll have open house? You always do."

"If I always do," Josephine said, as if reminding herself, "then I suppose I will again."

"And afterward?"

"Afterward what?"

"What I asked you before. You won't go to the barn as much, will you?"

At the sink Fran held her breath and waited. She was pleased to hear her answer, "I have to."

"Who's forcing you?"

"You don't understand, Frieda," Fran interrupted, wiping her hands on the dish towel, "Josie's working on a surprise for Peter, for his birthday."

"If everybody knows," Josephine said, "it won't be a surprise."

"Since when can't I keep a secret?"

Josephine couldn't help smiling broadly at that. "All right," she relented, "I'm modeling a head of Pete."

"If he's posing for it, what's the big secret?"

"He doesn't know anything about it. I'm working from sketches and memory. I want it done in time for his birthday."

"How do you stand him, Josie?"

"Pete?"

"No," irritably, "Ben Goudy. I bumped into him in the post office last week. I tried to be civil. I always feel it doesn't hurt to have good manners. And it shows breeding. Obviously, he has none."

"What," Josephine asked, steeling herself, "did Ben say?"

"I'm embarrassed to repeat it. Embarrassed for him." She took a deep breath. "I was wearing my new suit. Oh, I forgot, you haven't seen it. Well, take my word for it—it's stunning."

"I believe you."

"It's a gorgeous cherry red."

Josephine closed her eyes in pain. Not cherry red. Not with that ample figure!

"I didn't think you liked that color on you."

"I don't. I hate it. The salesgirl talked me into it. And she wouldn't have been able to if you had been with me. I know it was a mistake, but it was a final sale and I'll buy anything I think the store is losing money on."

"What did Ben say?"

"He said, 'Did you ever wonder why God dressed the robin in red and the elephant in unobtrusive gray?' "

"I'm sorry," quietly. "That was unforgivable."

"I've already forgotten the incident. It was that unimportant. Josie," she went on, eagerly confidential, "you've been so out of things. There's been so much delicious gossip."

"Like what?" Josephine asked, in spite of herself.

"Like Alice Daly having a miscarriage. And Madge Holden is divorcing Cy. It isn't definite and I don't like to be the one to spread false rumor, but—"

"What was that about Alice?"

"Your mother-in-law and I were talking about it before you came down."

Josephine felt an enormous weight lift inside her. She remembered the pain that hollowed Alice's cheeks and darkened the circles under her eyes. "Miscarriage?" She had been sure she had seen death there, but it was only the death of an unborn, unfeeling embryo. "That's too bad. Where is she? Memorial?"

"On the sixth. Gynecological."

"I'll drive over later and see her."

"I won't go with you," Frieda said. "Alice probably isn't feeling too cheerful, and being in my company always rubs her the wrong way. That's because I've always been honest with her. For God's sake, I'd probably ask her whether she was stupid or careless. But that would be me being honest. Not everyone," with dignity, "appreciates honesty as I do." Her lack of appreciation for Ben Goudy's directness was already forgotten. "Oh, I've got lots more juicy stuff." She dangled the prospect like a ripe plum. "We'll have to get together. You won't keep going to the barn after you finish the present for Pete, will you?" There was no cutting edge to her voice now. It was soft and said, please come shopping with me again. Please keep me from buying the wrong color.

102

For an answer, Josephine said, "If I want to finish Pete's present, I'll have to work on it. I'm late. I'd like to walk, but driving will be faster. Besides, I'll need the car to go to the hospital."

"Then you probably won't be home for lunch?" Fran asked. "You don't have to, honey."

It was true. She didn't have to report home like a well-oiled automaton. Fran was there—and happy to be, because it made her feel it was "our" house. She was there to feed the children and send them back, and if Ted happened by he never found either home or refrigerator empty. Josephine provided for that, too—by providing his own mother. Hadn't it been her idea six years ago to invite Fran to live with them? . . .

A few minutes later she headed for the River Road.

BEN WAS already at work when she entered the barn and went quickly and quietly to her own work.

He neither turned to welcome her nor acknowledged her presence by so much as a brief nod or grunt. He knew she was there, though. It was something she could feel, the same way she was feeling the silken clay under her fingers. He knew she was there, but was too busy to tell her.

At first that had bothered her. Then she learned to respect the reason. Without putting it into words, he had taught her that concentration in work had to be respected. It had nothing to do with good manners; it was not to be confused with poor ones.

But there was no excuse for the lack of manners he had shown Frieda. She would bring that up before she left today, but his reaction was impossible to predict. He might stare at her in amazement for confusing truth with rudeness. Or he might regard her with disgust for cluttering time with trivialities. Or he might be honestly puzzled and not remember the incident at all. . . .

No matter what he did or what he said, bringing up the subject would accomplish nothing except soothe her own conscience for neglecting Frieda all these months. That alone made it necessary.

She drew fingers over clay and tried to channel all her thoughts into that. "Love for the material," Ben had told her, "and love for the subject. You must have both." Thinking of Pete helped, too. She would think of her son with such intensity that she felt she was willing his breath into the clay.

This time it was going to turn out right. Twice she had been dissatisfied with what she was doing and deliberately turned her work back into a distorted mass. It was disheartening and discouraging, but never defeating. It was more like the turning of fresh earth and the planting of new seed.

She worked without stopping until her wrists felt boneless. It didn't matter. For the time being she was finished. Her hands lifted, fell into her lap, resting, and she sat looking at what she had done that morning.

"Well," she heard Ben say, "are you going to mash this one up, too?"

She spun around. "I didn't know you were there."

"Is this your final version?"

"This is the best I can do now. Maybe I'll do it better one day."

"Do you know what was wrong before?"

"All I was getting was a likeness. I have a photo album full of those."

"The others were bad starts," he agreed. "This is much better."

"I think I know why I wasn't satisfied with the first two. I couldn't find that double truth you told me to look for. It was all surface. The others did look like Peter, but there was never anything behind the eyes and the mouth was always wrong."

"I wish I had a dollar," he said, "for every time I've said there's something wrong with the mouth."

"Pete's always in a hurry. He runs a lot. I worked on this until I felt, looking at the head, that there was movement under it." Her palms were upturned in her lap, speaking with silent eloquence. "This is far from finished, but it is getting there. Finally."

After a moment, Ben said, "What you're doing is criminal."

I don't care, she thought, if it's technically bad. This one pleases me.

She flung out an arm to protect her work in case he decided to sweep it off the table. He might, if it offended him too much. She remembered doing the same thing when she found him in her kitchen months ago. Her first thought had been to protect her children. In a different way, this one was her child, too.

"Artists like me," Ben was saying, "give their whole lives just learning to be good. What right have you to be so good without suffering like the rest of us?"

She relaxed, letting her arms hang into the hollow of her lap as she sat on the high stool facing him. "Is this really good?" She had just finished telling herself that as long as the work pleased her, what he thought didn't matter. It wasn't true. What he thought meant everything.

"How was God careless enough," he said, "to make a mistake and give a big gift like yours to someone like you?"

She tried to control her voice, but her face showed that she was overwhelmed. "If you're right, Ben, why was it a mistake?"

"You tell me."

She hesitated before answering, then reddened and looked away. He was amusing himself and she hadn't been quick enough to recognize it. With great effort, she looked back at him and tried not to see that humiliating image of herself, the way she must appear in his eyes, the housewife who stopped decorating cakes, dabbled in art and took her pathetic first effort so seriously. The only way to get back at him was to put him on the defensive. She hoped her face didn't reveal how hurt she was. He had a tongue as sharp as any of his cutting tools. Hadn't he proved that with Frieda?

"Perhaps," she said, "I lack a certain sense of humor, but cruelty for the sake of cleverness or sarcasm in the name of wit is something I've never appreciated." The words sprang to her lips mechanically and she was trying hard to control her voice.

He frowned. "Is that what you think I was being just now? Clever and sarcastic?"

"Weren't you? With Mrs. Haines?"

"Who?" he said. "Who?"

"Frieda Haines. You met her in the post office. She was wearing red?"

He sliced the air with his hand and she drew back as if he had severed her in half. "Oh, God, you really want to bring that up?"

"Yes."

"All right. She had no business wearing red."

"It certainly wasn't *your* business."

"You're absolutely right, and next time, if I meet her in the supermarket and if she's bare-assed, I promise I won't say a word." It was vicious and obviously he was in one of his more unsociable moods. I don't like you today, she decided, and took even greater pleasure informing him, "And you were wrong about my friend."

He frowned. "You mean you like her in that outfit?"

"No, not her. The other one. The one I told you about."

"I'll be damned if I can follow you today. What started you in circles?"

You did, she thought resentfully, because you laughed at me without letting me hear it. Because we both know that the God I believe in isn't careless. He doesn't make mistakes. I don't have a big gift. If I'm lucky I have a little flair.

"I don't know any of your other friends," Ben was saying.

"I told you about this one. Remember? The one I thought was very ill. I found out today it's not that serious. She is in the hospital, but she's going to be all right."

He shrugged. "You were the one who said she was dying. I didn't."

"Well . . . I was wrong."

"Good. Glad to hear it. Now let's have lunch. It's on me today. Swiss cheese, fresh rye from the bakery, apples. It's a feast. I'll even open a bottle of wine. Let's drink to Jo who works blind, feeling her way, and produces something wonderful."

Stop laughing at me, she screamed silently. Or if you do, at least let me hear it so we can both laugh, because I've been wasting my time for months. Tell me, instead of teasing me.

"What about it?" he was saying. "Do we open the wine, or do we reheat the coffee?"

Suddenly nothing that was happening seemed real. It was like that dream she had the night before she came to the barn the second time. A nightmare sent her back and he was in that, too. Imagine remembering bits and pieces after all this time.

"You're not polite," she had told him. "I'm not used to people who aren't polite."

"What time is it? Come on," he had ordered roughly. "You're the one with the clock."

And in her dream she had been very apologetic. "I have a lot of things to do, Mr. Goudy. I lead a very busy life . . ."

Quick, she told herself, remember more before it slips away completely. It's slipping fast. It's important to remember. Remember how his hand smashed over the clay and destroyed it, disfiguring the nose, pushing in the eyes . . .

You're an evil man, she had thought, a destructive man.

Much more terrifying now than any nightmare was realizing what she had done. She had spoken the words. She had actually said them out loud: "You're an evil man—a destructive man."

He sounded confused. "Say that again."

"I didn't mean to say it."

"Why am I evil? Have I been destructive to you? How?"

Her heart was pounding. "Never mind."

She wrung out a clean wet cloth before wrapping it around the clay head. Excess moisture could spoil the surface; Ben had taught her that. Ben had taught her so many things. He had made her as happy on other days as he was making her unhappy today. Without looking at him, she knew he was watching her wash and dry her tools. She never left them in the pail to soak overnight.

"If you do," he once said, "they will crack," and hadn't even smiled when she answered, "I wouldn't leave them like that. These are my friends."

He hadn't ridiculed any of those foolish little bursts of exuberance. He had saved it up to taunt her now that she was almost finished with her first piece.

"Obviously," Ben said coolly, "you're not planning to work anymore today."

"Does it matter?"

"I thought it was beginning to."

"I'm going to the hospital to see my friend."

"Does that mean you're turning down my invitation to lunch?"

"I suppose it does."

"You have to eat anyway. Why not here?"

"There's a cafeteria. I can get something there."

He shook his head in amazement. "You don't really think I'm going to let you leave here without any explanation, do you? Without telling me why you said what you did?"

"I was only thinking it," she admitted. "I told you I didn't mean to say it."

"I'll be goddamned if I can figure you out at all today. I get it. You're still mad because I told your other friend that God dresses robins in red . . ."

"I forgot about that." It was true.

"No, you didn't," he said. "It's the only reason for you to be acting this way. Okay, I shouldn't have talked to her that way. I shouldn't have talked to her at all. For God's sake, what do you have in common with that tub? Never mind," hastily, "never mind. Don't answer. Just tell me, does what I said make me evil? That's putting it pretty strong."

"The work I've done here is the best that's in me," she said quietly.

"And I," he said, "have nothing but admiration for your work."

107

"Then was it nice to make fun of it?"

"When did I do that?"

"Just now. You wanted to open a bottle of wine," she reminded him, "and drink to me because I work blind, only feel my way and still manage to produce something . . . wonderful. You said that."

He was listening to her very carefully. "I remember exactly what I said."

"Wasn't that evil? Wasn't that destructive? I really had forgotten about Frieda." She smiled sadly. "Perhaps you didn't mean to hurt me, Ben. I never mean to hurt my daughter. When Elsie tries to do something that's beyond her, sometimes I'm impatient, and that's wrong, I know, but I never laugh at her. That's what I meant about being destructive. No one can be better than what they are. You should be more generous, because you can afford to be—just as I can afford to be with Elsie."

He took a big step and covered the space between them. Then he seized her wrists and held one in each of the big hands that had both attracted and repelled her the first time she saw them in the kitchen of her house. She held her own hands rigid, fingers spread.

"Look at them," he ordered. "Do you ever look at them and ask, 'Whose hands are these?' It's like repeating your own name over and over until they're just words and you don't recognize yourself in them at all. Keep looking at your hands and tell me who they belong to."

He let them go as suddenly as he had taken them. But she kept staring at them, surprised there were no marks on her wrists. He had really held them very gently. If she had wanted to, she could have taken them back herself.

She hadn't.

She must have been too busy telling herself: Why, he never laughed at me! He did mean it.

"I taught you to use your hands," he said. "Now what are you going to do with them? I warn you, if you use them only to turn down your husband's bed or wipe your kids' noses, they'll hurt. For the rest of your life you'll wake up in the middle of the night because your hands hurt."

"I am using them," she threw back at him.

"Not enough."

"I have to leave," she said. "My friend . . . in the hospital . . ."

It was an excuse and she knew it. But the way he was talking, the things he was saying embarrassed and bewildered her. They frightened her.

Without warning he caught her hands in his again, turned them palms up this time and, while she stood frozen, bent his heavy head and kissed them.

"Beautiful," he said. "They could work with marble. Don't be so easily satisfied with a little when you could have so much."

This time she didn't wait for him to free her. She tore herself away and rubbed her hands up and down on the sides of her tweed skirt. "What are you trying to do to me?" she demanded. "I'm shaking like a leaf."

"There are the milk white Italian marbles . . ." Ben was saying. Josephine had heard that special note of gentleness in a man's voice before, in Ted's when he talked of his children. "Carrara and Serravezza; the warm flesh color of French marbles, perfect for figures; the strength of the Belgian black. Each marble has a personality all its own. And when you choose one that's right for you, you'll know better than to try to dominate it. You'll try to understand it. I could help you understand, Jo, if you'll let me."

"Let me go," she said, knowing she had only to walk past him to the door.

"Marble," he continued as if he hadn't heard her, "changes color under different people's hands."

"*Please,* let me go."

"I'm not stopping you." It was Ben who walked away. "I'm not stopping you," he repeated from halfway across the barn. He was standing beside a virgin block. Mallet and chisel were lying beside it. "Only if you stayed, I'd start today. I'd show you how to chip off the outer layers of stone, how to find a warm body in the cold marble. I could show you how to search and shape."

Josephine's coat was within arm's reach. She put it on. Next winter, she thought, I ought to get a lighter-weight coat. This is so heavy. I never realized it. . . .

She wanted to get away from the sound of him hammering on the block of marble he had practically told her he would be willing to give to her.

At the door, she stopped. "If marble changes color under different people's hands, I think I know why."

"Do you?"

109

"It's the light," she said simply. "Different shapes can give off different shadows, and space can suck in light."

Satisfied, he returned to his hammering.

Once more she tried to leave. This time her hand was on the latch. "It's carving, isn't it? Rather than molding."

He turned to her and held out the tools.

She shrank back.

"Just hold them. Get the feel of them."

"It'll have to be another time. Alice Daly is in the hospital. . . ."

"You're afraid."

"Besides, I want to finish that head first. It's a surprise for my son. Remember? I can't think of anything else until I finish that."

He smiled. "You are afraid." She had never before wanted to leave there.

Now she ran.

Chapter Thirteen

SHE DROVE away too fast, going north. There was witchery in the sky. It drained color from winter branches that stretched over the road like silent specters and gave a grayish look to the rocks and stones and stumps of dead trees. She could see the frozen river, glassy and transparent. Suddenly, after about a mile she braked to a sudden stop and realized she had driven away from, instead of toward, the hospital.

On this particular day, to have gone in the wrong direction without thinking was unnerving. She looked around frantically. There wasn't quite enough clearance to make a U-turn, so she shifted into reverse and backed up.

When she got out to check the reason for the dull crunch, she found a dent in the rear fender. Ted would have laughed at her for taking that so seriously, "Why, everybody puts a dent in a fender from time to time, Josie. Especially wives."

But she never had before.

The sight of the damaged fender didn't make her as sick as the bits of colored glass from a smashed taillight. They collected like drops of blood on the icy ground. It was hard to believe the sun she felt last summer couldn't warm her at all now. She rubbed her hands together —the hands he said were beautiful, but too easily satisfied—and wondered what she had done with her gloves. If she had left them in the barn, she couldn't go back for them. After today, she could never go back, and that meant never finishing the head.

Even as she thought it, a gentle snow began and she remembered another day in winter when Peter was four. He had looked up at her startled and said, "Guess what? A snowflake just bit my nose." She had squeezed his mittened hand and loved him a little more.

If I leave that head unfinished, she thought, it could be bad luck for Peter. I won't take any chances. I'll finish it first; then I'll leave.

Having made up her mind she got back into the car, straightened the wheel and drove away quickly. When she passed the Goudy property, she went even faster until she could see the barn getting smaller in the small mirror. Still, her breath didn't come normally until she turned the bend of the road and couldn't see it at all.

Dave, at the auto repair shop, shook his head and said, "What have you got against this poor car, Mrs. Trask?"

"I was making a U-turn and didn't see the fence."

"At least you weren't as rough on it this time."

She was confused. "This time?"

"Never mind, Mrs. Trask. I can fix it so you won't even have to tell your husband. He was upset enough a couple of weeks ago."

Ted must have had an accident and let her take the blame. Such childish male ego was unworthy of him.

"I know you use the station wagon and he has the coupe."

And she knew which day Ted had taken her car. Carefully and chronologically, Peter had boxed the early editions of the weeklies that were stored in the cellar. He was going to help his father transfer them to the building in the square that still belonged to the *Digest*. Ted had decided using the station wagon would be more practical for carting.

"Since I promised him that room downstairs, I'll help him clear it. I won't tell him that this may be the first step to the Ditchling dump."

"Don't talk that way," she had said.

"If I can't save our paper, Josie, do we really want all those around to remind us? Maybe the whole idea was crazy from the beginning. What did I know about putting out a weekly? I was brought up in the middle of New York City. Saturday nights my dad used to carry the Sunday *Times* from the corner newsstand. We weighed it once. Six pounds. He used to call it the archives."

"The *Digest* wasn't a crazy idea."

"Maybe I should have gone into the import business, too. His wife never worried too much."

"Your wife doesn't either," she lied.

"It's just that I always wanted to live in a small town and have my own newspaper."

"You've told me so little lately," she said, at the same time thinking it was wrong to feel guilty. It was almost beyond her anyway, all that talk about block advertising and cooperatives. . . .

"Well, you already know Stan Ryder sold out."

"You expected it of him."

"I didn't expect it of Mike Weiss."

"The *Examiner?* When?"

"Yesterday." He was nervously chewing on the inside of his cheek. "I still don't want to sell out to Bartlett."

"Then don't."

He kissed her and smiled. "The fashionable new word in our vocabulary is 'supportive.' My wife is not only beautiful, she's also supportive."

Afterward, he and Peter had lifted heavy cartons of back issues into the station wagon. That had been two weeks ago. . . .

"How long will it take to fix the fender?" Josephine was asking now.

Instead of answering, Dave walked around the station wagon on the light snow that had only frosted the ground. He examined it from several angles. Then he wiped his forehead, leaving on it a streak of oily grime from his hand. There was an uneasiness in her that she didn't have a name for. Not yet. Whatever it was, it had something to do with Ted.

"Just the fender," she said. "That's all."

"I have to straighten it and spray it. The paint has to dry. I can't promise to have it ready until at least five-thirty."

"Can I use your phone? I want to call a taxi. I have to go to the hospital in Douglaston."

"If you don't mind riding in the tow truck, I'll drive you."

From inside the open garage, she heard the dull clang of a hammer. "You don't have to."

Dave tightened his belt. "I want to." Without another word, he upended a tire and rolled it with a light, knowing hand. Then he went into the shop to get his plaid mackinaw and tell his assistant he was leaving. A few minutes later, she was sitting next to him headed towards Douglaston.

Up until today, Dave had always been so easy to talk to. She never before had to buy words from him and was sorry now she hadn't called a taxi.

Finally he said, "It didn't really snow after all, but that storm a couple of weeks ago was bad."

"Yes," she said, and knew suddenly that there was another reason he had offered to drive her.

"The roads are treacherous. Especially these here to Douglaston."

"I'm a careful driver. I never have accidents. That fender—it's not a big thing."

"A love tap," he admitted, "next to that other time."

Annoyed she wanted to tell him there hadn't been any other time. That was her husband's fault. But if Ted wanted it that way, it wasn't important. The next moment a spasm of fright seized her.

"Don't you realize," Dave almost shouted and sounded more like himself again, "you could have been killed?"

"Was it that bad?"

"Come on now! You were probably so shook up after it happened, you couldn't get behind that wheel again. That's why you let your husband bring it in, wasn't it? You had to have been going damn fast, Mrs. Trask, with your mind on something besides driving." Ted must have been going that fast and thinking of something else besides driving. "Pardon me, but you scared the hell out of him."

"I didn't realize it," she said quietly.

"I asked him where it happened and all he told me was, 'Coming from Douglaston.'"

But he never told you I was driving, Josephine thought. You only assumed . . .

"You know you were lucky it wasn't a total. Listen, it's none of my business, it's just that I've known you both—how many years? Never mind, a lot—and I like you both. Tell me, who's in the hospital, Mrs. Trask?"

She neither stirred nor took her eyes off the curving highway. "Alice Daly," she answered automatically.

"She's that sick?"

"As a matter of fact, it isn't serious."

"Then why were you going like a bat out of hell coming back to Ditchling? I didn't let Mr. Trask know how bad I thought it could have been. Two doors smashed on the driver's side and the fender—the front one

114

that time. But I'm sure he knew. His hand was shaking. I had to light his cigarette for him."

Half to herself, she said, "Ted doesn't smoke anymore."

"He was smoking that day we looked at the wreck. If I wasn't lucky enough to salvage two doors of another wagon from the auto graveyard, it would have taken a month to get that thing back into shape."

That night Ted—offhand—told her he didn't like the way the station wagon was handling. He had left it for a tune-up.

"It's all right," she had said then. But it wasn't all right, because he hadn't told her the truth and she had been so wrapped up in her foolish hobby that she hadn't even suspected.

The accident had occurred on the road to Douglaston. . . . That's where the *Enterprise* was published. That meant that, of the original ten weeklies, only six were left. He must have found out that day. He must have driven back thinking about the *Enterprise* and almost been killed.

Dave let her off at the entrance to the hospital.

"I didn't mean to shout at you."

"I appreciate your concern," she said. "I mean it."

"Please drive more carefully. Don't let these hospital visits get you."

"I won't."

For the first time he smiled. "Then I won't tell Mr. Trask about this fender business. It'll be between the two of us."

"Thanks for the lift," she said. "I'll take a taxi back and see you at five-thirty."

"It'll be ready, Dave promised."

JOSEPHINE ALWAYS felt self-consciously healthy in a hospital. She was able to move with long easy strides past stretchers with patients helplessly strapped down to keep them from rolling off—or running off.

There was too much white. It bounced up from the polished white floor and was reflected on the white ceiling. It blotted up all the light from the corners. The odor of disinfectant and antiseptic filled her nostrils. She was sure it had been sucked into the flowers she had bought in the florist's shop.

At Information desk she had been told that Alice wasn't on six anymore. On her way to the reception desk, she passed yawning doors. In one room an old woman with sparse gray hair sat at the edge of a white bed. Her gaping white hospital gown exposed aged and shrunken buttocks, like wrinkled orange peel. There was an indecency in leaving the doors ajar. . . . In another room a man lay flat as a corpse on the raised bed. His jaw had fallen open. It framed a cavernous oval. Someone had taken out his dentures so he couldn't swallow them and choke to death. He was so still; maybe he was already dead. . . .

It's not my place to go in and find out, Josephine thought, and wondered why they had moved Alice down from the gynecological floor.

At the desk, a nurse stopped her.

"Mrs. Alice Daly," Josephine said. "She's in 406."

"Mrs. Daly isn't having visitors."

"You mean she can't?"

"I mean she doesn't want any. I'm sorry."

The trip to the hospital then had been for nothing. No, not really. If she hadn't driven here with Dave she wouldn't have learned about Ted's near-brush with a hospital or worse. She held out the flowers. "Would you see that she gets these?"

"Of course," the nurse said.

She had bought a card in the gift shop. "Please give her this with them."

"Of course," the nurse said.

Josephine had turned down Ben's invitation for bread and cheese and apples and wine. She had told him she would get something to eat at the cafeteria.

Since I'm here anyway, she thought, I might as well.

Downstairs in the cafeteria, she was carrying a tray with an egg salad, a cup of coffee and a plain Danish when she saw John Cullen.

He sat alone in the middle of the big room and managed somehow to make it into a very private corner. He seemed to have acquired even the air rights around the table and although every other was taken by three, or more often four, people, no one, for fear of being repulsed, had dared cross the invisible border that kept him at a distance. Only Josephine dared.

"Unless," she said, "you'd rather be by yourself."

He took the tray from her. "What are you doing here, Josie?"

"I came to see Alice. Why did they move her to four?" She broke the hard roll and spread it with butter from the stamp-sized pad. "That floor's a horror."

Nurses fluttered by like big white birds. "She wanted a private room. There wasn't one available on six."

"Why doesn't she want any visitors?"

"Do you want all of that Danish?"

She broke off a large piece. "Is she so depressed she doesn't want to see anyone?"

"That's it," he said.

"Did she really want another child so much?"

"You know all about it, I see."

"Frieda Haines knows all about everything."

Other doctors moved past, wearing dead white. "How's your sculpture?" he asked.

"That word makes it sound much more important than what I'm doing. Who told you?"

Unsmiling, he took the pastry and gave her back her words. "Frieda Haines knows everything. . . . He's an interesting man."

"Who?" She was sitting opposite those intensely blue, medically trained eyes. There was something clairvoyant in the way he looked back into hers.

"Goudy. He came into the office last week. He sprained his back lifting a piece of marble."

"Did you strap him?"

"Yes."

"He didn't tell me. I suppose it's all right now."

"I suppose."

Institutional food was tasteless. She ate it anyway and waited for him to speak first. When he didn't, she said, "I haven't seen you for a long time, John."

"We're both busy people." He stopped talking again and lapsed into contemplative silence.

For what seemed a long time, neither said anything. It wasn't the same kind of companionable silence she shared with Ben. She and John had always shared such good companionable talk. Through the years, she may even have talked too much about the way she thought and the things she thought about.

She shifted uneasily and wondered what he would say if she told him about going the wrong way earlier, after she left the barn. She wondered what his technical diagnosis would be about her hands. They were cold except for small centers. The centers were on fire as if a lighted cigarette had been pressed hard into the palms where Ben Goudy had kissed them.

117

"Something very upsetting happened a while ago," she heard herself say, and didn't wait for him to ask what. "I had to leave the station wagon for a minor repair. Dave told me Ted smashed it up a couple of weeks ago. It could have been serious."

"Ted never mentioned it?"

"He didn't want to worry me, I guess. It's worse hearing it the way I did."

"Is he that upset about the *Digest?*"

"Frieda tell you that, too?"

"It's all over town. Is there really a chance it could fold, Josie?"

"We won't let it happen."

"Good for you."

She looked away toward the window.

Only I'm not doing anything to keep it from happening, she thought.

"Kids okay?"

She nodded. "Is it possible Peter goes to bed at night and wakes up the next morning inches taller? It seems that way."

"He was two years behind his natural growth. He's catching up fast. When he was in the third grade I measured him. He said, 'Last year, Dr. Cullen, I was the second shortest in my class. This year I'm the shortest. How come I shrunk?' "

"Imagine you remembering that."

"Elsie still hate being a girl?"

"After I leave here," Josephine said, "I'm going to buy her a dress for the Christmas glee club concert. I don't expect her to appreciate it. Eventually, she'll get to like herself. She'll have a difficult time of it for a while, but it'll pass. I remember being an awkward adolescent myself."

"No," he told her matter-of-factly, "you've forgotten. I wonder if anyone told Elsie her mother never had acne or baby fat. Maybe you're one of the reasons she's having such a rough time of it."

"The truth is," she said almost defiantly, "I was exactly like Elsie. You were four years older and didn't pay any attention to me."

"Maybe you're right." He looked past her over the rim of his cup and stopped paying attention to her now.

"How soon will Alice be released?"

"Very soon." He put down his coffee and looked directly at her again. "How do you picture time?"

She raised her head at the sound of the word. "I don't understand."

"Do you see each week as a block to step over? Circles within circles?

Straight lines stretching up? Is it flat? Does it have form?"

"I've never thought about it one way or another."

"You probably have and don't want to tell me." He leaned back against the cafeteria chair. "A calendar fell off my wall this morning. It slid onto the rug without making a sound. When I looked up from my desk, it wasn't there. I wondered what the year would have looked like if no one had stapled it into a calendar."

The years are going by for him, and he has no one to share them with, she thought. That's why he's thinking this way. He's lonely.

"I'm having my usual New Year's Day brunch. Of course, you'll be there," she said.

"You're my second invitation. Frieda's giving a supper."

"I know."

"You doing it for her?"

"She wants to do it all by herself this time."

"God bless us, every one," he said, raising his cup. "There'll be an epidemic of ptomaine poisoning. I'd better not eat, myself—and be prepared with the pump."

She got up. "All she asked for was my vote of confidence."

"Sorry," he said, "I won't give mine. I'll tell Alice you were by."

"Well, I saw you," she said warmly. "We haven't talked for a long time, John."

"I have a strong feeling we're going to again soon," he said. "I'm sure we are. Good-by, Josie."

She left him sitting the way she had found him—all alone.

DOUGLASTON'S main street burst into life around the corner. There had been a small decorated tree in the lobby of the hospital and the gift shop had a Christmas look, but Main Street looked eager for brisk holiday buying.

A canopy of tinseled rope looped overhead. Cast-iron lamp posts had been painted to resemble red and white candy canes. Santa's head was impaled on telephone poles, and trash cans were gaily ribboned in red and green.

"Oh, God," Ben hissed.

She whirled around quickly. There were only strangers behind her. I just imagined his reaction to all this commercial garishness, she thought. He's right, though. It's awful. And she realized, with an uneasy start, it was her own reaction. There was something disconcerting about searching the corners of her mind and finding her own thoughts disguised in someone else's voice.

In the department store, she finally found a dress for Elsie—turquoise wool, wonderful with that vibrant copper hair. The style was feminine without being too fussy. The neckline was slightly scooped and edged in brown velvet. Two pockets were edged in the same velvet. Elsie loved pockets. She would love the dress and her mother for buying it.

"AFTER DINNER," Josephine said as they sat around the table, "model it for us. I left it upstairs in my room. It's a beautiful dress. It'll look beautiful on you."

"Why not?" Peter said, helping himself to mashed potatoes. "She has perfect measurements: twelve, twelve and twelve."

"Shut up," Elsie said and, without stopping, added, "I have a dress."

"The green one you wore to Betsy's party? It's too small. You complained then because it was tight under the arms."

"Josie . . ." Fran began.

Elsie didn't let her finish. "I have a new dress. Gran met me one day after school and bought it for me in the square."

"Well, well," Ted said, "how's that for a lucky girl? You have your choice of two dresses now."

Elsie shook her head stubbornly. "The one I got with gran is already shortened, so it can't be returned. Anyway, I like it. I picked it out."

All Josephine said was, "Oh," and she was conscious of smiling too much. Her lips felt glued onto her face.

"It's all right, isn't it, Josie?" Fran asked, anxiously. "We were going to surprise you."

"Of course. I'll just return the one I bought today."

"I'm sorry if I spoiled your surprise," Elsie said, but she didn't look sorry.

"It doesn't matter," Josephine said. "What's important is that you have something to wear to your concert next Wednesday."

Fran corrected her: "Thursday."

"She's right," Elsie said. "And I don't want broccoli. I hate broccoli."

"You don't have to like it," Josephine reprimanded sternly, "but never say you hate food."

Peter groaned. "Here we go again with the starving children in Asia bit."

"Don't be a fresh kid," Ted said.

Earlier Josephine had told John she had been exactly like Elsie at that age. It wasn't true. It was more than just the hair. Her own, she remembered, had been a pale ash. Nothing else was clear. To remember more now was trying to read blurred handwriting.

But I know I never had a face like a small fox, she thought; my chin was never so pointed. And I knew how to be still. Elsie doesn't. Even when she appears to, she's like a coiled spring. Touch it and it quivers. And I didn't frighten my mother. This one, she thought, frightens me sometimes. I don't know why. I don't know why I'm afraid of my own child.

"In case anybody's interested," Peter said, pausing to let the words take full effect, "my room's finished."

"Tell them I helped," Elsie prompted.

"You did," he admitted grudgingly.

"Well!" Josephine said. "Did you hear that, Ted? The room's finished! When can we see it?"

"Give us a few minutes' start after dessert," Peter said.

"Us? Oh, you and Elsie."

"Gran can come, too, if she wants. She's already seen it."

Fran laughed. "I donated my services to Pete in exchange for the privilege. Oh, Josie, wait'll you see what he's done down there."

If she wanted to, Josephine could have told *her!* Hadn't he been receptive to all her suggestions from the beginning—starting with the one for a Western saloon? When she gave him the spittoon, he gave her an enthusiastic, "Thanks. This is a great start!"

From then on, she dropped hints for him to gather up and use. "In the back of the bookstore they have lots of old movie posters, a few good ones from some Westerns. . . ."

Josephine wondered which he had bought. She liked the one from *High Noon* starring Gary Cooper and Grace Kelly.

Another time she said, "The riding stable probably has discarded horseshoes. Pick them up dirt cheap for wall decorations. I have some ideas about the tables, too. Find old patio stuff at a garage sale. Paint them bright colors and lacquer pictures on top. Our collection of *American History Illustrated* is full of pictures of the period. You have my permission to tear out anything suitable."

121

And not long ago: "In the attic, there's an old wood-framed mirror. Most bars in Western saloons had mirrors behind them." She remembered how he had exchanged a look with his sister. That was probably one of the ways she had helped him, carrying down the old mirror without breaking it.

One morning last week, just before she left to go to the barn, she suggested, "Get some cardboard and make up some posters—Wanted Dead or Alive for Stage Coach Robbery. Put in the names of your friends. They'd get a kick out of that, I'll bet."

"I'll bet," Peter said.

She gave him a dozen good ideas and would have given him more if he had invited her downstairs. He hadn't. He had asked his grandmother. It was foolish to feel left out, but she did.

The three of them decided not to wait for dessert. "Give us a ten-minute head start," Peter said.

"Fifteen would be even better," Fran said. The color was high in her cheeks and her skin was fresh and shining with excitement. It occurred to Josephine that her mother-in-law had the face of a sixty-year-old child.

"Did you notice," she asked Ted when they were alone clearing the table, "how young your mother looks?"

"She's happy living here. That's because of you."

"It's because of all of us."

"She's living in another woman's house. It can't be easy. If it is, it's because of you."

In the kitchen Josephine scraped the dishes carefully, placing them one at a time into the dishwasher.

In this house, at this moment, she reminded herself, but for the grace of God and Ted's naturally good reflexes, there could have been two widows—two instead of one set adrift from the safe harbor a man makes simply by his presence.

"I put a slight dent in the fender backing up," she said. "Never mind how it happened. I never did it before and probably won't again. I took the car to Dave. . . . It wasn't left for a tune-up a couple of weeks ago, was it?"

"He shouldn't have told you."

"No—you should have. Dave thought *I* had been driving the car that day."

Ted looked surprised. "I never told him that. I suppose he just assumed . . . since it was the wagon . . ."

"That part wasn't really important. I know you were coming back from Douglaston. The *Enterprise?*"

"I didn't want to tell you just yet. There's nothing you could do about it."

"I could have listened and given you—what is it the kids say they need when they get their report cards? C and S?"

He tried to smile and couldn't, so he went to her and held her close, widening his hands on her back as if he wanted to cover the whole of it. She could feel each of his fingers in the spread of them. "I need," he told her softly, "to make love to you tonight. Does that come under the heading of C and S?"

"Comfort and sympathy," she said, "and a lot more."

I've always loved him, she thought, from the first day I saw him in the admissions office on campus.

She loved Ted and it had nothing to do with money. He didn't have that much. If the paper failed, he'd have even less. Her love for him had nothing to do with power, because he didn't have that either, really. If he had died two weeks ago, only local people who knew him would have come.

But oh, my God, she thought, if I buried this man who loves me more than his own life, what would be left of mine? . . .The world doesn't always end with a bang or a whimper. More times for more people it ends with a pile of old, nearly new, or never worn clothes tied up in a bundle marked for the Good-Will Shop.

When he let her go, she saw that his eyes were red-rimmed, as if he had been crying silently for his dying newspaper.

"We'll think of something," she promised. "In bed tonight. Afterward."

From the basement they heard their son call, "You can come down now."

What she saw came as a shock. For a few minutes she was too confused to say anything. Luckily, Ted was beside her to say something for her.

"Hey, Pete, this is great. It really is."

"It's not a real basketball court. The ceiling isn't high enough and I don't have the space anyway."

"Well, this is the next best thing. How did you get those baskets up there? I see . . . braced them on wood blocks. Good idea."

"The Ping-Pong table isn't very steady. I got it secondhand for a good price."

Fran laughed delightedly. "He's a regular Yankee horse trader, your son. He practically got them to pay him for taking it off their hands."

Ted examined it. "I can help you level it so it'll be steadier. It's not too bad. I'll give you a game later."

"Mother," Elsie said—one day she had simply stopped calling her mommy and never called her mom—"Mother, what do you think of it?"

She *does* look like a little fox," Josephine thought. Those eyes! Were they always slanted? And why is she looking so satisfied? Because she knows this isn't what I expected to see down here?

Josephine wanted to take her daughter by those thin shoulders and shake her—let the copper hair bounce.

That was wrong! She was bewildered and upset and taking out her hurt on Elsie because the girl had been so ungracious about the dress and because she was looking so pleased now at her mother's obvious discomfiture.

"Isn't it great?" Ted was saying. "Look at your mother. She's overwhelmed and can't talk."

Josephine managed a weak smile. "It's wonderful."

"He made the bar out of orange crates," Fran said proudly, "and then painted it. Then he found those old barrels to use for stools. That's where I came in. I made the little pillows from some old material I had."

"Wonderful," Josephine murmured. "Wonderful."

"That idea you gave me for a Western saloon," Peter said, and she was relieved he finally put it into words. "It was terrific. It really was. You mad because I didn't do it?"

"Of course not. The room is yours. You should fix it your way."

"Not that you didn't give me some fantastic ideas."

"You didn't have to use them."

"He didn't," Elsie said, giving her a look of uncalled-for impertinence, "because he knew it wouldn't come out as good as you would have done it."

Her brother turned on her. "Did I ask you?"

She shrugged. "I knew it. You didn't have to tell me."

"I did it this way," he insisted, "because it's what I planned from the beginning."

"And you deserve to be congratulated," Josephine said, forcing herself to sound lighthearted. "Your father's right. I was overwhelmed and couldn't talk. Ted, look what he's done. Plugged in that old fridge we stored down here. Does it really work, Pete? Is it any good?"

With a flourish, he swung open the door. Inside were soft-drink bottles. Fran went behind the bar and brought up mismatched dishes filled with peanuts and popcorn. Elsie got the water glasses.

"What'll it be?" Peter offered magnanimously. "Coke or Seven-Up?"

"We're having a party," Fran said. "In Peter's other room. How do you like that? Now he has two rooms in this house. All I have is my one upstairs."

They spent the rest of the evening in Peter's room.

That's what we'll call it from now on, Josephine thought. And I was wrong to suggest anything for it. I'm sure this was exactly what he had in mind from the beginning. If he didn't ask me to come down while he was fixing it, it was because he didn't want to use my ideas and was afraid I'd think of it as a rejection.

"After your father plays Ping-Pong with you," she said, "how about giving me a game?"

"If he plays dad," Elsie challenged, "you play me. I'll beat you."

And she did, banging the light ball almost viciously across the net and returning it until at last she was winded but victorious.

"I did beat you," she said.

"You certainly did."

Impulsively, Elsie threw her arms around her mother and kissed her blindly. Surprised, Josephine held her tightly. She could hear the rapid breath and feel the heart still pounding from exertion. "Easy, darling."

"I'm sorry about the dress," Elsie said. "You didn't know I already had one."

"It's all right."

"Is it pretty?" She had recovered her breath, but her small pointed chin was trembling.

"I think so. Would you like to have it for Christmas?"

"I love you," Elsie whispered, then, embarrassed, left her and began to pass the popcorn.

THAT NIGHT Ted got into bed first. By the time Josephine got out of the bathroom—and she hadn't taken very long—he was already asleep. He lay on his back, an arm flung across her pillow.

Josephine knew that worry about the *Digest* had exhausted him. They

125

had planned to talk about saving the paper after they made love.

Noiselessly she eased her way in beside him and snapped off the light. Only in the dark did she have enough courage to remember back to that morning. So much had happened since to push it from her mind, so much and so many people: Dave and John and Peter's room downstairs, and Elsie's unexpected kiss. . . .

Now they were all gone she was alone, remembering the morning, remembering how she had worked with a joy too exquisite to last, remembering how Ben took her hands and held them gently.

"Beautiful," he had told her. "They could work in marble."

She fell asleep holding the memory close, the way she had often, in the early days of their marriage, fallen asleep holding her husband.

Chapter Fourteen

TED CAME naked out of the bathroom and she was startled because there was so much hair on his body. There was the soft brown bush under each arm, more on his chest that curved like a hard shield, and there was a grizzled nest at the junction of his thighs.

He shook the damp disheveled hair on his head. "I forgot to take underwear in with me." He had wrapped the towel like a scarf around his neck. "How stupid can I get?"

She picked up his boxer shorts and held them out. "It's not that important."

"I was more stupid last night," he apologized, "falling asleep before you got into bed."

Josephine had been up and dressed half an hour before he awoke. "Don't worry about it." She pulled the crumpled sheet taut and shook air into it.

"Before we went down to Pete's room, I told you I needed to make love to you. Then I conked out."

She smiled. "Last night wasn't the last night in the world."

"Were you very let down? I'm sorry, darling."

"Please," she said, deliberately busying herself with the blanket corners, tucking them in neatly. She couldn't bring herself to look at him

because, without warning, a disturbing fragment of a dream was returning to her.

She remembered being in the muscular grip of a naked, hairless man
—a stranger whose name she didn't know and whose face she couldn't
see. It had been too close to hers.

Embarrassed, she thought: Ted's right, I must have been sexually let
down, but I can't tell him about this. If she had ever before fantasized
in a dark defenseless sleep about making love to another man, she had
no recollection of it.

"You're right," Ted said, "it wasn't the last night in the world.
There's another coming up. I'll make a date with you now." He had
pulled on his pants and was zipping them up. His chest was still bare.

"You always put on your belt," she observed, "before you get your
shirt. Then you have to undo it. Isn't that the long way?"

He shrugged. "I suppose. It's habit. We do a lot of things out of habit,
don't we?"

"Yes," she agreed solemnly, "all of us."

That lean young look he once had was developing more every day in
his son. Ted's flesh wasn't as firm and the bones under it were broader
and heavier, but it was still a vigorous man's body. . . . But who, she
wondered, did that other belong to? That solid, unyielding, faceless
stranger?

Ted took a shirt from his highboy, then picked out a tie to go with
it. "Were you planning to go for a lesson this morning?"

"Yes," she said, "I was going to the barn." Even as she said it, she
knew what she had dreamed—what, not who, because it hadn't been a
real man at all. She had dreamed of the stone man in the studio. If the
face had been shadowy, it was because, in reality, the head looked down
over the powerful bent knee. She had never gone down on her own knees
to look up into the marble face carved over the smooth marble body.
Now, she understood why Ted's body had seemed so hairy.

I dreamed, she thought with an uneasiness that made her slightly
nauseated, of making love to a statue. It's ridiculous.

But it wasn't, she rationalized, if it was only a symbol. Yesterday, she
ran from Ben's outstretched hands that held a mallet and a chisel. She
had been so afraid of the marble he offered that at night fear had
. . . taken form. Oh, it was so simple to explain in this age of do-it-yourself
analysis . . .

"It won't matter too much if you miss a day, will it?" Ted was asking, as he flipped the wider part of the tie over the narrow end.

"Why? Is there something you want me to do?"

"Did you hear what my mother said last night?"

"She called it her room, Josie—not the guest room."

"Well, it's time, isn't it, she began to think of it that way?"

More than six years ago, shortly after Ted's father died, Fran came for a short visit. "I'm going to get myself a little efficiency apartment . . . in a residential hotel."

"You'll live with us," they had insisted.

"Only until I pull myself together. I can't live alone in that apartment anymore. I keep having the feeling our old friends don't like visiting now. It makes them uncomfortable."

"That's your imagination," they had said.

"It's true. Maybe it makes them wonder . . . I don't know . . . a little afraid people will visit their houses one day soon . . . and not find them there."

"Fran, don't," they had said.

"That chair of his—the big gold one with the ottoman? I'm the only one who sits in it now. It's as if I'm the only one who dares. I really think it frightens them."

"You're moving in with us," they had told her.

So Fran let an estate buyer pack up and cart away almost everything from the apartment in Manhattan. She insisted that Josephine and Ted take whatever they could use for their new house. Since the spare room wasn't even partly furnished, she donated her old bedroom set. "That way you won't have to go to the expense of furnishing it on my account. After I leave, sell it, give it away, do anything you want. But it'll serve a purpose while I'm with you."

"And make her feel more at home," Josephine told Ted confidently. . . .

Yet until last night, she had never referred to it as anything but "the guest room."

"Did you know she's paying forty dollars a month in fees to store stuff to put into that apartment she'll never have? It's her money, Josie, but I hate to see her throw it away. Last week I sent another quarterly payment. It almost killed me. Maybe I'm just more conscious of money going out these days."

"Every month all these years? That comes to—"

In a pained voice, Ted said, "Don't bother to total it. I already have."

"Do you have any idea what's there?"

"The storage company gave her an inventory list at the time. There's the Venetian mirror and the Victorian chair, and a French inlaid desk —those are worth something. The rest is probably pure sentimental junk. There are two cartons marked C.U. and O.P." He saw a slight frown cross her forehead. "Contents Unknown and Owner-Packed," he explained. "Ask her and she won't remember what the hell she put in them. Want to bet there's the yellow plastic saltshaker we used to take to picnics in Palisades Park? I'll bet it's still got caked salt in it."

They had turned their back on her one afternoon six years ago, and she called a storage company. What was done was done, but was there any sense in compounding a mistake?

"What do you want me to do?" Josephine asked.

"Go through those C.U. cartons. Make out a list of what's in them. Then she can decide what she wants to keep, give away or sell. Most of it's probably worthless, but some of it could be valuable."

"Why not send for the cartons?"

Because, Ted said—and Josephine ought to know her mother-in-law well enough after all these years—Fran was sure to unwrap one piece at a time and attach a lengthy anecdote to each treasure. She would stroke every half-forgotten relic and eventually dissolve into tears. "Write it down for her, Josie. She'll be less emotional sorting it out on paper."

"You want me to drive to New York today?"

"Well, if you put it off, we'll be in the middle of the holidays. You may not have the time. Didn't you tell me you were even going to cut out the lessons until after the first of the year?"

"Yes," she said, "I planned to."

"See what I mean? With all you'll have to do, you'll be too busy to take care of this. I'd like to get it settled."

It was an excuse for not going to the barn. Perhaps putting extra space between the sessions was for the best. Ben would have a whole day without her to get even more involved with his own work. Once he did, he might forget those wild things he had said yesterday. There was something else: she could put off until tomorrow looking at the statue of the nude man.

"All right," she answered steadily, pleased at being able to keep such strict control over her voice. "I'll go to New York today."

"You don't really mind about skipping a lesson?"

"I don't mind today. It's just as well."

He smiled understandingly. "Getting bored with them?"

130

"Oh, no," she said, startled because he didn't understand at all. "I'm not bored." She had kept her enjoyment of what she was doing secret, as if there was a shame connected with it, as if there was something sinful in the desire to work because that desire was so great.

"Then you're having fun at it?" her husband asked.

"Fun?" she repeated hollowly. "Yes. I suppose I am. I'm working on something I think you'll like. Don't ask me what. It's going to be a surprise."

SHE DECIDED TO stop at the barn just long enough to tell Ben she wouldn't be able to stay. "I have a family errand," she would say. "No, don't bother to turn around, Ben. I'll see you tomorrow."

And he would nod to let her know he heard and go on with what he was doing. There was a slim chance he would not be so deeply involved with himself. He might stop for a moment, half-turn and say, "Have you given any thought, Jo, to what we talked about yesterday?"

If that happened, she had an answer ready. "When I'm through with the head, I'll think about it. I have to finish that first for my son's birthday." She wouldn't tell him she was going to finish it only because it might be unlucky for Pete if she didn't.

She was so sure she would find him standing and working that it was a shock to discover him sitting, legs apart and knees angled, on the bench they shared for lunch or coffee. He was holding a large apple. When he saw her, he bit into it with his strong teeth. "It's good. Try it." Juice oozed from a corner of his mouth. He wiped it away on his sleeve and she looked away, not because it was an untidy action—actually there was something natural, healthy and alive in the way he did it. What made her uncomfortable was his offer to bite into the same piece of fruit . . .

"No, thank you."

"I'd offer you a whole one, but it's all I have." He held it out. "Finish it, if you like."

She gave her head a silent shake. "I won't be able to work today."

"I can see that from the way you're dressed."

Over a beige dress, she was wearing a fur-trimmed coat Ted had given her on her last birthday. It was a pale camel-colored wool, with a wide raccoon collar and cuffs. She was tall enough to carry it. On her head was a fur hood that tied under her chin. Ted knew cold air would make her ears feel close to bursting. Ted knew she had almost had to have a mastoid operation when she was little and that one of her earliest memories was leaning over the bathroom sink with her mother gently pouring warm oil down into her ears. Ted knew so many little things about her. She toyed with the fur on one of the cuffs, nervously separating and twisting strands of animal hair.

"I like your hat," Ben said.

"It keeps my ears from dropping off."

"It becomes you. Is it your friend again?"

"What?"

"Are you going to the hospital?"

"No. I have to drive into New York." In a rush of words, she explained —because she hadn't planned to stay and she was eager to leave—about Fran's cartons that had been stored in Manhattan for more than six years. Then, "Have a good day working. I'll see you tomorrow." She took a step backward and almost stumbled.

"What's the matter?"

"The statue." She hadn't realized she was standing so close to the stone man.

"What about it?"

"I've never seen his face. That just occurred to me."

Ben Goudy had a disconcerting way of hiding behind an odd half-smile, so that she could never tell what he was thinking by looking into his eyes.

"If you're so curious, bend down and look up into it."

"Not now," she said, remembering how the man had held her in her dream before he froze back into stone again here in the studio. "It's at least an hour and a half to the city. More if I hit traffic. And I have no idea how long I'll have to be at the warehouse." She was panting between sentences as if she had run to get there and tell him these things. "Not only do I have to go through everything in those cartons, but I also have to make out that list."

The secondhand stove never gave off enough heat, never warmed the barn enough, so why did she feel uncomfortably hot? Because Ben may have carved his own features into the stone that turned into flesh last night and pressed so close to hers?

"As long as I'm in New York," she heard herself rattle on senselessly, "I'm going to do some Christmas shopping. There aren't many days left, you know, and I don't get into the city that often." She took a deep breath and stepped back farther from the statue. "I'll look at the face later. I don't have time today."

Ben looked at her in amazement. "You have the goddamndest way of figuring time. Instead of babbling about nothing, you could have looked a dozen times over."

"Tomorrow." She walked away quickly out of the barn—self-conscious and half-running, feeling as vulnerable as Elsie. . . . She was a young girl hurrying to the safety of home before it got dark. . . . Inside the car was home. It was familiar and safe and away from both of them —the sculptor and his stone man who didn't have the good manners to stay where he belonged in the middle of her night. . . .

Josephine turned on the ignition. The noise of a stalled, protesting engine ground inside her stomach. She tried again. "I'll have to leave this with Dave," she thought in panic. "I should have taken the station wagon." The coupe had seemed more practical, easier to maneuver in the busy city. She tried again, jamming her foot on the accelerator and holding it there.

"You'll never do it that way," Ben said. "You'll flood her." He was wearing his leather jacket and had closed the barn door behind him. "Shove over. Let me try."

She did as she was ordered.

"In this weather," he said patiently, "at least with most cars, before you turn on the ignition, you should pump a few times, then let it sit for a minute."

"Are you going out?"

"I'm going with you." The engine caught.

Josephine was too surprised to answer.

"This is a good chance for me to see a new exhibition in one of the galleries. And I've been sitting on a letter from a friend of mine— unusual artist—who has some new things for me to look at."

The motor was purring gently now.

"Mind if I go with you?"

"No, of course not." The words felt thick on her tongue.

"That junk heap of mine got me here, and it gets me around town when I need it, but driving it as far as New York is chancy, especially in this weather. Sure you don't mind?"

"Didn't I just say it?"

"You didn't say you were glad either."

She managed a laugh. "What do you want? A written invitation?

Don't be so formal." She had recovered from her surprise at finding him next to her. "I'd welcome your company."

"Want me to drive?"

"No, thanks."

"I hope you know how to drive a car in the winter better than you know how to start one."

He let her get out, then eased the substantial bulk of his body over and waited until she let herself in again on the driver's side. Her husband, she thought, would have got out first and waited to close the door after her. They were nothing alike. She wondered what Ted would say when she told him Ben had driven into New York with her. She wondered whether to tell him at all.

Chapter Fifteen

"DON'T BE surprised if I fall asleep," Ben said as they started off, "that is, *if* I decide you're to be trusted behind a wheel."

"I am," she assured him and, to prove it, deftly swung the car smoothly off the River Road and onto the parkway.

"I'm tired," he told her. "I was up half the night."

"Working?"

"Just up."

She kept her head stiff and eyes alert to the road ahead, aware of the warmth of his big body sitting beside her. . . . She found herself hoping he would get tired and drop off.

I lied, she thought. I don't welcome his company. I was looking forward to staying away from the studio today because I didn't want him to talk the way he did last time we were together. I don't want him to tell me I'm wasting any part of my life making my husband's bed or taking care of my husband's children. It's none of his business and I don't want to hear about different kinds of marble. What have Carrara and Serrvezza or Belgian Black to do with me? That's his world.

"All right if I smoke?" he asked.

"If you want to."

"No lectures?".

"Your lungs."

"You're so right." He gave her an unexpected smile. "I'll even empty the ashtray when we get there."

"Fair enough."

"Do you like the radio when you drive?"

"Sometimes."

"Mind if I turn it on?"

"Press the middle button if you want news. It's nonstop."

"For a week," he informed her soberly, "I have not listened to the news. I have not read a newspaper. Every once in a while I do that. I recommend the practice to anyone who wants to stay saner longer. News is usually depressing. It depresses me mostly because there's not a god-damn thing I can do to change anything that's happening anywhere."

"Don't you want to know what's going on?"

"Not even in your Ditchling *Digest.*" He found a station that was playing a Rachmaninoff concerto. It sounded like a Byron Janis record-ing they had at home.

"What's going on," he continued, "will go on whether I know about it or not. Listen," he said, "this is going to be a long ride. Don't worry about making small talk with me, Jo. We never have."

"That's true," she said, and started to feel better for the first time since he joined her. Maybe the drive was going to be all right after all. Maybe Ben didn't plan to upset her by talking about anything. If he didn't they could drive in silence and concentrate on their own thoughts the way they concentrated on their own work in the barn.

She heard the announcer say it had been Byron Janis at the piano and was sorry she hadn't mentioned it.

A few traveling snowflakes disappeared by the time they stopped at the first toll booth. He reached across her with the correct change before she could get to her handbag, and they drove on through. The sound of the motor blended with that of the Tchaikovsky violin concerto coming from radio station WQXR.

With everyone else, she had always felt obligated either to talk or to listen. With him, she could spend hours doing neither. With him she could slip comfortably into her own calm without bothering to be socia-ble.

Little by little, a level at a time, Josephine descended into a state of relaxation until she was as much at ease as she had grown to be in the larger area of the barn. She had Ben to thank. He had taken his own thoughts and left her with hers. He withdrew into himself so much he even succeeded in creating an illusion of more width between them.

A sort of intimacy had been growing between them in the studio, and today, miles from the studio and fast adding more distance, they had, in some way, taken the air of it along with them.

They drove without exchanging a word, but once in a while she felt they were talking in their silence and wondered if he could hear her thinking: I don't really know anything about you, where you were brought up or how. I don't know anything about you except that Jess Goudy was your uncle and that, before you came to town I must have passed the barn a hundred times, never knowing that if I looked inside I'd find myself waiting for me. . . .

She could see the pleasure in his eyes as he looked at the carpet of winter along the sides of the parkway and was relieved he hadn't "heard." Reminders of last week's storm were all around them in all trees that were resigned to the snow piled on them like white foam. Branches shuddered under the weight.

I wonder, she thought, if you ever think of me the way you first saw me, almost as protective about my freshly baked cake as I was about my (to me) still freshly born children! I was so proud of that cake. I hated you for making fun of it. Do you remember? But remember it was all I had then. I didn't know any better. I hadn't learned any more. You hadn't taught me. . . .

She swerved the car dangerously when he said almost in answer: "The first American sculptor was a housewife. Did you know that, Jo? She modeled little likenesses of her family out of bread dough. Car all right?"

"I must have hit an ice patch. It's all right now. Was she really the first?"

"Her name was Patience Wright, a Quaker who married a farmer at twenty-three, had five brats and had never seen a statue when she began to make hers."

"Out of bread dough?"

"Putty, sometimes. Everybody who knew her thought she was a little peculiar. Does your friend Mrs. Haines think you're a little peculiar?"

"Tell me about Patience Wright."

"Eventually she opened a waxwork museum and became known as the celebrated Mrs. Wright. It was just before and just after the American Revolution. Washington, Franklin, Jefferson all knew her, or knew of her. She modeled a head of Franklin and a bust of Washington in wax.

That head of Franklin got her into trouble." He let out a spurt of laughter.

"Tell me," she said, anxious to laugh too.

"That was in France, in the early 1780s. It had something to do with wrapping it in a napkin and being stopped and searched for contraband. When the Paris police opened the bundle they thought they were seeing a corpse's head. Poor Patience was arrested as a bloody murderess."

"You said her husband was a Quaker farmer. How did she get to Paris where she was arrested?"

"They let her go when they discovered the head was made of wax. As for her husband, didn't I mention it? She was lucky enough to have him die and leave her to her work when she was forty-four."

Josephine stopped smiling and was suddenly neither interested nor amused. She felt the skin around her mouth tighten. "I'm going to pull into the next gas station."

He was looking at her through narrowed eyes. She strained her own to focus on the unbroken white lines of the parkway.

"Why did you take that so personally?" he asked. "I didn't wish a dead husband on you at forty-four."

"That sign," she said coldly. "Gas is less than a mile away."

"Now you're sorry you asked me to come with you?"

"It's like the first time we met," she hurled at him. "I didn't ask you into my house then, you know. I didn't ask you this time. You invited yourself."

"Up to now I thought it was a pleasant ride."

"Up to now I thought it was, too."

"Then tell me why you're angry."

Such innocence! she thought furiously. Why did you have to spoil our pleasant ride by saying something you knew you had no right to say, especially since I'm wedged behind this wheel and can't get away from you? . . .

"What you said did upset me," she told him, carefully spacing her words. "My reason for going to New York today is to go through some of my mother-in-law's things that are stored in a warehouse. You made widowhood sound like a cause for rejoicing. Maybe it is for some, but it's a lost cause for Fran."

"I understand," he said. "I apologize."

"I was upset. But it had nothing to do with me personally. You were wrong about that."

He squashed another cigarette end into the ashtray and didn't answer. They pulled into the gas station.

While they were waiting for the attendant to fill the tank, Ben said, "That exhibition . . . my friend who wrote me said the sculptor has an interesting technique. Would you like to see it with me?"

The anger that had built up inside her began to subside. "I have so much to do. My day is pretty well planned. . . ."

"I'd really be interested in your opinion."

"As a layman?"

"No!" he shot back. Now he was the one who sounded full of irritation. "As a creative artist yourself."

And the anger she felt toward him minutes before evaporated completely. "I don't know if it could be arranged . . ." she began.

"Anything can be arranged," he broke in, "if you want it enough. Don't be polite. Tell me if you're not interested."

"But I am! I'd like very much to see the exhibition."

"Then what's your problem?"

"I'm going to New York for a specific purpose, remember?"

"All right. We'll go to the warehouse first. Get it over with. Then we'll go to the gallery. After that you do your Christmas shopping and I'll go downtown to see my friend. We'll make plans to meet somewhere later."

In spite of herself, she laughed. "You have it all figured out—neat and orderly."

"I'm following your lead," he told her, acknowledging her joke. "You make such a big deal out of trifles sometimes."

"Well," she said, "trifles make perfection." She saw he was frowning. "You don't agree with that?"

"I was going to add, 'But perfection is no trifle.' "

She was impressed because he had taken her words, doubled them back on themselves and turned them into a thought that had much more meaning than when they stood alone. "That's very good."

"I thought so, too, when I first read the whole quotation from Michelangelo. See what a good team we make when we think in the same direction? I'll pay for the gas."

"No," she said, "I'd rather you didn't." For some reason, she didn't want him to pay for any gas that went into the car her husband had bought. There was money for that in her wallet, money Ted had supplied. . . .

"I'm sharing the ride. Let me at least . . ."

"You took care of the tolls. That was enough. I shouldn't have let you do that."

He looked puzzled. "Why not?"

On impulse, she said, "I'll tell you what you can do. Take over the wheel."

"I offered to drive when we left Ditchling, you know."

"I'm not used to city driving. It makes me nervous."

"All right. Shove over."

Once they crossed the last toll plaza, she felt the wonderment that renewed itself whenever she arrived within touching distance of the concrete beauty of New York. Shadowy pinnacles in the distance appeared to be moving fast to meet her instead of the other way around. In a short while now, she would see imposing glass towers and spectacular window displays along a Fifth Avenue choked with people and cars. There would be pavement musicians and vendors selling belts or chestnuts or cheap jewelry. There would be Salvation Army bell ringers and the man with the shepherd dog and the sign: "It's Christmas and I am Blind."

Every year at holiday time since her children were little, Josephine had made the pilgrimage to Manhattan. Every year they looked at stuffed animals in F.A.O. Schwartz's toy store, and one year, while a six-year-old Peter was studying a panda bear twice his size, a four-year-old Elsie took a stroll through the door and disappeared. Josephine tore out after her and found her squatting close to the cold sidewalk studying a mangy pigeon.

"Come inside," Josephine coaxed. "Inside there's a big monkey and a big horse and an enormous giraffe."

"He's better," Elsie said. "He's little."

"Well, there's a doll house with tiny furniture and tiny lamps with bulbs that light up and tiny mirrors."

"He's better," Elsie said, making a grab for the bird who hopped away. "He's real."

"What's the matter?" Ben asked. Under his easy manipulation, the country car, used to uncomplicated streets and quiet roads, was being thrown into the tumult made by hundreds of sophisticated city cars and rudely honking taxis.

"Oh, nothing," she said. But from that point on, she was uncomfortably aware that he could monitor her every change of expression out of the corner of his eye.

"You mean nothing you care to tell me?"

"I was thinking of Christmas. I never had to tell my son there was no Santa Claus. My daughter did it for me."

"Did you thank her?"

"No. I had the feeling she enjoyed doing it too much." Then she realized suddenly, "This is the first time we haven't gone to Rockefeller Center to see the big tree light up. I never get tired of it. Everybody always says 'Oh!' all together in one voice. I wonder why we didn't this year."

"I saw it."

"You did?"

"On the six o'clock news, after you left the studio one night. The reception on that little SONY isn't the greatest, but considering the fact that I don't have an outside aerial . . ."

"I just forgot."

"Is it really that important?"

"It's the first year since the children were old enough."

"Well, you may never get tired of seeing that big tree light up . . ."

"I don't."

"But maybe they do. Maybe that's why they didn't bother to remind you."

"No, they were involved with that room Pete was redoing in our basement, and I . . . well, you know, I got interested in . . . clay modeling because you happened to come to town. But there'll be next year, and the year after that."

"Where," he asked abruptly, "is that damned storage place?"

THERE WAS a barren, gray look about the warehouse that made Josephine feel she was visiting someone in prison; she could imagine that a prison must be something like this. The locked security door on Amsterdam Avenue opened only when a buzzer was pushed from somewhere inside. There was a massive brass gate that fronted the reception desk; it was as solid and as formidable as a cell-block door. The "matron" was polite and firm.

"You should have notified us in advance, Mrs. Trask. You're fortunate we have a man on duty who's authorized to unpack those crates. It's fourteen dollars to open and repack them again."

"Do I pay you now?"

The matron sighed. "You really should have let us know. Never mind. Since you've come all the way. The elevator's over there."

A black man, an unusually understanding guard named Louis, took them up to six. He actually referred to the compartments as "cell units"; behind them, his charges were condemned to solitary confinement until their release. Josephine and Ben followed him down a stone corridor that smelled of disinfectant.

"We turn here," Louis said. "Smell bother you? You get used to it. On the third floor, where we store rugs, you can't stay ten minutes before your eyes start to burn from mothball fumes. You get used to it."

It was all cartons and furniture, not people. There was nobody real living in those rooms, but every piece had been bought with care, often with love. Every piece had known what it was to be in a home and feel sun through open windows and see shades pulled down at night. They had been cleaned or polished or scrubbed or waxed to look their best when company came. Having company was always nice. Sometimes there would even be flowers in the vases instead of that terrible smell of disinfectant.

"Things," she imagined she heard Elsie say in a long-suffering voice. "They're not alive, mother!" Josephine wondered why she was thinking so much of Elsie.

It was probably because last night in Peter's room the girl had thrown her thin arms around her mother's neck. It was obviously something she hadn't intended. Josephine was even more moved because she could admit to herself something she had deliberately pushed from her mind for too long—the notion that this one of her children didn't really like her.

But last night hadn't Elsie whispered, "I love you . . . "?

"In here," Louis said, releasing a metal bar with a loud clang.

Fran's cubicle was one of the smaller ones. Josephine recognized familiar pieces of furniture stacked to the ceiling behind cartons marked, sure enough, *C.U.* and *O.P.* The gold-upholstered chair with the kick-pleat skirt and matching ottoman was once Ted's father's favorite place

142

to sit. Now it was upside down to conserve space. It bothered Josephine to see it that way.

The first time she had seen it was in the old apartment. He had stood up to meet her and said, "My son is right. There is a glow about you."

And Fran had smiled and said, "Tea, everyone?" She had served it with coconut patties and sugar cookies on the coffee table that was now jammed upright on top of the gold-upholstered chair.

"You're in a classy neighborhood here," Louis was saying. "That unit two doors down has stuff belonging to one of the Roosevelts."

"What's the average length of time people keep things in storage?" Ben asked casually.

"Yesterday we got rid of some books that had been here fifty years."

"What's the longest anything's been stored? Would you know?" For Ben it was only an impersonal, different experience.

"Since nineteen thirteen. Three cell units jammed full of stuff from before World War I."

"I don't understand," Josephine said, "why anyone would leave anything that long."

"Waiting for litigation from the courts to settle an estate," was Ben's guess. "The family's probably still fighting over who gets it."

"By the time it's settled," Louis said, "the heirs that are left won't want any part of it. An appraiser will make them an offer and we'll finally get rid of the junk."

And every piece, Josephine thought again, had once been bought with care and often with love.

"I'd like to look at the cartons now if you don't mind."

While they were being unpacked, she realized for the first time how difficult it must have been for Fran to live with her possessions in another woman's house. "Take anything you want," she had urged. "I want you to have anything you want or can use."

But one afternoon without telling them, she had secretly kept out a few special pieces, some furniture and china and bric-a-brac. Without consulting them, she had called the storage company. It was as if— Josephine understood now—Fran had come to a stubborn halt, as if she were saying, This far I will go and no further. This little I keep out for myself.

When the first carton was opened, Josephine saw a yellow plastic saltshaker. Under that, carefully wrapped in a dry cleaner's pink tissue, were a Belleek sugar bowl and creamer.

"That's a pattern they don't make anymore," Ben said.

"Some of the stuff," Ted had said, "might be valuable."

There was a small, glassless framed print of three birch trees. It had a yellow cast.

"If you tried to take it out," Ben said, "the paper would probably crack from age."

"Probably."

"I suppose it meant something."

"I suppose."

"But most of the stuff," Ted had warned, "is probably worthless."

Somehow Josephine knew that, offered the choice, Fran would give away the Belleek and keep the glassless print.

There was an inexpensive night table clock rimmed with seashells and a serene Kwan Yin lady.

"That's a beautiful piece of ivory," Ben said appreciatively, and Josephine said, "It doesn't seem to have bothered her to have been buried alive for six years."

There was a bone china-handled carving set and a chipped perfume bottle. There was a single blue satin hanger and a Venetian glass bud vase. There were demitasse spoons and miniature silk horses with tassels for tails and a large teacup with FATHER written in gold on the side and an inexpertly repaired crack on the rim. There were crystal glasses, shining where there was no sun.

She held one up and snapped her fingernail against its side. It rang like a bell.

"Come on," Ben said. "If you're going to spend this much time over every little thing . . ."

There was a crudely hand-tooled leather box on which a child had painted the words "Camp Pioneer." Inside were scrawled letters from a Ted she had never known and from his sister whom she could never know, the one who had been killed in that automobile accident. "Dear mom and daddy, I know you won't believe it, but they're drowning me in the lake and the food here is just awful, but Teddy's okay, except that he's in the infirmary. Love and kisses—Edie."

"My God," Ben said, "if you're going to go over every one of those letters . . ."

Josephine folded the one she was reading. "I'm through now." It was just as well. She was feeling queasy.

144

"Disinfectant getting to you?" Ben asked. "It's strong."

Josephine agreed. It was the disinfectant that made her feel sick. Carefully, she put away her list, tipped Louis, paid the woman at the desk and they drove across town to Madison Avenue.

BEN SAID they were lucky to find a metered parking space close to the art gallery. If necessary he could run out and feed the meter. "Now I want you to be honest." His voice was lighter now and full of anticipation. He was obviously glad to be out of the warehouse. "I want your opinion. I won't tell you what I think first. All right?"

"All right."

He had her firmly by the arm and was leading her into what had once been the concert salon of an early Manhattan residential palace. "Just tell me what you see."

Josephine closed her eyes. What she could still see clearly was the little girl's handwriting, "I know you won't believe it, but they're drowning me in the lake."

"Your first impression. That's what interests me."

". . . And the food here is just awful, but Teddy's okay. . . ."

Josephine wanted to be with Ted and ask him if he remembered why he had been in the infirmary and if he thought she and Edie might have been friends.

She looked around the vaulted art gallery and wondered what she was doing there. She didn't belong, especially with Ben Goudy.

"What's the matter?"

"Didn't you think being in that storage place was sad?"

"Living in your own past is always a waste; living in someone else's is just plain stupid. You're here now. Tell me what you see."

What Josephine saw was a huge block of molded steel. There was a gaping channel cut through the block. "The hole," Josephine said, "makes it seem weightless."

"Do you suppose that's the reason for it?"

"Maybe the sculptor thought that if you knew the right way to look through it you could see God." She stopped self-consciously. "I don't know why I said that."

Ben smiled approvingly and piloted her to the first figure.

Together they stood before the study of a woman. The body was reed slim and perfectly proportioned. In contrast, the feet that were joined to it were elephantine.

"According to legend," Josephine said, "the peacock was cursed with the ugliest feet in the barnyard because he bragged of being so beautiful. He was punished for being vain."

"Is that how you interpret the lady's big feet?"

After a moment, she said, "No. It made me remember that, but I'm sure it wasn't the sculptor's reason. This has nothing to do with vanity."

"Well, what do you think it has to do with?"

"She's earthbound. Gravity is keeping her on a solid block of earth. That's not just a pedestal for a figure, it's the exact spot where her body meets the world."

"You say that with such authority."

"You asked me what I feel."

"Appreciation of art," Ben said, "can't be taught. It has to be experienced."

He led her across the highly polished parquet floor, holding her arm even more tightly as he moved her to other agile, restless figures.

After a while, Josephine was surprised to hear him say, "I'd better put something in that meter or they'll tow your car away."

"Have we been here that long?"

"You must have enjoyed it."

Josephine thought about her answer. Then she said, "I found it stimulating and original."

"But you didn't like it."

"It's too abstract for my taste. I like what you do better."

"I'm a classicist," he answered. "But sculpture in any form has a right to exist, whether you or I like it or not. It was necessary for this sculptor to peel away what he considered inessentials."

"I've seen huge lopsided globs of stone that have absolutely no meaning for me."

"It's necessary," he said, "for others to design completely in space— make space part of the composition. Sometimes, if you study those globs, as you call them, long enough, they take on meaning—strength or sensuousness, sometimes even humor. What's important, Jo, is to remember that any creative form has a right to exist."

Then he told her to wait while he attended to the meter. She stopped him. "It's getting late. You want to see your friend . . ."

"And you," he finished for her, "have Christmas shopping to do.

146

Okay, let's go." And they left the gallery.

There was about a minute left on the meter. "I'll take you to lunch first," he said. "There's a place I used to like on Forty-sixth."

Josephine felt a stab of resistance. It was perfectly proper to let Ben Goudy take her to an art exhibition, but somehow wrong for him to take her to lunch.

"I know where I want to go," she told him uneasily. "I doubt if you'd like it."

"Where?"

"The junior shop in Bergdorf's. There's a luncheonette nearby, and I was planning to have a sandwich at the counter to save time. Elsie needs a bathrobe, and if I can find her a winter coat . . ."

"I guess you don't want to have lunch with me."

"That's not true."

"Don't lie to me, Jo. Tell me why you don't want to have lunch with me."

"It makes sense," she said, grasping for what could pass for an adequate explanation, "but I can see you're not going to believe me."

"Try me."

"Any nice restaurant would take too long. Every place is jammed around Christmas. We each have things to do, places to go."

"You're right. I don't believe you."

She was uncomfortable standing on Madison Avenue next to the car arguing about it. She was sure that they were being stared at. It was illogical; they weren't raising their voices, and there was nothing unusual about either of them to make a stranger turn.

Then why was she sure one of them was?

"It works," Peter had said at dinner not long ago. "Sit in back of anybody, in a movie, for instance. Keep staring at the back of his head. After a while, the guy'll feel it and turn around. It's weird, but it works."

She had laughed then, but now there definitely were eyes on the back of her neck. She could feel them, and her flesh turned cold under her winter coat.

"You're shivering," Ben said.

"It's freezing. Let's not just stand here." She opened her handbag and found her keys. "Take the car. If you don't, I'll have to worry about finding a garage. I told you I don't like city driving."

"You'll pick me up then?"

"Just write down your friend's address and the telephone number. I'll call first. Figure on about two hours. Is that long enough for you?"

"Two hours will be fine."

He leaned over the roof of the car, flattened the printed page of *Gallery Events* they had been given at the exhibition and wrote an address and phone number on it. "It's on Bleecker Street, off the Bowery. The studio used to be a barbershop. I'm telling you so you won't think I've given you the wrong address. There's still a barber pole in front."

"It's not the way I imagined artists lived."

"You saw yourself climbing four flights to a Parisienne-type garret with a slanted skylight. The whole romantic scene?"

"Something like that," she admitted.

"Next door to the barbershop, there's a Chinese laundry."

"Does somebody work there, too?"

He nodded seriously. "Lots of Chinese. They wash shirts."

She smiled, tucking the address and phone number into her handbag. "I'll telephone first. Enjoy your afternoon."

"You enjoy yours, and on the way home maybe you'll tell me why you wouldn't let me take you to lunch."

"I did tell you."

"No, you didn't." With not surprising dexterity, he tossed her keys into the air and lightly caught them. Then he got into her car and drove away, inching through the traffic toward an eastbound street.

People brushed past her without a pause, but Josephine stood where she was and watched her car inch along the avenue. If I want to, she thought, I can go to Bergdorf's first.

In all honesty, she had no intention of paying their prices for anything Elsie would outgrow before the winter was over. She inhaled cold air. It was as if his leaving had given her permission to breathe again. She could have lunch somewhere other than the lunch counter if she wanted to. She had only suggested it to discourage Ben. When she couldn't see the car anymore, perhaps she would walk over to Fifth Avenue. She was free and could do whatever she wanted. She could go to Steuben and look at glass sculpture and not be challenged to explain why she felt this way or that about any piece she admired.

She could walk farther down to Saint Patrick's Cathedral and then across Fiftieth Street to Saks. She could drop money in the iron pot of a Salvation Army Santa Claus like the one that had bewildered a three-year-old Peter. Elsie had been too young to go on that particular excursion. Josephine had given her little boy some change from her purse and told him to give it to Santa "to help buy toys for the poor children."

Santa had bent down to take the money, patted the child on the head and said, "Bless you." And Peter had turned to his mother confused and said, "But I didn't even sneeze."

Every year there was so much more of Peter. It was a contradiction, but the bigger he got, the easier it was to lose him.

"It's weird," he had told her, "you can actually make a person turn around and look right at you if you stare at that person long enough."

When Ben turned off Madison and she couldn't see the car anymore, she turned and looked right into the face of Tony Haines.

"Well, well," he said, "and does Ted know you're giving the car away to strange men, Josie?"

Chapter Sixteen

SHE WONDERED how long he had been standing there watching them. "That was no stranger," she said. "That was Ben Goudy."

"That's like saying 'That was no lady; that was my wife.' "

"I don't see the connection."

Tony gave her an insinuating laugh. "There isn't any. It was the rhythm, the way you said it." He winked. "All God's chillun got rhythm, and every little movement has a meaning of its own."

"Tony," impatiently, "make sense."

"You haven't said you're glad to see me. Aren't you glad to see me, Josie?"

"Of course I am."

"Where's my wife? She's been talking about coming into Manhattan. Break it to me gently. Where did you leave her? Tiffany's? . . . I'm only kidding."

"Frieda's not with me." Belatedly, Josephine realized how Frieda would have jumped at the chance to drive to New York. Why hadn't she asked her? "It was a spur-of-the-moment thing. I only decided this morning. There was something Ted wanted me to do."

"Oh," he said, and looked up Madison Avenue as if he could still see the car with Ben Goudy at the wheel. "He's not the struggling artist; he looks if he could afford to take you here."

For the first time, she noticed that they had been parked in front of a restaurant where windows were painted to simulate stained glass.

"Prices in there are pretty steep."

And Ben and I stood here in the cold, Josephine thought, making such an issue about having lunch together. Now Tony is taking it for granted we did.

"Unless," he was saying, "Goudy can put you on an expense account."

"We went to an exhibition of sculpture around the corner. Then he went his way; now I'm going mine. We're not having lunch together."

"Good. I'll put you on my expense account." With no warning, he moved closer. And she stepped back. His breath smelled of tobacco and toothpaste.

"Thanks, anyway, but I have a lot of shopping to do."

"You've got to have lunch somewhere. Why not with your friendly next-door neighbor?" He ran his fingers through hair that was parted to one side to give it a fuller look, and seemed reassured there was as much of it at that moment as there had been when he left home. "You two go to many exhibitions together? According to Frieda, you spend your time with him in the barn."

"Do you remember Jess Goudy?" Josephine asked. "Ben's his nephew."

"So what?"

"His uncle and I were very good friends."

"I see," broadly, "and now you and his nephew are good friends."

Josephine was beginning to see how Tony and Frieda deserved each other. "Ben is a sculptor."

"Frieda told me."

"He's been giving me lessons. I'm working on a head of Peter. I expect to have it in time for his birthday. At least, I hope to have it. I planned to work today, but Ted asked me to drive to the city and go through some of his mother's things in storage. On my way, I stopped to tell Ben I wouldn't be there for my lesson and he said that as long as I was driving in . . ." In the middle of her monologue she stopped, confused. "Why am I telling you this?"

He grinned. "Because you're feeling guilty?"

"For God's sake, Tony—"

"Listen," he said soothingly, "we're old friends, remember? You and Ted, Frieda and me."

She tried to remember if Tony always smiled so much under that lean straight nose, under that thick youthful moustache. His slate gray eyes looked at her with such intensity she was certain there was very little on his brain. Funny, she had never before thought of Tony as empty-headed. The truth was she had never thought much of Tony at all.

"As far as I'm concerned," he was saying, "there's nothing wrong in going to an exhibition with teacher."

"That's right." She wondered if he always had such a fatuous smirk.

"And you'll tell Ted all about it tonight?"

"If he wants to hear about it." Her husband, she was sure, would have absolutely no interest in a block of stone with a hole in the middle or a bronze lady with too-large feet. '

"By the way, it's not true about the paper, is it?"

"What have you heard?"

"You mean what has my wife told me? Nothing goes on that my wife doesn't know about first, you know. Any chance the paper will fold?"

"Not a chance. We're not going to let it happen." We! That editorial license again! She had used it in the hospital cafeteria in Douglaston when John Cullen asked if Ted's accident with the car had anything to do with being upset about the *Digest*.

"I wish there was something I could do to help," Tony was saying. "That's not very original, I guess."

Not very original, but the simple words made her feel a little less angry with him. It was true they were old friends. For years, hadn't the Trasks and the Haineses shared barbecues in the summer and Christmases in the winter? Hadn't their children given each other birthday presents and chicken pox? Tony probably hadn't set out to offend her; he simply wasn't—she had never stopped to think about it before—a particularly bright man. To be perfectly honest, Frieda wasn't particularly clever either, so maybe they *were* meant for each other.

"Why don't you have lunch with me?" Tony asked.

"I do have to have lunch somewhere. Do you know a place where it won't take too long? I have so much to do." She started to say, "Before I pick up Ben Goudy, but she amended, "Before I start back home."

"He has your car."

"Ted was worried about my driving in all this traffic."

"Oh? Was he?"

By his look of disappointment, she could see he believed it had been her husband's idea for Ben to take the car. There she was telling a half-truth again. This time she was pleased with herself, and the fact that it was Tony kept her conscience from bothering her.

Tony didn't know what was making her smile, but he was keen enough to sense a change in her. "I know just the place."

"Not too crowded?"

"We'll feel like the only two people there."

"It can't be very popular."

"Exclusive is the word. Only 'in' people know about it."

"All I want is a fast sandwich—cheese or . . ."

"This place specializes in Swiss, American—Roquefort and coffee to go."

"Sounds like a drugstore."

"You can get aspirins, Band-aids, rubbing alcohol, you name it."

"Then it is a drugstore?"

"Let's go. It's not far."

Afterward she couldn't remember what they talked about during the short walk, or if she had just listened and looked into store windows while he did the talking. All she could remember was that suddenly they were standing in front of a refurbished brownstone on a street somewhere in the west fifties.

"It's upstairs."

"What is?"

"My pied-à-terre." There was a boyish affectation in the way this middle-aged man said the words that made her bite her lip to keep from laughing in his face.

What a fool he is, Josephine thought. I never realized that either. "Frieda never told me you had an apartment in the city."

"Frieda doesn't know. Oh, it's not what you think, Josie. A few other guys and I split the upkeep. It's cheaper than a hotel whenever one of us has to stay in the city to work late. And much more comfortable. Makes sense, don't you think?"

"If it makes sense, why doesn't she know about it?"

"It would give her too many ideas. That's not what you think either. The minute she found out about this place she'd be ready to come in twice a week to go to a good restaurant. You know my wife and good restaurants. Say, it would end up costing instead of saving me. The guys all agreed. None of the wives know. Now you won't tell mine, will you?"

Annoyed, she told him, "You had no right putting me in this position. I'll forget about it and find another drugstore."

"Hey, now wait a minute. You act as if I had intended to make a pass.

153

I can't believe it. . . ." Now it was his turn to be offended. "All I wanted," he said, sounding hurt and younger than his own little boys, "was to make you a sandwich."

His own little boys, she thought, had partially grown up in her house. If I walk away now, nothing will ever be the same between us again. And if we're all going to go on living next door one another . . .

"All right," looking at her watch, "but just for a few minutes." She was sorry now she hadn't gone to lunch with Ben. Had there really been anything wrong in it?

Up the steps and inside the vestibule, Tony unlocked a second door. While he did, she glanced at the mailboxes—3-B was labeled *A. Haines.*

"I'm the one who signed the lease. That's why I'm the only one listed."

He's inept at lying too, she thought. It was too late for her to back out.

"It's not a walk-up," her best friend's husband said. "There's a self-service."

The elevator was stifling and rose slowly. Tony used a second key to open apartment 3-B.

"Well," he announced, "this is it."

He sent his coat flying. It landed in a heap on a small bench. There was something so theatrical in the performance that she looked away, embarrassed, and was startled by her own reflection in a mirrored screen that flanked the entrance hall.

He had taken her into a high-ceilinged L-shaped room. Two walls were painted a deep chocolate brown and two a flat white. A banquette was covered in a tiger-striped fabric. The colors of the throw pillows echoed the walls.

"It's the African look. I did everything to play it up."

A glass coffee table floated on a zebra-stenciled area rug. In two large bamboo buckets were tall artificial trees.

"Leaves need dusting. That bother you?"

"No."

What bothered her were the artificial plants and own growing uneasiness. But Tony wouldn't dare. He lived next door, he knew Ted . . .

"Frieda's always telling me you're a nut about dust. She says you can eat off the floor anywhere in your house." He grinned. "But I don't have to tell you about Frieda. She'll eat off anything . . . anywhere."

Josephine wanted to say, "That's in rotten taste. A husband shouldn't

154

talk about his wife like that, especially a wife who feels about you the way yours does."

Before she could say anything, he managed to remove her coat. It mysteriously vanished and she heard a latch click.

"The kitchen," he said, leading her into it, "is superefficient. You'll appreciate that. There's a drawer for pots and pans under the stove, and over the sink there's storage for glasses and dishes."

The built-in cabinet, he informed her, housed bottles of wine, soda, tonic and mineral water. "My private wine cellar." On the wall was a knife rack framed like a picture. "Receptionist I know at the agency gave me the idea." She wondered how many ideas Tony had given the receptionist.

There were small white Scandinavian stack stools. "Everything had to be scaled down to take away from the size of the room. That's why I had the smoked mirrors put in. Opens it up, don't you think?"

She smiled out of politeness and moved back into the living room.

"If you want to go to the john, you can see in the bedroom on the way."

"No, thanks."

"There's a jungle motif in there, too. Bedspread's batik—black and brown. In the bathroom the toilet seat is called 'Safari.' You really ought to see it."

"I don't have much time, Tony."

"If you gotta go, you make the time. Just remember—it's off the bedroom."

"I'll remember."

There was a small walnut bar against one of the white walls. Coins were sunk into the top. "Real ones. Cost me plenty, but it's unusual. What can I make you?"

"Nothing."

"I have to drink alone?" He shrugged and with practiced hands poured two full jiggers from a bottle over a cube of ice into the fat glass.

Pointedly she looked at her watch.

"Okay," he said, "okay, I promised you a cheese sandwich. Swiss or American?"

"Swiss," but she felt sick and empty, not hungry.

"Coffee? Or wine? A loaf of bread," he singsonged, waving the fat glass, "a jug of wine and Josie. That's a nice dress."

"You've seen it dozens of times, Tony. It's not new."

"Well, it's very nice. Simple but nice. Why are some materials full of static in the winter? That why it clings?" She felt his eyes travel over her body. "Let it alone. Looks good. Did you say you wanted wine with the sandwich?" He had finished his drink and poured himself another.

"I'd rather have coffee." What she really wanted was to leave. "Why don't I make everything," she suggested, thinking how fast she could do it and get out. "I'm more used to a kitchen than you are."

"Hey, you're my guest. Just make yourself comfortable. There are magazines on the coffee table."

He disappeared into the kitchen and she heard him open the refrigerator. Without looking at the cover, she opened one of the magazines. What she saw when she looked down was a series of photographs of a nude couple doing calisthenics. "Take it off together—but take it off first!" Quickly she closed the magazine and went to the window. Across the street was a unisex beauty parlor.

I won't tell Frieda about this, she decided. She wasn't even sure she wanted to tell Ted.

"If you're in the mood for window-shopping after you leave," he was saying from his super-effiency kitchen, "I'll tell you where there's a place that features a red bathtub for Christmas. A big square red tub with green plants all around it. Would a big red bathtub appeal to you, Josie?"

"Not particularly."

"Imagine how rosy you'd look in one! And there's another place farther down on Madison where they have the damnedest bed you ever saw. They call it a playpen. Little light bulbs all around and a mirrored canopy. Think I'm making it up?"

That time she didn't bother to answer.

"How would you like to sleep in a playpen, Josie? Bet you wouldn't sleep much."

I could be out that front door before he even knows I'm gone, she thought. Where had he put her coat? There were two doors beyond the mirror screen. One of them led to the bedroom; the other door would be the closet. But which door? She hadn't paid much attention because she had been too taken aback by her first view of Tony's lair. The whole thing was a playpen. And no one, she was sure, shared the upkeep. When he stayed in the city, it wasn't to work.

The room was overheated. Real plants would have wilted. Josephine opened her handbag, took out a piece of tissue and wiped her face. Her cheeks felt flushed and damp. I've got to get out of here, she thought, crumpling the tissue, and I don't care anymore if I do it gracefully. She didn't know Tony had moved behind her with noiseless steps until she heard him laughing softly.

"I might have known a leopard never changes its spots. You fit in perfectly with the jungle motif."

"What are you talking about?"

"You couldn't resist getting rid of the dust, could you, Josie?"

Without being conscious of it, she had taken the crumpled tissue and wiped one of the stiff, lifeless leaves. Her fingers closed around a plastic stem.

"What's the matter?"

Her nervousness, she knew, was spurring him on in all the wrong ways. In his hand was a fresh drink.

"Guaranteed to warm a lady on a cold day," he offered.

She looked at Tony and said in a level voice that surprised her, "I'm not staying for lunch after all."

"Thanks, but no thanks?"

"Something like that."

"You just came."

"And I'm just leaving."

"What do you think I have on my mind besides Swiss cheese?"

"I don't intend to stay and find out."

"I'm not falling for this, you know," he said. "It's a phony bit. You only *look* like somebody ought to prop you up in Saint Peter's next to the Virgin Mary and put candles around your feet. All those Catholics would want to kiss your big toe instead of hers and never know the difference. Jesus," he said, *"I'd* like to kiss your big toe."

"Shut up," she whispered hoarsely. "Just shut up."

"I am aware," he told her in a sodden voice, "that I am trampling on one of the most sacred establishments in our town—Josephine Trask's fabled virtue. Did you know there was always something exhausting about your virtue?"

In spite of herself, she asked, "What are you talking about?"

"Tiring and tiresome. Only I'm onto you. Everybody thinks you're perfect. Perfect wife. Perfect mother. Perfect everything. Most people shower or take baths; everybody thinks you lock yourself into the bathroom and polish your virtues. God, how they glow!"

"My son is right," Ted's father had said the first time he met her. "There is a glow about you." She shook off the memory. It tarnished what had been meant as a compliment to remember it here.

"By comparison," Tony went on, "you make everybody else feel like a slob. Of course, some people are natural slobs. Now you take my wife." He grinned. "Who's the comedian who says, 'Take my wife. Please!' "

"I don't know. I don't think it's funny, Tony. I don't think any of this is, either."

"Poor Frieda. I didn't mean it. Poor fat Frieda. I'm just trying to make you smile. What can I say to make you laugh?"

"Tony," she said, "don't you understand? I'm not interested. Where did you put it?"

"What?"

"My coat."

"I threw it out of the window and the sanitation department picked it up. It's on its way to the city dump. If you go out without it, you'll freeze. Now you'll have to stay here with me until we get to know each other better. Don't you think it's sad we've known each other so many years and don't know each other at all?"

There were two doors. One of them had to be the closet.

He saw her trying to decide. "The lady or the tiger," he laughed, using his finger to move the lump of ice around in his glass.

There seemed to be another lump, in the back of her throat. She couldn't swallow it.

"Which is the closet and which is the bedroom? Do you know what I would like for Christmas, Josie? To see you in the middle of a big white bed."

"Tony," she said, "you're making such a fool of yourself."

"And to think that for years I pitied Ted. I was so sure you were as frozen as this cube of ice. How serious is it between you and Goudy?"

She took a chance, went past him to the second door in the foyer and flung it open. Her winter coat had never looked more beautiful. Even though she was overjoyed to see it, she yanked it roughly from the hanger. Tony was at her side immediately. On the way he had put down the fat glass. Both his hands were free now and then they were covering her breasts.

"Don't go, Josie," he pleaded.

The liquor smell . . . she was so afraid she was going to throw up; she felt weak as well as sick. Then anger seemed to restore her strength. She gave her body a sudden wrench, shook herself free and shoved her arms into the sleeves of her coat. It was a soft thick wall between them. She fumbled with the buttons and wondered why the holes seemed so much narrower. Forget the buttons. Just leave.

If he tried to keep her from leaving, she knew she couldn't fight him and win, even drunk as he was. "Stop it!" she ordered. She was really ordering herself, not him—telling herself not to cry. She wanted to cry, but not in this place. . . .

Tony didn't try to keep her from leaving. Surprisingly, he stood aside looking suddenly bewildered and shaking his head as if he didn't know what she was doing there.

In the hallway, there was a fire exit. Shamed and outraged, she ran, nearly falling, down two flights of stairs. Behind her she could hear Tony's unsteady voice: "You said you wouldn't tell Frieda about the apartment. You promised, Josie. Remember we're old friends."

At that moment, what she wished more than anything in the world was to be far away from him and home. . . . There was a cab coming down the street as she left the brownstone. She got in and gave the driver the address on Bleecker Street.

THE BARBER pole Ben had told her to expect was there. Desperate, she pushed the bell and waited for what seemed a long time.

The door was opened finally by a woman. Josephine had expected a man, although Ben had never said his friend was a man.

There was an aristocratic magnificence about this woman. A generous dusting of white powder on her beautifully boned face made eyes that were thickly outlined with black pencil appear larger and more velvety. She wore no lipstick and appeared to have almost no mouth. Her dark hair was boyishly short. Blunt-cut bangs covered most of her forehead and pointed up those exaggerated eyes.

Josephine looked down at small boots, noticing that although the woman was very tall, she was delicately boned. Slim fingers held open the door.

"Yes?" The single word said, I don't know you. What do you want?

The entire day was taking on nightmare proportions. She had awakened haunted by one. It was the reason she had come to New York. Going was supposed to let her put an extra night, a less disturbing dream, between herself and the nude stone man.

"Yes?" the woman said again.

Josephine stood riveted, teeth chattering in the cold, unable to answer. Everything we dream, she thought, is symbolic because nothing—and no one—is ever what we see in the dream, but merely a representation of ourselves in other forms.

And one day, would she hide from the prying eyes of her own children a plastic saltshaker?

"Jo," she heard Ben Goudy say in an anxious voice. "Is that you, Jo?"

And the lady sheathed in layers of cloth, toying with long amber and gold beads, said, "It's your friend, is it?"

More than anything in the world, Josephine had wished to be home. With these two, one she had never met before, she felt she was.

"Come in," the woman said. A remarkable sweetness in the woman's voice drew Josephine inside to a large tiled area that had been partitioned off to make two rooms. Yards of exquisite Chinese silk were artfully draped over the partition.

"What happened?" Ben asked. "You look terrible."

"There was such a crowd." Another half-truth. "I felt sick." That was the whole truth.

"Maybe all that disinfectant in the warehouse got to you."

"Yes." She smiled at him because the shared experience bound them together. "I promised to telephone first," she said apologetically. "I'm sorry."

"It doesn't matter," the woman said. "Let me have your coat. Introduce us, Ben? My name is Tish."

He grinned. "You just introduced yourself."

Tish didn't bother to hang her coat the way Tony had. She threw it over a large leather hassock, then put a cigarette into an oddly shaped holder. It was gold and jutted out before it tipped up.

"We just finished eating. Did you have your lunch?"

Ben answered for her. "At a fast-food counter near Bergdorf's."

Josephine shook her head. All of a sudden she was feeling much better and ravenously hungry. "No, I didn't, and I'm starved."

Her hostess blew a cloud of smoke. "You can have some of my moussaka. It's delicious. Ben!" She waved the hand with the gold cigarette holder in his direction. "Tell Jo I'm a fantastic cook."

"You just told her yourself."

"What's moussaka?" Josephine asked.

"A casserole of eggplant and lamb." Tish used long expressive fingers to draw it in the air. "It comes out of the oven puffy and brown and gorgeous as a soufflé."

"Thank you."

It was served with a custardlike topping, a crisp salad and a glass of white wine. "Don't talk," Tish commanded. "Just sit there and enjoy it and let Ben finish looking at my new shit."

"It's wonderful shit," he said, "even better than your moussaka."

"Really good?" she asked, exactly as Josephine had about her own work.

She sat alone at a small table and ate and watched them leaf through a portfolio.

"You know it's good," Ben was saying.

"Yes, naturally. Of course I do." She let loose another cloud of smoke, at the same time widening those velvety eyes.

"You've got more than enough for that exhibition."

"You know why I won't let him take them. It's an exchange. He wants to ball me."

"Then find someone else."

Josephine ate the exotic food, drank the dry wine and forced herself to listen as if they had begun to talk while she was half-asleep. In some ways, what was happening began to take the shape of another dream. None of this seemed real either. She knew where she was, but was beginning to wonder who she was.

For some reason, she liked this woman. Tish was even more exotic than her cooking. Her dress was . . . individualistic and marvelous, although she, herself, would never attempt anything like it. Still she couldn't help wondering how it would feel to dress like that.

The fact that Tish's face was mostly eyes and hardly any mouth because it wore no lipstick made the foul words that came out of the mouth seem more acceptable. They emerged, blew away like the smoke and weren't important. All that was important was what she did.

"I'd like to see your work."

From halfway across the room, Tish looked more closely at her. "And do you have as good an appetite for painting?"

"I'd like to see yours."

"All right," Tish said, "look at them then."

Josephine moved across what had once been a barbershop. For the first time since this strange day had begun, she felt completely awake, completely alive and completely happy.

She knew Ben was watching her, waiting for her reaction.

The painting she held in her hands had been done with a peculiar fury

—in broad brush strokes. A sort of wanton brutality covered from each large canvas. All of it was strong and compelling. The combination of paint and pen and ink was exciting.

Exhaling puffs of blue smoke, Tish stood beside Josephine, who sat cross-legged on the tile floor forgetting she had, only the day before, picked up the beige dress at the cleaner. "You don't paint like a woman."

Good-naturedly, Tish shot back, "How the fuck does a woman paint? What did you expect? Butterflies and roses? I'm not a woman. I'm an artist."

"I think it's wonderful." There was no mistaking genuine admiration. She smiled up at her. "You would hate the way I decorate cakes."

Ben said harshly, "Don't pay any attention to her. She does more than decorate cakes. And she gets better all the time."

"I'd like to see what she does," Tish said. "Will you let me?"

Josephine looked to Ben.

"She'll let you," he promised.

"All artists," Tish said, "are basically egocentric. They have to be. I want to talk about *my* work now. Do you have a favorite?"

"Yes. And it's the only one I don't want to look at again."

"Look at it anyway. Which one?"

"The house."

Tish gave Ben a significant look. "Why don't you like it?" she asked her.

"It frightens me." She forced herself to stare at a somber painting of a burned-out ruin. She could imagine the smell of burned flesh. There was a chilling desolation about the bleak house. Rotted slats resembled wasted human ribs. Behind it was a sense of barren wasteland. Josephine shuddered and turned away a second time.

"I hate it, too," Tish said.

"Why did you do it?"

"I don't know." She smiled sadly. "I wish I did. It frightens me. I wish I could shake off the premonition of danger it gives me." She jerked her head at Ben. "Tell her what happened with it."

"I came here once and found her in a dead faint."

Josephine almost asked, "How did you get in?" but stopped herself. So he had a key. . . .

"I had worked on it most of the night," Tish said. "There aren't many skylights with northern exposure left in New York today. It doesn't matter. Photographers' lights work miracles. Besides, skylights are dan-

162

gerous in this city. Anyone can get in."

"You worked on this most of the night," Josephine prompted. "Then what?"

"It was as if someone else's hand was moving mine. By the time I stopped it, it was finished. I went"—she indicated the partition—"to bed. And dreamed of this . . . thing." Josephine knew all about nightmares. "But in the dream I was locked *inside*," she continued. "I woke up and ran back out in here, trying to get away." She blew some smoke and finished, "I was terrified. I turned on the lights and found myself face to face with that house all over again on the easel. I knew I couldn't run away from it. I suppose that's when I passed out."

"If it frightens you," Josephine said, "why don't you get rid of it?"

Tish looked away in amazement. "Because I created it. Besides, it wouldn't prevent whatever it's trying to tell me from happening."

BEN DROVE all the way back to Ditchling. Neither of them said much until they were out of the city. There had been little snow to see in the streets of New York City because of the cars, but it was waiting where they left it, along the sides of the parkway.

"Winter," Ben said, "gives us snow, but it's an Indian gift. The snow will melt, and take with it more than it brought."

"You mean it will take the old year?"

"Yes, and would you want to know what this new one has in store for you?"

"No one," Josephine said, "really wants to know. Not if there's no mistake and no turning back."

"Remember what happened to Lot's wife when all she did was look back once," he said.

Josephine turned on the radio.

"No news, please."

"I was trying to find the kind of music we had driving in."

When she found it, she said, "I like Tish."

"She likes you."

"Did she tell you?" pleased.

"She didn't have to. I've known her a long time. There's no other woman quite like her."

"She's talented."

"She's more than that. Underneath those mummy wrappings there's a hell of a human being."

"Do you think I'll ever see her again?"

"And that," Ben said, putting on speed, "is up to you."

For the rest of the way they listened to music. As he took the exit turnoff, Ben asked suddenly, "What happened after I left you on Madison Avenue, anyway? I haven't known you as long as I've known Tish, but I'm beginning to read you pretty well, too."

"I told you. I got sick from the crowd."

"Have it your own way."

"I don't think I'll be coming to the studio again until after the holidays." She said it in a polite, almost impersonal voice. Her features, she knew, had already rearranged themselves to match the voice.

"Why not?"

"There's so much to do. So many activities. You might enjoy coming over for some of them."

"I doubt it."

"Ted and I have open house on New Year's Day every year. Will you come?"

"I won't be here. I'll be in New York."

"When did you decide that?"

"Just now."

"But your work . . ."

"If yours can wait, so can mine." He brought the car to a stop alongside the barn. "See you next year." As he got out, he said, "Jo? Wouldn't you really like to know what this new year will bring us? I would."

She took the wheel. As she drove away she saw his tall figure standing motionless looking after her. It was startling to see him turn and move back into the barn. It was as if the stone man had returned of his own free will to the space given him close by the woman who was still a prisoner in stone.

She left them together in the studio and went home.

Chapter Seventeen

IN THEIR bedroom the following week, her husband asked, "How often have you been going to the barn?" It was the night of Elsie's glee club concert.

Josephine looped the length of soft silk around her neck. "I've been there a lot lately. Working."

"You've never told me what you're working on."

"If you really want to know, I'll tell you."

"I'd rather be surprised." Then he surprised her by adding, "Did you buy Goudy a Christmas present?"

A present for Ben? The idea had never occurred to her. "I wouldn't know what to give him," honestly. "If I thought of giving him anything, I would have told you."

"I know you would. But Josie, honey, you can't take up a man's time and not give him anything for it. It's not right."

I've made you dissatisfied with everything you have and everything you are, Ben had told her. *You haven't found it out yet. . . .* Ben thinks he's already taken something from me, she thought, clutching the hairbrush; I'm not sure what it is, but I don't dare tell that to my husband.

"Anyway, I've mailed him a check. Christmas is a good time to send it. Besides, didn't you say you'll only be going a few more times?"

"It's all I need to finish what I'm doing. How big a check did you send?"

"A hundred dollars. If I break it down into hours, I know it isn't enough. Have you been using his materials, too?"

Wordlessly, she nodded and wondered why she never offered to pay for what she used. She had taken everything so naturally, as if it had been her right. Or was it simply a reaction to the natural way he had given it, as if it had been his right?

"I hope he won't be insulted." He put on his jacket. "It's not much, but it's something, and it's all we can afford."

"More than we can?"

"Never mind, darling. As long as you've enjoyed it."

"Ted, I want to talk about the *Digest.* I want to know where we stand. Don't put me off."

And Elsie knocked at their bedroom door. "I wanted to tell you," she announced, "that Pete isn't going to my concert tonight." Her indifference was too obvious. "I also want to tell you not to try to talk him into it. I don't care."

If you didn't, Josephine thought, you wouldn't look so hurt.

"Of course he's going," Ted said. "What'd you two fight about now?"

"Nothing. He's going to Mitford instead."

Judy Ryder lived in Mitford. Peter hadn't mentioned her since the night of the press association meeting. Josephine tried to remember what the girl looked like. All she could recall was an advancing Judy with heaving young breasts . . . and a retreating Judy with youthful, melon-hard buttocks.

If Peter had seen her after that night, she would have known. Some children took pleasure in things if they hid them. Peter wasn't like that; being secretive made him uncomfortable. It wasn't the son she knew so well. She tried to push away an unpleasant thought. Lately was she the mother *he* knew so well?

"What's in Mitford?" Ted was asking.

"Some stupid play. It has to be stupid if they gave Judy Ryder the lead. Her father's downstairs. He's driving Pete over."

Josephine said, "I didn't hear the doorbell."

"Pete was at the window. As soon as he saw Mr. Ryder's car, our front door was wide open! If you want to know what I think, I think he's in a big hurry to get to Mitford—and not to see that stupid play, either."

Elsie was wearing the dress her grandmother helped her buy. It was the wrong shade of blue; it didn't do a thing for her. Only I, her mother admitted silently, waited too long to get the right color.

"Anyway Mr. Ryder doesn't want to go before he says hello to you."

"Tell him we'll be right down."

When they were alone, Ted said, "How do we handle this?"

"Peter's too young to be thinking seriously about a girl." Josephine tried hard to convince herself. "You've got enough on your mind without cluttering it with nonsense."

"Oh, I'm not worried about that. If the kid's developed a crush, it'll be the first of many. It's that I haven't seen Stan since the night of the meeting. Remember how he almost yanked my arm out of its socket shaking my hand?"

"He asked you to print up a copy of what you said, so they could read it over and . . ."

". . . Remember, if the going gets rough.' "

It was such a perfect imitation of Stan Ryder's beefy voice that Josephine laughed in spite of herself.

"He didn't have the guts to tell me to my face he was throwing in with Bartlett. He put it in a letter. How am I supposed to act, Josie? I don't feel particularly friendly. Maybe it was dream-world stuff, but I still think if we had all stayed together . . ."

"Maybe that's why he's here. Let's go down and find out."

Winter and summer, Stan Ryder boasted an overripe tan—from the sun in season, the ultraviolet bulb out of season. He told people he'd decided that he wasn't going to outlive his skin anyway. "If I look better this way, screw the experts who say it's lousy for you."

Next to his florid face, Fran's looked like alabaster. It really does, Josephine thought again, deserve to be modeled in that material. If only I were good enough now. . . .

Stan got to his feet as they came into the room. "Josie, you get better looking all the time. This guy must be taking good care of you."

"Always." She tried to smile graciously, but didn't know if she was succeeding and didn't care. She didn't like the man or his daughter, and wished Peter weren't going out tonight.

"How does an ugly puss like Ted rate a gorgeous mother and a gorgeous wife?"

Before Josephine had a chance, Fran protested, "I think my son is handsome enough."

"Oh, Mrs. Trask, I'm a big kidder. Tell her, Ted."

"I never know if you're serious or not. That letter, for instance. Was it a joke?"

"I guess it would have been nicer to tell you face to face. The truth is—and it takes a big man to admit it . . ." Because his smile was forced, it coarsened his features even more. The bronze tan couldn't hide tiny veins that marbled his nose. ". . . I was embarrassed after the way I shot my mouth off. You remember the things I said that night?"

"I remember." Suddenly Ted looked tired and defeated. "Never mind, Stan. It doesn't matter whether you told me to my face or dictated it."

"Yeah, that, too. The least I could've done was not dictate it. It was like the time I sent my secretary out to buy my wife an anniversary card. Mabel never lets me forget that. She found out and tore it into pieces right in front of me. That what you did to my letter?"

"I just read it," tonelessly, "and threw it away. Your decision. I can't argue it."

"Putting out a boondock paper isn't where my head is. Real estate. That's where the money is."

"You don't have to explain."

"Nobody in Mitford gives a hot crap anyway." In a fast aside, he said, "Sorry, ladies." And to Ted, "People in my town couldn't care less if the weekly is full of canned news and boilerplate or not, as long as they got space left over for the local ads and the wedding, birth and obit announcements. They just don't care, Ted. And Bartlett's deal was a fair one. You gotta admit it."

"Mr. Ryder," Peter said—he was wearing his best suit—"we won't be late for the play, will we?"

"By God, I almost forgot kitten's debut as a star. Pete tell you she's a star?"

"Pete," Josephine said, looking at him, "didn't even tell us he was going out tonight."

"That kid of mine is a shrewdy. She rounded up her own cheering section—got her whole crowd coming."

"I didn't realize Peter was one of Judy's crowd."

"Nice kids," Stan Ryder said. "With what you hear going on these days, we ought to be damn glad we got nice kids with nice clean interests. Peter's the only boy Judy-kitten knows outside Mitford. She said, 'Daddy, since you'll be driving through Ditchling on your way back, pick up Petey.' "

Josephine heard Elsie mutter, "Petey! Oh, boy!"

Stan didn't hear her. He had even stopped smiling. "Mabel asked me, too, Josie. She's always liked the both of you. She'd feel bad if this little business difference stopped us from being friendly."

"There's no reason why it should."

"Of course not." Ted's voice was as hollow and as polite as hers.

"Then you'll change your mind about the twenty-eighth? We're having the thing catered."

"I told Mabel when she called—our neighbors invited us to a holiday party several weeks ago." Josephine didn't care for Mabel Ryder any more than she cared for the husband or the daughter, but given the choice, she would almost rather go to the party in Mitford than the one next door. It was too late to refuse Frieda, though, even if being in the Haines house meant being around Tony again.

Don't think about it. Don't think of what you'll say when you see him next time. Just think of Peter. "When will you be home?"

"Oh, mom," embarrassed.

"Not late," Stan Ryder promised. "I give you my word on that. After the play we're throwing a party at the house. Ginger ale to toast a successful opening night."

Elsie narrowed her eyes and asked with calculated innocence, "How many times are they going to do the play?"

"Just tonight, Little Miss Redhead. Why?"

"Well, won't everybody be celebrating because it's the closing night, too?"

Stan Ryder tossed back his big head and burst into a peal of good-natured laughter. His head was so oversized that for a wild moment, Josephine was afraid it would snap from the folds of his thick neck and roll over her freshly vacuumed carpet. "You got a good sense of humor. Now you hold onto that, Elsie, because, believe it or not, some boys like that almost as much as a girl who's good-looking."

169

FRIEDA waved frantically when she spotted them coming into the school auditorium. She mouthed the word "Here" and pointed to empty seats beside her.

Ted sighed as they went down the aisle. "I hope it's not a long concert. Those chairs give me splinters."

Frieda wouldn't be bothered by the hard seats. She was more well upholstered than the last time Josephine had seen her and she was wearing the cherry red suit.

"Perfect for Christmas, isn't it, Josie?"

"Especially with that green scarf."

"You hate the combination."

"I didn't say that."

Frieda pulled off the scarf. "I look like a Christmas tree. A fat Christmas tree. Hello, Mrs. Trask. Ted, you'll have to take care of all of us. Tony's working late."

"It's my gain."

"With the pounds I've put on, it's a bigger gain than you know. Josie, do I look like an elephant in this? The truth."

"It's a very festive color," Fran offered helpfully and saved Josephine from answering.

"He said God dressed the robin in red. I'm sure some hell of a robin."

"Who said that?" Ted asked.

"It's not important," Josephine said quickly. She picked up a program that had been lying on the seat. "Jennie Daly has her usual solo."

Frieda lowered her voice. "I saw Sam earlier. You know, of course, Alice is still at Memorial."

"No, I didn't."

"Sam told me how she developed the flu and they're afraid it could develop into pneumonia, so they're keeping her longer. I happen to know she had a breakdown after that miscarriage. Flu, my foot. She's in psychiatric."

"Where do you get your information?"

"Not from the *Digest,*" Ted said. "We only print reliable news."

Frieda shrugged her plump shoulders. "Nobody's asking you to print it, but it's reliable."

"If it is," Fran said, "we ought to send her flowers or a bed jacket or something."

"It's up to you, but if she's in the cuckoo's-nest section, she won't appreciate it. Frankly, I'd save my money."

170

Mr. Neeriam, the choral director, appeared onstage and the audience fell silent. On behalf of the faculty, he welcomed the parents and proudly he said, "We present your own youngsters in an evening of seasonal melody." He was happy so many of them could attend.

"Poor Tony," Frieda said. "He felt rotten about missing this. He hasn't seen you in so long."

When the curtain parted, it revealed representatives from both the lower and upper schools. Frieda's twins, Gerald and George, were in the group of younger children standing on a raised platform where they could be more easily seen. On the other side of the stage, less fidgety, more composed, were the older students. Every boy wore the required navy jacket, white shirt, dark tie and slacks. Every girl looked as if her dress were new.

Frieda whispered, "Good thing my kids take after their father and not me. Ever hear Tony sing? He has talent."

Josie knew some of Tony's other talents.

Jennifer Daly was with the seniors. This would be her last Christmas concert. A lovely child, Jennie. She had the youthful suppleness of the marble girl in Ben's studio who covered her face and wept without making a sound. Josephine wondered where Ben was. With Tish? In their world . . . not hers! But then why had she felt so at home from the moment she stepped inside the renovated barbershop and heard the door close on the world outside?

It was disconcerting not being able to keep her thoughts from jumping incoherently. She never used to have a problem keeping her mind or her body still. . . .

"Chairs getting to you?" Ted whispered.

From her other side she heard Frieda, "How did Alice and Sam get a beauty like that? If she were older and had that figure, I'd hate her."

Jennie was as motionless as the statue, but her waist-length hair was alive. It was brushed and smoothed, the color of the highly polished mahogany piano where any minute now the choral director would take his place.

Was Elsie hidden somewhere in the back row? Josephine had no illusions about her own child's thin, undistinguished singing voice. With dozens of others to drown her out, it wouldn't matter.

Mr. Neeriam apologized to the audience for an unintentional oversight in the program. "The narrator who will introduce our songs and tell you a little about each will be Elsie Trask."

Ted applauded enthusiastically. "Say, Josie, what do you think of that?"

Josephine applauded, too, with less enthusiasm. Seeing her name emblazoned on a souvenir program would have been so important to Elsie. She had a need right now to feel important. It might even have made her begin to like herself. Instead, her brother, who hadn't bothered to come, would have to take the word of others that she had been chosen.

One of the teachers must have suggested to Elsie that she concentrate on an object to keep from suffering stage fright. She stood alone, downstage, looking thin and woebegone, wearing that shade of blue that washed her out even more under the strong lights, and stared with fixed intensity at the big clock at the rear of the auditorium. Her eyes appeared twice their normal size, and the tomboyish assurance she affected most of the time deserted her at the moment she needed it most. It was replaced by a little-girl wistfulness—a vulnerable, terrible eagerness to please.

" 'Deck the Hall,' " woodenly, "is one of the gayest and most popular of all Christmas carols. . . ."

She doesn't sound gay, Josephine thought, and how small she looks. Oh, please, let her get through this.

". . . It is based on a traditional air."

The fringe of copper hair on her forehead probably felt heavy and damp. She protruded her lower lip and blew. A curl bobbed up and then down again, and a ripple of laughter ran through the audience. A flush of embarrassment animated Elsie's pale skin. Josephine's hands were painfully folded in her lap as if her wrists were handcuffed.

"It will be sung by the entire ensemble." She took a step backward into blessed anonymity; then to everyone's surprise came boldly forward again, this time dangerously close to the edge of the stage. "I forgot I was supposed to say, 'We're glad you came tonight and we hope you enjoy the concert.' And what I just said before is going to be the first song. Anyway, I'm saying it now." She stepped back again.

Somebody laughed. The laughter spread, but there was affection in it. Elsie sensed the audience was on her side now. She smiled impishly and blew the curl again—deliberately this time. They applauded. Why, she has style, her mother thought, pleased, and it was unkind of Stan Ryder to tell her that she isn't pretty. He's an unkind man and Elsie is prettier than she realizes.

The audience kept applauding until the first song was underway. Josephine exhaled deeply and relaxed her hands. It was going to be all right.

For the next two hours the hall was radiant with carols.

"There is some dispute," Elsie informed them, "as to whether 'The First Noel' originated in France or England. No one, however, can argue about its timeless appeal. . . ."

Other Christmases, Josephine recalled, were long past. Somehow, only this one mattered.

". . .'I Saw Three Ships' has long been popular among the seafaring English. It is sung tonight by the senior boys' chorus."

In years to come, she thought, this Christmas will be most remembered.

" 'O Little Town of Bethlehem' was written by a Philadelphia minister more than one hundred years ago, following an inspirational visit he made to Bethlehem's Church of the Nativity on a Christmas morning. . . ."

Josephine couldn't dismiss—any more than she could explain—the profound feeling that this Christmas would be the one that mattered most to her—the one that would be her most remembered.

Jennifer Daly closed the evening's program. Each note sounded the way the girl looked—clean and freshly washed. Why, she was the girl from the barn come alive. The hands at her sides were in tight balls and no open fingers could cover her face. She was still crying silently, but in the music now, and for the first time since anyone could remember, Jennifer Daly's voice broke.

As if it had been spontaneous and not planned, the entire ensemble behind her rescued her with a reprieve:

> Hear soft and sweet—this lullaby,
> All angels smile above.
> A mother is holding her child,
> A mother is singing with love.

Jennifer was crying openly now.

"It's because she's graduating this year," someone in the row behind said to someone else, but Josephine was sure Jennie was crying because this was the first year her mother wasn't there.

At Frieda's party, she would make John tell her about Alice.

CHRISTMAS CAME closer. Josephine festooned the balustrade with green ropes of pine boughs, braided with stripes of red licorice. She wired together pairs of large candy canes and tied them to the greenery with bright red ribbon.

Oranges and lemons were studded with colored gumdrops and grouped on the sideboard next to clusters of white candles.

Butter cookies cut into hearts and stars and angels were taken from the freezer. Josephine remembered that she had started her holiday baking the day after she returned Ben Goudy's portfolio.

Look at your hands, he had ordered. *They're trembling. What's the matter with you?* And he gave her some clay and told her to find whatever was hidden inside. It had been a long time before she went back again. And once she finished that head of Peter, she would never go back.

Obligingly, her husband supplied rational reasons. They couldn't afford the luxury of a hobby for her, and it was unfair to impose on Ben Goudy. She tried to forget the real reason, but it rolled into a burr and stuck in her memory. As a child, she put away clay because she didn't know what to do with it. As a woman, she was putting it away because she did know.

The day before Christmas Josephine took the shortcut, walking in her own invisible footsteps to the River Road.

She went because Ben Goudy was away and she had a compulsion to be by herself in the barn. He had given her a key she never used. The heavy door had always been unlocked and welcoming.

In the quiet he left behind, Josephine put her warm hands on the cold marble hands of the sobbing young girl. They resisted her. She would never be able to move them apart and find out if the girl was anything like Jennie Daly.

Then she got down on her knees and looked up into the face of the kneeling stone man.

"Into everything you create," Ben once told her, "there will be something of what you are and something of what you want to be." She stared at the unsmiling mouth and was sure she heard him say, "As long as you're here, Jo, take a good look at the woman. You've wanted to. You just didn't want me watching." She went back to stand before the prisoner.

Ben told her that whatever he wanted to say was said. That meant he had no intention of ever finishing this. And the woman would never be completely released from the stone.

"I wish I could help you," Josephine said aloud. "I can't."

The next thing she knew she took her smock from the wall. The studio was in a state of chaos. After she swept the creaky floor, gathering together fragments of plaster, cigarette butts and ashes, pieces of wood, assorted debris and dust—dust everywhere—in the corners and along the cracks of the walls, she filled a bucket of water and scrubbed every inch of it. She soaked rags in detergent and scraped and wiped stools and ladders. She washed the familiar percolator, emptying it of cold and stale coffee grounds. She wrung out the rags and hung them to dry over the sink.

Without giving herself time to think, she shook out the sheets on the roll-away she had watched him bid for, tucked them back tightly, smoothed the blanket and plumped the pillow.

The last thing she did before she left was to look at her own work. Ben was right. It was good, and she could get better. . . .

Only there was no time. It ran out even before she started. Even at that moment, she should be home. It was where she belonged, especially on Christmas Eve.

She locked the barn door after her. Coldness stung her cheeks and made her eyes tear. It had to be the cold that made them tear. . . .

THERE WAS a lovely leisure about Christmas morning. Home was the world and their world was safe.

"It smells like Christmas," Peter said. The turkey that would have a garland of cranberry strings when it was brought to the table was already stuffed and roasting.

Except for the opening of gifts, even their movements were unhurried. Fingers closed around another ritual: frothy hot chocolate steaming in mugs.

Peter tried to hide his disappointment when he didn't find the backgammon set he wanted under the tree. Elsie told him he was getting it for his birthday two weeks later.

"Elsie," her grandmother scolded, "don't you know how to keep a secret?"

"Sure. But it would have ruined his Christmas."

The backgammon set, Josephine thought with a secret smile, will pale next to my gift to him. And this next year, Jo, she told herself, you will give yourself a priceless gift: no regrets and no remorse.

Josephine wondered if she had actually thought the words or if she had heard them. They were so clear. Someone else must have said them. Only there was no one else in the room who could have.

Ted saw her frowning. "You think I spent too much on your perfume, don't you, Josie? Come on. I know what you're thinking."

Do you? she thought, screaming inside herself. Then explain it to me. Tell me what it means. I'm frightened. But all she said quietly was, "I know what it costs an ounce."

"I wanted to get you something extravagant and useless. It's like thumbing my nose at our bank account. Be grateful. If the account were healthy, you probably would have got something practical, like a garbage disposal."

Frieda called to wish them a merry Christmas. "And don't forget the twenty-eighth. Our house. I told Tony I'd kill him if he has to work that night. He promised faithfully he'll be here. Say, Josie, I'll bet you've even forgotten what that husband of mine looks like."

"No," Josephine said, "I haven't forgotten."

FRIEDA WADDLED toward them with difficulty on high-heeled pumps that bound her swollen insteps. She was flushed with the excitement of her party and whatever had been in the empty highball glass she was clutching.

"Hi, you Trasks. You're late. How long does it take to walk next door?"

There was an unbecoming girlishness in her manner and in the way she had fluffed her hair around her round face. Instead of concealing her bulk, the flowing caftan turned her into an advancing oversized flowerpot. She was breathing hard. "God, Josie, how skinny you are! You look like a shiny black eel. Have you lost weight?"

"I don't think so. It's probably the dress. You were with me when I bought it. You liked it."

"It's elegant," Fran said quickly. Josephine wished she weren't always so protective. It made her feel stifled under a giant wing.

"I thought you'd dress it up," Frieda said, "especially for my party. Oh, never mind me. If wearing that one little pin makes you happy . . ."

"I gave it to her for our anniversary," Ted said.

"Never mind me. I'm just jealous of your wife because she looks like a shiny black eel. Did I say that before?"

"Yes," Josephine told her.

"So sue me. I'm having a good time at my own party. Why not? Drinks are on the house. And it's my house. Dammit, where the hell is Tony? He was here a minute ago. The way he disappears! That's being a rotten host. He should be with me. Fran's right. You do look elegant, but I don't like your hair that way, and I wouldn't have said a word, but since you asked—Tony!" Her voice jumped an octave as he joined them. "Be honest—brutally honest—because Josie appreciates it when people are honest. Don't you think she looks unsexy with her hair pulled back and stuck up like that?"

"When you're here, sweetheart," Tony said, with a disarming smile, "no other woman looks sexy to me." He was moving the lump of ice around in his glass with his finger, exactly as he had done in his "pied-à-terre" in Manhattan. Josephine didn't like the reminder; she turned her head away and felt him staring at her profile. His eyes were boring a hole in her cheek. "Let Josie wear her hair any way she wants if Ted likes it."

Ted said, "I like Josie any way—any time."

Fran returned a friendly wave to someone across the room and excused herself. When the two couples were alone, Josephine wondered if she had subconsciously dressed so simply, combing her hair so severely in the hope Tony might overlook her. Her appearance was having the opposite effect.

In a room full of trailing chiffon, rustling taffeta and light-catching sequins, Josephine was a stark silhouette. In a room women with sparkle in their ears, on their wrists and around their necks, she emerged dramatically instead of receding into the gathered glitter. Her host's eyes were fixed on her.

Her hostess was close beside him, stroking his jacket. "Well," Frieda said, "was I right, Josie? Did you forget what this handsome devil looked like? It's been months, hasn't it?"

Tony's eyes were still on Josephine. Except for nostrils blowing out smoke from his cigarette, and a tip of his moustache that twitched slightly from nervousness, he was absolutely motionless.

All at once she knew that they couldn't go on living next door to one another with the specter of that Manhattan efficiency apartment taking up the space between their two houses. She had to root it out by pretending that it had never existed for her.

"Didn't I tell you, Frieda," she said deliberately, "that I ran into your husband a couple of weeks ago?"

"I didn't know that," Ted said.

"She didn't tell me either." Frieda screwed up her face like a spoiled child who wasn't getting her way.

"We were both surprised," Josephine said. "Imagine meeting someone you know in the middle of a city like New York. Sometimes, I can go for months in this little town without seeing friends. Is John Cullen here yet, by the way?"

"He called. He may not be able to make it," Frieda said. "It must be rotten being married to a doctor. I don't care what anyone says. If his wife hadn't been hit by that car, she would have died of boredom."

"Shut up, sweetheart." Tony turned toward Josephine without really looking at her.

He's still afraid to look at me, she thought. But she was looking directly at him when she said, "Remember, Tony? We almost went right past each other without even saying hello. But then, you were in such a hurry to get back to your office."

Reassured, Tony emptied his glass in one gulp. Whatever he was drinking shone brightly in his eyes. "She was with what's-his-name Goudy," he told them. "They had gone to an art exhibition."

Instantly alert, Frieda parted her lips with a half-smile. Josephine had never realized before how sharp her teeth were, like a small cat's teeth. Her head was beginning to throb. I must have pulled my hair back too much, she decided. The elastic is wound too tightly and there's a hairpin sticking somewhere in my scalp.

They had just arrived and already she was anxious to go home.

"Why didn't you tell *me* you went to an exhibition with Ben Goudy?" Frieda accused.

"Because," Ted said, smiling pleasantly, "she didn't think it was interesting enough to talk about. She told me I wouldn't have liked it much—too abstract." Tough disappointing my hostess, he thought, but I knew all about Goudy going to New York with my wife. I knew because my wife told me.

He squeezed his wife's hand. "Looks like it's going to be one hell of a party, Frieda," he said.

"Come see my buffet table, Josie," Frieda said. "Tell me honestly what you think." On the way, Frieda's drink was freshened by the bartender hired for the evening.

"Just white wine for you, Josie?"

"It's what I want."

"Keep that up and you won't enjoy the party."

"Wanna bet?"

Frieda's table looked as if it had been torn from the Christmas issue of a magazine and brought to life. "Three magazines," Frieda admitted. *"Town and Country, House and Garden* and *Vogue."*

For a centerpiece, she had constructed a tree of radish roses, celery fans and green olives.

"Ask me how long it took to make," she dared.

"How long?"

She grinned. "Don't ask. Boy, did you walk into that one!"

There were assorted aspics, assorted cheeses and assorted fruits. There was a baked ham decorated with chunks of pineapple and cloves. Biscuits in bun warmers were turned golden brown.

"You like the tablecloth? It's new."

"Very much."

"That's my Lenox china," proudly.

"I remember it."

"I almost forgot it. The stuff's been on my top shelf for years. You're not kidding me, Josie? You really like the way everything looks?"

"Everything's lovely, Frieda. Really." She meant it.

They heard Marge Holden before they saw her. She was making a curious swishing noise in stiff taffeta. "The table's gorgeous," she said. "It's a shame to spoil it by taking a thing from it."

"You will, though," Frieda predicted, beaming. "The food's as good as it looks."

"You're so lucky, Frieda," Marge sighed. "I wish I had a next-door neighbor to do something like this for me. It's perfect, Josie."

The compliment was so unexpected and undeserved that Josephine was momentarily thrown off balance. Before she could answer, Marge swished away again.

"The hell with it," Frieda said softly. "I'm going to get another drink."

"I'm going to tell her she's wrong. It's not fair."

"Oh, don't bother. Marge wouldn't believe you."

Josephine was left standing alone at the buffet table. Almost immediately Tony joined her.

"Listen, Josie," he whispered, "you covered up but beautifully."

Eyes blazing and upset about what had just happened, she turned on him. "What are you talking about?"

"Going to my place. If you don't slip, I won't. It only concerns us anyway. Right?"

He's acting, she thought furiously, as if something did happen between us in that awful apartment. Maybe he's so drunk he believes it did.

"I want to find my husband," tightly.

"Tell me one thing first. What are you wearing under that second skin? More skin? Oh, babe!"

The Trasks were the first guests to leave the party. By that time, neither host nor hostess was in any condition to notice. Frieda had picked all the olives from her carefully constructed centerpiece and was tossing them around the room with abandon. "The hell with it," she singsonged. "Oh, the hell with it."

THE HAINESES, twins in tow, were the first guests to arrive on New Year's Day.

Frieda pulled Josephine aside. "I haven't dared call you since my party. When I looked around, you were gone. I didn't say anything to insult you, did I? Of all the women in this stinking town, you're the only one who gives a damn for me."

"I'm a little concerned about the way you drank at your party."

"Oh, that," dismissing it airily. "How many parties do I give? It was a big success, Josie. Were you with me when Marge said how gorgeous my table looked? I don't remember."

"I heard her. Come and have some orange juice."

"What's in it?"

"Champagne."

"That's better. What else? I'm starved."

This year she was serving omelettes, hot fruit muffins and coffee. The year before it had been Swedish pancakes with jam or sour cream. And next year she might offer quiche in individual stoneware bowls.

Or maybe there wouldn't be a table next year. . . .

"Is John Cullen coming?"

"He isn't sure."

. . . Or maybe the table would be here and she would offer the biggest surprise of all: she wouldn't be here.

Why, she wondered giddily, did such a thing even occur to me? We always have brunch on New Year's Day.

She gave Frieda an empty plate, and then left to sit on the upholstered seat on the bay window.

Ted joined her. He was holding a glass. "You should have asked your artist friend."

"Ben's in New York for the holidays. I haven't been to the barn since before Christmas."

He started to ask if she missed it, but realized in time it would have come out, "Do you miss him?" instead. He wasn't, he decided, used to champagne in his orange juice, especially on an empty stomach.

Obviously Frieda was enjoying it. She downed her second.

"Happy New Year, darling," he said; and kissed her.

She kissed him back, but for the first time, she was afraid to face the coming year.

At the same time, she was impatient for it to happen.

Chapter Eighteen

"I've come back," Josephine told him. She could hear the words sing in her ears. "Didn't I tell you I'd be back after Christmas?"

Outside, across the road from the barn, a stream gushed over rocks coated with ice. Inside, it wasn't warm enough to make the hands lazy or cold enough to stiffen the fingers. Ben was mistaken. The old stove did a fine job.

She hung up her coat, sat on the three-legged stool and pulled off her boots. Free of winter's encumbrances, she slipped into the smock she had taken home to wash after that last time alone in the studio. There was a fresh, clean smell about it.

"Did you have a nice holiday?"

"It was all right." His broad back was to her.

His hair, she noticed immediately, had been bluntly cut. That tail of reddish hair long enough to be held by an elastic band was gone. The first day they met, it had irritated her like everything else about him. Now she was sorry to find it missing.

"Did you see Tish?"

"She asked to be remembered to you," still not turning.

"That's kind of her." She hoped she sounded as pleased as she felt. When Ben didn't look at her or say another word, she went to her turntable. If he didn't feel like talking, it didn't matter. They would talk later during a break.

Putting aside the head for a moment—there was so little left to do actually—Josephine picked up a soft lump of clay and began to work it between her palms. She twisted and bent the wires of a small already-constructed armature she had discovered on the shelf. It seemed a perfect height, although for what she wasn't exactly sure.

To be fair to Ben, the old year had ended on a more positive and compatible note for them than their last working session, when he had grabbed her wrists, challenged her to tell him whose hands they were and demanded to know what she intended to do with them. The very next day hadn't he driven to Manhattan with her and made that visit to the storage warehouse a little easier?

She and Ted had talked it over. The storage charges were paid up for the rest of the quarter. Time enough to think of a graceful way to tell her mother-in-law there is no room in our house for leftovers from your house—sell what is saleable, give away whatever strangers can make use of, throw away the rest. There's no space in a shrinking world for a yellow plastic saltshaker that doesn't even have a stopper on the bottom.

Josephine pressed the agreeable clay over the skeletal form and re-called how later that afternoon in New York Ben Goudy had been her refuge when she ran from Tony Haines. That magical interval on Bleecker Street had been powerful enough magic to make her forget for a moment the ugliness of what went before it. She recalled the length of Chinese silk draped artfully over the divider in Tish's makeshift apartment, colors vivid enough to wipe out the memory of words: "Do you know what I would like for Christmas, Josie? To see you in the middle of a big white bed."

She was really glad Tish had asked to be remembered. They were nothing alike, she and that flamboyant, brilliant artist, neither in speech nor in way of life. But in that brief time spent with her, Josephine had been strangely drawn to her.

She looked down at the figure and, with some surprise, saw it was beginning to be Elsie in jeans and a T-shirt—thin shoulders and sharp little bone wings in the back.

On this day that would probably be her last one at the barn, she repeated what she had done on her first day: she felt until she found something deep inside the clay. As in that first session, she had no idea what was going to happen; it simply did.

183

WITH LONG fingers, Josephine drew the tightness from the taut chords in her neck. Even as she wondered how long she had worked for her body to feel the effects, she thought impulsively, Fran will be disappointed if I stop now. Doing more in the house has been good for her. And if I've done a head of Peter, it's only fair to complete this figure of Elsie. If I don't, she'll suspect favoritism, which isn't true; but she'll be hurt again and Ted wouldn't want that to happen either. I'll keep on, she decided, just until this figure is done. That's all.

Then, as on that day when she cáme to return the portfolio, she heard Ben say, "Don't you think you ought to take a break?"

Again, the smell of fresh coffee brewing. She realized she was even repeating the same words. "Three hours?" looking at her watch. "I don't believe it."

"Three hours," he said, and sounded surly.

His own work probably wasn't going well. Josephine washed her hands and joined him on the bench.

"I opened a couple of tins of sardines," he told her. "And there are hard rolls."

"I usually make the coffee. Next time. Tell me about your holiday."

"Nothing to tell."

"Do you want to hear about mine?"

"Not particularly."

"Did you spend Christmas with Tish?"

"She took scissors and chopped off my hair."

"I noticed. It's neater, don't you think? She's a marvelous cook. What did she make?"

"For God's sake, you're so damned concerned with food. That's what comes of wasting too many years in a kitchen. I don't have any frigging idea what she made."

"I just asked. There's no need to use that language or that tone."

His voice had a chameleonlike quality: it changed color abruptly. "I don't remember what we ate, but I do remember some of what we talked about: Christmas when she was a little girl in Hungary."

"Oh? Was that the accent? It's faint, but it's there. I should have recognized it. When I was a little girl, an old man lived next door to us. He was Hungarian. We liked each other, the way your Uncle Jess liked my Elsie, I imagine. Anyway, I used to enjoy his stories. Budapest sounded like such a funny name to me then. Children find things to giggle at. I used to laugh and he did, too, and told me it was a wonderful city to laugh in."

"That old man must have left Budapest years before Tish." It was disconcerting the way his voice, like a stringed instrument, kept sliding and changing tone. "Thirty years ago Russians kicked in the front door of the house and kept her family prisoner for forty-eight hours. The soldiers had never seen a flush toilet. They thought they were supposed to wash meat in it. And the closet of the baroque living room, that was what they thought should be the bathroom. Tish spent part of this Christmas remembering that other one."

Because she was sickened and not sure what to answer, Josephine said only, "I'm sorry it wasn't a nice Christmas."

"Oh, she only mentioned it in passing. It's remarkable how casually human beings can pass off, like pissing off, horrors they suffered, as if those horrors happened to someone else. In a way, it's true. It can only happen to someone else, if it doesn't happen to you. And if it does, it changes you, and then it really did happen to someone else." He was through eating and lit a cigarette. "Actually, it was a pleasant enough holiday. I have a lot of friends in New York. I went to another exhibition, took in a few life classes. Studying and drawing the human body is one of the good ways to learn about it."

"Well," she said, "I'm glad. Then it wasn't being away that put you in the mood I found you in when I came this morning. It's your work?"

In a mocking voice he said, "No, it isn't my work, Mrs. Trask." There was no mistaking the anger in his voice.

"What's the matter?" she asked bewildered. "What did I do?"

"You were here while I was gone, weren't you?"

"Yes. I was here."

"I didn't ask you to be my studio helper."

"This barn looked like a battlefield. I thought you'd be pleased, and I didn't do it just for you. I think of it as our studio. I hope you don't mind."

"The bed isn't ours. I wish you hadn't made it."

Uncomfortably, she told him, "It needed making up, so naturally, I—"

"I'd rather you hadn't touched it."

"Is that the reason you're angry?"

"No."

"Tell me, please."

"I got a check in the mail. From your husband."

So that was it.

"Do you think I put a price on what I've given you? Your husband hasn't got that much money."

She would have to be careful choosing her words. "I didn't ask him to send it, Ben. I didn't know anything about it until afterward."

"One hundred dollars! Did you know it was for a hundred dollars?"

"He told me. That's a lot for him right now."

He scanned her face closely, then looked away. "And you had nothing to do with it?"

"Did you really think I did?"

"You don't think I have any intention of cashing it, do you?"

"No," she said. "I wish Ted had told me before he sent it. He meant well—but I wouldn't have let him."

He turned toward her again, fixing unwavering eyes on her, and said nothing.

She wanted to tell him how sorry she was. Instead she simply looked back in silent appeal.

"I think," he said quietly, "you're very sorry."

"I am."

"Don't be, Jo. None of this is your fault."

"I wish it hadn't happened."

"You couldn't help it," he said. "You're not to blame."

"I know," she said.

He picked up a spoon and swirled it around and around in his cup. It was an odd thing for him to do, since he took his coffee black, without sugar. Apparently it was as necessary for him to do as it was for her to watch the spoon move around and around until she felt she was growing smaller and being swept into the center of the circle.

I just apologized for my husband, she realized, ashamed of herself as well as Ted. I offered excuses because there was a lack of sensitivity in what he did. He hadn't deliberately offended Ben. He simply hadn't understood, just as he hadn't seemed aware of any change in her these past months. That was it, wasn't it . . . ?

Frieda had noticed and sulked, and Fran had noticed and encouraged the change because it let her feel more important. And Pete had been conscious of a subtle difference or he wouldn't have felt free to be secretive and join Judy's crowd. Elsie, with her curiously pointed chin and foxlike eyes, hadn't said anything, but nothing escaped her.

The only total blank had been in Ted, who looked without seeing, listened without hearing and thought good thoughts about everyone, like the good Dr. Bovary, who stared down at his wife, the arsenic-induced suicide and asked, hurt and confused, "But Emma, weren't you happy?"

"It's a bad joke," Ben said finally. "I've taken his wife away from him, and he tried to pay me for it."

The intoxicating smell of the studio—of plaster and clay, freshly shaved wood and marble dust—wasn't as strong as the restrained sensual energy that came from him.

Josephine wrapped her arms around her breasts and shivered. She had been mistaken. The stove wasn't very useful after all, she thought, giving herself time to recover from her astonishment at what he had just said.

To be perfectly honest, had it been of such genuine surprise? Hadn't she expected it to come sooner or later? Wouldn't she have been disappointed if it hadn't? The idea that somewhere deep inside her she had wanted him to say what he did sickened her in a way different from the story of the soldiers who washed their meat in the flush toilet.

He was waiting for her to say something. Instead, she went back to her worktable and nervously began to manipulate the clay. She had found other things in it. Maybe she could find the right words.

"Did you really enjoy your holiday," Ben asked without warning, "or were you a little bored?"

The fact that she wasn't answering was as good as admitting she was. Quickly, she ordered herself: tell him you loved every minute of it. Frieda in cherry red waving them down the auditorium aisle, and Marge Holden in stiff taffeta, Tony's intimate, indecent insinuation and the New Year's Day brunch she thought would never end. She wanted to say something and envied him because he could, and with so little effort.

"Being bored isn't a bad thing, sometimes," he was saying. "It gives you space to think . . . and make decisions. When you took time out to come to the barn—"

She forced herself to say, "I didn't plan it." There was almost overwhelming relief at hearing her own voice.

"Of course not. But you made your decision that day, didn't you?"

After being grateful just to be able to talk again, she wanted to scream: "You deliberately twist everything I say! Always. It wasn't anything like that."

Instead, the accusation came in a vehement, furious whisper, meant for only him to hear, even though there were just the two of them in the barn and no one else could have heard anyway.

187

"What's the matter?"

"I have a son."

He frowned. "You have a daughter, too."

"My son," Josephine said and it sounded idiotic, but she knew she must have a reason for saying it, "is in first year geometry."

"What's that got to do with us?"

"It has everything to do with me." Now she really was close to screaming. "A triangle can't break out of three sides. It can't be done." She was conscious of his staring at her. "And that means you're wrong about me. And anything you imagined about us." It still sounded idiotic, but she was sure he understood.

"What did you say when you came today?" he asked. "Your very first words."

"I don't remember."

"You said, 'I've come back.' "

"I didn't mean to you." Scrupulously, she began to tidy her worktable with hands that were surprisingly steady again. And she had not only recovered her voice, she had mastered it. "That check wasn't my fault. This probably is. I don't know how it happened, but you've got it all wrong."

"I don't believe that."

"Believe what you like."

Unexpectedly he said, "I see you're making a mud pie of your little girl now."

"Don't call it a mud pie. Please." Did it really make any difference anymore what he called it?

"What else is clay? One day you'll put it away for good and work only in marble. That's living material."

She took a deep breath and said, "I have some finishing touches left on the head. Then I'm putting away clay for good."

He laughed. "I admire your nerve. So you think you're ready to work only in stone now?"

This conversation was dizzying. She was on one pendulum, he on another and they were swinging in opposite directions. She wanted to vomit.

"I didn't say that."

"I should hope not. You've got years of work ahead of you. It's different for a woman from learning how to play the piano or write a novel. It's a lot harder. You'll have to stand on your feet until you feel like dropping. Learn to lift heavy weights. Bend iron. You'll have to study anatomy—every muscle, every bone. You'll work until you feel bloodless because you'll have given your own blood to the marble."

"Listen to me—"

There was no stopping him. "And when that happens," he promised, "you'll soar like an eagle until your wings break from your body. I envy you that first flight. I want to be there, darling."

"Shut up," she said hoarsely. "I never gave you the right to call me that."

"Months ago," he said, "you cut yourself in half. I'm curious. Does it hurt very much?"

"Yes! Are you satisfied?" The separate pendulums had stopped and started again; this time they were moving together.

"Step up," he said, "and meet Josephine, the lady magician. She sawed herself up the middle and doesn't know how to put herself back together again." He laughed shortly and leaned toward her. "If you cut a snake in two, both halves will wiggle, but the human body isn't like that."

"You're talking nonsense."

"I'm talking sense. You can't be two women."

"That's how much you know," she shot back. "I've always managed to be at least half a dozen women at the same time. Children have different personalities—like your marbles. You can't dominate them either. You have to try to understand them. So I've tried to be one kind of mother to my son, another to my daughter. I am also a wife to my husband, which is quite different from being a mother. I tried to be a daughter to Fran, and for Frieda I was a friend. I have to be many people for many people. I've cut myself not just up the middle, but into slices to match the hours of the day. . . ."

"But I got to know the only one that mattered—and the only one you never had any time for."

She covered her face with her hands because his head was too close. She dropped them again quickly when he said, "I know this isn't easy for you, Jo. But you've got to make a choice."

"I have. I'm going to finish that piece, and then I'm not coming here anymore."

He gave her a look of contempt and then he deliberately turned away, as if he needed a moment's rest from the sight of her. It gave her a chance to move closer to the hook where she had hung her coat.

"You can have the world you want," he said quietly, "if you're not a perfect fool. I refuse to believe I misjudged you. Whatever you are, you're not a fool."

"I'll have to come back again. I can't work anymore now, and I have to have that head for my son's birthday. The truth is it's all I ever really intended to do."

"Then why did you put it aside and start something new?"

She was torn between telling him too much and the desire not to lie. The truth could be a trap. If she fell into it, he wouldn't help her out. She couldn't tell him that as long as she left something there unfinished, she would have to keep coming back.

"I suppose," she said, "I could take this home, finish it there. It wouldn't be as easy."

"Do anything you please. Go to hell if that pleases you."

"Is this the way it's going to end with us?"

"Tish can go to hell, too," he said.

"What's Tish got to do with anything?"

"She watched you come together that day. She sensed that all the other people you had ever known up to that point in your life were only transient figures—"

"That's because she didn't know my family."

"Shadows," he continued, as if he hadn't heard her, "to be reproduced on some faraway wall in some foreign place with fingers moving before a bright bulb. No more real than that."

All of a sudden everything she had felt that day washed over her. She remembered how everything beyond the barber pole that stood in front of the studio had taken on an unreal quality; the only truth had been inside.

"Tish didn't know what she was talking about," Josephine lied. "I'm leaving now. Please don't make it too difficult tomorrow. It's only one more day. I'll probably be here less than an hour."

She moved quickly, pulled her boots on, yanked her coat off the hook and pulled the scarf out of the pocket. The palms of her hands were moist.

"I won't look at you or say a word if that's what you want," he offered with affected politeness.

"It might be better—"

"Maybe you'd prefer it," caustically, "if I weren't here at all."

"It's your studio."

"A little while ago you said you thought of it as our studio."

"After today, it can't be. Not anymore."

He turned his back on her, the way he had when she arrived.

This time she didn't drive in the wrong direction, but she was almost at the square before she realized she hadn't even said good-by.

Chapter Nineteen

A TERRIFIED dreamer, returning to consciousness after a plunge through nothing, reaches out for something to hold onto. The doorknob of the *Digest* office was reassuringly solid. Josephine gripped it under her woolen glove, then opened the door.

Once inside, the delirious feeling of falling through space left her and she went back to the safe and the normal, where Millie, in her cubicle, had another very bad cold.

The prominent nose was red. Lips, already swollen, were cracked at the corners and dabbed with zinc oxide ointment. "Your husband's at a meeting of the press association," she announced glumly, "what's left of it. Ten little Indians standing on a Linotype machine and Harris Bartlett picks us off one by one until now we are seven." Deliberately averting her head, she pulled a tissue from the box on her desk. "After today, we may be six."

"Another paper?" Josephine said upset. "Which one?"

"The *Graphic*. Habersville." She blew hard into the tissue. "I shouldn't have done that. I just blocked my ears."

Josephine smiled sympathetically and decided that Millie looked like a sad sick horse on the way to the glue factory. Instantly, she was ashamed and wondered if the unkind thought crossed her mind because she had once looked at Millie as Ben Goudy might have. She was once so sure Ben could produce something not only interesting but actually beautiful with such a face. After what happened today, it gave her a perverse pleasure to contradict everything she had ever thought, if it had to do with him.

"What time will he be back?" She wanted to sit with her husband in his familiar office and look across at his familiar face.

"He didn't say," running a red-knuckled forefinger down a list of subscribers' names.

Josephine looked down at her own spread hand, the one with the wedding band. What kind of shadows could be reproduced by long fingers before a bright bulb on some foreign wall? I have no intention, she thought belligerently, of changing my life for him, and remembered to say graciously, "I'm sorry you couldn't stay longer New Year's Day."

"Well, you know how they are. I don't have to tell you." The ailing mother and the demanding father were always "they" or "them." "If I'm not with them, she wets the bed and he stops talking. That's worse than listening to him complain." It was said with no trace of complaint.

"Have you tried to make arrangements for a homemaker? Through Medicare? They're both probably eligible because of age, and your father's a veteran."

"Taking care of them gives me something to do. If I didn't have that, what would I have?"

"You could have the world if you want," Josephine heard herself say unexpectedly, as Ben had just said, which meant she was still thinking of him. She was careful not to end with *if you're not a fool.*

Millie looked surprised. "What do I want, Mrs. T.?"

"I don't know. Didn't you ever want anything?"

The rawboned woman with the fading yellowish hair thought about it. "I always wanted," she admitted, "to be pretty."

"Good looks aren't important."

"You're so right. You only miss 'em if you don't have 'em." She snatched another tissue from the box and held it. "I often wondered what it would be like to be you."

"Why me?"

"Your husband says you've got a magic touch. You should hear him brag about you. According to him, there's nothing you can't do."

"I wish it were true."

Millie looked straight at her. It was disconcerting because the rheumy eyes appeared unblinking. "It must be nice to be beautiful and smart."

193

She blew her nose again and added, "And loved. If I had all that, you know what I'd be, Mrs. T.? Damned grateful. Now tell me it's none of my business." She fed a sheet of paper into the typewriter.

"Are you crying, Millie?" Josephine asked, confused.

"It's this rotten cold."

"You're upset about the *Digest.* That's it, isn't it?"

"I better finish typing up the ads while we've still got some."

Then it was the newspaper that was upsetting her. "I waved to Bernie at the copy desk when I came in," she said with artificial lightness. "He grew a beard over Christmas."

Bernie was a journalist major at the university who earned course credit and a small salary for his off-campus job at the *Digest.* He was nineteen. The curly beard made his unlined face look even younger.

Millie stopped typing. "Bushy, isn't it? First time you've seen it, Mrs. T.?"

"I just told you. He was clean-shaven before Christmas."

"He started that chin rug over two months ago."

"Oh, no, not two months ago . . . he couldn't have. It was more like . . ." She stopped because it was true.

"I suppose you've been too busy to come. Never mind. We had a nice little tree. I fixed the place up, not as good as you maybe, but I don't have your magic touch. Just the same, considering this could be our last year . . ." She left off and went back to typing furiously.

Josephine was too dumbfounded to answer. I didn't decorate the office this year, she realized, and Ted never once mentioned it. She could find an explanation for him more easily than she could find a reason for herself to have let this happen.

Their house had been dressed for Christmas, and along with everything else there was to do for the holidays there should have been, as in every other year, time set aside for the *Digest.*

Now, listening to the clack-clacking of the machine, she tried hard to remember where that time had been carefully put, then somehow carelessly misplaced. When Josephine did remember, she wished she had not. It would have been better to have spent the rest of her life just trying.

She remembered starting out for the square, and the cold sun and the dry wind, and how it had occurred to her to make a short detour and stop at the barn for a few minutes. Ben was away. It might be the only chance she would ever have to be there alone.

By the time she had finished cleaning the studio, making his bed and getting down on her knees to look up to find out if the stone man really did have a face; by the time she had studied his finished work, her one unfinished small piece and the one of the woman she insisted was unfinished, no matter how much it satisfied him to leave her that way; by that time, it was evening. There was only enough light left to fill a single star. So she had gone home again and forgotten about her husband's newspaper.

Less than an hour ago, Ben had said, *That was the day you made your decision, wasn't it?*

"I planned to come," Josephine told Millie nervously. "Something happened."

Millie kept typing.

"I'm sure you did a fine job of the decorations. . . ."

Clack, clack-clack.

"And you're wrong, Millie."

"What am I wrong about?"

"This won't be our last year."

Millie didn't answer.

"Will you tell my husband I waited for him?"

Clack-clack. "Sure, Mrs. Trask." Not Mrs. T. this time. Josephine felt awkward and unwanted. She never felt that way here and was as glad to leave as she had been to get there.

Since she didn't have a cold, there must have been another reason that she saw everything outside as if through a wet pane of glass.

If the paper died, she wouldn't be the one who had dressed it for its last Christmas. Millie had done it. If Elsie was never again chosen to introduce a school presentation, it would be her grandmother who had bought the special dress.

In the window of the dress shop were mannequins wearing spring clothing behind signs advertising Christmas clearance sales. For the first time she could remember, she was glad Christmas was over. There was too much about this one she wanted to forget; most of all was admitting to Ben Goudy that it had been a bore. If it was, it must have been her fault, just as it was her fault she hadn't put the finishing touches on the head today.

If she had finished, there would be no need to go back again tomorrow. If he's as sensitive as he pretends, Josephine told herself, he won't be there. He'll stay in the big house until he sees me leave with the clay head wrapped in a cloth.

Nothing had worked out the way she planned. The plan was to surprise her son, then return the bust to Ben, who would send it out to be cast. She trusted him when he told her that although the original clay would be destroyed, the head would be returned to her in bronze. Now it wouldn't be. Perhaps, the really important things in life don't always work out, just because you chart them to travel in a certain orbit. John Cullen had tried to tell her that once. She couldn't remember exactly how he had said it.

Behind her, he was saying now, "Josie, this is nice—running into you. Going to buy that dress?"

"No," turning to him. "Actually, I was looking at the sign."

He smiled. "My wife's favorite three words in any shop used to be 'Reduced for Clearance.' "

Josephine smiled with him and wondered how lonely it was for him to live by himself in a gabled house on Brookledge Street. "Do you realize how long it's been since I've seen you?"

"A whole year ago?"

"You sound like my children when you say it like that. They'll go on making jokes about the new year until February. We missed you at our brunch."

"I wanted to come. It wasn't possible."

"And Frieda's party? You weren't looking forward to that!" It was a good-natured accusation.

"I admit it."

"You didn't use your patients as an excuse not to come, did you?"

He stopped smiling. "There's nothing I can do for some of them. Why should I let them do anything for me?"

"I wanted to ask you something. You probably won't be able to answer though."

"Try me."

"It's something you told me a long time ago. . . . No, forget it; you wouldn't remember and it doesn't matter." She noticed he wasn't carrying his black leather bag.

"I was taking a walk. I have no office appointments, and I'm not due at the hospital until later."

"Where did you go for your walk?"

"To the best possible place in this or any other town—directly to no

196

place in particular. There are usually surprises on the way."

"Did you find one?"

"You," he said. "Where are you headed?"

"I dropped in at the *Digest*. Millie's not sure when Ted will be back. I wanted to have coffee with him."

"Have it with me instead."

"All right," looking toward the diner across the street.

"We could go to my house."

Josephine had been in his office in the separate wing, but not, she realized, inside the house itself for over three years. Or was it four?

"Nothing's changed," John said, "but somehow it just looks like furniture now. The woman who takes care of the office does that for me, too. It's clean."

"I'm sure it is."

"You'll recognize the same pictures on the wall. Same lamps. Same rug. The wing chair needs reupholstering, but it needed that before Louise had her accident."

He makes it sound as if she sprained her ankle, Josephine thought. He's a doctor. He sees people die all the time, and he still can't bring himself to say, "Before my wife was killed."

Frieda had raced across the yard that day. "Oh, my God! Did you hear about Louise Cullen? Some son-of-a-bitch hit-and-run driver. No one even got his number. She was tossed in the air like a rag doll, someone said. One of my damn kids came home saying she smashed into the side of the bank building so hard she was decapitated. I couldn't help it, Josie, when he told me that I walloped him right across the face. You don't think that could be true, do you?" . . .

It happened around this time of year. Louise had gone to the supermarket. The milk, Ted said, and the eggs ran out of the broken bag and into the gutter. He printed her picture, a smiling head shot on the front page of a special edition, and wrote a beautiful tribute that everyone in town talked about. It hadn't been good enough to put the eggs together again, and she was still dead.

"We'll drive there," Josephine said. "My car's parked around the corner, in front of the *Digest.*"

They started walking back to where she had left it.

"You liked Louise, didn't you, Josie?"

"Everyone did."

"You're not just saying that?"

"No."

"I'm glad." He said, "It was four years ago today."

"I didn't realize. Is that one of the reasons you were walking nowhere in particular?"

"One of them."

On the way to his house, they stopped at the German bakery. She went in with him and he bought a coffee cake, fresh from the oven in the back. It smelled of hot raisins. Ten minutes later he handed the box to the woman who cleaned and cooked for him. "Use the old Wedgwood coffee set."

She looked startled. "The one on the top shelf?"

"That's the one."

"It hasn't been taken down since I came to work here, doctor. It's probably covered with dust."

"Well," patiently, "if you wash it, Mrs. Landry, it probably won't be."

Mrs. Landry glared resentfully at Josephine.

She left them alone in the living room and they could hear her noisily dragging the step stool across the floor to reach the shelf of the cupboard. Then they heard a rush of water from the sink tap.

"For my benefit," John said good-naturedly, poking at the fire. "She's extremely unpleasant, isn't she?"

"I thought it was because I was making extra work for her."

"Don't take it personally. Mrs. Landry is the most unpleasant woman I've ever known. Occasionally, I wonder how far my Hippocratic oath would be stretched if I had to make an incision in her fat belly to remove something."

"I'd sure you'd do a perfect job."

"Either way," stone-faced, "I'd hate myself afterward."

"Why don't you get someone else?"

"You think I should?"

"If she's that unpleasant."

"I don't like firing anybody. It makes me uncomfortable." Carefully, he placed another log, then came to sit beside her on the overstuffed sofa. "I have a plan though. I intend to outlive her."

Josephine laughed outright. It was the first time she had laughed all day. It had a cleansing, restorative effect.

"I'm glad I ran into you," he said. "Today, especially."

She was glad herself. "Louise loved her Wedgwood."

"It was never dusty when she was here."

"She took it out for me one day after I had an appointment with you. I could have used my stomach as a table."

"Pete or Elsie?"

"Pete."

"He has a birthday coming up next week."

"Imagine you remembering that!"

"He'll be fourteen."

"That's right."

Mrs. Landry brought in the tray and set it down on the coffee table.

"Thank you, Mrs. Landry," John said gravely.

"These things were awfully dusty, doctor."

"They look fine now."

She left without further word.

"While you pour," John said, taking up the knife and poising it over the coffee cake, "I will pretend I am about to remove her gallbladder."

Josephine managed at the same time to pour the coffee and study him. Loneliness etched on a face can add depth to the expression, she thought, and quickly tried to forget it because that kind of thinking meant part of her was still in the studio where Ben was saying preposterous things. Quickly, she ordered herself: . . . talk about something that has nothing to do with him.

"Did I tell you what I'm giving Pete for his birthday? A head of him modeled from memory and sketched on the backs of old envelopes and in the margins of the morning—" she heard her voice trail off—"paper."

And there she was looking through a wet pane of glass again, only this time at a piece of cake she was holding. For the sake of something to do, she took a bite and found it unpleasantly tasteless.

"What's the matter, Josie?"

"Nothing." She had always been able to open her mind, spread out her thoughts and sort them out in front of him. Now she couldn't talk to him anymore, and he was the only one who never asked anything of her. Ben Goudy had taken, as well as given. "I suppose I'm getting a delayed reaction to the holidays. Isn't it a fact people feel more depressed that time of year?"

"More of them try to commit suicide and usually wind up permanently maimed. There's another statistic for you. Why should you be depressed?"

Why should I be? she asked herself. To Millie, I'm beautiful and smart and loved and should pay heaven back by being grateful.

"You haven't answered."

"Yes, I did. You didn't hear me. I was talking to myself again. It's not very satisfactory. We argue a lot."

"There's more than one you, Josie?"

"Enough of me," softly, "for every hour of the day."

Unexpectedly, he said, "Tell me about Frieda's party."

"She did everything without my help; Marge didn't believe it. It was too bad. Frieda worked so hard; she wanted a little credit. It wasn't much to ask. She probably dislikes me for it."

"If she does, it started long before the party."

"What are you talking about?"

"Those stories she's been inventing about you and that sculptor, Goudy."

Josephine felt the blood siphoned out of her, then much too quickly, pumped back in again. It went directly to her head and set her brain on fire.

"Don't, Josie."

"It's not true," she began, and remembered the way Ben had said, "It's a bad joke. I've taken his wife away from him and he tried to pay me for it."

"Everyone knows Frieda," John said.

"She must really hate me. I think I know exactly the day it began. It was my fault."

"What could you have done to deserve this?"

"She asked me if I really enjoyed the lessons. I told her I wondered what I had done with myself before and didn't I realize how bored I had been. Don't you understand? That meant with her. She said she was glad I developed a hobby, but it started then. I'm sure of it."

"You really enjoyed your lessons that much?"

"It doesn't matter. After tomorrow, I won't be going anymore. I'll have finished the head. It's all I ever planned to do. That's the truth, John."

"Then forget it. Other people will forget it, too, when they find out you've stopped going."

"Will they think they forced me to stop? I don't want to go anymore. I've had more than enough, but I wouldn't want anyone to think that was the reason. It would be like an admission."

"I shouldn't have told you."

"I'm glad you did. It explains a lot. Millie, for instance. The way she looks up to Ted has nothing to do with his height. In her own special way, she loves him, and she thinks I've been . . ." She stopped self-consciously.

"Sleeping in the barn with a stranger?"

"Was it necessary to put it like that?"

He nodded. "That way you'll be able to face whatever it is you may have to outlive." He smiled and covered her hand with his. "Ride with it. You'll see. It'll take less time than for me to outlive Mrs. Landry. It's a small-minded town, but it has a short memory. They'll forget."

She stared numbly at their hands, the large one comforting the smaller one under it, and understood why Tony Haines had been disappointed that day in New York. Frieda had led him to expect more than he got.

"If I had known about this before, I could have spared myself some . . . unpleasantness. Is everyone talking about it?"

"I'm sure you won't believe it, but most of them are concerned with more important things."

"At this moment," tonelessly, "I don't believe it."

"The Kileys, for instance, had their baby this morning."

"Boy or girl?" Josephine asked, and almost forgot about herself.

"Boy. Seven pounds three ounces."

"Gwen all right?"

"Perfect. So's the infant. As a doctor, I know it's not possible, but when he was minutes old, he looked at me and seemed to be trying to communicate."

"But they can't see, John."

He smiled enigmatically. "No, they can't, can they?"

"You don't sound convinced."

"How convinced are you," he asked, "that when a child is born, it's not already capable of thinking?"

She looked past him to the window where a persistent wind was rocking the bare branches of the tree. "I never thought about it."

"Think about it now."

"When a child is born," Josephine said reflectively, "if he or she can think at all, there must be a sublime anticipation of what life could be."

"It would be a natural result," the doctor said, "of nine months of constant warmth and constant nourishment. Only there's no way of proving it."

"Because we never remember."

"If we do, it's buried deep in our subconscious."

"Part of that lost memory all of us have," Josephine said to herself, only loud enough for him to hear this time. "And I wonder what kind of sublime anticipation I had."

"See Gwen when you get the chance."

"Of course. And thanks for telling me."

"I knew you'd be glad."

"And it was a good way to get my mind off what we had been talking about, wasn't it? I'm sorry, I'm still thinking about it and for the first time in my life I wish I were dead."

"Stop it, Josie." He sounded angry and kicked at a spitting piece of wood that had splintered from the flaming parent log. "I told you because I wanted to remind you of a banal truth. People are born, people die." He looked at her with those intensely blue eyes and said flatly, "Alice Daly is dying."

She couldn't answer at first. "I don't believe it." They were just words to fill in the silence.

"Now tell me honestly, how important is that stupid gossip about you and Jess Goudy's nephew?"

"Not very."

"Everyone who knows Frieda Haines will look to the source and when they find out about Alice, they'll remember who started the rumor about her miscarriage and her breakdown. Did you believe it?"

"I tried hard. I wanted to." And she found herself telling John how she had looked at Alice on the day of the luncheon. With a sense of release and relief, she talked freely about Ben, all about how he had warned her not to deny that fourth and final dimension behind the masks people wear. Ben had been sorry about her friend, but he was convinced that if Josephine saw death there, it was probably true.

"What day was that?" curiously.

"November third."

"I didn't know myself then."

"I was sure you didn't. Later I talked myself into believing I was wrong. Ben said he was glad, but I don't think he believed it." She took a deep breath. "I tried to visit her. Visitors weren't allowed. Remember? I met you in the cafeteria."

"Sam didn't want anyone to know." He sighed deeply. "Not letting them know would keep it from happening—is anyone reasonable at a time like that? But I did try to tell you."

Josephine remembered sitting with him at the Formica table and discussing time. How, he had asked her, did she picture it? Was each week a block to step over? Circles within circles? Straight lines? Was it flat or did it have form?

"Why," she was asking him now, "is there more for some and less for others?"

"You might as well ask me if a newborn child knows the answer and then forgets. If that memory weren't a lost one, I suppose we'd all make the most of what we can be sure of."

Josephine stood up. "For me, sooner or later, wherever I am, it's always time to go home."

He got her coat from the guest closet.

"You didn't invite me here just for a sociable cup of coffee, did you?"

"The diner wasn't the place to tell you any of these things. I thought it would be easier here. I even hoped Louise's Wedgwood would help. It didn't."

"You'll let me know about Alice?"

"As soon as I hear."

At the open door, he reminded her, "There was something you wanted to ask me. You said I probably wouldn't remember."

"It matters even less now."

"Ask me anyway."

"It was the day you told me I was going to have my first child. We had what Pete would call a heavy conversation, all about the consummation of order being another word for perfection. And I told you that long ago I had decided on the exact direction my life was going to take. I believed it was the only sensible approach to living, but you told me life is much too full of unknown factors for anyone to plan on the ultimate."

"Did I really?" John asked her with a faint smile.

"Human beings," you said, "aren't tossed like planets and satellites into orbit. No mortal, you said, moves alone with invisible ties in such mathematical precision."

"Well, well," he said, "that was heavy. I said all that?"

"It came back to me . . . in a rush."

"Then you don't have to ask me anymore, do you?"

"No." They said good-by and she walked away quickly without looking back.

"Drive carefully," she heard him call after her. "The roads are icy."

As she started the car, she was remembering that day almost fourteen years ago, remembering that she had said, "All my ties are invisible, but

I know they're there. All I have to do is keep order in my own physical universe. The rest is simple."

And John had answered, "I think I should be a little afraid of you, Josephine Trask. Instead, I think I'm a little afraid *for* you."

Now she was afraid for herself because she had known Alice was going to die before any doctor knew and because tomorrow would be her last day at the barn.

"Tomorrow," she said in a loud clear voice because she had turned the corner of Brookledge Street and there was no one to hear, "I'll see Ben for the last time."

She was sure—as sure as she had been about Alice—that he had no intention of staying in the big house until she left. Instead he would do his best to make her as uncomfortable as he could, treating her with the veiled intimacy of a secret accomplice—because for months, only he had known about her mysterious other life.

Chapter Twenty

"QUICK! WHERE is it, in the car? Bring it in. We'll hide it."

Josephine closed the kitchen door behind her. "What are you talking about?"

"The birthday present," Fran said with whispered excitement. "Don't worry. Peter's downstairs in his room with Elsie."

"I don't have it," she said. "I couldn't work today. It just didn't go right."

"Maybe you were out of practice."

"That's probably the reason." She unbuttoned her coat. "What smells so good?"

"Spaghetti and meatballs. You left the chicken out to defrost, but the children don't like the way I bake it as much as they like yours."

"I'm sorry I didn't get back in time. Thanks, Fran."

"Oh, I don't mind, honey. I never do. By the way, there'll only be the four of us. Teddy's gone to Habersville."

"I know. To try to talk Mark Petrie out of selling to Bartlett."

Fran blinked in disappointment. "Who told you?"

"Millie. I was at the *Digest.*" Her mother-in-law at her heels, she went into the foyer to put away her coat. "What time did Ted call?"

"He was here—early this afternoon. He wanted to tell you what was happening."

The coat was lopsided on the hanger. She straightened it. "Was he very upset?"

"About the *Graphic?* Well, naturally—"

"I mean because I wasn't here." She hadn't been home the day he found out about Stan Ryder either. Stan was the first. Ted came home both times to tell his wife and found his mother instead.

"He was surprised," Fran said. "This morning you told us you planned to be at the barn only a couple of hours."

"That's what I planned."

"I'm so ignorant about these things. What do you do when the work doesn't go right? Stare at it to figure out what's wrong? I can't imagine you of all people spending hours not doing anything."

Josephine gave her a quick, anxious glance. Whether she was in the house or not, she was sure Frieda still visited daily. She had to talk to someone and Ted's mother was a good listener. She must have listened often lately, as Frieda added more vodka to her juice on cold mornings to warm herself. How much had she warmed to the subject of what was happening in the barn?

"Table's set," Fran was saying.

"Tell me," deliberately allowing her no preparation for the question, "exactly what you think I do in the studio when I'm not working."

"I know what you're going to say," Fran chided with innocent good nature. "You're going to tell me sometimes just staring at your work is valuable, too—like breaking up and studying plaster figures Ben Goudy made. Isn't that what you once told me?"

Relieved, Josephine smiled.

"Laugh at me. I don't care. Didn't I tell you I was ignorant about these things? I can't wait to see what you've been doing." She sniffed. "Something's burning."

In the kitchen, Josephine started the salad. "Actually," she said, "I left the studio early. I told you I went to the paper. That was about two."

"Teddy was here then. What a shame. Try this—" holding out a wooden spoon. "What does it need?"

Josephine tasted the thick spiced sauce. "Not a thing." She went back to cutting radishes. "I didn't come home after that because I met John Cullen. "We went to his house for coffee. Louise's accident was four years ago today."

"Four years. Was it really? What a sad day for the doctor! I'm glad you were with him, Josie. Did he talk much about her?"

"He talked a lot." No need to tell Fran everything they talked about; she would find out soon enough about Alice.

"I know what you're thinking, honey."

"Do you?"

"That it was more important to be here with your husband if he needed you."

"It was."

"But Ted didn't find the house empty. That's what's really important. He had someone to listen to him. Josie? If the other papers sell to Mr. Bartlett, we'll be alone. The *Digest* isn't big enough or strong enough to stand alone."

Josephine hadn't realized how imminent their last edition could be. Ted had done a good job of keeping it from her. Or maybe she hadn't realized it because most of the time lately, when he talked, she saw only his mouth moving and heard nothing while she studied the way his ears were set on his head and drew an imaginary line across his face where the brows would be placed. . . .

Fran took the collander off the wall and dumped the spaghetti into it. "Ted said that the only cause *not* worth fighting for is one nobody else cares about. He didn't know if anyone outside this house really cared if there was a *Digest* or not."

"I should have been here."

"I told him it was too bad he couldn't go from door to door and find out how people felt. Then I had an idea. Probably not a good one. I'm ignorant about things like that, too."

"What is it?" Ridiculously, Josephine felt a little envious of a conversation her mother-in-law had shared with Ted, one that rightly belonged to her.

"Put it in the paper,' I suggested. 'Ask people if they do care.' I don't even know if he heard me. He was thinking about tonight. The publishers who are left are meeting at the *Graphic.* Did I tell you that?"

"No."

"All he wanted was coffee, but he's had too much of that lately. Caffeine works on the nerves. I wouldn't let him out of here before he had a good lunch. I made sure he drove away with a good hot meal under his belt."

"I'm glad." Fran's skin was even more translucent than usual. A soft blush, nothing to do with the heat from the stove, quivered on her cheekbones. She's getting younger all the time, Josephine marveled. She even walks lighter. At this moment she looks like a young girl whose lover told her he'll be coming back soon.

"Everything's ready," Fran said. "Call the children."

At the door to the basement, Josephine said, "I'll definitely be through with that head I'm doing tomorrow."

"And after that?"

"After that, nothing."

"I don't understand."

"This whole business is taking up too much of my time. It's not worth it."

"You can't stop," Fran said, upset. "You're doing so well."

"You haven't seen what I've done; how do you know how well I'm doing?"

"I know you, honey. How many times have I told you that you have golden hands?"

"There's more for them to do at home."

"Please don't stop because you think you've put too much on me."

"I'm stopping because I don't want to go there anymore. Besides, we can't afford—" she forced herself to say, "—a hobby for me anymore. Ted and I talked about it. He knows I'm quitting."

"Josie," Fran called after her as she ran down the stairs, "if it's money, I have a little extra. I could easily let you have some."

Josephine pretended she hadn't heard.

AT THE dinner table she was disagreeably aware that her daughter was surreptitiously watching her eat. Without intending to, she reached across the table and lightly slapped Elsie's hand.

"I can't wind spaghetti, if you do that. Why did you do that, anyway?"

"You looked as if you might be coming down with a cold." It was all she could think of to say. She was ashamed of what she just did and tried to explain it away. "Your eyes seem murky."

Elsie gave her a clear cool look. "There's nothing wrong with me."

"I wanted to find out if your hand was cold—or hot."

"Was it?"

"No. You're fine."

With sickening horror, it occurred to her that the stories Frieda was spreading might have reached her children. That would explain why Elsie had been watching her. She had to find out. "Remember the day we came into the kitchen and discovered a man we had never seen before?"

They stopped eating and looked up.

"What made you think of that all of a sudden?" Fran asked. "I'm glad I wasn't here. I would have been terrified."

"I remembered it when I saw him today. For my lesson." She looked directly at them. "Were you two as frightened as I was? I never did ask you."

Peter shrugged. "I could have handled him if he had tried anything funny."

His sister gave a short laugh. "I'd like to have seen that! What would you have done? Give him your famous karate chop?"

"Maybe."

"He would have annihilated you."

"Spell *annihilate.*"

"I can't."

"Don't use any word you can't spell."

"I can spell *bullshit,*" Elsie said, her eyes flecked with the overhead light, "and that's what I think of your karate chop."

Fran was appalled. "Elsie! Such language!"

"I don't like it either," Josephine said, but she was reassured. The mention of Ben Goudy had only produced another squabble. It didn't even touch her.

"Does he run a regular school?" Peter was asking. "How many in it?"

"I'm his only pupil. After tomorrow he won't even have me."

"He can't be a very good teacher," Elsie said.

"He's very good," loyally. "I'll let you judge for yourself when I bring home what I've been working on. Don't ask what it is. It's a surprise."

Elsie swallowed the last of the milk left in the bottom of her glass. "Too bad you're not going to take more lessons."

"That's what I was telling her," Fran said.

"Because I was thinking," Elsie went on, "I could pose for you."

"Cut off your arms," Peter said. "You'd make a great Venus de Milo."

"Peter," his grandmother said, "bite your tongue."

"He's sick," Elsie said. "Real sick." She looked at her mother again. "I'll tell you how I know I could make a good model. We're doing this pantomime for the spring pageant. Scenes from the American Revolution. I'm going to be Molly Pitcher looking at the cannon."

"Which end?" Peter asked grinning.

Elsie ignored him, and her grandmother said, "Rehearsing for spring? So soon? The closer we get to it every winter, the more I think this time the snow won't melt in time. It always does."

Elsie waited patiently for her to finish; then she continued, "I'm the only one who can stand practically without breathing. Miss Palm said I was like a statue."

"I'm sure you were," Josephine said.

"Well, you want to?"

"Very much," Josephine said. Mentally, she added: I already have. It's a quick study, an impression, and I did it in only three hours, but it's you. Ben Goudy recognized it immediately. He said I was making a mud pie of my little girl.

"Okay," Elsie said. "When? You want me to show you how I stand when I'm Molly Pitcher?"

"No!" It was harsher than she meant it to sound. "Didn't you hear what I said? Tomorrow's my last time." She softened her voice. "I'm sorry." She was sorry. Having one of her children with her in the studio would have changed the whole tone of the sessions. Everything might have been different.

Elsie returned to winding long strands of spaghetti. "Never mind," exactly the way she had said "never mind" when she offered to turn a flower on the cake and her mother refused—afraid she would spoil it. That small hurt would be nothing compared to the one she would have when she saw the study of Pete who hadn't even offered to sit for it.

Her daughter already resented her. Josephine could find an easy explanation for that. Every book she had ever read about child-parent relationships agreed on the natural resentment a daughter usually feels toward a mother. It was based on female competition.

The books also agreed on sibling rivalry. When Elsie saw the clay head of her brother . . .

I'll bring them both home, Josephine decided. The figure of the girl was rough, not the way it should be, but there was no reason why it couldn't be left that way. An impression. If it did have an unfinished look, she would say, "But it's a whole figure. Peter's is just the head."

Elsie would weigh the merits the two, then throw her arms around her mother's neck the way she had the night they all went downstairs to Pete's room, and she would whisper, "I love you," the way she did then.

For the first time since she left the barn earlier, Josephine was happy.

She didn't regret the hours spent on the figure when she should have been completing the head. It turned out for the best, she told herself, pleased. Now they'll both be satisfied. And everything else that happened in the studio would fade into time. The Josephine she had been in the barn would take her proper place in memory alongside the Josephine she could never be again: the little girl her father once lifted onto the painted wooden horse and said, "Be careful, Josie. Hold on. I don't want you to get hurt."

Because he loved her, he had held her himself while the horse slid up and down the brass pole and she got dizzy to the music. In the end it made her sick. The barn had been a carousel. Now it was time to get off.

"After the dishes are done," she announced, "I will beat anyone in a game of Ping-Pong."

Sibling rivalry disappeared. "Which one of us," her son dared, "do you want to take on first?"

LATER, ALONE in the double bed upstairs, she tried to keep her body awake and alert until her husband came home. She wanted to know what happened at the meeting and why he hadn't said a word about her neglecting the *Digest* office. The clock radio on the night table read eleven-thirty. In the dark, the numbers would be luminous. The next thing she knew, they were. Someone had turned off the lamp. It was three-thirty.

She looked at the sleeper next to her. Ted had come quietly into the room, undressed and slipped in beside her. It wasn't important when. The only thing that was important was to try to hold onto some tangled images of her dream before they thinned into transparencies and shredded into nothing.

The house she had just moved through in her dream had been her house, but there were so many rooms! Why hadn't she ever bothered to go into them?

One was a bedroom. White bounced from floor to ceiling and blotted out the corners. There was no place for shadows to hide. Alice Daly was in a bed.

"Isn't it terrible?" she was saying. "Louise's lovely Wedgwood, broken to pieces all over the street."

"I tried to see you," Josephine told her apologetically. Then she heard someone screaming and was embarrassed because she was the one making all that noise and there was a picture of a nurse holding a forefinger to her mouth and the word, "Shhh."

But Josephine was already running down the road across from her house, taking the shortcut to the barn. Ben Goudy put strong arms around her and said, "You're trembling, Jo."

"Alice's face," Josephine had told him. "She doesn't have one."

"I can't help it if you saw death there," he said gruffly. "Why are you so stubborn? Admit it when I'm right. Cut a snake in half, both halves wiggle. The human body's not that way. You can't cut yourself in two."

JOSEPHINE TURNED on the lamp. She asked the light to wash away the rest, and it did. Ted moaned and moved restlessly, so she switched it off again and pulled the blanket close.

People, she knew, dream every night, but they don't always remember. What bothered her was that this was the first one she remembered so clearly since the night before she started her lessons. And it was a nightmare.

"If they start again," she said softly, needing to hear the sound of her own voice, "I'll be afraid to go to sleep."

Chapter Twenty-one

THE NEXT time she opened her eyes she saw her husband's face. Because it was so close to hers, it appeared abnormally large. She pushed herself into a sitting position, at the same time backing away from him.

"I was going to kiss you," he said. "Good morning, darling."

"Good morning."

He smiled. "I've been watching you sleep."

She smiled, too, but she was thinking: People shouldn't watch other people sleep. There's something indecent about it.

She couldn't remember any of the invisible strands of her lost dream —a spider's web without spiders—but like all the others it was very private and intensely personal. Knowing that Ted sat next to her on the bed, saw her face all undressed and whatever was in her mind spilled out on the pillow, was embarrassing.

"I hope you had nice dreams."

"I don't remember."

"I never remember mine either."

She thought, when I'm dead, I don't want the casket opened. It must be terrible to lie there and have people look at you and not be able to talk back.

That brought back a lost piece of the dream. Something about Alice. "What time is it?" She looked at the clock dial that wasn't luminous anymore. "Quarter past seven," answering herself. "And you're ready to leave." She should tell him about Alice. The Dalys were part of their world.

"Today's Thursday."

"That's right. You go to Middleburg." She decided against telling him. There were enough unpleasant things on his mind. Why add another before it was absolutely necessary? "You started to kiss me good morning."

"You got away from me."

"I was half-asleep." She held out her arms, gently held him to her and ran her hand over hair the same texture as their daughter's. He smelled of pine after-shave lotion and his jacket scratched her skin.

"You go to bed practically naked," he said sternly. "One day you'll catch pneumonia."

"I like the freedom. I couldn't sleep in a gown with long sleeves and elastic at the wrists."

"No one's asking you to go to extremes." He stood up suddenly and began to move restlessly about the room.

"What are you looking for?"

"My cigarettes."

"On your dresser. I can see them from here. You're back on them?"

"I may not smoke at all. It depends."

"On what?"

"Bartlett. If I can get in and out of the plant without seeing the bastard."

"Going there can't be easy for you." On an impulse, she said, "I'll go with you."

"Really, Josie?" pleased. "Take that long drive and hang around till I've finished?"

She sat up, twisted around and felt for her slippers. "I can be showered and dressed in ten minutes."

"What were you planning to do today?"

"Finish what I've been working on in the studio."

"Thanks, anyway," Ted said. "Do what you have to do." He dropped the cigarette pack into his jacket pocket. "I'll do what I have to do." The words at the end were almost a harsh whisper.

The sound of it frightened her. Suddenly only one thing mattered: the *Digest*. They helped it grow and were proud when people said nice things about it.

214

You don't sell a child, she thought. You just don't turn it over to someone you don't even like. "Don't say yes to him today."

"Don't worry. That's not why I didn't want you to come. In the end I may be forced to sell, but dammit I'm going to make him sweat a little."

"The man doesn't sweat and he has no bowels."

"Why, Josie," in mock disapproval, "that doesn't sound like you."

"What happened in Habersville?"

"We couldn't talk Petrie out of it. He's asking Bartlett to draw up a contract. I don't blame him. He doesn't see any point in putting off the inevitable."

"This," Josephine said, "was the first year I didn't decorate the office for the holidays."

"Millie was a poor second best."

"Why didn't you say anything?"

Ted turned to face the mirror and began to readjust the knot of his necktie. "I knew you hadn't forgotten."

"You're so sure?"

"Yes. Because I know you so well," he said, keeping his back to her. "I'll bet you started out for the paper one day—"

"I did."

"But it bothered you too much . . . knowing it could be the last time . . ."

She didn't answer.

"I understood," Ted said, putting his cigarettes in his coat pocket. "I'm going to get a second cup of coffee. I just came for these. Want me to bring you a cup?"

"No, thanks. What time did you make the coffee?"

"Fran made it."

"Your mother never gets up this early."

"Well, there's someone down there who looks a lot like her. She says she'll make sure the kids are off to school on time, and to let you sleep. Did I wake you? I'm sorry."

"This is nonsense," getting out of bed. "I've never in my life slept while the rest of the house is awake."

"Have it your own way."

"Ted," she said, "if the paper goes, what do we do?"

"Whatever it is, we'll do it together . . . won't we?" He looked grateful for the answer she hadn't given him.

Josephine closed the window. Chill winter air and pallid sunlight were coming into the room. "Of course," she said.

A half-hour later, the school bus took Peter and Elsie in one direction toward the school. The station wagon had already taken Ted in the other direction toward Middleburg and the printing press.

"After you leave," Fran said briskly, "I'll polish the silver and shine the copper pans."

"Didn't Cecilia do that yesterday?" The cleaning woman came on Wednesdays.

"She did a slap-dash job of it, honey—not the way *we* like it. I was sure you'd notice and say something." Over the rim of her cup, Josephine looked at the undersides of dangling pots. Only the centers were conscientiously bright. She remembered when she used to wait impatiently for the woman to finish. Then she would thank her, pay her and do the house her own way. The habit always exasperated Frieda. Fran had regarded it with fond and indulgent amusement.

"This house shouldn't have needed much. I gave it a thorough going-over for the holiday."

"You never finish with a house. Isn't that what you used to say? Clean it one day, and the next, it needs doing all over again. Buy something new and something else needs replacing. By the way, have you noticed the runners on the stairs? They're beginning to look worn."

"They'll have to stay that way," Josephine said tightly, because she hadn't noticed. "If the paper goes, we're going to have to cut back on a lot of things." She glanced at her watch. By now, Ben would be wondering why she was late. Last time he saw her, he told her to go to hell. Today was the last of it. Tomorrow, someone at the university's fine arts department would be able to suggest where to send the work, or take it, to be cast. She didn't need Ben.

Oh, but one day, she had vowed, and carelessly let him overhear, she would do everything—every step from first to last, even learn how to cast it herself. When he told her she had a lot to learn, she had answered, "I have time."

"Time for what?" Fran asked, and Josephine realized she had said it out loud.

"To start a beef stew in the slow cooker." She set the crock pot on low, where it would simmer for eight hours. "And don't bother with the silver or the pans."

"I don't mind."

"The difference is: you don't mind, I enjoy it."

Offended, Fran said, "All right, honey." She was still smiling, but the smile looked pasted on.

If you don't mean to be mean, her father used to say, why be mean? Josephine wondered why she found the older woman so irritating this morning. Poor blameless Fran hadn't done anything except offer to be helpful.

It isn't her fault, Josephine decided. It isn't even mine. It's Ben, upsetting me even before I get there, stirring up the air from the barn to this house, whipping it full of tension . . .

"It's going to rain," Fran said. "I can always tell. Something in the air."

Josephine was so relieved not to have imagined it that she kissed her. "Why, Josie—!"

The skin on the cheek wasn't as firm or elastic as it used to be, and Fran's body held the scent of the light cologne they gave her at Christmas, the same cologne she had used for years. It seemed less delicate. Maybe that's what happened when you grew older. Something in the aging of the oil glands affects the scent. Marble could stay perfect through centuries.

"Any special reason for the kiss?"

She nodded. "Today's my last lesson and I couldn't have taken any if it hadn't been for you."

"It's too bad," Fran murmured. "You liked going so much."

"I did," she admitted, "for a long time."

"Right here in this kitchen, you told Frieda you didn't know what you had done with yourself before."

Josephine remembered.

"You told her you hadn't realized how bored you had been."

"Why don't you leave?" Ted's mother asked suddenly. "You're always in such a hurry to get to your lessons. That's why I don't want you to stop."

"Why don't you believe I've had enough?"

"Those things you said to Frieda—"

"Forget what I said to Frieda."

"How much does he charge for a lesson? Consider it a loan."

"I wouldn't take your money."

"Then it isn't the money—"

"Money has nothing to do with it."

"Of course it does. And you're foolish. If going there made you that happy—"

It was such a rapid exchange, they sounded as if they were having an argument.

"Why," Josephine asked her quietly, "are you trying to push me into this?"

Fran blinked, confused. After a moment she said, "What's the matter with me? I'm sorry."

Just then, John Cullen telephoned from the hospital in Douglaston. "She's gone, Josie," he told her.

Josephine hesitated, then said, "All right." She was sure he would understand why she hadn't said thank you.

"It happened around three-thirty this morning. I promised to let you know, but I didn't think you'd want me to wake you then."

He hadn't needed to. She could see the dial of the bedside clock, Alice in a white room and a white bed . . .

Josephine hung up, feeling Ben's arms around her again, hearing him tell her how sorry he was she had seen death. Why didn't she admit it when he was right? Why was she so stubborn?

"What's the matter, Josie?"

She realized she was hugging herself to keep from trembling, but the arms felt stronger and bigger as if they belonged to someone stronger and bigger.

"Oh, no," Fran gasped when Josephine told her.

"I knew yesterday. John told me."

"It explains a lot. You haven't been yourself. And I thought you were upset because your lessons were ending. That's why I kept at you about them. But it had nothing to do with that, did it?" She sighed heavily. "Something was in the air. I can always sense it."

There was security in being able to call Ted in Middleburg.

"I still have time to get it into this edition," he said in a clipped, matter-of-fact, newspaperman's voice, "and do a follow-up later. Tell me what you know."

"John Cullen called here a few minutes ago."

The door behind her opened and closed. Josephine knew Frieda was in the house. It wasn't necessary to look at her to know she had thrown her coat over a kitchen chair and was listening carefully.

"Alice has been dying for months. Only the immediate family knew. She was gone at three-thirty this morning."

Behind her, she was pleased to hear a sharp intake of breath. Was I really Alice's friend, she wondered with a nervous shudder, if I'm taking such satisfaction repeating this news?

"Memorial Hospital in Douglaston?"

"Yes, Ted, Memorial." What she was really doing was talking directly to Frieda at the same time turning her back on her—telling her it would be a long time before anyone would take her gossip seriously, and that included anything to do with Ted's wife and the man living in the barn at the Goudy place.

"I'll come home after I leave here," Ted was saying.

"I want to go see the Dalys," she said. "I'd rather go with you. I'll wait for you." She hung up and finally turned around. "You heard all that?"

Frieda mumbled something inaudible.

"Josie knew yesterday," Fran was saying. "Dr. Cullen told her."

With difficulty, Frieda managed, "I'd like to go to the Dalys' house, too." She looked at Fran. "You going, Mrs. Trask?"

"If Josie doesn't think there'll be too many of us."

"It's better to have them send us away than not to have us come at all," Josephine said. "We'll know if we're intruding."

"Are you going to call Mr. Goudy?" Fran asked.

"Why him?" Frieda said sharply. "He doesn't know her. I mean, didn't. Jesus, this is awful. All of a sudden Alice is . . . *didn't* instead of . . . *doesn't.*"

"Ben never bothered to get a phone," Josephine said.

"Won't he wonder why you're not there today, honey?"

"I'll drop him a note." For Frieda's benefit, she added, "I'll tell him I'll take my last lesson in a few days—after the services."

"You're not going there anymore?" Frieda said. "How come?"

"I got more out of it than I expected. I was only going to do a head of Pete. I ended up doing something of Elsie, too. Please, don't mention it to either of them."

"The way you were talking, I was sure you were going to go on and on with it."

"Did I ever say that?"

"I don't remember." She sounded unsure of herself.

"And today," Josephine said, "is no time to talk about it."

"Isn't our Pete friendly with their Andy?" Fran asked.

"Andy's older," Josephine said. "He's sixteen. Jennie's eighteen."

219

"Remember her at the school concert," Fran said, "crying and singing at the same time? Everyone was sure it was because this is her last year at the high school."

"It was her last year for a lot of things," Josephine said, remembering her own mother.

You never really get over missing your mother, she decided. Hers once bought her some clay. She couldn't help wondering how different her whole life would have been if she had tried, instead of being afraid of spoiling the musky-smelling block of green clay. . . .

TONY HAINES didn't go to the funeral. Tony had integrity. It was one of the qualities, his wife said, that made him different from the others he worked with side by side in the Madison Avenue agency—side by side, except that he refused to kiss anyone's rear end—in other words, play the game. Tony wasn't like that. If he did play the game instead of just doing his job, even though it meant putting in so much extra time at night, he'd be a lot higher up the ladder. It was his choice, and Frieda respected him for it. He wasn't a hypocrite, which is very rare today, and that, she said, was the reason he didn't attend the church services.

"What he told me, his exact words were: 'I never really took to Alice. It may sound lousy now that she's passed on, but I never could warm up to unattractive women and she didn't like me very much either, so going to the funeral would be hypocritical.' Well, for God's sake," Frieda said, "you've got to give him credit for integrity." She cut herself another slice of coffee cake. "You make this, Mrs. Trask?"

"Josie did."

"Lately I never know. Why does going to a funeral always make me hungry? I have a theory. It's got something to do with being glad I'm still able to enjoy eating. That sound awful?"

"Perfectly understandable," Fran said.

Frieda turned to Josephine.

"If you want it, you're welcome to it," Josephine said.

Frieda looked disappointed. It wasn't, Josephine knew, what she wanted to hear. She wanted me to remind her of her diet, tell her how much butter and sugar went into the recipe. She wanted me to care.

"My rotten kids," Frieda said, "wanted to go today. Anything to cut school. What about yours?"

"Elsie said she's never been to a funeral. She thinks she's missed something. I told her that wasn't a good enough reason to go to this one."

"I didn't know about that," Fran said shocked. She inserted the needle in the material she was holding. "When I was little, I used to sing a song, something about 'I went to the funeral just for the ride—just for the ride.'" Her voice trailed off. "Imagine remembering that," she said. "I wonder why sewing always calms me."

"It's putting your three fingers together," Frieda told her.

"What does that do?"

She shrugged and stuffed the last of the cake into her mouth. "I don't know. I read it. It's a yoga thing. Maybe I should try that instead of gorging myself." She glanced hopefully and appealingly at Josephine again.

"Watering my plants calms me," Josephine said. It occurred to her that Fran had been taking care of the pots of ivy and philodendron on the windowsill for so long they were strangers to her.

"Did you write Mr. Goudy and explain why you never showed up that morning?"

"I cut the notice out of the *Digest* and mailed it. I'm sure he understood."

"Ted," his mother said with quiet pride and confidence, "will write a beautiful piece about Alice."

"Aren't you stunned about Sam and the kids moving away, Josie?" Frieda asked.

"He asked for a transfer the day Alice went into the hospital."

"That long ago?" Frieda said. "And nobody knew?"

No, Josephine thought, not even you—but she said only, "He told me there are too many memories for him here."

"Those kids were born in this town. Their friends live here. It's ridiculous."

"It's up to Sam."

"But you just don't pull up roots and change your whole life after more than twenty years."

"Some people," Josephine said, "pull up roots because the weeds are choking them."

Frieda cocked her head to one side. "That's a peculiar thing to say."

Josephine frowned uncomfortably. It had been a depressing morning. It had rained during the service. On the way out to the cemetery, her mother-in-law had said, "I hate leaving that poor girl all alone in the rain." The morbid, unsettling thought stayed with her and made it difficult to concentrate. She wondered exactly what it was she just said to have Frieda give her such a crooked half-smile.

"Are you really going to close the house for him, honey? It's a lot of work."

"What's that?" Frieda demanded.

"Sam's leaving town tomorrow," Fran explained.

"So soon?"

"He wants to get started in his new job right away. Isn't that what you said, Josie?"

"Yes," Josephine said. "Jennie and Andy are staying with friends."

"And you're supposed to close that big house?" Frieda said. "I call that nerve."

"The movers will take care of the big things."

"But everything else?"

"I'll do everything else."

Sam Daly had told her that his wife felt closer to her than to anyone else in Ditchling. Josephine felt guilty because, although she had been fond of his wife, she had never felt particularly close to her.

"Alice would like it," he said, "if you're the one who goes through her personal things. Give away what has to be given away. Take anything you can use for yourself. You'll do it, Josie?"

"If you want me to."

"It would be too hard on Jennie."

"Yes," Josephine agreed, "much too hard."

"My first thought was to give away everything—furniture, dishes, pictures, everything. I can't afford that. I'll learn to live with it all, Josie, but somewhere else will be easier. Don't forget, whatever you can use for yourself . . ."

"I don't need anything," she insisted.

"She'd like you to have something. Her sisters want her fur coat and her jewelry. I'll mail it to them. The clothes aren't your size. Still, there's bound to be something."

"Don't worry about it," Josephine had told him. "Don't worry about anything."

"Well, if you're going to be such a soft touch," Frieda sighed resigned, "I guess I'll have to help."

"You don't have to."

"Let you do this by yourself? Say, what kind of a friend do you think I am?"

Josephine didn't answer.

As it turned out, she wondered how she could have done it without her. Overnight, Frieda's efficiency matched her energy. She helped compile a comprehensive inventory of the contents of the two-story house. She refolded towels and linens, wrapped dishes and glasses in old newspapers and carefully put them into big cartons. She pushed up her sleeves and vacuumed the rugs. Together they turned them into long rolls, tied them and left them for the moving men. She wiped and dusted records and books. She forgot to eat until reminded. She seemed content.

"I keep thinking of you doing this alone, Josie. You couldn't have done it without me, could you?"

"No, I sure needed someone."

"You needed *me*," Frieda told her.

Every morning for almost a week, she appeared at the back door. She had already eaten a good breakfast, she announced, and refused coffee. "Work to do," she would singsong. The vigor she flaunted was a natural vigor. It didn't come from adding vodka to morning juice. "Come on," she would urge. "Let's go, Josie."

She balked only at entering Alice's oversized walk-in closet and coming out again with hangers of dresses, skirts and pants suits over her arm. "I can't do it. Even the thought makes me nervous. It's as if she's in there."

"You know that's not true."

"I know she didn't like me. If one of those hatboxes came down on my head, I'd be terrified."

"Don't talk nonsense."

"You go on, then."

"All right," Josephine said.

Frieda watched, too, while she went through bureau drawers. "Sam will want this photograph album," she said. "Maybe not now, but later."

Frieda shook her head silently, then straightened her shoulders and said, "There's something especially lonely about used bras and girdles, isn't there. Why, Josie?"

"Probably because they were more personal than dresses or skirts—worn closer to the skin."

"I wish you hadn't put it exactly like that. What are you going to do with these? Do you want them at Good-will?"

"I don't know. I'll pack them with the rest and let them decide."

"God," Frieda said, "this is depressing."

"You want to go home?"

"Oh, no," Frieda said. "I'll finish up with you. By the way, I wanted to tell you, that was some powerful piece your husband put in the *Digest.*"

Josephine was too embarrassed to admit she hadn't read it. Frieda sounded so impressed; she was sure Ted had outdone himself writing about Alice. That night he had asked her himself what she thought of it, and because she had come home too tired even to open that week's edition of the *Digest,* she lied and said, "I was proud of you. Everyone in town will talk about it."

"You really think so?" he asked. It seemed so important to him that she promised herself she would set aside a quiet time and read it once the Daly house was closed. . . .

On the last day, when everything was either packed or given away, she and Frieda applied fresh makeup, combed their hair and had lunch together at the Town Line House.

The delicate chair creaked under Frieda's weight. Her round face was flushed with undeniable pleasure and she was perspiring slightly.

"Isn't this fun, Josie?" She stopped self-consciously. "I don't mean about Alice, of course. I mean having lunch together. It's been ages. Poor Alice. Forty-three years old! It scares hell out of me." She ordered a chef's salad without dressing, looked across the table for silent approval and continued, "When I was a kid, I mean really young, I thought people lived to be a hundred. When you got to be fifty, you had fifty years more, and Jesus! it was going to be forever before I got to that first fifty, which meant I had half a century left to go after that. That meant I was practically going to live forever. I'm talking too much, aren't I?"

"It's all right," Josephine said. She really wasn't listening. She was too busy looking at her, wondering when she'd find the opening to accuse her of being an unblushing liar—unless she really believed those lies.

"It's been so long since we've really talked," Frieda said, "except that I'm doing most of it. It's terrible about Alice, and I wish to God I hadn't said such shitty things about her all the time." She waved a protesting hand. "It's true, and confession is good for the soul. I said she was a mess. Well, she wasn't a beauty, God knows that, but from the way Sam went to pieces when they lowered her into the ground. . . . Frankly, I don't like anything about dying. The whole thing's shitty, and Alice is the first of our crowd to go. Sure, there was Louise, but that was an accident, so it doesn't count. What happened to Alice is different and I wish to hell she hadn't done it. It really was a lousy way to start the New Year off for everyone."

In spite of herself, Josephine couldn't keep the corners of her mouth from twitching. "I'm sure she didn't do it on purpose."

"No, of course she didn't. And isn't it just like me to say something so stupid?"

It was on the tip of Josephine's tongue to remind her that she had said a lot of stupid things lately. This was a perfect opening.

"After we get through here," Frieda said, "how do you feel about coming back to my house? Remember the draperies I had made for the living room? I decided they're better in the bedroom. All those birds and flowers are too busy, don't you think? So now I've got to get spreads to match, and Tony's going to have a fit."

"I thought the draperies looked nice in the living room," she said, and the moment was gone.

"How about it? Do we go to my house?" She smiled and said, "Josie?" She said the name as if it was a pleasure to roll it around on her tongue, as if it were a happy memory of times past.

"All right. We'll go to your house," Josephine said, and forgave her for the rumor. Without expecting to, she felt a certain protective tenderness toward Frieda. Because she needs me, Josephine thought, and when I'm not with her, I don't even miss her.

"By the way, Pete's invited the twins to his birthday party tomorrow."

"I'm surprised. They're so much younger."

"He's smart, your son. I guess he thinks it's better to invite them and ignore them instead of having them crash the party through the trapdoor in the cellar. What's the matter? You don't think he should have asked them?"

"I was just trying to decide how I'll decorate the cake."

"If I know you, it'll be a masterpiece. Remember the rodeo you did once? All those little figures twisted out of marshmallow? So much work!"

"I remember," Josephine said, but she was thinking of the work still left in the studio. She knew she couldn't put off going back even one more day. Tomorrow was her son's fourteenth birthday. She knew she had to finish the head. For the first time, she admitted to herself that she had been grateful to Sam for giving her a good and reasonable excuse to stay away from the studio.

She admitted to herself that she was afraid to be with Ben Goudy again.

Chapter Twenty-two

AT BREAKFAST Elsie said it was only fair that since she saved her own money from her allowance to buy a dart board for Pete's downstairs room, she should be invited to the birthday party. Pete said it wasn't actually a birthday party; only young kids had those. What he was having was just a "thing," because it happened to be his birthday.

Fran reached across for the butter, deliberately brushing close to Josephine and whispering, "Make him invite her."

Josephine gave a quick shake of her head to let her know she was not going to interfere.

"I suppose," Peter was saying, "I'll have to have a cake."

"No law says you have to," Elsie replied gravely.

"On the other hand," Ted said, saving face for his son, "it's an excuse to have one."

"That's true," Peter said.

"It is," Josephine said, "an excuse to decorate one."

"I wanted to talk about that decoration," he said. There was a shadow on the table where he leaned on his elbows, chin on his fists.

"Don't put your elbows on the table," she said.

"It's okay."

"It's not okay."

"You heard your mother," Ted said. "Get your elbows off the table."

"You shouldn't yell at him on his birthday," Elsie said.

Peter studied his sister with unspoken approval for a moment. Then he said, "I'm not inviting girls. You'd be the only one."

"I don't mind."

"I could use someone at the bar."

"Sure," Elsie said, "and I paid a lot for that dart board."

Ted stood up. "I'd like to stay with you nice people, but I have to get to work. And won't the school bus be here soon?"

"He really shouldn't have to go to school if he's got something contagious," Elsie said.

"What does he have that's contagious, pet?" her father asked.

"A birthday. I'm getting it next month."

Straightfaced, Ted looked at Josephine. "Are we going to risk an epidemic?"

"Absolutely." She smiled up at him and lifted her face to be kissed. Surprising herself as well as him, she put both arms around his neck, pulling him closer to her. When they broke apart, Ted looked self-conscious at this unexpected display of affection so early in the morning.

"Well," he teased, "are you planning to go away on a long trip after I leave?"

She didn't answer, wondering why she had kissed him as if she were saying good-by.

"I know why," Fran said wisely. "Because fourteen years ago today we were waiting to find out if Peter was going to be a boy or a girl."

"There was never any doubt about it," Josephine said. "I always told you it would be a boy." To her husband she said, "Will you be back in time for the candles?"

"I wouldn't miss that."

"That's another thing," Peter said. "I may not have any."

After Ted was gone, they talked about the cake. There would be a single candle for luck and nothing as stupid as a marshmallow rodeo. Since Elsie had told him on Christmas morning that he was getting a backgammon set for his birthday, he suggested that the decoration, in chocolate and white icing, simulate the board. He suggested leaving out the words "happy birthday," because that was stupid, too, and he thought Elsie's suggestion about not going to school was a good one. He didn't press the point.

In an offhand way, Josephine asked if Judy Ryder had been invited.

"I told you. Just boys."

"Except for me," Elsie reminded him.

"What about the boys in Judy's crowd?" Josephine was still trying to be offhand.

"I don't really like any of them. Judy's okay, but I'm not asking girls."

"I see," his mother said. It didn't sound like a question, but obligingly, as if it had been, he answered it. "Mitford isn't exactly around the corner. So I haven't seen her much. Practically not at all lately."

"I see," Josephine said again, hoping she was still sounding noncommittal instead of relieved. At the window Elsie saw the bus coming, and then they were gone, too.

"That head you modeled—does it really look like him?" Fran asked.

"You'll have to judge for yourself."

"You only have a couple of hours work on it."

"Less than that." She got out the mixing bowl quickly.

"Why don't you go to the barn first? Get that over with," Fran said.

"I'll make the cake first," and she knew she was putting it off again.

"I suppose you're right. It'll really give it a chance to cool and be easier to frost."

"That's it." She was sure that must have been her reason; it made the most sense. . . .

Then too soon the cake was upside down on the rack. Ingredients and utensils were put away. The kitchen was cleaned, the rest of the house was straightened. The only thing that made any sense now was to leave.

It was too mild a day for January. The sudden change in the weather drained her of energy even before she reached the barn. She parked in front and remembered back to a time when nothing disturbed the well-ordered regimen that regulated her days.

Inside the studio she sensed an air of expectation, an anticipation of something inevitable.

Ben didn't say a word to her. He waited until she hung up her coat and put on her smock before holding out a piece of paper.

"What's that?"

He didn't answer.

Is this, she wondered annoyed, the way he was going to act toward her on the last day?—not talking to her? Writing her notes, for God's sake? Months ago, she had accused him of sulking like a little boy when he couldn't have his way, but she never expected him to be so childish.

Maybe all good artists were not only basically egocentric, but childlike. It was their unashamed, constantly renewed awe of beauty, even the beauty of a single exquisitely drawn line.

She pulled the paper from him. She had never seen his handwriting and wondered why it looked so familiar, the distinctive hard, downstrokes of the pen. . . .

Women, she read, *have never been lacking in intellect, and it is well known that, when they are instructed in some subject, they are capable of mastering what they are taught. Nevertheless, it is true that the Lord did not endow them properly with the faculty of judgment.* Tight-lipped, she glanced up at him. He smiled encouragingly and she continued: *And this He did in order to keep them restrained within the boundaries of obedience to men, to establish men as supreme and superior.*

"By the way," Ben said, "I read what your husband wrote in his newspaper. Very effective."

Josephine was too furious to answer. She tore the paper in half and deliberately let it fall to the floor she had worked so hard to clean one day during Christmas.

Ben looked surprised. "Why did you do that? It was for you."

"Yes, I was sure it was meant for me."

"You thought I wrote that?"

"Or that you copied it somewhere for my benefit."

"I guess I might have if I had seen it first. But it was from Tish, along with a letter I got this morning. That's a coincidence, isn't it? She didn't know you were coming today. Neither did I. She asked me to give it to my 'little friend.' "

The torn pieces of paper were at her feet. With Ben watching she couldn't very well bend down, pick them up and save them to tape together again later. It was too bad. She really would like to have kept something that Tish had sent. The handwriting was like her work—bold and strong.

"Why did she refer to me as your 'little friend?' I'm as tall as she is."

"But more vulnerable."

Uneasily, Josephine wondered just how vulnerable she was. She wished she hadn't come, but it was too late for wishing. She was already there.

"I don't have much to do," she said. "Less than an hour's worth. I told you that last time."

"You told me a lot of things last time."

230

"Well," awkwardly, "I'd better get started." For a moment she hated him for being able to stand as cool and as still as one of his statues while she couldn't keep from twisting the button on her smock or pushing back hair that kept falling over her forehead. Even her blood seemed to be moving too quickly in her veins. . . .

"Did you have lunch before you came?" he asked.

"I had coffee at breakfast."

"That's all?"

"I don't need any more."

He broke the wide-legged stance finally, went over and sat on the bench near the stove. "Do you know Rodin's work?"

"I've seen some pieces in the Metropolitan."

"Rodin said that nature is a stern mistress. Try to play tricks with her and she'll punish you." He patted the empty space beside him. "You have to eat, Jo, if you want the strength to do good work."

In spite of herself she smiled back. "What about starving artists who turn out masterpieces?"

"Don't believe it. No one can accomplish anything really great on an empty belly, except maybe a revolution. And there have been very few completely satisfactory revolutions. I have the kind of cheese you like . . . and the bread. I have sardines and fruit. Are you really in such a damned hurry, if all you have left is less than an hour's work?"

From the moment she had come back to the barn, Josephine had felt self-conscious at being there, not so much because of what had happened last time but because of what John Cullen had told her some people in that small community believed.

"It doesn't really matter," she heard herself say in a clear voice.

"What doesn't?"

"If I stay a little longer."

"Good!"

That intense vitality, she thought, I'll miss that about him. I'll miss a lot I've had here, but it can't be helped. "I'll make fresh coffee."

"We'll have wine instead, since you're not coming anymore." He poured it into water glasses. "What'll we drink to?" he asked.

"Do we have to drink to anything?"

"I'll drink to you, Jo, and that first day you came here and asked me what I didn't like about your cake. Remember? 'It's only made of sugar,' you said, 'but when I did it, it was very important to me.'"

She had swallowed most of the wine. Her stomach must have been empty because the liquid rushed through her. She hoped he wouldn't ask her why it was so necessary for her to be home soon. She didn't want to tell him she had to decorate another cake. Nothing would force her to tell him that, but Ben had a way of making her say things she didn't want to.

"Ted was very fond of Alice Daly," she told him. That, at least, was a safe subject. She was glad she remembered it.

"Who?"

"Ted. My husband."

"Who's Alice?"

"The one who was in the hospital. My friend, the woman who died." Uncertain now, Josephine nodded.

"I remember," Ben said. "You were very upset when you came one day. You had seen something in her face."

"I knew she was going to die."

"That's right." He frowned. "I don't get the connection with your husband."

Patiently, she said, "You told me you liked what he wrote about her."

"I didn't read it."

"You said it was effective."

"I'm sure it was."

Confused, Josephine said, "What are we talking about?"

Ben went over to the shelves that lined part of the wall and brought back the current edition of the *Digest*. The newspaper looked out of place in this room. "I was talking about his editorial," Ben told her.

Lately she only leafed through the *Digest*. This particular week, with so many other things to do, Alice's funeral, closing the Daly house, Peter's birthday, she hadn't even opened it. It didn't mean she didn't care.

On the front page was a simple, passionate statement to the readers, telling them of the threat to the paper, asking them how important the *Digest* was to them and letting them know that unless it was, he didn't want to fight for it. But if they really wanted a free press that would continue to be independent politically, taking firm stands on community issues, stirring up controversy and setting the people to thinking constructively about their town, then somehow he would find the means to keep on publishing it.

Ben was watching her curiously. "This isn't the first time you've seen that, is it?"

"Of course not."

"You look as if it were."

"The truth is," she lied, "Ted read me the typescript after he wrote it. It isn't that it looks better in print, just more official."

The wine gave her courage to put down the glass and pick up the torn pieces of the note. "If I had known this was from Tish instead of you, I wouldn't have wanted to destroy it."

"Why would I want to write notes to you?"

"You wouldn't. It was stupid, worse than a marshmallow rodeo."

He raised his eyebrows. "I think the wine's gone to your head. Better eat something." He held the loaf of bread against him the way a peasant would, and cut a thick slice.

"Those weren't Tish's words, though. They don't sound like her. Who wrote it first?"

"A seventeenth-century art historian named Passari. He couldn't imagine there would ever be women painters like Mary Cassatt, Georgia O'Keeffe or Rhea Sanders." He dropped a piece of cheese on the bread. "Or sculptors like Malvina Hoffman, Louise Nevelson or Josephine Trask."

Josephine winced. "Please don't put me in such company. I feel foolish. I haven't done anything."

"That's true. But you could. Jo, the gods are generous, but they don't have much of a sense of humor. They won't laugh if you throw the gift they gave you back in their faces."

It had been a mistake to accept his wine.

"Where are you going?" he demanded. "I cut this bread for you."

"Then eat it for me. I have work to do. Then I'm going home. I have something even more important to do there. Decorate a cake."

"You have a right to feel foolish," Ben said. "You *are* a fool."

"Thank you. Now please don't talk anymore." At her worktable, she unwrapped the damp cloth that covered the clay head. Immediately, she forgot Ben was even in the same room.

Peter might not even like this study. It was less handsome than expressive. In the face was a restless vigor of a half-child, half-man. There was a sweetness in his eyes as well as the smile. Only there was something wrong with the mouth. There was no blood in the lips. There was no breath or voice behind them.

Always look for the secret of movement, Ben had cautioned her. *Otherwise, whatever you do will give the impression of something par-*

alyzed. What you have in your hands, Jo, is more than a motionless lump of clay. There's sorcery in it. You can make it act. You have the power to make it talk. What do you want it to say to you?

Josephine was startled to hear him asking her now, "Does your husband think you're beautiful?"

She couldn't think fast enough to say anything but, "Yes, Ted thinks I'm beautiful, but I don't believe it." That was honest as far as it went. There was no denying the uneasiness she felt knowing that the teacher was studying *all* of the pupil this time—not just her hands.

"You're right," he said. "You're reasonably attractive. I've seen better-looking, and plenty of women with more interesting faces. Tish has it all over you. But when you're working, Jo, there's a radiance about you I've never seen in anyone. You should work all the time, for vanity's sake."

"I've been given credit for more virtues than I have, but the one I know I have is lack of vanity. That's because I really don't care how I look. Reasonably attractive is good enough."

"Then care for something more important—the work."

"Please have the good manners," she said, "to let me finish the work I'm doing now."

"I'm sorry," Ben said. "You're right."

The close familiarity that happened so quickly between them became, even more quickly, a kind of hostile intimacy. They stood a short distance apart, and for a moment simply looked at one another. Josephine had the feeling they were stalking each other. Even when they were saying nothing, they seemed to be talking. She forced herself to get back to what she had been doing. A few minutes later, she was completely lost in it again.

When, finally, the mouth seemed to move, she heard Peter say, "Since it's my birthday, I suppose I have to have a cake."

"Of course," she promised quietly. "And I'll decorate it the way you want. You've given me an easy job. A backgammon set will be simple."

Once she was satisfied with the mouth, the rest was pure joy. One ear was too flat and needed depth to give it dimension. The hair was worked over carefully with loving fingers until she felt she could actually run them through living strands. "You should comb your hair."

"It *is* combed," she could hear him say. "Stop messing with it."

"Why don't you get a haircut? I thought I told you to get a haircut."

"I like it like this."

"Then comb it. You really should comb your hair, Pete. Look at the way it stands up in the back. It's silly. No, it's wonderful. This looks just like you."

"I'm through," Josephine said, putting down her tools. "I've finished."

"You're pleased?"

"I think so."

"Don't lie to me." He smiled. "You know you are."

She smiled, too. "Yes, I know I am." Without intending to, she said, "And I'm grateful to you, Ben, for teaching me what you have."

"Sculpture can't be taught. It was in you to begin with."

"Well," awkwardly, "I'd better take this and go. There's a lot I have to do before—"

As she lifted her arm to look at the face of the gold watch, he grabbed her wrist and held it in a viselike grip.

"You look at that goddamned watch of yours once more, especially if today is really the last time—"

"It has to be—"

"—And I'll pull it off and break it."

"I don't have to look at it to know I have to leave." She stood perfectly still, waiting for him to release her. Once he did, she massaged her wrist, not so much because it still hurt but because she wanted to rub away the feel of his hand.

Carefully, she wrapped the damp cloth around the clay head.

"You're going to leave it like that?"

"I've been too much trouble to you already, don't you think?"

"I warn you, Jo, don't say you've taken up too much of my time."

"I thought I'd ask someone at the university's fine art department about having it cast. Someone there will know."

"I was going to take care of that for you. I offered."

"And I appreciate it. I just told you. I've been enough trouble."

"And the figure you started?"

"It'll have to stay unfinished." She took off her smock and folded it. "It can stay an impression."

"Will that satisfy you? It's a good beginning. You could make it a lot more than just an impression."

The smock was already folded, but she made an even smaller parcel of it. "Unfinished," she was surprised to hear herself say. "If it satisfies you, it'll satisfy me."

"What's it got to do with me?"

"It doesn't bother you to leave the woman in the stone that way." It wasn't what she planned to say. She wondered frantically if there was any way to get back the words. . . .

Not once taking his eyes off her, Ben moved back and stood in front of his statue. If she wanted to look at him now, she would be forced to look at that piece of sculpture. He knew how she hated it.

It doesn't matter, she thought, because in a minute I'll be out of here and I'll never have to see it again.

"Why do you keep saying it's unfinished?"

"The woman is still half in the stone, isn't she?"

"I told you once, the woman I found in that block isn't strong enough to free herself. That's what's really locking her in. I'm not."

"That's a poor excuse to leave work undone," Josephine said bitterly, wondering why it was worth arguing about. "Never mind. I don't care."

"In that case, it won't matter what name I give it. From now on, I'll call it 'Josephine.'"

"Don't you dare. That . . . thing has nothing to do with me."

"Oh, come now. You recognized yourself in that a long time ago."

"That's not true."

"Then why don't you ever look at it? I've seen you walk by her with your eyes turned the other way."

"That day I cleaned up . . . *your* studio, I did look at her. I stood in front of her and looked at that ugly piece. . . ."

"Look at her now," Ben dared. "Then tell me that you don't see something of yourself there."

She did as she was told, fixed her eyes on the statue and was frightened to hear a great smothered sigh come from somewhere inside the cold marble body. Then it began to sob. It wasn't until Josephine felt the tears streaming down her own cheeks that she realized both the sigh and the sob had come from her.

"Tears won't melt marble."

It was humiliating, standing out in the cold before him, the way she was with nothing to cover her. If only she could remember how to crawl back into the stone, go back inside, so he couldn't see her. Her thoughts were running wild.

A moment later, even more wild, his arms were around her. "You have it in you to be great," Ben said. "Don't you realize it's like being chosen?"

236

Her voice became as rigid as her body. "Let me go. Please."

"I told you that I've made you dissatisfied with everything you are and everything you have. Why don't you admit it?"

This time she knew what the words meant. She had known it all along, really. Instead of admitting anything, she simply said, "And I told you once to let me go, Ben. I mean it."

He dropped his arms heavily to his sides. "Decide," he said, "how important your work really is to you. If it is, then I'm important, too."

His eyes held her more tightly than his arms ever could have. She felt as if she were drowning in them. She looked past him to the tormented half-figure of the woman, with spread fingers grabbing at a teasing freedom she couldn't quite reach. She recognized as her own the strong neck rising from rounded shoulders.

Part of me, she thought, is going to die today. She wasn't sure which part of her, and for a moment she was a bystander, curious to find out. She had the sensation of having moved outside her body, of waiting to find out whether Josie was going to leave the way everyone expected her to, or whether Jo was going to stay, the way Ben Goudy wanted her to.

"If you need your work," he said, "you need me."

"I need you," she said. Once she said those words, the others came easily. "I'm not the same person anymore. I need you, Ben."

"That's it," taking her in his arms again. This time she didn't hold herself rigid. The heat from his cheek was against hers.

She gave a sharp little moan and hid her face against him. "What a terrible thing it must be," she said, "to wake up in the middle of the night because your hands hurt."

"And that," he said, "is the least the gods will do to you."

She closed her eyes blotting out everything around them. She stood as still as stone, feeling his fingers move down her forehead, over her nose and out to her cheeks. The broad tips traveled down around her jaw to her chin.

It was as if he were modeling her face, carefully pressing out the features or gently dressing a wound. When they reached her mouth, the fingers outlined the contours and stopped. Josephine started to hold her breath until she realized she had none left to hold. Still without looking at him, she knew he had lowered his heavy head. Somehow she recovered her breath again, and almost choked on it. Then he kissed her.

At that moment, her eyelids seemed to fly apart. Her eyes were forced open and she realized she had lost her bearing. It was waking up in the middle of the night not knowing which side of the room she was facing. This big room kept spinning dizzily in space. If she didn't hold onto someone, she knew she would fall, so she held onto him.

Suddenly, they were somewhere else. They had to be, because she couldn't see the man kneeling anymore. Instead, there was the bed Ben hadn't wanted her to make up because it wasn't their bed.

"He's gone," she said.

"Who?"

"The statue."

"Jo," Ben said softly. And that made everything all right. She was Jo who came to the studio, closed the big door and left Josie outside. She was sorry for Josie who lived all those years with a husband, children and mother-in-law—but was always alone. There was a bitter sweetness in admitting to herself that Josie had always really been alone. *Even I wasn't with her,* Jo thought.

And everything that was happening now was all right. It didn't matter because it wasn't happening to Ted's wife.

And when his bare fingers stroked her bare neck, that strong neck rising from those rounded marble shoulders, she didn't try to control the tremor that spread through her. She was just glad because the stone man was finally with the unfinished woman. She was glad because she knew he was the only one who could make her feel complete.

Chapter Twenty-three

SHE HAD fallen like a plummet line into something uncontrollable and foreign. When it was finally over, there was a carved out hollow in the pit of her stomach and she had never been so hungry. That was when she realized she hadn't eaten since the night before. All she had had that day was coffee and too much wine—she couldn't remember what they had been celebrating. There was nothing to celebrate now. The only thing to do now was to go home. The fire had gone out in the stove. The studio was icy cold and the high window showed her that winter light was fading fast.

Her clothes were thrown on a chair. Josephine never treated clothing carelessly and had no recollection of how they got to be there. They looked terrifyingly alive—not merely discarded, but offended and accusing. The next hour, they seemed to be telling her, is going to be the worst hour of your life.

Quickly, with unsteady hands she got dressed again. Ben was asleep. Slow heavy breathing told her he was asleep; otherwise his smile, full of triumph and satisfaction, forcing his mouth open slightly, would have made her afraid that any second he would prop himself up on one elbow and talk to her. She had to leave before that happened. One word, 'Jo,' could pull her back again. It was Jo who had left caution and discretion outside the heavy door and closed it tightly.

Over the cracked porcelain sink was a small mirror. In it, a white-faced woman covered the lower half of her face with stiff, spread fingers. On one of the fingers was a wedding band. Everyone who really mattered in that woman's life called her Josie, and . . . Ted had promised to be back in time for the candles. . . .

As quickly as she could manage she left the studio, quietly in the half-darkness that threw a veil over the still and silent figures. The light that could change the color of marble was almost gone. There was barely enough left for her to find her way out.

Minutes after that, she made the turn that put the Goudy barn out of sight, and braked the car to a sudden halt. It bucked. The shock of it pitched her forward and the unexpected sound of her own crying was demoralizing. It was more like retching than crying.

When I open my eyes, she promised herself, it will only be two o'clock. Three, at the latest. It'll be a rush to get everything done in time for the party—decorate the cake, make the sandwiches—it'll be a rush, but I can do it.

Even while she made the promise, she knew it was one she couldn't keep. She looked at her watch, the small gold one Ted had given her . . . the one Ben had threatened to break. . . . Ten minutes to six and the birthday present for Peter, the only reason she had gone today, was half a mile back on her worktable. She had had so much trouble with the mouth. Finally, it curved upward in a quizzical young smile that was Peter. By this time, those corners must be turned downward in disappointment because she had forgotten all about him. For an insane moment she imagined the two of them: Jo's boy in the studio and Josie's boy at home, both faces full of terrible disappointment because she had forgotten them.

If a car came out of nowhere, she thought, the way it did with Louise, and tossed me into the air like a rag doll somebody threw away, then Pete wouldn't care where I've been all these hours. He would only care that I wouldn't ever come back.

The station wagon was alone on the lonely road. There were no other cars in sight. And if there were, she knew, she wouldn't really run out in front of it and let it hit her, because in spite of everything, she still wanted to live.

"When I got to the barn—" Josephine said softly, and had difficulty recognizing the sound of her own voice. Nervousness pitched it higher and thinned it out. At the same time, there was something reassuring in knowing she still had a voice. The last words she remembered saying out loud were: "I need you." For all she knew, saying that could have dried up her power of speech. "When I got there, Peter," she repeated, rehearsing it even more slowly, since it was necessary to convince herself first if she wanted to convince him, "Mr. Goudy and I had lunch together. We often do when I go for my lessons. It was my last day and there was plenty of time, Pete. Then I got to work, but it took much much longer than I expected. You see, I couldn't get your mouth exactly right. Please try to understand why I didn't bring the head home. I ran —when I realized how late it was. But you see, dear, Mr. Goudy had been sharpening one of his steel-edged tools and there was a bad accident. Blood everywhere . . ."

Or, she thought, I could tell him that Ben had been chipping off the outer shell of a plaster cast and was careful not to drive the chisel too deep and damage the surface. He was more concerned about his work than his hand . . . and there was blood everywhere. Or he was constructing an armature, cutting a pipe with a metal saw and something tragic happened. Or perhaps he had been on a platform that should have been braced and reinforced. It gave way and he fell. She had been frantic.

"There's no phone in the barn, Pete, so I couldn't call Dr. Cullen or even call home to tell you what happened. I wanted to drive to the square for help, but Mr. Goudy is a stubborn man. He wouldn't let me. He insisted he'd be all right if I stayed and helped him." Josephine took a deep breath.

I was never a blatant liar, she thought, sickened, but it's the only way I can go home.

As she started the engine again, she wondered why Ted hadn't come looking for her. If he had, he would have found a woman in the barn with Ben Goudy. Josephine wouldn't have recognized the woman as Ted's wife, but Ted would have believed it was. Each of them would have been right.

The best thing to do was not to think at all and she managed very cleverly—she wasn't sure how—to blow invisible glass around her thoughts and carry them like that in her head, undisturbed and out of reach. She kept her eyes on the road as she drove, held her head steady and was careful of bumps along the way. When she reached the house, she saw that Ted's car wasn't in the driveway.

Too quickly, she was inside the house where there was an uneasy quiet. Automatically, she hung up her coat. It took all her courage after that to open the door leading to Pete's room.

On the way down, she was acutely conscious of the tap of her shoes. They were loud, but not as loud as the beating of her heart. That was an odd kind of beat. It skipped and stopped. Not until she reached the bottom and saw Pete tossing darts at the board did she realize it hadn't been her heart thumping after all.

The guests had gone home. Only Fran, Peter and Elsie were left. The bridge table was littered with cardboard plates, half-eaten sandwiches and broken pieces of potato chips. There were scattered M & M's, and empty cardboard cups on the tile floor Pete had laid down so carefully. There must have been a small disaster because there was an ugly gash in the green felt on the pool table. The larger disaster was a single slice remaining from a cake she had left to cool. Someone else had gone to the trouble of putting chocolate icing on it.

Elsie, her narrow face looking older than usual, was sitting close to her grandmother. When she saw Josephine, she moved closer. "Hello, mother. I guess you're home now."

There was no mistaking that greeting for a welcome. Peter was kinder, saying nothing. He simply waited.

Fran didn't wait. She jumped up and said, "I told them something must have happened, honey. I told them that's why you couldn't get back on time for the party. Tell them," she pleaded, asking for help, "that something awful happened."

Josephine waited for her heartbeat to quiet and let her breathe normally again. When it didn't, she knew she couldn't put it off. It had never been so hard to say, "I'm sorry." She said it again and added, "Oh, darling, I'm so very sorry."

"Did something happen?" he asked hopefully.

"Yes, Pete."

Her answer brought the beginning of a smile from him. She had to strain to focus her attention on his face because it hurt to look at him. Go on, she ordered herself, tell him about the steel-edged tool Mr. Goudy had been sharpening and all that blood. Boys always appreciate hearing about blood. Remember the platform that gave way. Tell him how Mr. Goudy fell against one of his marble blocks. Tell him there was no phone, just a lot of blood.

She put both hands on his shoulders and heard herself tell him, "I forgot."

Behind her there was a gasp from Fran. Josephine didn't turn. Her eyes and her son's eyes were locked now. There was no looking any other way. "I've always told you that the most important thing is to tell the truth. If I don't believe it for myself, I had no right trying to teach it to you." She stopped, gathered strength and repeated. "I just forgot, Pete."

He stared at her, holding his head very still. She dropped her hands. There's still something wrong with the mouth, she thought dismayed. It's too set and too hard for Pete. She didn't recognize the mouth.

"One of the twins," Elsie volunteered, "I forget which—ate too much and got sick. Naturally. They're both pigs."

"Your cake, Pete—" Josephine began.

"I put a nice frosting on it," Fran said with forced cheerfulness. "And all he wanted was one candle. I knew where you hid the backgammon set. He likes it very much. You like it very much, don't you, Pete?"

He gave a short nod, but still said nothing.

"He's planning to give lessons. And charge for them. Didn't I always say I had an enterprising grandson?" She rattled on. "Some of the boys want to learn how to play, and our Pete's going to teach them."

"I had another present for you," Josephine told him.

"Give it to him," Fran said. Unspoken were the words: For God's sake, give him something. What's wrong with you anyway?

"I forgot that, too, when I realized how late it was."

"Too bad you didn't have an accident," Elsie said calmly.

"Elsie!" Her grandmother gave her a reproachful little slap.

"It's all right," Josephine said.

"I just meant so you would have had a good excuse. It would have been easier. I bet you wish you'd had an accident."

Josephine felt a lunatic fear mixed with a grudging, horrified admiration for this child. Elsie's perception was uncanny. Maybe she even knew what happened in the studio. . . .

It was a preposterous idea.

Unexpectedly, she saw Pete grin. "Hi, dad, I saved you a piece of cake."

Ted was at the top of the stairs. Maybe it was because she was looking up at him, but he appeared taller and more erect than when he left that morning, while she felt she was shrinking more into herself.

Maybe she could disappear altogether. . . .

"I'm sorry I didn't get back in time," Ted said. There was no real apology in his voice.

"That's okay," Pete said.

Josephine watched her husband run lightly down the stairs to the basement room. Only a man with no problems could run like that. She knew something good had happened to him.

Something had happened to her, too, since they were together that morning. She hoped he wasn't going to kiss her. It was too soon. Her face twisted because she was biting the inside of her cheek.

"You all right, Josie?"

"Fine." She tried not to stiffen when he did kiss her. The three of them, she knew, were watching.

"Now," he said, "somebody ask me why I wasn't here. I said I wouldn't miss the candles."

"Only one, dad."

"Manage to blow it out alone, Pete?" he asked straightfaced.

"Yup."

"Congratulations. I've changed my mind. I want to hear about the party first. Then I'll let you have my news."

"One of the twins," Elsie said, "ate too much and got sick."

"Well, naturally. They're pigs."

Out of habit, Josephine told him, "That's what Elsie said. It's not nice. . . ."

She had to tell him before they did.

"Ted—" she began.

"It was Pete's party," Ted said. "Let him tell it."

"It was great," Pete said. He kept going, warming up as he went along. Josephine listened, astounded. "You should have seen the way the cake was decorated—like a backgammon board. There were twenty-four points. I counted them. With a bar in the middle. And mom made the stone pieces of chocolate and white frosting."

His mother looked at him in gratitude, but he avoided her eyes.

"This all that's left?" Ted asked, picking up the single piece on the plate.

"You're lucky we were able to save that for you," Fran said. "We had a lot of boys here."

"I was the only girl," Elsie said. "I took care of the bar. Want a Seven-Up or Coke or anything?"

Ted told her he'd have a Coke. While he was drinking it from the open can, he glanced at the disorder and said it had obviously been a successful party. "Sorry I missed it."

So am I, Josephine thought helplessly. Oh, so am I!

"Mom made enough sandwiches, but the kids finished them."

"What kind?"

"All kinds."

Josephine let him lie because he was covering up for her in front of his father, and couldn't remember loving him quite so tenderly. Peter may not have understood why she hadn't been there, but he had forgiven her, for now.

"Who did that to the pool table?"

"Kenny. He's a clumsy ox, dad. I told him."

"Well, I think it can be fixed." He sat on the edge of it, dangling a leg. "Now for my news. If any one of you nice people goes down to the *Digest,* be careful not to trip over a very large carton full of letters and postcards." He smiled at his mother. "Want to guess what's in it? It was your idea, Fran."

"Oh, no, it wasn't," she protested, almost embarrassed.

"Didn't you tell me it was too bad I couldn't go from door to door asking people how they felt about our paper?"

"That's all I did," Fran said.

"It started me thinking, and the editorial came out of that. Doesn't she deserve the credit, Josie?"

"Of course," Josephine said. "And it was a wonderful editorial." She didn't tell him she had read it for the first time that day in the barn, or that Ben had been the one to give it to her. "Did it really bring results? Did you get that much of a response?"

Then he told them about the phone that had been ringing all day, and the bank loan that was going to make it possible to buy the press, and the man on the north side who offered deferred rent on a warehouse he wasn't using to house a new printing plant.

"And Mike Weiss, Josie—The *Examiner*—he told Bartlett he changed his mind. He's going with us instead. I know for a fact that the *Graphic* hasn't actually signed the new contract yet. I'm sure we can hold on to that one, too. I think we can get them all back, except for Stan Ryder and we didn't need him when we needed him."

"Are you going to be too excited to have dinner tonight?" his mother asked.

"I'm starved. I didn't have time for lunch."

"I guess he forgot," Elsie said pointedly.

"We'll go get dinner started," Fran said. "You stay here, Teddy. Look at the presents. There's a shrunken head somewhere."

"I don't believe it really is," Elsie said.

Upstairs in the kitchen, Fran turned on her, careful to keep her voice low. "What really happened? You should have been here."

"Peter lied for me just now," Josephine said. "He can't hate me too much."

"He didn't lie for you. He lied for his father. He didn't want his father hurt. I'm beginning," she said, "to know your children better than you do, Josie. Little by little I've taken your place here. I've given you that luxury you said you wanted—time for yourself, you said. Just what have you done with it?"

"You made it easy for me," Josephine said in an almost inaudible voice. "You made it easy for both of us—for Ben and for me."

Dumbfounded, Fran stared at her.

"You really want to know what happened there today? Do you really want me to tell you what made me forget where I was supposed to be?"

Fran didn't answer her at first. Then she said tonelessly, "I don't believe it—" which were just words.

"You did everything," Josephine said, "but close the door of that barn for us. Today I watched it slam shut. I didn't do a thing to try to stop it. I couldn't. Does that tell you everything you want to know?"

Her mother-in-law hunched her shoulders as if a cold wind had come into the room.

Josephine didn't feel shame at making this confession. She didn't feel anything but tired. She was sorry about a lot of things. It was too late to change them now. She was sorry she knew as much as she did about the human face. Everything the other woman was feeling was transparently on it.

Then, as she watched, she saw a light leave Fran's face. For a moment there was nothing on it. It was as if something inside her had turned it off. It was frightening. "And when you were ready to get dressed and come home again," it said, "I hope you washed your hands. Did you have the decency to wash your hands first, before you came home and put them on that boy?"

Hearing words come from a face like that was even more frightening. Josephine covered her own with those same hands.

"Are you crying for what you did to Peter?" Fran demanded. "Or to Ted?"

Dry-eyed and dry-lipped, Josephine said, "I've disgusted you once. I might as well a second time. If I cry any more today, it won't be for my son or for yours either. It will just be for me. When you come right down to it, people always cry for themselves."

Without another word, her mother-in-law left the kitchen.

Quickly, Josephine went after her and stopped her as she started up the stairs. "You won't tell Ted."

"You're so sure of that?"

"You don't want to hurt him any more than Peter did and that's going to be my excuse to myself for not telling the truth."

Halfway up to the room that until recently she called the guest room, Fran said, "Tell me honestly you haven't been happy these past fifteen years. Tell me to my face that Teddy hasn't made you happy."

"Being happy isn't always enough."

"It was always enough for me."

They faced each other like enemies. "And what have you got now that it's over?" Josephine asked. "Is that all I have to look forward to—living in another woman's house?"

Her mother-in-law let out a strangled sound and ran the rest of the stairs. She carried Josephine's voice up with her. "Is that what you call enough?"

Chapter Twenty-four

PETER WAS lying in front of the fireplace, his face pillowed on his arms. There was an insolence in the way he sprawled as if he relished the way his ungainly position was disturbing the neatness of the room. His mother had never seen him look so lonely.

The way I am, she thought, remembering again that being lonely has very little to do with being alone.

He hadn't heard her come into the living room, so she stood for a minute watching him. It was more than a week after the party, and the three who knew she had forgotten to be there treated her like someone who had visited a long time ago, then gone away and come back. Now they had nothing in common and it was hard to find things to talk about. Josephine, with a strained smile, did most of the talking. The only one who smiled back was Elsie. Josephine wished the girl would be more like her brother and grandmother. It was a smile that chilled her mother's blood.

I really am afraid of her, she admitted to herself.

Her mother-in-law obviously had no use for her anymore. Her son was uncomfortable whenever he found himself alone with her and invented excuses to get away.

Ben Goudy, she couldn't help thinking, would tell me I wouldn't even be missed in this house. It might be a relief for everyone if I left. Except

Ted, of course, and eventually even Ted would get over it. So what's keeping me here?

"Peter," she said, sounding almost apologetic, "do you mind getting off the floor? I want to vacuum."

Slowly, deliberately, he sat up, and she saw a mix of oddly shaped pieces of a jigsaw puzzle littering the rug.

There was nothing apologetic in his voice. "It's okay if I do it here."

"Did you hear what I said? Take that somewhere else."

He picked up a piece and carefully set it into place.

"What's the matter with your room downstairs? Isn't this the sort of thing you wanted it for? Work on that downstairs." It was a plea; not an order. Last week was still much too close to both of them.

The window was open slightly at the bottom. The smell in the air was mostly winter, but there was a far-off, faint scent of spring. For an instant, an edge of light from a strong sun played along the ridge of his mouth. Then he began to chew on the lower lip, spoiling the effect. It was a pity after she had caught it so perfectly.

With a start, she remembered that the mouth she caught perfectly was on another face that only looked like his. When that other used to look back at her, she could tell it liked her more.

Ben was right. The face wasn't the only mirror of the soul. Each muscle in the body expresses all the varieties of feeling. Peter shifted into a cross-legged position and bent over the puzzle. In shifting, he turned away from her. With his face hidden, his body told her everything he was feeling—disappointment in her and resentment of her.

"Pete!" firmly.

Startled, he turned and glanced up. She smiled and was pleased because for a moment the smile confused him and gave her the upper hand. What kind of a contest is this? she thought. The time she took to think it gave him the advantage again.

He seized it quickly. "This is almost done. After that, I'll glue it and push it under the grate until it dries."

Since he had never before been openly disobedient, she was at a loss to know how to react. "No—" she began.

"What's the difference? There's no fire in there. Why does it bother you?"

She said, "Pete . . ." once, and floundered, not sure what to say or do next.

Fran's coming into the living room wasn't unwelcome.

"Pete's making a mess in here," Josephine said.

He studied another odd-shaped cutout, then, disgusted, tossed it back into the box.

"Go downstairs with that," Josephine told him again. There was helplessness in her voice at his defiance. It was even worse having it show in front of Fran.

Peter looked to his grandmother. "Do I have to take it apart just because she says so?"

"Honey," softly.

His mother blanched. Once she would have chided, "She? Who's she? The cat's mother?" And he would have answered sheepishly, "Mom. I meant mom."

Now, still cross-legged on the floor, he swung around and shot back, "You. I meant you." There was daring in the simple pronoun. Spitting it at her the way he did made it almost obscene.

"Petey, dear," his grandmother said, as if she hadn't heard, "aren't those interlocking pieces?"

"Kenny brought it to the party. You were there. You remember." It was another obscenity directed at his mother.

Instead of answering, Fran said, "Why don't you get a spatula from the kitchen? Lift it up in sections onto a board. Do it carefully, and you can put it together again easily downstairs."

His mother watched him get to his feet.

"Are you going to see me off on the boat, Pete?" Fran asked unexpectedly. "It's a ship really. You could probably tell me the difference. I don't know much about these things."

"What ship?"

"Didn't your mother say anything to you? She knows all about it."

No, I don't, Josephine thought, and you know it. But I can guess. All she said was, "I was sure you'd like to tell him yourself."

"I'm going on a cruise with my friend, Anne Harris. She doesn't want to go alone and it does sound as if it could be enjoyable."

"You're leaving here?"

Fran hesitated for a moment before she said, "The cruise is only for a few months, honey. I'll send you and Elsie postcards from every port. We're going to stop in Port Everglades, Curaçao, Honolulu—"

"When?"

"Two weeks from Thursday." She deliberately avoided Josephine's eyes. "Remind me later. I'll show you the brochure—pictures of the stateroom and the dining room. There's a swimming pool on the deck. Imagine! If they have one of those shipboard costume parties, maybe you can dream up something unusual for me to dress up in. That is if I decide to participate. I'd probably feel foolish."

Immediately he suggested, "Your friend can string a bunch of cameras around her neck, pin colored postcards on a big straw hat and wear sunglasses—like a typical stupid tourist. And she could pull you with a rope."

"Pull me?"

"Sure. Tie it around your waist." He forgot Josephine was even in the room. They both seemed to have forgotten.

"Put some dark makeup on and wear a grass skirt," he explained patiently. "It would be like she was bringing you back as a souvenir from Hawaii."

Fran let out a spurt of laughter. "Me in a grass skirt! Oh, Peter!"

"It doesn't have to be real. Cut out long strips of newspaper."

Gravely, she thanked him for the suggestion. Josephine was as surprised as she was pleased at this unexpected show of imagination.

There was so much about her son she didn't know, so many things just beginning to develop, but he made it clearer every day that he intended to keep much of himself to himself and apart from her.

"Pete," she said, "I've changed my mind. Leave the puzzle for now. Move it somewhere else later. It's a lovely day after the bad weather we've been having. Don't waste Saturday indoors."

"Okay," he muttered, and didn't tell her where he was going or when he'd be back. He just left.

"When did you decide to take the cruise?" Josephine asked.

"I've been thinking about it," vaguely, "for some time."

"It sounds exciting."

"I didn't tell Pete, but when we come back, Anne and I plan to take an apartment together."

"Have you told Ted?"

"Not yet."

"You're part of this family now—" Josephine began.

"In case you hadn't noticed, I'm a terrible coward. If there's a chance there isn't going to be a family anymore, I don't want to sit around and wait for it to happen. That's one of the reasons I'm leaving. . . ."

Josephine wanted to shout at her: Stop it! Don't put ideas into my head.

". . . Isn't it lucky I still have those things in storage? I'm not exactly sure what I'll find, but it'll give me something to start housekeeping with."

She could imagine Fran sitting in the gold-upholstered chair with the kick-pleats and matching ottoman that was once Ted's father's favorite place to sit. On the wall would be the glassless framed print of three birch trees. She'd cry for the daughter who didn't live long enough, and even more for the son who lived long enough to have a faithless wife.

Josephine knew she'd better say something because too many unpleasant words were being spoken in the silence. "What can I say?"

"Is there anything you haven't already said?"

I could remind you how sorry you are for Frieda who drinks too much and ask you to be a little sorry for me, Josephine thought. There's a particular intoxication in that studio. For a long time I tried to fight it. I lost because it was stronger than anything Frieda gets from a bottle.

Fran wouldn't understand.

She could say: Whatever else I am, I'm not capable of deliberate cruelty. I never meant to hurt you.

Fran wouldn't believe her.

She could say: Right now I'm living in another woman's house, too, only it's worse for me than it ever was for you because this used to be my house.

Fran wouldn't care.

So instead, she said simply, "The children will miss you."

"They're your children."

Josephine felt the whole of her face harden at a reminder that was more of a rebuke.

"You don't understand," Fran said. "I have more than one reason for leaving."

"I shouldn't have told you what happened that day. Telling you was wrong."

"Is that what bothers you most? Never mind. Now it's my turn to shock you. What I have to tell you is worse in a way. I've had over a week to lie awake at night and think about it."

Josephine frowned, waited.

"One day, weeks ago, when you were gone, Ted came home. We talked about the things that were worrying him. Before he left, he kissed me very sweetly the way his father used to. I don't know exactly how long I sat there with my eyes closed, but I do know that I was really happy for the first time in years. Then your daughter came home. She called, 'Mother?' And I heard myself answer, 'I'm in here, darling.' "

"Don't tell me anymore. Please, don't—"

"Elsie didn't realize what had happened. Neither did I, completely, until I went upstairs. I had been ironing and I wanted to put away some personal things in your bedroom—underwear, nightgowns. . . . Suddenly I realized those weren't your personal things. They were mine." She gave herself a moment to find the courage to finish. "I really tried to convince myself I had made a mistake. I couldn't. Do you understand now my other reason for having to leave this house?"

Josephine understood something else. She knew why her mother-in-law had seemed to grow younger every day. Fran needed to be younger if she wanted to feel comfortable with a husband as young as Ted.

Two WEEKS later, Ted and the children were going to New York to see Fran off. "She'll be very disappointed when we show up at the pier without you," he said.

In bed, Josephine pulled the blanket closer. "No, she won't." She was sure his mother would be relieved. Even hiding behind polite words, they could still see each other.

"Sure she will. She's crazy about you. I can't get over the two of you keeping this a secret—the cruise and what she plans to do when it's over."

"You heard what she said. She wanted to wait until after Peter's birthday. She was afraid he might be upset."

"Is he, do you think?"

"It's possible. Have you noticed the way he's been acting lately? He won't do anything I ask him." She tried not to sound too upset herself. "He doesn't obey me at all."

"He's really a good boy, Josie. If he got a little out of hand it's my fault."

"Why yours?"

"I've been so involved with my problems for months, the poor kid's probably felt it. I'll make it up to him."

"You have nothing to make up."

He shook his head. "Even though he's acted excited about the paper, he's still only fourteen. I'm sure it bothered him when I wasn't here for

253

his birthday party. I did promise. Maybe that's why he's behaving this way. He'll get over it."

"About the party—" she began. As much as she wanted to say, I wasn't here either, the words wouldn't come.

"Are you a little angry with me, too?" he asked.

"Why should I be?" surprised.

He smiled slightly, as if it were difficult to smile at all. "I haven't been around much for you either."

"Ted—" she began again.

"Everything will be different from now on," he promised hurriedly, not really wanting to hear what she had to say. "That head you're making." He sat on the edge of the bed. "I didn't even ask to see your work. The truth is, I didn't even give it a thought until this minute. Where is it? Pete's room?"

"No. I didn't bother to bring it home. I'd rather not talk about it."

He stroked her forehead, pushing back a rebellious strand of hair. "Didn't come out the way you wanted it to?"

"No. I'd like to forget it. Don't be late. I sent a basket of fruit to the boat. Tell Fran I hope she has a wonderful trip."

"I'll kiss her for you."

Josephine smiled woodenly.

"You do think she'll be okay, living alone afterward in New York?"

"She's lived there before. And she won't be alone. She never intended to stay here indefinitely. Otherwise she would have got rid of those things in storage long ago."

He nodded. "And wouldn't have called it the guest room."

"She's doing what she wanted to do. Don't try to talk her out of it."

"She was a big help to you, though, wasn't she?"

"Yes," more to herself than to him. "She filled in, made it possible for me to be, well, mind-free, and time-free. . . ."

"Then you'll miss her."

"In other ways, but I can take care of my own house by myself."

WHEN THE three were gone, Josephine showered and went downstairs. She hoped Frieda didn't know she had stayed behind. She needed to be alone. She needed to go from room to room remembering how she felt when she decorated each one, hooked the fan-shaped rug in the foyer, made the curtains in the dining room, mended the leg on the chair in the den. She wanted to try to make friends with her house again. She planned to work very hard on it from now on, because nothing she did for it lately seemed to be appreciated. When she polished the silver, it didn't shine as much. When she waxed the furniture, it lacked luster. She watered the plants, but they were dying. The house was a living thing. Nothing she did for this one lately seemed to please it. She had the feeling she could do little to displease it either. It submitted without really responding. As if by unspoken agreement, they managed somehow, she and the house, to keep Ted from noticing. But she knew it didn't really like her anymore.

John Cullen came at eleven-thirty. It was unexpected, but she was always glad to see him.

She took his sheepskin jacket. "I never had a secret desire to move to California or Florida or Arizona," she told him. "I've liked watching the seasons change. It's always given me—" She shrugged and hung up his jacket.

"A feeling of continuance?"

"Something like that. But this particular time I'm beginning to wonder if winter will ever end. Who's come down with what on this street? Who's your patient?"

"You are."

She questioned him with her eyes.

"Ted called me."

"He didn't tell me."

"He was probably afraid you'd stop me from coming."

"I would have. There's nothing wrong with me."

"He said you had a bad night."

"Restless," she said. "That's not enough reason for you to make a house call."

He followed her into the living room where a long time ago she had transformed the space in front of the bay window into an indoor garden. There were tall plants in walnut tubs, small ones in clay pots.

Frieda once complained that she couldn't even get a cactus to live. And everybody says that's the easiest. "Do you talk to your plants, Josie? What the hell do you say to that philodendron to make it climb over the wall?"

"What happened to your philodendron?" John was asking.

"It's dying," matter-of-factly. She tapped her finger on the tip of a heart-shaped leaf. It fell. "You're the doctor. Maybe you know why they've all taken a sudden turn for the worse."

"From the looks of the soil, you're overwatering them."

She smiled sadly. "I gave them plant food twice this week. The directions said once every three weeks is enough."

"Don't you believe in following directions?"

"I am from that school of mothers," she told him, "who believe that you can buy love with food, so I'm overfeeding them and they're dying." She switched off the light tube under the louvre. "I don't want to fight them anymore. I don't care."

He frowned almost imperceptibly. "Didn't you want to say good-by to Fran?"

"I couldn't get out of bed. I didn't sleep well last night."

"I know. That's why I'm here."

"I'm sorry to miss the party—the one she and her friend are having in their stateroom—but I was just too tired. After a good night's sleep, I'll be fine."

"What's wrong, Josie?" he asked sharply.

"I wish," she said, "I could see you once in a while and not have you look at me with those X-ray eyes. I would like very much not to have you ask me if I'm all right or tell me that something's wrong."

"It's a pose. I try to make everyone think I really can cure them. Just between us, people are as well or as sick as they believe they are and die only when they get good and ready."

While he was talking, she had started the fire and they were sitting in front of it. "You honestly believe that?"

"In the terminal wards of the hospital, I've seen people wheeled in who have no medical right to live through the night. They're already dead; they just don't know it. Afterward, I've seen those same people get up and walk out." He smiled ironically. "I've seen others brought in, and I *know* I can make them well. I know exactly what to do, what medication to give, how much, how often. But there's a certain look in the eyes, and nothing I or anyone can do will save them. They've made up their minds to die instead, and they always do."

"Is this a new medical theory, or is it all yours?"

He looked at her intently. "It's been around a few years. About 400 B.C., Socrates said: 'There is not illness of the body, but for the mind.' "

"But deep inside every living thing isn't there that biological will to live?"

"Only if that biological will has a psychological drive."

"I don't understand."

"People have to have something to live for, Josie. In some circles, there's a belief that every man, and woman, has a mission. Once it's fulfilled, they have no further need to stay on this earth. Mozart died at thirty-six. So did Raphael."

"Think of what Mozart might have composed and what Raphael might have painted if they had lived longer."

"Maybe they gave all they had to give."

"I don't believe it," she said.

"Well," he said, "there's no way of proving it, is there?"

"What a deep philosophical discussion we're into, and it isn't even noon. Stay and have lunch with me."

"I would," John said, "if I didn't have to be in Douglaston."

She got up with him. "George Bernard Shaw," she persisted, "lived to be ninety-three or four."

"Four," John said.

"Well, he gave himself time to say all he had to say, didn't he?"

"I remember reading a copy of a letter he sent to a friend. He wrote he ought to clear out because his bolt had been shot and overshot. He had an accident that same day and died of complications not long afterward."

Josephine got his sheepskin jacket from the closet. "There's no arguing with you," she said lightly.

"I didn't know we were."

"I started snapping at you the minute you came."

"Only because you refused to admit anything was wrong with you."

"There isn't."

"In that case, there are patients who need me."

"I'm not your patient." She placed her hand on his arm. "But I want you to be my friend. I've always wanted that."

"Friendship, like love," John Cullen said, "is a creative instinct."

Quickly she withdrew her hand. "Are we talking about creative instincts now?"

"That particular one is a compelling force, Josie. You've always had it—in everything. Everything you touch comes to life. Just tell me something, why are you letting your plants die?"

She would have felt safer somehow if she could have closed her eyes and not looked at him. "I never had an instinct to be destructive," she said. "I loved those plants. I always felt I was growing or flowering with them. Now there's something belligerent in me that's willfully destroying them. I know I'm letting them die and I don't know why."

"After I leave," he suggested quietly, "put the light back on."

"All right," she said.

"And stop killing them with kindness. Be yourself."

The only trouble is, Josephine thought, I'm not sure who I am anymore.

"Since your husband did call me, and frankly, this was out of my way, I may decide to send you a bill."

"That's all right," pleasantly.

"Did I tell you my fees are going up?"

"Constantly."

"This time I may mean it, so why don't you tell me what's wrong?"

"I think it's possible," she heard herself say, "that I have arthritis."

"Oh?"

"What is it exactly? I'd like to know."

"Just like that? Standing here at the door?"

"I thought it would be some time before that could happen to me."

"Osteoarthritis," John said, "is part of the aging process of the body. It's most likely to strike joints that receive most use or stress over the years. But there's another kind—rheumatoid arthritis. Eighty percent of those cases occur between the ages of twenty-five and fifty."

Josephine managed a smile. "I think I'd rather hear about what causes it."

"It's one of those diseases whose causes are still unknown."

"Not very helpful."

"What makes you think you have arthritis?"

She looked down at her widened fingers. "Last night I woke up in the middle of the night because my hands hurt. It's a terrible thing, John, to wake up in the middle of the night because your hands hurt."

He took one of hers by the wrist and held it up. "This doesn't look arthritic. But come to my office and we'll check you out."

"I'm sure you're right. There's nothing wrong with me. I was probably sleeping with my fists clenched."

"Is that the way you usually sleep?"

"Lately I wake up and they're like that."

"If you don't want a checkup, come and talk to me anyway. I didn't prove it today, but I'm usually better at listening than I am at talking."

She opened the door for him. "I'll remember."

Without another word, he left her and she felt a faint sorrow at losing such a good friend. Josephine knew she wouldn't go to talk to him. There were too many things she was afraid she would tell him. Because something had happened to her, something had ended with them.

She closed the door and went back to switch on the fluorescent lights.

Chapter Twenty-five

PETER SHIFTED his bike to top speed.

Mrs. Haines, he decided, was okay. Anyway, she had always been nice enough to him, and if she was getting fat as those blimpy monsters of hers it was her business. He had heard her tell his mother about this Feiffer cartoon. In it was a father having a serious discussion with his five-year-old kid and he was saying something like: "Look, I have to tell you this isn't working out. When you were a little baby I thought you were pretty swell and I took you out in your carriage and all that and I've tried, and maybe you have, too, but this just isn't working out, so here's a check for ten thousand dollars. Go to Florida and leave me alone."

Mrs. Haines had laughed so hard, those big boobs of hers shook. It was embarrassing, but if a woman had big ones, he guessed she couldn't keep them from shaking.

His mother didn't have anything like that. Anyway, he didn't like to think of things like that when it came to his mother.

It was all right to think of Judy's boobs, though. The way she pushed those pointed hard things against him whenever she got close let him know she didn't care if he did think about them a lot.

He shifted his bike into first because he had come to the hilly stretch on the way to Mitford, and thought how great it would be if he could get a better bike—maybe not a top-of-the-line like a Motorbecane Grand Record, but a Super Mirage wouldn't be bad either. And maybe he could, now that they were going to do their own printing and be part of a cooperative. Peter wasn't exactly sure how that was going to work, but it sure put his father in a good mood lately. He had been in a rotten one most of the winter. Never really lousy, though, because his father was generally easygoing. You couldn't exactly push him around, but you could always get around him if you used the right technique, and that was practically the same thing.

He pedaled faster. Judy had told him the party was going to be at eight-thirty. The Ryders were leaving at eight and if he got there before anyone else, he could help her set up the food in the recreation room.

"And we'll be alone for a little while," she had promised.

It was the same as promising he could cup his hands and cover those hard-pointed boobs that really weren't hard at all when you pushed them in a little. If he could buy a better bike, he could get there faster. With money, you could buy a lot of things.

He thought of the father in the cartoon giving the kid ten thousand dollars to go to Florida so he could get rid of him. For ten thousand bucks, he thought, anybody could get rid of me. He wondered if he could make it to Florida on a bike. He would take out a few hundred first, buy a top-of-the-line and head south.

He pressed to reach the crossing and avoid the changing light.

The reason the cartoon was funny was that no five-year-old kid could make it alone to Florida or anyplace else. At five you're pretty stupid. But Peter knew he could make it. In the first place, he looked more than fourteen. It was too bad he had told Judy Ryder he was fifteen now. If he was going to lie, he could just as easily have said sixteen and she would have believed him.

With ten thousand, less the price of the bike, it might be fun to try to go it alone. He passed the sign that read, "MITFORD, A GOOD PLACE TO WORK, LIVE AND BRING UP YOUR CHILDREN."

What stupid bastard put that up? He was glad Ditchling only had a sign that said "A Friendly Town" and nothing else. He wondered if you went through New Jersey if you biked to Florida. He used to know a boy who moved to New Jersey. They had been in the sixth grade together and had been pretty friendly. His name was Eddie something. If he couldn't remember the last name and didn't know where in New Jersey, he'd better forget the whole thing. Besides, he wasn't sure if you had to go through New Jersey. It was south. That much he was sure of. He wasn't too great in geography. He was even worse in algebra. If he didn't flunk that this term, plus French, he'd be surprised.

And maybe his father would say something about that, but his mother wouldn't.

That was one good thing about the way they were with each other these days. He could get away with murder and she wouldn't say anything. Well, maybe not murder exactly, but a damn lot. She was still feeling cruddy about not bothering to turn up on his birthday. Never mind forgot—just not bothering. He was sure she had remembered. You don't forget something like that, particularly when you spent so much time the same morning talking about how to decorate a cake. It was probably too much trouble to do it the way he wanted it. If it was that much trouble, she shouldn't have asked in the first place.

It wasn't that he had wanted her to hang around. Nobody wants his "mommy" to hang around when a bunch of kids get together, but not to show up at all and calmly say she forgot! She said she had forgotten something else, too. Something she had been working on in the barn with old Goudy's nephew, the one who walked in on them last fall. He hadn't bothered to knock that day. Another one who didn't bother! They were two of a kind—Ben Goudy and his mother. And who cared about either one of them?

Anyway, if she really had made something for him, where was it? The absolute proof it never existed was that she never got it afterward to give to him. Not that he wanted anything from her anymore. It was fine with him the way things were. When he graduated high school, he'd be damned if he'd go to the university and commute. The hell with that. In the first place, who wants to go someplace where everyone would point at you and say, "So you're Josephine and Ted Trask's son. My my my, we hope you'll do half or even a quarter as well as *they* did yah yah yah." The best thing was to go someplace far away. The farther the better, and the sooner the better because ever since January—and here it was way into March—he wasn't that happy being at home anymore.

Sometimes he felt he and his mother were in the middle of a big arena, and they were walking around in circles waiting for somebody to make the first move. And Elsie was sitting in a front seat watching and eating popcorn. Well, not actually eating popcorn, but she gave him that impression—smiling and waiting and not really caring which one of them won.

262

The only good thing about this sort of undeclared war he was having with his mother was that she didn't bug him about where he was going or when he'd be back. It was like she didn't dare and that made him feel even taller. Tonight, for instance, she had said, "Peter, your father's at the new plant. He won't be home for dinner. I'd rather you'd wait until he comes so we can talk about whether or not it's all right for you to ride all the way to Mitford in the dark."

"I've got lights," he reminded her, "and reflectors."

"I'd still rather you waited until he came home."

"What time?"

"I'm not sure."

"Well, I'm sure what time I have to be at Judy's. And if I want to make it, I have to leave by eight o'clock."

She hadn't tried to stop him. Not that she could have, but she hadn't even tried. It was crazy, but he wished she had.

The Ryders lived in a big brick house on Stafford Street. It was a much bigger house than theirs, but the Ryders had more money. Judy once told him it was her mother who had most of the money and she never let Judy's father forget it. Peter didn't think it was the sort of thing you talked to outsiders about, but in a way that was one of the things he liked about Judy. She didn't hold back. In anything. He didn't think about that part of it too much. It made him nervous. Once he almost fell off his bike thinking about it.

He was a little nervous in a different way about tonight. Judy talked a lot about the parties she threw for her special crowd. Maybe she didn't actually talk, but she hinted a lot about how sensational they were and how much he'd like them if he was lucky enough to get an invitation.

Peter met some of that crowd only once, on the night Judy starred in the school play. When the play was over, her father puffed down the aisle with a bunch of red roses and he tripped. Everyone laughed except Judy, who handled it like a real pro. She took the flowers and pretended he hadn't even embarrassed her. Afterward, they had what Mrs. Ryder called an opening night "fête." There was an ice-cream cake and Peter remembered his piece had part of the *T* from the word *STAR*.

He had kept pretty much to himself that night, afraid someone would ask what grade he was in at the Ditchling school and find out how old he was.

All those other times he had seen Judy he had been alone with her, which wasn't bad either. It was pretty good actually, because the Ryders were always going out when he came. They told them to enjoy themselves watching television or whatever, and the whatever had been something else! To put it mildly, he was getting to know Judy extremely well. When he thought of how well he could get to know her, there he was, getting nervous again.

Then she invited him to this party. He tried not to show how pleased he was being part of what you might call the inner circle. Judy probably felt he was mature enough to fit in.

Peter swung his leg over the bar of the bike as he brought it to a stop at the side of the house. It surprised him to see several other bicycles leaning up against the big oak in the front yard.

The entire house, even the recreation room, where the party was supposed to be, was dark. It didn't seem possible that he had made a mistake and come on the wrong night. And if it was the right night, why were so many others here ahead of him? He was supposed to be first.

"You're the last," Judy told him, annoyed, when he rang. She opened the side door and gracefully slid out. Peter thought it was funny that she was wearing a coat.

"What do you mean last? You said eight-thirty."

"Eight. I told you they were leaving at seven tonight."

"I'm sorry."

"If you can't be punctual, Petey, better forget the whole thing and don't expect to be invited again. We like to do things together and on time."

"How many times do I have to apologize? Okay, I made a mistake. If you want me to go home, say so."

She thought about it for a moment, then said, "You can kiss me. After that we'll go inside. I'm freezing."

Pete didn't understand why she should be freezing since it wasn't that cold. He was wearing only a jacket over his best suit and there she was all wrapped up in a red wool coat. It wasn't too dark for him to tell the color or how good she looked in it with that long silky black hair and that white skin. He decided kissing her wasn't a bad idea. When he did, the coat flew open and he realized with mixed horror and excitement that the white skin went straight down to her high-heeled shoes.

"Hey," he said, which wasn't absolutely the most brilliant thing he could have said, but he was damned if he could think of anything better.

"What's the matter?"

"You're naked."

"Why do you suppose I'm wearing this? You didn't expect me to come out without anything on, did you?"

Speechless, he shook his head.

"It's your fault," she said. "No one asked you to be late. Everyone had clothes on at eight o'clock. Even me."

Somehow, Peter managed to find his voice. "What do you mean, everyone?"

She opened the door she had let close tightly behind her and drew him inside. "Come on. Join the party."

Inside it really was dark. There was weird music coming from the stereo, thin squeezed-out notes—fingernails-on-glass kind of music.

At first he could see only tiny red dots floating in the room, and shadowy figures moving slowly in a kind of weird dance to match the music. The smell was something he recognized immediately—sweet and heavy; it sat in his throat. It wouldn't go up or down. It just sat there and made him feel sick. He'd smelled it in the locker room of the school more than once. More than once someone would offer him a joint. He always said, "No, thanks."

When he was a lot younger, his mother once said, "If you're ever dared to do something, Pete, and don't want to, sometimes it's easier if you have a comeback. If anyone ever calls you 'chicken,' try saying, 'I'd rather be a live chicken than a dead duck.'"

He never happened to use that, but he supposed it wasn't bad advice for a young kid. At fourteen, he could simply get away with "Forget it. Thanks, anyway." If you said it as if you meant it, nobody bothered you.

Up until tonight, it had worked. Up until tonight, it hadn't been Judy who was doing the asking.

She threw off her coat and giggled. "If you feel overdressed, get with it." She reached out, and damned if she didn't pull down his zipper, and not the one on his jacket.

"Hey," he said, and pulled it up again.

"All right, do it yourself, but hurry up. Then I'll introduce you."

"Judy," he said with exaggerated dignity. "I think maybe I better make it another time."

"What are you talking about?"

"I just don't think I'd fit in, that's all."

The figures were getting clearer by the minute. Peter had to concentrate on Judy's face, so he wouldn't stare at them. Concentrating on her face and nothing else wasn't that easy.

"I think you're scared."

"No, I'm not."

"You keep swallowing, but you're not eating anything. Don't tell me you're not scared."

"I'm not," he insisted again.

"Well, what are you?"

He was stunned to hear himself admit, "I'm fourteen. I'm just not ready for this yet. Maybe when I'm fifteen. Maybe even next month. But right now I don't want to stay."

He didn't tell her what else he wanted to do. He wanted desperately to go to the bathroom.

"Fourteen," she said. "No kidding? You act a lot older. Never mind. I won't tell them. Come on. Get with it, Petey. Don't be a fuck-up. . . ."

He was afraid she was going for his zipper again so he turned, opened the door and ran back to where he had left his bike, got on unsteadily and rode furiously in the direction of Ditchling.

It's a good thing it's night, he thought. During the day, he could ride with no hands if he wanted to. At night he couldn't afford to think of anything except keeping his eyes on the road and everything around him. His father had written more than one editorial about night bicycle accidents.

His father! Peter hoped he wouldn't hear about this. It would be even worse somehow if his mother did. She had been right about Judy Ryder. Not that she had ever actually talked against her or tried to get him to stop seeing her. She was too smart for that, but she had her own special way of making it obvious she wasn't happy when he mentioned casually he was going to Mitford. If he wanted to be honest, it was one of the reasons he had gone out of his way to see Judy so much. It bugged his mother. In a way, what happened tonight was all her fault.

Instead of taking Route 4 to the highway and then off to Main Street leading to Ditchling, he took the Old Country Road. It was darker and there were no lights except for his bike lights and the moon. Ordinarily he wouldn't have chosen that route, but he still had to go to the bathroom. It was safer to piss against a tree on a deserted road than on the highway with cars driving by.

Afterward he didn't feel much better. He got on the bike again and started pedaling. Damn bike. It kept sticking and skipping and now there seemed to be something wrong with the steering.

266

"Mitford," he shouted. There was no one within a mile to hear him. "A good place to live, work and bring up your children."

If what he'd seen tonight was a sample of the way they brought them up, the hell with Mitford. "The hell with Mitford," he shouted louder because he could imagine how they were all laughing at him in Judy's recreation room.

Then he made the turn that took him to the River Road. There were only a few scattered houses on the River Road—Rama Kennels on a slight rise (Peter could hear dogs barking), then a wooded area for about four hundred yards, then the white colonial house where he and Elsie had gone once with his mother to look at antiques. That seemed a hundred years ago. Elsie probably couldn't remember it at all.

In those days, they had been dragged from one place to the next because they were too small to be left alone. They never knew where they were going; they just went. He could still remember the antique lady who sold them the andirons. She had given him a tin soldier. He still had it somewhere. She gave Elsie a paper fan. Elsie probably lost that the next day. He had the kind of stupid sister who couldn't keep anything without losing it or breaking it or just generally messing it up so it wasn't any use to anyone.

He was pretty good about things. Right now he was pretty good at thinking of anything except what had happened in Mitford. Think about the antique lady instead. Wave to the light in the second floor bedroom where she was probably getting ready for bed. Wave even though she didn't know anyone was there. No. Better keep both hands on the handlebars. There really was something wrong with the steering; the bike swerved to the side where frost had melted leaving the ground moist and spongy. He had to work harder to get it back on the road.

The River Road Inn. They had all gone there last summer, including his grandmother who had lived with them. The inn was boarded up. It probably opened only in season.

Peter wondered how much farther it was to Highland Avenue. There were lights on Highland Avenue. The next thing he knew, he lurched forward over the handlebars. He heard the crash of the bike going down and saw the lights go out.

"Great," he said aloud. "Just what I need to make a perfect evening."

He had a sudden, searing thought. He was actually sitting where he was because a giant hand had picked him up between a huge thumb and forefinger and deposited him in the middle of the brambles because of all those nights with Judy when his own hand had been warmed in places maybe it had no right to be; and if that wasn't a stupid hang-up from Sunday school, he didn't know what it was! He sure had hated Sunday school. Talk of being bored, bored, bored. He was glad when he wasn't forced to go anymore, but maybe this wasn't exactly the time or place to think about that. He could still feel that huge thumb and forefinger pinching the scruff of his neck.

The underbrush was spotted with light from the moon. Then the moon disappeared and there was blackness all about him. Peter tried to get up. That was when he realized he had hurt his knee.

It was funny that very often something didn't hurt at all at the time you hurt it. It was after you realized you had that it bothered you. Then the pain was awful and getting worse.

Gingerly, in the dark, he felt his knee. The pants to his best suit had a big hole. Inside the hole he could feel blood.

When the moon finally reappeared, Peter dried his bleeding knee with his sleeve. He had no handkerchief, and his best suit was ruined anyway. Try to explain that to his mother if he ever got home. He wasn't sure he ever would.

With great difficulty, he managed to stand. With even more difficulty, he righted the bicycle. It was impossible to tell how much damage had been done, and it didn't matter now, since he couldn't ride it anyway.

Once back on the road, he limped slowly and painfully, pushing the bike along with him, using it for support. When he came to the next house, he would ring the bell and ask to use the telephone. With luck, his father would answer.

The next house, when he finally reached it, looked deserted. It was, Peter remembered, the old Goudy place. That meant that the lighted windows in the adjacent barn marked the place where Jess's nephew was living. Of all places for him to have to ask for help—the place his mother had been on his birthday.

In a way, he was curious to find out for himself what was so damned fascinating for her to have forgotten what day it happened to be or what time it happened to be.

He let the bicycle fall noisily in a heap. At the door, he felt with flattened palms for a bell. If there was one, he couldn't find it, so instead he kicked with his good leg.

Putting all his weight on the bad one hurt like hell. Then slowly, the heavy wooden door creaked on its hinges and opened. In the artificial daylight that flooded the studio, Ben studied him.

"Why, you're Jo's boy."

Peter never remembered anyone calling her that before, but he was sure Ben Goudy meant his mother. "I've had an accident with my bike and I'd like to use your phone, if it's okay."

The door opened wider. "Come on in."

Inside, the barn was like a museum. Peter looked around at the figures. He wondered why these didn't look naked and Judy and her crowd did. Maybe it was because these weren't real. Somehow he didn't think that was the reason.

"I was working," Ben Goudy told him. "I didn't expect company."

"I'm not company," Peter said ungraciously. "I just want to use your phone."

"Sorry. You can't."

His knee really was hurting now. He limped to a bench and sat down. It was a mistake, acting bad-tempered and demanding, but damn it, his leg was killing him. And now Ben Goudy wasn't going to let him use the phone?

"I don't have one," he explained. "If I had, you'd be welcome to it."

"Oh, great. That's just great."

"What happened to you, boy?"

"My name is Peter, if you don't mind."

"This isn't a road to bike on at night. There are no lights out there."

"No kidding."

"Be a fresh kid with me," Ben said roughly, "and I'll toss you out on your ear. I didn't invite you here in the first place."

"We didn't invite you," Peter reminded him, "when you came to our house last September. That rainy day. Remember?"

Ben stared at him for a few seconds under those thick reddish eyebrows. Then he laughed good-naturedly. "Touché."

"Look," Peter told him patiently, "I've got trouble enough right now without having you talk in French. I'm flunking French."

Then Ben Goudy was down on one knee, gently examining Pete's injured one.

"Did you pose for that statue?" Peter asked. "How could you copy yourself?"

Ben smiled. "I didn't pose for it. I had a model. But in everything an artist does, I think he puts a little bit of himself."

"You sure put a lot of yourself in that," Peter said. "For a minute, when you bent down, it was like the statue. . . ." He shook the wild thought from his head. "Forget it. I'm feeling dizzy. The truth is, I don't know what hurts more, my knee or my stomach."

Ben got a first aid kit. "You hurt there, too?"

"I never got dinner. I'm starved."

"I think I can find something after we fix the knee."

Once the bruise was washed, swabbed with antiseptic and bandaged, Peter started to feel better. He was beginning to feel very good again by the time he curled his fingers around a hero sandwich—a long length of fresh Italian bread split up the middle and generously filled with slices of cheese, cold roast beef and salami. He didn't like coffee and didn't want beer. There wasn't anything else to drink, so he settled for a glass of spring water.

The evening was turning into less of a disaster. This guy was a lot nicer than Peter had expected him to be—really interesting. And he had plenty of talent. There was enough evidence of that. He hesitated before asking, "Did my mother do any of this?"

"Everything you see is mine."

Suddenly Peter wasn't hungry anymore. He set down his unfinished sandwich. "Most of the winter, she was busy coming here all the time. She must have done something."

"Not enough," Ben Goudy said. Somehow he didn't sound as friendly anymore.

"She was here on my birthday. That was the last day she was here."

"Was that your birthday?" Ben asked; then he remembered. "Yes. I remember she told me."

"What I want to know is why did she lie?"

Ben stared at him again, then said quietly, "About what?"

"A present for me. She said when she left here she forgot about it. I think that's because there wasn't anything in the first place. That's it, isn't it? Not that it really matters."

Ben Goudy stood very still for a minute, looking altogether like one of his stone people. Then he went to the other side of the barn. "Come here."

"It's hard to walk."

"Come here anyway. It's worth it."

Peter joined him at a wooden turntable and watched him slowly unwrap the damp cloth that covered a clay head.

"What do you think?"

Instead of answering, Peter turned toward the table and looked at himself; then he said, "It looks like somebody cut off my head. So how come I'm smiling?"

"Be serious. Do you like it?"

"She did this? My mother?"

"Yes. She did this."

"Pretty good, isn't it?"

"It's better than that."

"I mean it really does look like me."

"A snapshot can look like you. This practically breathes the way you do."

"It's weird," Peter said.

"No it isn't. It's wonderful."

"How could she have done that without having me pose for it?"

"I suppose," Ben said, and he seemed to be choosing his words carefully, "because she loves you. If it's ever hard for you to remember that, Pete, try to remember this head, and then try to forgive her."

Peter looked at him sharply. Obviously Ben Goudy knew everything about how she had forgotten to be home on his birthday, forgotten the present. "It must be hard," Peter said, "making something like this."

"It took dozens of very precise drawings first, and then I saw her destroy other heads before she was finally satisfied."

"No kidding?"

"When she worked," Ben told him—but now he didn't really seem to be talking to him—"she had no sense of time. It didn't exist. In the beginning that frightened her."

"Do you read much sci-fi?" Peter asked.

"What? What did you say?"

"Science fiction."

"Oh. No, not much."

"You ought to read *The Time Machine*. H. G. Wells. It's great."

"I'm sure it is."

"If a person loses time, if that person doesn't know how it happens, can't actually explain it, then you can't really blame that person for losing it, can you?"

"I suppose not." But Peter knew Mr. Goudy was only being polite. He had no idea what he was talking about. It didn't matter, because he knew. He finished the sandwich. "You don't happen to have anything for dessert?"

"There's an apple. And a doughnut I was saving for breakfast."

"That'll be okay."

"After that, I'm going to take you home." Deftly, he tossed the apple to him. "It's been a long time since I've seen your mother," Ben Goudy said.

Chapter Twenty-six

THE VOICE over the telephone was like the man, heavy and florid. "Now don't get me wrong, Ted. I'm not saying I'm not goddamn disappointed and disgusted Judy let herself be influenced by a bunch of perverts, and I goddamn let her know it. First thing tomorrow Mabel's packing her up and she's going to live with my sister in Cleveland for a while."

"I don't believe this."

"It's true all right. If Mabel hadn't developed one of her migraines so we came home early, we never would have walked in and found them naked as jaybirds, the lot of them. I did what I just told you, what any levelheaded father would have done under the circumstances: marched them up the stairs to the living room the way they were—sort of a come-as-you-are party of my own—and called their folks one by one while they sat there, not saying a word, trying not to look at each other. I made my Judy sit right there with the rest."

Close by, Josephine listened to Ted's side of the conversation.

"Stan," Ted said, "you're an ass. If no one's ever told you that before, you're an unmitigated ass."

"Now wait a minute," Stan Ryder said. "Tonight I blew that crowd to smithereens the same as if I had thrown an atomic bomb into the middle of them. Dollars to doughnuts they won't be able to look each other in the face again. Not after tonight."

"Or at themselves," Ted said. "I don't know how much damage you did to those kids tonight, but I'm glad I don't have it on my conscience."

"You saying what they did was right? Because if you are, you're as much of a pervert as they are and I don't know how they sucked a good kid like Judy into anything sick as this is."

"I'm saying what you did was worse. . . . Look, why the hell call me about it anyway?"

"What is it?" Josephine asked, puzzled.

Ted waved her quiet with a quick impatient shake of his head. "You suggesting I run a lead story in the *Digest?*"

"That's exactly why I'm calling. Harris Bartlett and I got to be pretty chummy. I can still get a local tidbit into the *Leader,* even if I don't own it anymore. Print one word about tonight and I'll have another piece written. I'll tell how your precious Peter was here, too."

"Pete?" Ted said in a dazed voice. "Our Pete?"

Josephine saw him grip the telephone so tightly the veins on the back of his hand swelled. "Please," she said, "what is it? Did something happen to him?"

"I don't know how," Stan said, "but that slippery young eel managed to get away before I could round him up with the others. But he was here all right. Judy told me, and by God, whatever other mistakes the kid makes, she never lies to me. In her whole life, she's never really lied. At this point in time, it's not much, but it's something. . . ."

After Ted hung up, Josephine listened with quiet horror while he repeated the entire conversation. Then she told him simply, "Pete wasn't there."

"Judy Ryder said he was."

"I don't care what Judy Ryder says. Pete didn't get away because he wasn't there."

"Then where was he tonight? You never actually told me. You let me think he rode over to Kenny's on his bike."

"Because Kenny lives at the end of the street. I didn't want you to worry, knowing how far Pete was going to ride at night. I knew you would, and please keep your voice down, or you'll wake Elsie."

"Then he did go to Mitford. Come on, Josie, admit it."

"Yes, then he changed his mind," she said stubbornly. "If Stan didn't find him with the rest, it's because he wasn't there."

"Intuition, or wishful thinking?"

"A little of both."

He was pale and serious. "Because you think you know him? God, Josie, how well do any of us know our own kids? The Ryders thought they knew Judy."

"Peter wouldn't get into anything like that."

"Then where is he?"

"I don't know, and it's where he is now that bothers me a lot more than where he was earlier."

Ted went to the telephone again. "I'm calling the police."

"Don't bring the police into this yet."

The phone rang again. Ted made a grab for it. "Pete?" he said into it. "Where are you?"

"Hi," Frieda said brightly, "what's happening?"

"We don't know where Peter is, Frieda."

Josephine sighed. Now Frieda was going to get involved and enjoy every minute of it. "Tell her she doesn't need to come."

"I'll be right over."

Resigned, Josephine opened the breakfront to get another cup. Just before Stan Ryder called she had plugged in the percolator. They had planned to sit in front of the fire and talk about the hour spent earlier that day in the small two-story brick building on the north side of town across the field from the railway station.

"Why two more cups?"

"I only meant to take one. I wonder why I did that."

"Maybe you figured Tony's coming, too."

"Maybe." She put the extra bone china cup on the mantle, uncomfortably aware that it appeared to be patiently waiting to be taken down again. "Don't call the police," she heard herself tell him again. "Pete's all right."

"Intuition again?" He waited for an answer that didn't come, then went to the window and stared into the darkness.

Looking at his rigid back, Josephine remembered the person he had been earlier that day. . . .

The mustiness of the old warehouse was already absorbed into the new smell of paper stock and printer's ink. She watched him inhale deeply, watched him walk past the type saw. There was an electric droplight hung over it. At the Linotype, he tapped keys and let the slugs fall. She watched him look around at the machine that would soon be clacking and spinning while the building trembled.

And she knew exactly how he felt. Real understanding, she thought, is touching just for a moment what is deepest in another human being. Ben Goudy had understood.

With a flourish, he pulled a revamped masthead and gave it to her. "Now it's everything we want, isn't it, Josie?"

Josephine had smiled and thought, no, it's everything *you* want. That's not the same thing.

But Ted was satisfied. It wasn't the first time he had put words of his own behind her smile.

But she could still say, "This is wonderful," and mean it. . . .

"You're both making too much of this," Frieda said after she poured herself a cup of coffee. "It's the kid's Easter vacation, he's fourteen, he went to a party. So it's eleven o'clock. Big deal."

By unspoken agreement, Josephine and Ted had confided little in her.

"Ted spoke to the girl's father. The party's been over a long time."

"Anyone I know?"

"No."

"From experience," cutting herself a piece of crumb cake, "I can tell you Pete's got a good excuse. A long time ago I stopped letting myself go gray when Tony's late. He always has a legitimate excuse. He'll have a good one tonight. He'll tell me, 'The train schedule was off'—which it probably was. You know how damned unreliable that broken-down line is. Or the car he was getting a ride in as far as Greenwich broke down. I'd believe that in a minute, no matter how phony as hell it sounds. Cars today are made for obsolescence. Everybody knows that. We'd be better off riding bikes. Pete take his, by the way?"

"That's another reason we're concerned." Josephine wondered if Ted was going to stand motionless at the window until he saw his son come safely up the front steps.

His son.

For almost two months, the boy hadn't seemed like hers at all. And she missed him. She was sure he didn't feel the same way and wondered idly if he ever would again. It was more than missing a birthday party. If she really had forgotten, she could have shaken him, big as he was and said: Enough of this! It wasn't the end of the world. For all those years up to that day, I proved a thousand times over how much I love you.

To hold this against me for the rest of your life is unfair, Pete.

But because she knew the real reason she hadn't been home on time, she could never say it.

Frieda dusted flaky crumbs from the front of her dress. "Doesn't he have lights and reflectors?"

Josephine nodded.

"Well, that's good. Just the same, riding at night can be dangerous. How far is Mitford? Seven, eight miles?"

"Yes."

"Wouldn't the most direct way be on Route 4 to the highway, then on to Main?"

"I think so."

"Well," cutting more of the cake, "why doesn't Ted take the car and go look for him?"

"Frieda," Ted said, turning around suddenly, "sometimes you're very smart. I don't know why we didn't think of that ourselves."

"I'm not only smart, I'm sexy. Ask Tony. No, don't. He may not be discreet and you still print the only newspaper in town."

Ben Goudy's old Chevy drove up as Ted, his coat carelessly thrown on, opened the front door to leave.

"What's this?" Josephine heard him say.

"Mr. Goudy strapped my bike to the roof of the car, dad," Peter called. "It's all bashed up."

"Never mind the bike. What happened to your leg?"

Then Josephine heard Ben's voice. "The boy's all right . . . a bad bruise . . . no bones broken."

She sat stiffly erect on the couch in front of the fireplace, afraid that if she moved at all she would fall apart.

"Well," Frieda said, "look what the big cat brought home. Your Pete."

Ted moved back into the room from the foyer. He was grinning with relief. "It's okay. Pete's here. I'm going to help get that bike down."

Deliberately, Frieda pushed away the cake plate. "I don't really need this."

Her heart beating with nervousness, Josephine went to the mantel and took down the single cup. Frieda remarked that, since Ben Goudy had brought Peter back, the polite thing to do, of course, was to offer him some coffee, but Josie would understand why, under the circumstances, considering that unfortunate encounter in the post office, she herself had

277

no intention of being anything but coolly cordial. . . .

Josephine couldn't help noticing how Frieda tucked in her stomach as she said it, at the same time idly running practiced fingers through her hair.

A few minutes passed and then there was a blur of voices, men's footsteps on the front steps leading up to the house, and the sound of the front door opening and closing. She heard Ted say, "I know my wife wouldn't want you to leave without seeing her."

"I'd like to see her," Ben said.

Josephine felt her whole body incline toward that voice. With controlled panic, she wondered if Frieda noticed, but Frieda was too busy tucking in her stomach.

"Hello," Ben said. Josephine was grateful that he pointedly refrained from calling her Jo.

Everything about him looked bigger than she had remembered—the plaid squares on his shirt, the massive silver buckle on his belt, the broad ends of his fingers.

"Hello, Ben." To Peter she said, "How did this happen?"

Ted, who hadn't stopped smiling since he had learned his son was safe, repeated everything he had been told in the garage while they were carefully lowering the broken bicycle. He told them about Peter taking the alternate River Road route, about the fall, the broken lights, the cut knee and finally the refuge of the Goudy barn.

"Peter wasn't at Judy's party," he said looking at his wife. "He only stayed a few minutes."

Peter shrugged. "Long enough to know it would have been a stupid party. Frankly, I didn't want to waste my time. I'll tell you about it later. Maybe."

"If you want to tell us," Josephine said, with a ghost of a smile. The smile was meant for her husband and was full of triumph. "Ben," she said, "you remember Mrs. Haines."

Ben nodded. "I was rude to you the last time we met."

"Were you?" airily. "I don't remember. I only like to remember pleasant things about people. How nice of you to bring Pete home, Mr. Goudy."

"He's a nice boy. And even if you don't remember, I'd like to apologize. It'll make me feel better."

"Make believe we've kissed and made up."

Josephine winced.

278

"Well, anyway," Frieda amended coyly, "make believe we've shaken hands on it."

Ted laughed and offered his own hand. "I'd like to thank you, Mr. Goudy," he said, "for taking care of my son."

Josephine lowered her head so they couldn't see her face and busied herself pouring coffee. She couldn't look at them clasping hands. The thought that those same hands that were touching each other had both touched her made her pulse churn her blood until it grew hot.

"Peter," she said, "if you didn't stay at the party, I'll bet you're hungry."

"No. Mr. Goudy made me a sandwich."

"You must be tired after everything that's happened."

"Beat. I think I'll go up to bed. My knee's throbbing a lot." He hesitated before he said, "Maybe you could bring me up a glass of milk?"

"Would you like me to?" hopefully. It was the first time in two months he had asked her to do anything for him.

"If it's not too much trouble."

"No trouble." She felt happy because he was home, because she had been right about him and because, for some unexplained reason, the hurt had left him. It didn't matter that another kind was making his knee throb. The more important hurt seemed to be gone.

He said good night to them, held onto the bannister and made his way slowly to the second floor.

For the moment, Josephine wasn't acutely conscious of Ben Goudy being in her house. For the moment, he was just another guest. She asked Frieda to finish pouring the coffee for her. A few minutes later she stood outside a closed door holding a small tray.

"Come in," Peter said when she knocked.

He was sitting disconsolately on the edge of his bed wearing his pajamas. Two fingers were shoved through the hole in his trousers. "I wrecked them," he said in a gloomy voice.

"Maybe they can be fixed."

"I doubt it."

Josephine set the tray down. "Your father and I were worried about you. The suit isn't important."

"I just got it."

"As long as you're all right. Except for the knee you are, aren't you?"

He drank some of the milk before he answered. "Mr. Goudy showed me that clay head you made."

"What did you think?"

"I told him it was like someone cut off my real head, so how come I was smiling. I thought that was pretty funny, but he didn't laugh. He's very serious, isn't he?"

"When it comes to his work."

"He told me when you work, it's like time doesn't exist."

"That's true."

"Did it happen that day?"

"It could have."

"You didn't mean to forget," Pete assured her.

She gave a superficial smile. "No, it just happened." On impulse she sat next to him on the bed, pulled him to her and felt him offer no resistance. Her breath was coming in short spasms, and she tried hard to hold back tears.

"Don't do that," Peter said.

For a moment neither of them said a word. Finally, she released him and stood up again. "Let me see the pants."

He held them out and she examined them. "There's a man in the square who does excellent reweaving."

"You really think you can get it fixed?"

In an undertone, she answered, "I can only try."

Before she left him, she asked why he hadn't brought the clay head home and had to settle for his lame explanation that they had been preoccupied with the bike. Maybe he hadn't really liked it after all and didn't want to hurt her feelings. It didn't matter.

Halfway down the stairs, she heard Ted saying, "If you don't plan to keep it, why haven't you turned the property over to a broker?"

"He might try to sell it."

"Isn't that what you want?"

"Right now," Ben said, "what I don't want is a lot of strangers tramping about and annoying me—" He broke off when he saw Josephine. "The boy all right?"

"Fine. Did I thank you for being so kind to him?"

"Of course I would be. He's yours."

Frieda glanced from one to the other, then said, "Since I've taken over as hostess, how about a cup of your own coffee?"

"I don't want any. Thanks."

"Mr. Goudy was telling us how talented you are, Josie."

"He was being kind to me, too."

"I'm sorry my wife stopped her lessons, Mr. Goudy," she heard Ted say.

"Are you really, Mr. Trask?"

"It was good for her to have a hobby. Was she your star pupil?"

"Ted," Josephine said, "please."

"Don't be modest, darling."

"I don't have pupils," Ben said. "Your wife and I have been working together."

"Since you're a professional, it's generous of you to put it that way."

"We had—still have, I think—mutual admiration for each other's ability." He reached into his jacket. "By the way, you sent this. When I knew I was coming here, I stuck it in my pocket."

Ted stared down, not understanding, at a check he recognized immediately. "I thought you just hadn't bothered to cash it yet. You're giving it back to me?"

"I don't run a school. I haven't any use for that kind of money." He waited for Ted to take the check from him. When he didn't, Ben put it on the coffee table, bending close to where Josephine was sitting.

"I've heard that artists are notoriously bad businessmen."

"We're a strange breed."

"For God's sake, Ted," Frieda said, "don't complain if somebody gives you back money." Her eyes were shining with exaggerated brightness. "Mr. Goudy, would you like to drive me all the way home? I live next door."

As soon as they were gone, Ted said, "You know, I like him."

"For bringing Peter home? So do I."

"It's more than that. There's a directness about him. And an honesty."

He seemed to be looking closely at her, she thought . . . or was she imagining it? She wanted to tell Ted not to like him. She was remembering what Ben said a long time ago: "I've made you dissatisfied with everything you have and everything you are, but you haven't found it out yet . . . I feel guilty enough without your liking me."

Because this time she was the one who felt guilty, she began to clear the table and didn't say a word.

Chapter Twenty-seven

A FEW days later, they began work in the new plant. Ted sent her two dozen yellow roses. That night he found them on the mantel in the crystal vase Fran had given them.

"They're beautiful," she said.

"You've put them all together."

"What's wrong with that?"

"I'm used to having you do things with flowers."

"These are lovely enough without having anything done to them."

She didn't tell him she had thought of letting a few of the roses grow out of a china blue teacup, of floating some of the pale petals in the amethyst bowl. Instead, she had just arranged them neatly, if unimaginatively, in the vase, and returned to cleaning her house.

Once, she told Frieda, she believed there was beauty in order. Since she had stopped going to the barn, she dedicated herself to that belief with a fervor approaching religious fanaticism. She bent her knees to it while she scrubbed the floor and the stairs and the woodwork. She took pride in every fresh cut, in every broken nail or torn bit of skin.

"Your hands," Ted said, taking them in his. "What are you doing to them?"

She stood quietly and allowed them to be examined. "It's not important."

He turned them gently, palms upward, and kissed them as Ben had kissed them. "Don't hurt these. They're so beautiful."

She examined them, too—a steady, searching appraisal. "They're not so beautiful anymore."

"You don't sound upset about it."

"I'm not." She smiled to prove she meant it.

"Listen," Ted said, "I know the reason you let the cleaning woman go—we were on such a tight budget before the changeover. It'll be different now. Give me a little while to get ahead. Then I want you to hire someone to help with the heavy work."

"I don't want anyone to help."

"Why do all this if you don't have to?"

"I enjoy housework." She forced a laugh. "I know that isn't usual."

"Neither are you," he said. "Don't overdo it, Josie."

"I won't."

"Well, spring cleaning doesn't last forever."

"No," she agreed. "Nothing does," and added, "and don't say foolish things."

"Like what?"

"Like I'm trying to punish my hands."

"Did I say that?"

She frowned, unable to force a laugh now even if she wanted to. "I thought you did. Didn't you?"

ABOUT NINE o'clock that same night, Frieda went to the barn. She found Ben Goudy working with a wide chisel and a heavy mallet. A shower of flakes and ribbons from the wood covered the floor.

"The only reason I barged in," she explained, "was because there isn't any bell. Barns don't have bells, do they?"

"This one has." A figure was coming to life under his sure swift strokes. "I rigged it myself. The trouble is no one seems to be able to find it. Or they don't try very hard."

He was critical without being rude—very different, she decided, from that day in the post office. She wondered how much the Goodwill thrift shop got for the cherry red suit she had donated. "If I'm bothering you, say so."

"And what will you do?" he asked. "Go away?" When he said it, he let her have half a smile. Half was enough encouragement.

283

"It really is a studio. Unbelievable what you've done. From the out-side, who would guess what's in here? Those lights turn night into day."

"What can I do for you, Mrs. Haines?"

"Why don't you call me Frieda? I still think of my mother-in-law as Mrs. Haines."

"And you don't like your mother-in-law."

For an answer, she said, "You wanted to know what you can do for me. I promise not to take up too much of your time."

"Can I count on that?" pleasantly.

She brushed away the remark with a jerk of her shoulder. "Up until the other night, I would have taken that the wrong way. I really got to know you then."

"In less than an hour?"

"Don't make fun of me, Mr. Goudy."

"Mr. Goudy," he told her, "was my father. I didn't like him much either."

Frieda shifted her weight from one leg to the other, hoping that under the strong lights he would notice them. No matter how much excess cargo she carried elsewhere, her legs had always stayed slim and well curved. Even Tony said so. Especially Tony. "Okay," she said, pleased. "Let's make it Frieda and Ben. Now I know you want to be friendly. That other is just a pose."

"What other?"

"The snide little remarks, your passion for unsociability, trying to stare me down from under those bushy eyebrows. Comb them straight up and cut them across with a scissors, by the way, and they'll look neater. . . . What were we talking about?"

"My eyebrows. You were about to offer to cut them for me, I think."

"No, your negative personality. I've got one, too, if I want to be honest. Ask almost anyone who knows me. Except Josie. Josie likes me. She likes you, too. I wonder if she'd think our two negatives could make a positive."

He seemed to be thinking about it; then he offered her a cigarette. She took it and neither said a word. There was an excitement in prolong-ing the silence between them. There was an excitement in this disturb-ing blend of awareness and disinterest. Later, she intended to wait up for Tony—no matter how late. She would tell him only about the awareness.

"Artists," she would say, "have always been attracted to well-upholstered women. Remember Rubens and his three graces? I'm practically Chicken Little compared to those fat hens. . . ."

"It might be just as well," Ben Goudy said, "if you don't tell Josie you were here. She doesn't know, does she?"

"No." It had been a mistake to inhale so deeply.

"Don't mention it then," he suggested.

"You probably didn't think I meant it that night when I told you I'd drop by sometime to see your work."

"I hoped you meant it." With a sweeping gesture, he indicated the whole of the room. "Here's what you told me you wanted to see."

Her eyes wandered carelessly around the studio before she made her fast pronouncement. "Marvelous!"

"I've always had an aversion," he said solemnly, "to critics who spend too much time analyzing an artist's work. It's the initial reaction I value most. Frankly, I've never had one more spontaneous."

Unruffled, Frieda said, "I'm not stupid, Mr. Goudy."

"I thought we were on a first name basis."

"If we are, don't make fun of me. I suppose I asked for it, but I assure you I want to look at everything carefully, if you'll let me. But I want you to know first that this isn't a purely social visit."

"I'm disappointed."

She tilted her head slightly and tried to read his expression. It was inscrutable. She couldn't tell if he was making fun of her again or not. "Do you want to hear my real reason for coming?"

Obligingly, he put down his tools and sat, knees spread apart, on the long bench. His jeans, she couldn't help noticing, packed hard-muscled thighs. "You have my complete attention."

Frieda plunged into it. "I'm here on behalf of the—" No matter how hard she tried, she couldn't push out the words "Ditchling Cultural Society." She compromised: "The club Josie and I both belong to is sponsoring an art exhibition next month. The fine art students from the college will submit their work, and all proceeds are going to the school scholarship fund." She shot it out in one breath.

There, she thought, that's my excuse for coming here. That's what I can tell Tony. I came in the interest of the community. Could I help it if his interests were prurient? Don't blame the man completely, Tony. Those lights were very strong and I happen to have very good legs. Haven't you always said that? So, in a way, I suppose what happened was as much my fault as his, and you don't have to tell me where you were tonight because, goddamn it, I stopped believing you a long time ago. So just shut up. And if what you do isn't any of my business, then what happened with me tonight isn't any of yours. Don't ask. And go to hell, Tony. . . .

"I've already told . . ." he hesitated, before saying the name—"Josie that I'm not the person to ask."

Frieda looked confused. She had forgotten what they had been talking about. "What?"

"To judge the contest. I'll tell you what I told her. I'm never sure where I'll be from one week to the next. The truth is I'll be leaving here soon."

"Oh? How soon?"

"I haven't set an exact date. I'm sure, though, I won't be around a month from now. You'll do better getting someone else."

"Josie already asked you? I'm surprised. When she said she preferred not to, I said don't bother." She didn't bother to tell him that particular conversation happened last September and hoped she was giving him the impression they had discussed it more recently. "This is terribly embarrassing."

"Never mind. It gave you an excuse to come."

"Excuse?"

"Reason would have been a better word. Give me your coat. In exchange, I'll give you a glass of wine."

"Wine?" Frieda repeated without much enthusiasm.

"What would you say to a beer instead?"

"What would you say to mixing them?"

"There's a limit to my creativity. I've got a bottle of Scotch. Perhaps, you'd rather—"

"I'd rather," she said shortly. "Then I'll look at your work. I warn you, Ben, I'm brutally honest."

He found the bottle of Scotch, poured a drink for each of them and they drank to her brutal honesty.

"I can't picture Josie spending so much time here."

"Why not?"

"This floor. Does it always look like this? Josie's so neat—even more so lately, somehow."

"In what way?"

"She's practically a fanatic about her house. Her idea of spring cleaning is to start in the cellar and work her way up to the attic. Her hands are all calluses and cuts. It doesn't seem to bother her."

If it bothered Ben, it didn't show on his face. "Is that what she's doing now? Cleaning cellars?"

"Oh, Josie's always busy, especially since her mother-in-law left. She never seems to have enough time to get everything done. I suppose that's why she isn't taking any more lessons here—too busy."

"You heard me the other night. I don't run a school."

"I forgot. That's why you gave Ted back the check, isn't it?" Drink in hand, she began to move around the studio, "Then Josie was special?"

"She was special."

"Funny, she never brought home anything she did."

"There was only one head. It's being cast, and a figure of her little girl—unfinished. Would you like to see it?"

"Oh, yes," Frieda said. "By the way, now that I'm getting a good look at what you do, your talent overwhelms me. You'll see, Ben, before tonight's over, I'll talk you into judging our contest. I can be very persuasive."

He was in front of her now at a worktable. Gently, he removed the cloth from a small clay figure.

Round eyes opened wider, Frieda said, "Why, that's exactly like Elsie. Josie did this?"

"It's a quick study. I'm still hoping she'll come back and finish it."

"Just this," Frieda wanted to know, "and a head that's being cast?"

"Not quite," he told her in a barely audible voice.

"I didn't hear you."

"There's something else she left here. A figure of a woman in stone."

"She worked with stone? That's hard to do, isn't it? Which one is it?"

He nodded in the direction of the statue that Jo had once looked at and told him, "I thought you were working on something beautiful. Now it seems ugly . . ."

"I can't believe Josie did that," Frieda was saying.

"She didn't really."

"You just said . . ."

"I said it's something else she left here. Actually, I did it and called it 'Josephine.' "

Frieda finished her drink quickly and held out the glass to be refilled. "She posed for this?"

"In a way." His eyes were fixed on her face, but she had the unpleasant sensation he wasn't really seeing her.

"No wonder you're sorry she isn't coming anymore."

"What do you mean?"

"That's not finished either, like the little statue of Elsie. Although, to be perfectly honest, that one looks done enough to me. But you can't finish yours without Josie, can you?"

"I'm not even going to try."

"I've got a confession to make." Suddenly she wanted to stop talking about Josie. Deliberately she drew her lips together and tried to look appealing. "I wasn't telling the truth the other night. I did remember you were rude to me that day we met in the post office."

"Your friend Josie said my remark was unpardonable."

Damn her, Frieda thought, annoyed. It's me I want to talk about. "I have a theory about men who make unkind remarks about women."

"I'd be interested to hear it."

"I think they're attracted to them but don't want to admit it to themselves. If you hadn't been physically conscious of me you wouldn't have said what you did. Right?"

"You're so right."

"Did you really mean it when you said you're leaving here soon?"

With a slow smile, Ben Goudy said, "Yes. And once I do, I'll never come back. Wouldn't it be too bad to have you remember me for—what was it you said?—my passion for unsociability?"

CLOSE TO midnight, Josephine stood at the bedroom window, saw Frieda leave her car and walk unsteadily to her front door. She saw her fumbling to fit the key in the lock.

There were no lights in either house. Josephine knew Frieda's boys were spending spring vacation with their grandparents in Maryland and that Tony hadn't come home. She would have heard the taxi as it drove up from the railroad station.

The dark of a deserted house, Josephine decided, is deeper. When there are people quietly sleeping inside, even the color of the dark changes. It's warmer. She wondered if thieves know when it's safest to break in because the house itself tells them. A light left burning or a radio left playing means less to a sensitive ear than a house screaming, "I am alone." It was the kind of thought that comes only at night.

Below, the figure of Frieda finally let herself into the cold, dark house and shut the door. A moment later the foyer lights went on.

288

Ted yawned. "What are you doing at the window?"

"I woke you, didn't I?"

"I usually know when you get out of bed."

For the first time, she wished she had a separate bedroom where she could lie or stand awake without being afraid of waking her husband— a room where she could dream and not be afraid he was sitting beside her on the bed looking at her face while she did.

"Can't sleep?"

"Frieda's just come home. I think she's been drinking."

"Then she has no business driving."

"I wonder where she's been."

His hand gently touched the back of her neck and sent a shiver through her. "She'll probably tell you tomorrow. Come back to bed."

FRIEDA DIDN'T come over until Ted and the children were out of the house. A tour of the new plant was planned as the high point of the Easter vacation week. Josephine was certain Frieda had waited until they could be alone before coming across the yard. Not only was her walk steadier; there was a definite bounce in it. Frieda might not have lost weight last night, but she moved as if she were pounds lighter.

She sat in the big Queen Anne chair, looking pleased with herself and watched Josephine move the vase to the mantel. The reflection in the mirror gave back two dozen more roses. The room was suddenly full of roses.

"Those are gorgeous."

"Ted brought them."

"He's the kind of husband women ought to be able to order from a catalogue. Or did he do something he shouldn't have?"

"The plant opened officially yesterday. These were in celebration."

"Well, congratulations to you, too."

"It's all Ted's doing." In fairness she added, "With some help from Fran."

"Too bad she isn't here to celebrate."

"Yes," Josephine said. "She sent a cable from the cruise ship, though." The color of the flowers matched the sunlight that played on the walls and on the ceiling. "I saw you come home last night."

"Spying on me?" good-naturedly. Go on, she dared silently, ask me where I was. I'm going to tell you anyway, but go on and ask me.

"You shouldn't drive if you've been drinking. You put more than your own life in danger."

"I didn't come for a lecture," peevishly. "In the first place, I wasn't drunk. And how could you prove it by sneaking a peek from your bedroom window?"

Josephine felt her face redden. "It wasn't anything like that. Forget I mentioned it."

"Don't you want to ask me where I was?"

"Only if you want to tell me."

"Oh, come on, Josie. You're dying to know. Let's not play games. I was at the barn. Ben and I just lost track of time. Didn't that ever happen to you there?"

Josephine stared at her. "You were at the barn? Why?"

"You never told me how extremely talented he is."

"I asked why you went there."

"Why do I have the feeling you're shaking your finger under my nose. Don't. It makes me nervous. I shouldn't have told you."

Josephine sat opposite her, consciously composed herself and folded her hands on her lap.

"For God's sake," Frieda said, "now I feel like I'm in the principal's office. You want to know why I went? If you stopped to think, you'd remember the art contest is next month. We still don't have a judge. As chairman of the committee, it was up to me to do something about it."

"I already asked him, a long time ago."

"You might have told me."

"I thought I did. Ben said he'd be a wrong choice because he's—"

"Unreliable."

"Exactly."

"That's exactly what he let me know, almost right away. He won't be here a month from now, but you know that." From the way Josephine frowned, Frieda saw that she hadn't known it.

"What else did you find to talk about?"

"I have a great appreciation for art, Josie. You may not believe it, but I have."

"You talked about art until almost midnight?"

"I don't like being cross-examined."

"I'm not cross-examining you."

"You're mad because I was there, aren't you?"

It was an unexpected thrust. "Mad is an inaccurate word."

Frieda bent forward. "What's the right word?" It was more a feline hiss than a question. Frieda was scratching over a big tom with speckled yellow eyes, and Josephine was ashamed of having let herself be drawn into a catfight over Ben Goudy. She drew back in distaste.

The unpleasant odor of tension was strong enough to overwhelm even the fragrance of two dozen roses. "Never mind. Forget I said anything."

"Oh, come on, Josie. Admit you'd like to have changed places with me last night."

As much as Josephine tried, she couldn't work up any just anger in retaliation. It had been a lot easier that day when John told her about the rumors Frieda Haines was spreading around town. Frieda didn't know it, but at the time she had only been premature, even prophetic. . . .

"For tonight," she was chattering now, "I'm going to pick up a couple of steaks and some frozen french fries. I intend to fix a decent dinner for him."

"Is he expecting you?" quietly.

"The man's looking forward to it."

"Frieda," Josephine said helplessly, "you probably don't believe I'm thinking of you. Don't go back there."

"Oh, I'll just bet you're thinking of me! Well, try thinking of me this way: tonight, for the first time in almost a year, I won't give a damn whether Tony comes home or not." She was on her feet, making a visible, muscular effort to hold in her stomach. "I'll be glad to tell Ben you were asking for him."

Josephine didn't answer.

"All right, I won't then."

Frieda went past her to the front door with a slight twist of her ample hips.

Josephine waited a few minutes, then left the house.

Chapter Twenty-eight

THE RIVER Road, she discovered when she turned the car into it, hadn't been washed out to sea at all. She wasn't really surprised. What did surprise her was that here, as everywhere else in town, the trees were full of new green and new promise. Josephine must have been vain enough to think that because she had chosen to ignore this little back road, spring would forsake it altogether.

She parked in front of the barn and got out, slamming the car door. It was a commitment. Once Ben knew she was outside, she couldn't turn back. The deliberate slam served another purpose. It would rudely interrupt his work. He would be even more outraged because it came from Jo, who should understand how important it is not to shatter concentration.

This lack of understanding, she hoped, would be enough to catch him off guard. There were only two things she must remember, she thought, as she walked over the familiar gravel, now sun-warmed: not to look at her work, be tempted to lift the cloth that covered it; and, even more important, not to look at the woman in the stone.

It was Ben who took her off guard. Instead of finding him at work, she found him sitting at the old kitchen table he had borrowed from the big house. Years ago, she had sat at that same table with his uncle. Jess had never once mentioned having a nephew named Ben.

There were two cups on the table. There was a familiar upturned crack in one. Next to the cups was the percolator she had bought. Behind that, ridiculous and touching, a few early wild flowers curled over an empty coffee can. He looked across the big room and said, "Good morning, darling."

If she wanted to run, she should have done it that first day she came here, half a year ago. The barn was bathed, as it had been then, in mysterious color, and now she understood immediately that it was the sunlight vibrating that produced the enchanted dome. And all around her she could still hear the sound that frozen movement makes.

Fascinated, she watched him pour the dark steaming liquid and felt her resolve run from her into the cups. When he finished and put the percolator down again, she was drained.

"I make better coffee than I used to."

"I didn't come for coffee."

"Drink it anyway."

Without a word, she took the cup he gave her and drank, watching him over the rim of it. She was a ringmaster, gauging the quick lethal movements of the lion. His eyes, not his claws, would give away the moment he would spring.

"The coffee's slightly burned," he said. "I expected you earlier."

"You couldn't have."

"Why?"

"Because I didn't know myself until a little while ago."

"I knew last night when I told Frieda not to tell you she was here. I'm really surprised she waited this long." The speckled yellow in his eyes glinted. "I knew you'd come," confidently. "Look around you, Jo." But his eyes wouldn't let her. "All right, look at me instead and tell me how much you've forgotten."

"I came here to talk about Frieda."

"You came here the first time to return a portfolio."

"It's true," she insisted.

"After what happened between us the last time I can't believe that."

She ignored this. "Frieda's been unhappy for a long time. It would be easy to take advantage of her."

He looked amused. "Very."

"She doesn't know I'm here."

He laughed unpleasantly. "If she did, she'd tell you to mind your own damn business."

293

"This is my business. I introduced her to you. I know she didn't leave here until almost midnight."

"She came about nine," he volunteered.

Josephine finally allowed herself to lose her temper. "Don't tell me you sat here all those hours discussing contemporary art."

"We didn't discuss art at all. What's the matter, Jo? When she told you, did you wish it had been you?"

Suddenly, everything that had been sealed up in her exploded with enough force to blow the barn apart. Her hand flew out and struck him across the face. He grabbed her wrist and held it.

"It's true," he said triumphantly.

"What I really *wish,*" she said with more bitterness than she had ever known, "is that I had never met you."

He let her go. "I'm sorry. I'm sorry I said that."

"So am I." The smock she meant to take with her last time was back on its rusty nail. It had been hung up again neatly and with great care. She ripped it off. "And I'm sorry I came here today. You're absolutely right. What happened last night or what happens tonight is none of my damn business."

Ben reached the door before she did.

"Get out of my way," quietly.

"I can't let you go like this."

"You can't keep me if I don't want to stay."

"About Frieda: nothing really happened. It could have, if I had wanted it—"

"What inspired such superior control?"

"You should know women like that don't interest me. If I can't have one I can talk to afterward, I want one who doesn't talk at all. God, she doesn't stop. How have you put up with her for so long?"

"You didn't have to put up with her at all. You could have asked her to leave."

"Keeping her here last night was the only way I could be sure of getting you here today. I was also sure she'd tell you I'm leaving soon. Is that the real reason you came? To find out when?"

"Are you really leaving?" It was maddening to hear the anger draining out of her own voice.

He nodded. "Would you have let me go without saying good-by?"

"Where are you going?"

From the pocket of his jacket, he took a crumpled envelope and handed it to her. The letter inside must have been read and reread. "Go on," Ben said.

Obediently, she looked down at the paper, but her eyes refused to focus. "What does it say?"

"Before I left Paris, I entered a group of figures in a salon competition. They've been accepted."

"That's wonderful," Josephine said, giving him back his letter. "I'm so happy for you."

"I'm going to Paris in a few weeks. I want to touch my figures, touch the base where I cut my name in the stone." He moved closer to her. "And, of course, you're coming with me, Jo."

"Of course I'm not," she said, drawing back.

"I'm not a good teacher," he went on. "I haven't the patience to be a teacher. But there's a man I worked under. I want his opinion of your talent. I'm sure I can talk him into taking you on. You've reached what we call the breaking-through point. You're ready to leave everything you've done here and go on to your next level as an artist."

"You have the most fascinating arrogance," Josephine said. "You listen only to what you choose to hear. You admit only what you don't choose to ignore. Doesn't the fact that I haven't been here since that last day say anything to you? Doesn't it tell you that once I got home to all the familiar things, I realized I had made a terrible mistake?"

"The only mistake you made was leaving."

She forced herself to meet his eyes. "You won't believe this, but it was never you, Ben. It was everything else here—for a time—but it was never you."

"Don't tell me you didn't come to see me today."

"I didn't."

"All right. Then you came because you missed all this. I'll accept one or the other and be satisfied with either."

"I came to ask you to leave Frieda alone. That was my only reason. There is nothing here I missed."

She found the way to prove it by walking over to the worktable that had been hers, lifting the cloth from the last thing she had done and looking down at it dispassionately before covering it up again. "The other is gone," she noticed.

"I took it to New York to have it cast. Your son knew I was going to. I made him promise not to say anything. It was to be a surprise."

"That was very nice of you, Ben." She said it graciously. Then she went over to the woman in the stone and stood before it unflinchingly. "You were right to stop when you got this far. It's the idea that counts. This is such an interesting one."

Without turning, she knew he was standing beside her. "She's you!" she heard him say. He sounded unsure of himself now.

"If it is, there's nothing I can do about it."

"But I can."

Before she realized what was happening, Ben picked up the heavy mallet, lifted it high in the air and brought it down savagely on the stone. A large chip fell away.

"I could free you both," he said. He raised his arm again. This time she stopped it midair.

"Don't, don't spoil your work to make a cheap point."

"What cheap point are you trying to make?"

Her hand slid heavily from his arm and he let the mallet drop noisily to the floor of the barn. "Just tell me you've been happy since you were last here."

All her strength seemed to go from her into him. She hated him for taking it without asking. He wasn't even leaving her enough to give him any kind of an answer. What answer?

"Jo," he said, "time's run out. We both know it. When I leave here, I won't leave alone. You'll leave with me."

"You're crazy." This time he wasn't blocking her way.

At the waiting car, she managed to open the door, slide in and turn the ignition before he came after her. He dared her to drive off by going to the front of it and taking a stance. His feet were planted in the gravel of the drive, his thumbs hooked into the belt at his waist. "I gave you enough time," he called to her across the hood, "to find out how well you get along with me."

She tightened her hands on the steering wheel. Her foot was resting on the accelerator; her heart was pounding.

"When I leave here," he called to her, "I won't leave alone. I meant that. You're going to leave with me, Jo."

She gritted her teeth, closed her eyes and pushed down hard on the accelerator. When she looked again, she was on the road that led home. If he hadn't jumped away in time she would have run him down. The knowledge of that made her shudder. She was trembling when she reached the house. Elsie was sitting on the back steps.

"Daddy said he gave us the dollar tour of the plant, and now we're all going out to lunch."

"Really?" Josephine said in surprise. It was the steadiness of her own voice that surprised her most.

"Since we can afford to have lunch at the hotel and since he bought so many flowers, I guess that means we're not going to be poor after all."

"Is that what you thought?"

"Oh, I thought we'd probably sell this house and move to one of those three-story wooden ones on the south side—the kind with the back porches and the cats in the garbage cans and sheets and underwear and things hanging from the windows."

"You were afraid that might happen?" amazed.

"I thought it might be interesting," she said with a regretful sigh. "If you want to know the truth, I'm a little disappointed."

"Where's your father?"

"Downstairs in Pete's room. They're playing pool. I think that's a dumb game and it's not just because I'm not good at it." Elsie stood up. For a moment, her small, perfectly proportioned body took on the exact posture of the small, perfectly proportioned clay figure.

At the same moment, Josephine seemed to see Ben again, standing in front of the car. Her foot began to throb as it had throbbed on the accelerator just before she pressed it down. Remembering, her ankle turned under. She caught herself on the bannister and went down on the top step.

"Mother! Are you all right?"

Josephine forced herself to make light of it. "I tripped, that's all."

A pointed, frightened little face seemed to be floating over her. She reached up to pat it reassuringly, and without knowing she was going to do it, cupped it with both her hands and found she still had fingers enough to touch the curly hair. "Were you worried about me, Elsie?"

"How come you fell?"

She could have told her it was because she had been remembering how she almost killed a man. Instead, she said, "I was clumsy." She got up and brushed the folds of her skirt.

Elsie followed her into the house and Josephine was conscious of being watched through darting, questioning eyes.

"Why didn't you do anything fancy with the flowers?"

"They're fine this way."

"Wouldn't they look better if they were fancier?"

"I suppose," Josephine answered, distracted and only half-concentrating. "Do me a favor? Hang up my coat?"

"Sure." Elsie was back immediately when she heard the crash of china.

"Don't touch that," her mother warned. "You'll cut yourself." She bent to pick up the pieces herself.

"You never break dishes."

"I'm really very clumsy today."

"You're the only one I know who doesn't ever break dishes. Don't you think it's funny you broke one right after you fell down?"

The sound brought Ted from downstairs. "You never break dishes," he said.

"I wish everyone wouldn't treat this as a major disaster. They're old dishes we've had too long anyway. We have plenty of others I can use for lunch."

"Didn't Elsie tell you we're going to the hotel? I made reservations."

"I forgot. It's a wonderful idea. I wasn't in the mood to make lunch."

"I've asked Frieda to join us."

Josephine stopped smiling. "Why?"

"Aren't you pleased?"

"Of course," she lied.

"Where are the big scissors?" Elsie interrupted.

"In the utility table drawer."

"Okay if I borrow them?"

"As long as you put them back where you found them."

Elsie took the scissors and left.

"I thought you wanted to make this a family outing," Josephine said.

"Frieda's like family. And I felt sorry for her. She's alone. Her boys are away, and Tony only drops in when he's in the neighborhood. Have you noticed?"

"More and more lately."

"I wouldn't have invited her if I didn't think you'd like the idea."

"It was very thoughtful," she told him, but wondered, confused, why Frieda would even want to accept after what happened between them earlier.

When Frieda came, she appeared to be in even better spirits than Ted. "This dress is new," she announced. "How do you like it, Josie? You know how important your opinion is to me."

"Very becoming," Ted said when his wife didn't answer.

"Sorry," Josephine apologized. "I was wondering why Elsie wanted the scissors."

"I'll bet she wanted to cut something." Frieda laughed and pressed a hard forefinger into Josephine's shoulder to drive the point of the joke home. It hadn't been necessary to press quite so hard.

"You've got the sweetest husband." She smiled, but Josephine could see Frieda was really laughing softly to herself, making it obvious now why she had wanted to join them. Her presence would be a constant reminder through lunch of where she planned to have dinner later.

"On our way home afterward," Frieda said, "would it inconvenience you very much to stop at the supermarket? I promise not to take long."

"Sure," Ted said. "Why not?"

"I want to pick up a couple of juicy steaks, some frozen french fries and greens for a salad—"

"Sounds as if Tony's in for a good dinner."

"Oh, it's not for Tony," Frieda told him, deliberately avoiding Josephine's eyes. "I don't know if he's even coming home—and I don't give a shit."

"Hey!" Ted said, taken aback.

"The dinner's for Ben Goudy. Josie knows all about it."

"Very neighborly of you," Ted said. He looked at Josephine. "Did you really know about this?"

"We had a long talk about it earlier," Frieda said. "Your wife doesn't approve."

"I'm not sure I do, either."

"I asked you before, Josie. When I see Ben, do you want me to say hello for you?"

"Frieda," Josephine said, "have more pride. Don't throw yourself at someone who isn't interested in you."

"You know something," Frieda said bitterly, "you can be goddamned insulting—taking it for granted Ben couldn't possibly be interested in me!"

"He isn't."

"What makes you so sure?"

"Because," Josephine heard herself tell them both, "he told me so himself this morning."

"You asked him?" hoarsely.

"I didn't want to see you hurt."

299

There was no sound in the room until Frieda said, "You make me sick."

"I suppose it doesn't really matter what advice I give you. You'll do as you please anyway."

"That's right!" She swept up the handbag she had put on the table and got as far as the door, then unexpectedly changed her mind. "Oh, forget the whole thing," she said good-naturedly.

"Still going tonight?" Ted asked.

"I've decided against it."

There was a menacing mildness about her. Only Josephine detected it.

"There's no point in going now. Your wife," with quiet venom, "took all the fun out of it."

"You heard her. She was trying to keep you from getting hurt."

"We both heard. Only one of us believed her. Do you really believe that was her only reason?"

"Why not?"

"Ask her."

"I'm asking you."

"Ben Goudy could have been interested in me if . . ."

"Excuse my very dull middle-class morality," Ted said, "but you happen to be a married woman, Frieda."

"Well, I've got news for you. So is your not so dull middle-class wife." She turned on Josephine. "And if Ben hadn't been interested only in hearing about you and talking about you last night, things might have ended a lot different."

"If he talked about me," Josephine was trying desperately, for Ted's sake, to make it sound convincing, "it's because you two had nothing else to talk about—nothing in common."

"You two must have had a lot in common—your work and all. You ought to go there sometime, Ted. There's something you should see—a statue of a woman. He calls it 'Josephine.' "

"Frieda," Josephine said frightened, "stop it."

"A nude," she went on. "How do you like that, Ted? The statue of Josie is a nude." It was an ugly outburst that contorted her face.

Ted was standing close enough to his wife to sense the muscle tremors running through her. He remembered how, when she had thanked Ben Goudy for taking such good care of their son, the artist had answered, "Of course I would. He's yours." That night he had felt a little sorry for

Goudy, who didn't have Josie the way he did. Now he felt he should feel a little sorry for Frieda, who didn't know Josie the way he did. He couldn't work up any anger toward her. All he could do was tell her quietly, "I think you've said too much."

Frieda looked first at him and then at Josephine. "Oh, my God," she moaned, shaking her head. "What happened to me just then? Have I always been such a bitch? I don't think so. I really don't."

"You didn't know what you were saying," Ted said.

She was hiccuping faintly. "That's where you're wrong. I knew exactly what I was saying. You know something else? For a long time, I've been ready to have an affair with anyone who'd have me, just to prove I was worth having. But I'm not worth anything this way, and I'm going to tell him that whenever he comes home. Only this time he won't be bored because, goddamn it, if he is, he doesn't have to come home at all—not anymore."

She looked as if she wanted to cry. Instead she began to laugh nervously. "I don't think I'm going to take you up on lunch, Ted. Do you believe this? I'm actually turning down food. That would be a beginning, wouldn't it? It's not much, but it's something."

ONCE FRIEDA was gone, Josephine said, "About that statue, he just gave it my name; I never posed for it."

"You should know me better than that," he said. "I never thought that you did."

"Sometimes," Josephine said, "being trusted is the same as being loved. It can be a terrible responsibility."

"And you're the kind of woman who couldn't live without being both."

Everyone, she thought, seems to know what I need to live, everyone except myself. "Do you still want to take us out to lunch?"

"Not in the beat-up pants I wore to the plant. I wouldn't want my family to be ashamed of me. Give me a few minutes to change. Meanwhile round up our gang."

Before he went upstairs, Ted suggested that later—not now, because she probably wouldn't want company, but later—when they got back, Josephine might think of going over to be with Frieda.

"I planned to," she said, thinking, he really is a very nice person. No wonder his mother bled for him. Fran wouldn't believe it, but in my own way, so do I. If Ben Goudy has his way, part of me always will.

She opened the door leading downstairs and called, "We're leaving soon, Pete." Then she went to look for Elsie.

What she saw in the living room horrified her. She let out a convulsive little cry. "Oh, my God," she said in a rasping whisper she knew was verging on hysteria. It wasn't really because of the roses that had been chopped and hacked and put back into a crystal vase, or the petals and pieces of stems on the rug, as revolting to her as pieces from a dismembered body. It was everything that had happened that day.

"Elsie, what have you done? Why?"

Elsie didn't answer. Instead she stood with deliberate defiance in the middle of the room.

"Answer me! Why did you do that? They were beautiful. Why did you have to spoil something that was beautiful?"

The girl bent her elbow, raising it so that the back of her hand covered a guilty face. She looked ready to ward off a blow. "Get away from me," she said. "Don't come near me."

Then her mother realized Elsie hadn't been defiant after all. She had simply frozen in terror. Her arm dropped to her side and, although she continued to stand in the center of the room, she seemed to be backed up and flattened against the wall.

"All I was doing was trying to fix them!" It might have been the dead of winter the way she was clenching her teeth to keep from chattering. "That's all I wanted to do. I wanted to surprise you. I should have known you'd say I spoiled it."

Josephine went to her quickly and tried to put her arms around the thin shoulders.

"I said get away from me!"

"Forget about the flowers," Josephine said. "It's all right."

"I should have known better than to try to do anything you do. You do everything better."

"Stop it," Josephine ordered. "Don't say that."

"You're always afraid I'll spoil things."

"That's not true."

"Yes, it is. I know it is." The tears that streaked her face wet her lashes, pointing them into angry spikes. "I can't help it if I don't know how. I can't help it if you always do things better than I do."

It was one of the saddest voices Josephine had ever heard come from anyone. What have I done to her? she wondered, appalled, suddenly remembering Elsie at five coming into the kitchen proudly to show off some Easter eggs she had spent hours decorating. Only Ted was there before her. "Look what your mother's done. Aren't these beautiful eggs, Elsie?"

Elsie had looked, admired and then smiling sweetly, put her own basket on the floor and deliberately stomped on it. After all those years, Josephine could still hear the sickening sound of shells crunching under the small shoe.

"Mine aren't any good," she had said. "I don't want anybody to see them. . . ."

"I'm sorry, darling," she apologized now, years later. "I never meant to spoil anything for you. I never meant to."

She was referring to Easter eggs and to dozens of other buried and remembered incidents. But Elsie's face was flaming with hopeless resentment.

"Darling," she began, "when I was your age—"

"You were better then, too. I bet you were. In everything. Always. I'll never do anything the way you do it. And you know what? I don't care."

"You're right," her mother said. "Don't care. Because it really doesn't matter. You'll grow up to be a different kind of woman than I grew up to be. Probably much better, probably much happier. Don't try to be like me, and don't envy me."

This time Elsie was too startled to protest when Josephine put her arms around her. "Listen to me," she said. "This is something I've never told anyone. I'm telling you. Ever since I was a little girl, no matter what I did, it never seemed to be enough. I always looked for other things to do, more and more things to do. And when I finished, I always felt cheated. I was always dissatisfied."

She let her daughter go then and repeated softly. "Don't envy me." When she tried to blink back her own tears, her lashes felt sticky and clotted. She went to the breakfront and got out another vase. "You cut the stems a little too short for that one," she told her.

"That's not the way you acted before."

"I was upset before, but it wasn't about this. This was just an excuse. I used it as an excuse. I was wrong. Never mind. Here. Take this and rearrange the roses."

She hesitated. "I won't do it the way you would."

"No," Josephine said, "you'll do it your way." She held out the vase as an offering. "Oh, please," she said. "Please do it your way, Elsie."

Chapter Twenty-nine

TISH STRETCHED out her hand. Josephine took it and they began to run from the house that reared up behind them, a bleak house of chilling desolation with rotted slats resembling wasted human ribs. They were running in the darkness to get away from it before it collapsed and fell on them.

"But it isn't real," Josephine said. "It came out of your imagination and I'm dreaming this. Only I don't know how to wake up. That frightens me much more than your house."

"Just run," Tish warned. "Don't look at it."

Josephine looked anyway because she knew all she would see would be broad brush strokes on a large canvas. Then in her dream she heard herself laugh. "It's all right. It's not the house you painted. It's my house."

At that she felt the slim hand slip through her fingers. Tish was gone. Josephine tripped and fell into a kind of pit; then the darkness was gone, too. It was summer again. She was moving about a garden, planting rather than picking tiny blooms. Beds of roses, masses of begonias, clusters of violets burst into life under her fingers.

"You can't see the garden for the flowers," Ben Goudy was saying. "How do you expect it to grow choked like that? He was dressed as he had been that first day, his coat heavy with dampness.

"It's only decoration," she shot back. "What right have you to come into my life, uninvited and through the back door, telling me how to live?"

"Put the kettle on," he ordered. "Fill it full of water and seal it tight."

"Why?"

"Because when it boils, the kettle will swell and burst and tear your house apart."

"Then I'll free it," she said. "I'll let the vapors out. It's wrong to close it up."

"That's it, Jo." He smiled and sounded pleased. "You finally understand what I've been trying to tell you. Open it up. Free it and it'll sing."

"I think you ought to see John Cullen," Ted said groggily, and Josephine knew she wasn't dreaming anymore. "You never used to have such trouble sleeping."

She tried to dismiss it. "Lately I make the slightest movement and you're awake. Maybe you're the one who ought to see the doctor."

With a satisfied sigh, he fell back on his pillow. "Tomorrow," he said, "we'll have turned out two full issues of each paper and doubled our advertising." He yawned. "That's what's wrong with both of us—too much excitement." The last syllable of the word trailed off and he was asleep again. The digital clock told her it was almost five.

I won't sleep anymore, she told herself. I'm not even going to try.

Later today the members of the cooperative and their wives were going to gather at the plant for a wine and cheese party to celebrate the successful printing and distributing of their individual papers. And today, Ben Goudy could be coming for her. Hadn't he said he wouldn't leave without her?

For two days now since her son put her on guard, Josephine had been expecting him. "I saw Mr. Goudy," he told her.

"Oh? Where, Pete?"

"At the barn. We got to be pretty good friends that night."

She wanted to shout at him, tell him Ben wasn't really his friend. Instead, she said quietly, "How is he? What did he have to say?"

"Not much, actually. I felt in the way, if you want to know the truth. He had a friend of his there."

Josephine was certain it had been Tish. She remembered the beautifully boned face, the blunt-cut bangs that covered most of her forehead, the exaggerated eyes and the brilliantly embroidered silk shawl. "Did you think she was rather odd looking, Pete? Some people would call that kind of look exotic. She's really a very fine artist. I saw her work."

"Who?"

"Mr. Goudy's friend."

"This wasn't a woman. It was a man. He introduced me. I think his name was Moore."

"Oh."

"They were wrapping the statues in bandages, like mummies. Anyway, they looked like bandages. Mr. Goudy said to give you a message."

"What is it?"

"That he's leaving here as soon as everything's packed. I asked him if he's going to come over and say good-by."

"What did he say?"

"To be sure to tell you he wouldn't leave without coming."

Then he was off again on the repaired bicycle, leaving his mother rigid where she stood.

Inside the bedroom, a soft gray was beginning to fill the room. Outside, a bird began to chirp. "He'll come today," Josephine told herself. "I know he'll come today."

She was neither happy nor sad. She was a bystander in her life, waiting to see how it would come out. She hadn't slept enough lately, but it wasn't that she was too tired to care; she was just too tired to fight anymore.

The wine and cheese party came off as smoothly as the issues had come off the new press. Everyone was in a celebratory mood.

Mike Weiss of the *Examiner* put a friendly arm around her and said, "We pulled it off, Josie." And his wife, Meg, suggested they make the cooperative a real family and get together socially once a month.

It's possible, Josephine thought, I may never see any of these nice people again.

"You okay, Josie?" Ted said.

"I think I'm a little drunk."

He laughed. "I better take my drunken wife home. It's time we broke up this party anyway."

It was warm enough not to have needed coats, but the night air cleared her head. When they reached the house, they saw that the lights were on in the living room. "That's funny," he said. "The kids are never in that room when we're not here."

She knew Ben was waiting for her. They both knew she wasn't even surprised to find him there.

"Well," Ted said, "Mr. Goudy." His voice was noticeably cooler than it had been the night Peter was brought home.

"Have you been here long?" Josephine asked. Her own voice was even less welcoming. She was glad. It hid the truth that she was absurdly glad to see him. Not seeing him, pretending the River Road had been washed out to sea, wouldn't accomplish anything. By coming he was forcing her to settle whatever it was that needed to be settled.

He was sitting on a bench in front of the fireplace, a small sketch pad propped up in front of him. Elsie was sitting on the floor, chin stiffly and self-consciously thrust forward.

She jumped up, snatched the pad from him and ran to Josephine. "This doesn't look like me."

Josephine stared down at a blur of lines.

"Why, it's a terrific likeness, pet," Ted said, pleased.

"Mother?"

Josephine closed her eyes hard, then opened them quickly, forcing them to focus. The small face under tousled hair made the eyes look even larger, the pert nose, the teasing obstinate mouth full of an early morning innocence, the young curve of the neck were all Elsie.

"It's excellent."

"Only it doesn't look like me."

"She's fishing for compliments," Peter said disgustedly.

Josephine frowned. "Don't you know this is how you look?"

"Well, it's my hair anyway—messy, as usual. I was going to comb it. He said not to bother."

"I think this should be framed."

"Why?"

"Because it's a pretty picture, even if you don't think it's anything like you."

"Keep looking at it," Ben suggested. "After a while maybe you'll realize it's you."

Josephine looked at him gratefully. For a moment they smiled at each other and there was no one else in the room. Everything she had disliked about him that other morning was gone—his arrogance, his malicious presumption. This was the Ben who had walked her home in the new snow, talked to her about his work, encouraged her about her own and warned her not to like him too much. He had warned her.

"Did you have a special reason for coming, Mr. Goudy?" Ted asked.

"I went to New York today and brought something back."

For the first time, Josephine noticed a form covered with newspaper on the table. She watched Ben slowly and carefully unwrap it.

"Not much of an unveiling," he apologized. When he finished, papers were strewn on the floor, and on the table was the portrait of Peter, permanent in bronze.

"I knew all about that," Peter said. "I promised I wouldn't say anything."

Ted went to it immediately and turned the head around. He squinted and then bent to see it even better. "You did this, Josie? I'm hardly an expert in the field, but it looks damn good to me. What's your opinion, Mr. Goudy?"

Instead of answering, Ben said softly, "Don't you want to see this?" Even more softly he added, "Jo." Or perhaps he just thought the name and she heard it. She went to the bronze, reached out her fingers, but didn't touch it.

"She was so worried the day I told her we'd send it out and have a cast made. She didn't want the clay to be destroyed in the process."

"Clay?" Ted said. In the wonder of this work his wife had done, he forgot for a moment that the man who brought it was the same one who named a nude statue after her. "It's done in clay first?"

Still ignoring him, Ben talked directly to Josephine. "She said, 'This mud is mine. It has part of me in it. What if someone makes a mistake?' You see," he said with a tight-lipped smile, "I told you it would be all right."

Elsie laughed. "Is that what you said, mother? This mud has part of me in it? That's funny."

"This really amazes me," Ted said, picking up the piece and studying it closely. "You were always so secretive about what you were doing, Josie. I had no idea—"

"Maybe she thought you wouldn't be interested."

Ted put the bronze down, remembering again just who Ben was. "My wife knows I'm always interested in anything she does."

"I never knew anyone to work with such complete joy. I think she felt guilty about being so happy."

"Guilty, Josie? Did you?"

She had been standing by helplessly, listening to them without saying anything, listening to her own uneven heartbeats. Her voice, when it finally came, sounded like someone else's. "Did you two have dinner? I left it in the warmer."

"We were having it when he came," Peter told her.

Elsie shrugged. "It's probably cold now."

"Heat it up again. I brought dessert. It was supposed to be a wine and cheese party, but somebody donated a cake."

"I still don't think that drawing looks like me, but that does look like Pete."

"I modeled something of you, too."

"That's nice."

Josie knew Elsie would have to see it first to believe it. The only way to see it was to go to the barn and get it for her after he left—if he left alone.

She was facing the staircase where Ted's mother had turned on her. Fran had dared, "Tell me to my face that Teddy hasn't made you happy."

If it was true, as she had answered, that being happy isn't always enough, Ben was right in coming tonight.

"I have a conceit about my own particular talent," he was saying to Ted, "but I don't think I could have done that head any better."

"You couldn't have done it as well," pleasantly. "It's true, Mr. Goudy. My wife did put something of herself in it, because there's something of her in that boy—the real one. As I told you, I'm hardly an expert. The truth is it's way outside anything I know or even understand, but I do know this: if that's any good, it's partly because Peter's mother did it."

Peter's mother's fingers stuck as if something were gluing them together. It took all her strength to pull them apart. In a sudden rush, she remembered how Ben told her she had reached the breaking-through point in her work. She could either stand still or forge ahead.

Forging ahead the way he wants me to, Josephine realized, means letting go of another woman. It means destroying her. The moment I do that, I'll destroy too much of myself. There won't be enough left of me to work, not with the same complete joy. Ted isn't an expert. It *is* outside everything he knows or understands, but without really understanding, he's just told me why I can't leave.

It was too bad she would never be able to explain it to Ben. He would go on being angry with her because he had given her so much and thought she was just throwing it away. They were both, she knew, waiting for her to say something.

"Won't this bronze be good to have when Pete is a man?" she said to her husband.

Ted smiled. "That won't be for a while, Josie."

"I can wait." She knew Ben understood she was saying: And here is where I'll wait.

The sketch pad with the penciled drawing of Elsie was on the mantel. Josephine looked at it again. "She is pretty, isn't she?"

"Yes," Ben said, looking steadily at her.

"She hasn't found it out yet. When she does, it could be a worry." And she knew he understood: And I'll be right here, when I'm needed, to worry about it.

He waited until she moved closer to her husband before he said, "Tomorrow I'm going to New York. I'll stay at a friend's studio for a while. Then I'm going to Europe."

"What about the house?" Ted asked.

"I've taken your advice, Mr. Trask—turned it over to a real estate agent. They can get rid of it. I don't want it."

"Well," Ted said, "good-by then. And good luck."

"Are you going to be staying with Tish?" Josephine asked. "If you are, give her my best."

Ben frowned. "I wouldn't have told you."

"Told me what?"

She noticed he couldn't keep the muscles in his jaw from contracting. Whatever control he had saved after her clear choice appeared to have left him completely. His hand, she noticed, was shaking slightly.

"Tell me, please."

"Tish is dead."

Josephine sank down on the couch and stared dumbly at him. She wanted him to admit he only said it to be cruel, because he was angry with her. For the second time, they seemed to be all alone in the room.

Someone asked, "Who's Tish?" For a moment she didn't even recognize Ted's voice.

"When I got your bronze," Ben said, "I was so proud, I wanted to show it to her. The street was roped off. There had been a fire in the studio."

"And the painting? The house that frightened her?"

"Everything burned."

"A friend of yours, Josie?"

She remembered Ted was still there. "Remember I told you about the artist Ben introduced me to that day when we drove to New York?"

"The one who lived in the converted barbershop?"

Without looking at him, she knew Ben deeply resented her for sharing any of that part of the day with Ted, who was an outsider.

"She was magnificent," Josephine said. "What happened was a kind of self-prophecy."

"I don't understand," Ted said.

"In one of her paintings, she predicted how she was going to die."

"I'll be honest, Josie. I don't really believe in things like that."

Ben smiled as if he were a little sorry for him. "A scientist," he told Josephine, "who predicted the end of the world would have mixed feelings if he turned out to be right. I'm sure it was like that for Tish. She foresaw exactly how her own world would end, and part of her was probably pleased she had been right. God, she was tough. And she was . . . magnificent."

And knowing her, Josephine thought, is something else we had to-gether.

"I have a lot to do before I leave tomorrow. Say good-by to your family for me."

"I'll go to the door with you," she offered hastily, afraid he would try to take her hand.

He didn't, not there in front of Ted, not at the door, either. She was let down, though, when he didn't even try.

"Good-by, Jo."

In the small foyer, she thought, I'll never see the studio again the way it was, the one I thought was mine too.

"I dreamed about Tish last night," she recalled suddenly.

"I'm not surprised. She liked you."

"I'm glad. Anyway, good-by, Ben."

I wish, she thought, there was some way to tell you that if I'm disappointing you now, think of the terrible disappointment I'm sparing you.

He looked at her as if he were memorizing her. "You're right," he said. "You would have disappointed me. Good luck with your figures."

It had happened for the last time, that telepathic hum between them, indiscernible to anyone else but as clear as the full-throated note of a bell.

Without warning, he took the hand he hadn't even wanted to shake a minute before and held it briefly to his mouth. Since he had already said good-by once, he said nothing now. He turned and walked away from her.

Months ago, he had come through the back door to stay until the rain stopped. When it was over, he had left and she felt certain he would forget ever having met her. When he left now, by the front door, she was as certain that long after it closed, he would never forget her.

She closed it and went back into the room. Ted was standing at the table studying the bronze head. "I'd like to think it had something to do with me, Josie. I'd like to hear you say you let him go, not just because of Pete and Elsie, but because of me."

"Is that what you're thinking?"

"The night he brought Peter home, I knew you meant something to him. Do you want to tell me what he meant to you? I saw the way you looked at each other."

"Ben Goudy's work is his religion," she heard herself say. "And he tried to make it mine. But he worships a god who demands more than I could give it."

"That's all there was to it? Tell me it was, and I'll believe it because I want to, whether it's true or not."

"It was never really Ben," she insisted. "I told him that once. You can believe it, because it's true."

"All right," Ted said. "It's over, then. He's gone now. That's the end of it."

THE STUDIO had been transformed. All the marble, bronze and wood figures she had come to know so well were gone, along with the wire sculpture of the elongated horse, and the fierce fighting cocks she had watched him make by bending wide strips of metal and fashioning twisted wires for tail feathers. She would probably never see any of them again.

The woman in the stone, the one he called Josephine, was gone with them.

She stretched her arms and remembered how the woman had stretched hers out of the rock, trying to grasp a freedom she couldn't quite reach. Perhaps she had wanted too much *now*. There was a whole energy of truth in that one word. For now, she thought, I have to put that part of my life in escrow because I don't know how to work without letting it consume me, letting it block out everything and everyone else. Maybe it'll be possible for me to turn it off like a faucet and one day turn it back on again. That's something I'll have to find out.

But one thing she was sure of: the next time she lived, she would be more careful before she made her commitments. She would get to know herself first, before she let others need her too much. . . .

All alone, on a small table in the corner, was the little clay figure she had come for. He hadn't taken what he called one of her "mud pies."

Oh, I'll think of him, she thought, sometimes, not often, but once in a while. I know I'll think of him.

Carefully, she picked up the little figure of Elsie, wrapped it in a damp cloth and left the place completely a barn again.

Outside, she leaned against the broad side of it, and knew that what she learned long ago was still true: the great difficulty in life did not so much arise in the choice between good and evil as in the choice between good and good.

She wondered idly if the stamp of her back would remain on the wood after she went away.

There was no imprint left when she moved. A little disappointed, she covered it with her hand. The spot wasn't even warm.

But the air was—and it was full of the healthy scent of spring. Josephine breathed deeply, and started home.